LAST TANGO IN CYBERSPACE

ALSO BY STEVEN KOTLER

Stealing Fire: How Silicon Valley, the Navy SEALs, and Maverick Scientists are Revolutionizing the Way We Live and Work (with Jamie Wheal)

Tomorrowland: Our Journey from Science Fiction to Science Fact

Bold: How to Go Big, Create Wealth and Impact the World (with Peter H. Diamandis)

The Rise of Superman: Decoding the Science of Ultimate Human Performance

Abundance: The Future Is Better Than You Think (with Peter H. Diamandis)

A Small Furry Prayer: Dog Rescue and the Meaning of Life

West of Jesus: Surfing, Science, and the Origins of Belief

The Angle Quickest for Flight

LAST TANGO IN CYBERSPACE

STEVEN KOTLER

ST. MARTIN'S PRESS
NEW YORK

LAST TANGO IN CYBERSPACE. Copyright © 2019 by Steven Kotler. All rights reserved. Printed in the United States of America. For information, address St. Martin's Press, 175 Fifth Avenue, New York, N.Y. 10010.

www.stmartins.com

Designed by Devan Norman

Library of Congress Cataloging-in-Publication Data

Names: Kotler, Steven, 1967– author.
Title: Last tango in cyberspace / Steven Kotler.
Description: First edition. | New York : St. Martin's Press, 2019.
Identifiers: LCCN 2018055450| ISBN 9781250202079 (hardcover) |
   ISBN 9781250202086 (ebook)
Subjects: | GSAFD: Science fiction.
Classification: LCC PS3611.O749295 L37 2019 | DDC 813/.6—dc23
LC record available at https://lccn.loc.gov/2018055450

Our books may be purchased in bulk for promotional, educational, or business use. Please contact your local bookseller or the Macmillan Corporate and Premium Sales Department at 1-800-221-7945, extension 5442, or by email at MacmillanSpecialMarkets@macmillan.com.

First Edition: May 2019

10 9 8 7 6 5 4 3 2 1

BRICK BY BRICK, MY CITIZENS.

BRICK BY BRICK.

—Emperor Hadrian, on building Rome

SOMEONE KNOWS SOMEONE

He steps off the plane and into a shimmering world. They've hidden the airport beneath a thick coat of dazzle. Depth of field in every direction. A parade of razor-thin screens, angled atrium glass, and staccato mirror work. Everything scrolls, winks, and blinks, but softly, like Sunset Strip on mute.

He can feel it, all this kinesis, like a twitch in his brain stem. It's old code, an ancient alert system. Any shiver in the outer peripheral registers as another living creature, another consciousness, potentially an opportunity, possibly a threat. This airport shivers too, even at this late hour.

Walking deeper into the terminal, he passes a crowded bar. A long row of shiny: gleaming marble counters, brushed chrome stools, and translucent hanging lamps. Enough live bodies that the vibe is happy-hour horny. The flavor is surprisingly poly-tribe, which is new slang for the global mash-up, the hybridization of signs, styles, and meanings that is somehow now: Liberty International Airport, Newark, New Jersey.

In Chile, he once got good dollars to em-track an early poly-tribe. This was over a decade ago, one of the first jobs of his em-tracking career, and back before anyone was paying anything for a skill that no one yet knew existed.

Except for the Japanese.

At the behest of some faceless Osaka-based mega-corp, he spent a month in Chile, hunting new and exploitable micro-demographics—a task, they suspected, for which em-trackers were particularly well-suited.

They were right.

He'd uncovered one of the early subcult melds, the first internet generation to carve their identity from a global menu of counterculture. Style-wise, they borrowed saggy hip-hop gear from West Coast rappers, cartoonish Gyaru makeup from the Japanese cosplay scene, and angular Emo hairstyles from the Washington, DC, post-hard-core crowd. Their attitudes crossed anything-goes California bisexuality with edgy Brit-punk sneer, a combination that led to a completely novel form of rebellion: wet-kissing strangers on the street.

This airport, he figures, is poly-tribe light—the safer upscale version.

Just past security, a tall Chinese man with dark glasses and a dapper cap holds almost his name on a sign. The placard reads JUDAH ZORN, so he almost walks on by. For a long time now, everyone's called him Lion. His real name actually is Judah, but a job in Jamaica turned that into "Lion of Judah," which stuck, and makes sense, but only if you speak Rasta.

It takes him a couple of steps to remember his real name.

Lion backtracks. "I'm Judah Zorn."

"Bo," extending a hand for his carry-on.

Bo starts toward the exit. Lion falls in a step behind him, noticing a series of white scars above a bar code tattoo on the back of Bo's neck. A new poly-tribe sign? Maybe Rilkean—though the Rilkeans are mostly a myth.

Like everything else, these facts get slotted. The data fed into the maw of Lion's adaptive unconscious, fodder for his pattern recognition system, fodder for his talent. A long time ago, Lion was a journalist. Now there's no real name for his job. An empathy-tracker, he's heard it called, also a wayfinder. Neither are exactly right. His old editor once gave him a T-shirt that read TRUTH SEEKER. That's probably closer, but not the kind of thing one puts on a business card.

The early researchers described em-tracking as a hardware upgrade for the nervous system, maybe the result of a genetic shift, possibly a fast adaptation. Studies revealed an assortment of cognitive improvements: acute perceptual sensitivity, rapid data acquisition, high speed pattern recognition. The biggest change was in future prediction. Normally, the human brain is a selfish prognosticator, built to trace an individual's path into the future. The em-tracker's brain offers a wider oracle, capable of following a whole culture's path into the future.

Also a decent way to make a living—which explains why he's on the East Coast.

Down an escalator and around a corner. In a seventeen-foot Chanel ad, Lion catches the reflection of his straight-world uniform: layered blacks and grays, like a secret bruise. Gray hooded sweater, dark wool coat. Black jeans appear to have slid up above black boots. From the waist down, he could be his earlier punk rock self. From the waist up, for a while now, he's not sure what the signifier signifies.

Bo takes a right turn at something menacing, maybe Eddie Bauer. Magazine stand. Starbucks. Out into the New Jersey night.

The SUV is idling at the curb, clearly an impossibility in today's hyper-security, or someone knows someone, that much for sure. Bulky black and scary polished. Bo opens the door, and Lion climbs inside.

The whisper-click of expensive engineering as the door shuts itself, the exhale of plush seats as he settles in. Like the upholstery is breathing and standard now, almost everywhere. Too comfortable is what Lion usually thinks; tonight he needs the swaddle. His post-plane system quivers with more human contact than he typically prefers. Emo-stim overload, the kids called it, one of the downsides of em-tracking.

The SUV glides into traffic with just enough motion that a paperback copy of *Slouching Towards Bethlehem* slides across the dashboard. This catches his attention. *Slouching* was one of the books that made him want to be a journalist. Could Bo really be a Joan Didion fan? With the bar code tattoo, a possibility. But the other option? Lion shivers at the idea that Arctic, his temporary employer, would have spent the money to dig that deep.

Bo glances right, hunting for something on the seat. The bar code on his neck contracts as he moves. In the scrunch, Lion can make out a single question mark, which is telltale Rilkean, their marching orders: Live the questions.

So maybe a myth no more.

But he doesn't have time to think about this. Bo found what he was looking for, and appears to be passing it to him over the partition. A skinny rectangular box, ornate and etched with dragons.

"From Sir Richard," he says. "You can, of course, smoke in the car."

In his grip, the box's exterior gives a little. It's the sigh of skin, of fauna, not flora, very soft, utterly wrong. Lion feels the flash that is almost, but not yet, angry.

"Not leather," says Bo, silencing his escalation. "Tissue engineering. Stem cells. Lab grown."

Puzzled replaces perturbed.

"Yeah," continues Bo, "animal friendly. But it's not my department. I was told to tell you this if you needed to know."

Lion catches Bo's eyes in the rearview.

"Sir Richard assured me—you would need to know."

As they pull into traffic, he's no longer wondering. Arctic clearly dug. But it's now so easy. How little remains hidden, how little it seems to matter.

"You know," says Lion, "I haven't met Sir Richard."

Bo doesn't answer, simply accelerates the SUV into silence. Lion tries to enjoy the ride. He flew into Newark intentionally, despite the longer trip into the city. LaGuardia, at night, like being lost in a funeral parlor. And he likes this view of New York better.

But it doesn't distract, or not enough.

Lion knows his information is available in any net search, even though he's paid for scrubbing. The suspected origin of his talent remains, like a Snowden stain, viewable via any browser.

So maybe it's nothing.

Opening the box, it's not nothing. Lion unearths one pouch of organic rolling tobacco, two packs of rolling papers, and five black vials marked with marijuana strains and blends. So either his agent is uncomfortably thorough, or the unmet Sir Richard leaves nothing to chance.

Proof of the latter sits in a vial marked GHOST TRAINWRECK #69. Ghost Trainwreck is the more familiar marijuana variety, crossing Neville's Wreck and Ghost OG and cranking out 30.9 THC, thus the nomenclature and the notoriety. But what he's holding—#69—is a rumor. Urban legend for most; for Lion, on that Jamaica job, something else he saw coming.

Which is when he knows for sure. That ratchet-click of certainty deep in the reptilian dark of his brain stem. Somebody knows somebody; somebody did their homework.

GANGSTERING ET CETERA

Thirty minutes later and Lion's a little high as he walks into the Ludlow Hotel, which is the way he likes it. Through a door and into a dim corridor: a few low-slung chairs in oranges and reds, a rough-hewn table, stained gray, and a short check-in counter, dark woods. Beyond that, the lobby bar and an atrium, in tall plated glass, so the effect inverts, like walking inside to get back outside.

Crossing the entrance hall and heading to the check-in counter and, apparently, singing along with the sound track.

"Little hustler, probably die, gangstering et cetera."

Was that out loud?

It's a trick, of course. That thing the neuro-crowd has been doing to music lately, the trigger buried in the rhythm. It fires up the amygdala, a dash of flight-or-flight to create hyper-salience, hippocampal overactivation for enhanced recall, more Big Brother kind of shit. "Direct-to-memory" is how they describe it. Singing in public was his experience.

But before those ramifications fully land, the desk clerk hits him with the "We've been expecting you, Mr. Zorn."

He sees a skinny suit and a lilting afro.

"Lion," he says. "Just call me Lion."

Arctic's information is on file, so nothing's required but a signature. This he can manage. The clerk slides a key across the counter. A black fob attached to a swatch of animal leather, and just about the only thing Lion doesn't like about the hotel.

"Killing for stuff we don't need," he says, tapping the swatch on the counter and another thing he didn't really mean to say out loud.

The clerk lifts an eyebrow; the afro goes Tower of Pisa to the left. Neat trick.

"Good night, Mr. Zorn."

It's late, so good night to you too.

Starting toward the elevators, Lion crosses beneath a cluster of Victorian pendant lamps, but rapid pupil dilation caused by sleep lack sends the light bouncing around the lobby like pinballs. Makes it hard to walk and definitely a sign that his internal clock has begun the countdown.

So not a decision, the decision to head straight to his room.

T minus three minutes as he passes blondes, brunettes, the lobby bar on the right, the Dirty French restaurant on the left, then Bo, standing by the elevators.

"You left this in the car," handing him the dragon box for the second time in an hour.

Lion takes the box. He feels that fleshy feel again, but it's quickly overridden by the skunk of Ghost Trainwreck. Scents are primary signals, processed the fastest of all information feeds: straight to the brain's reactor core. Lion's core scents skunk. Pretty sure they can scent it up in Harlem too.

New York is still a holdout state—but Bo doesn't seem to care, so maybe Lion won't either.

A bellboy arcs a pair of Henk suitcases around them. They're the older, nonautonomous model, but still more machine than luggage. Each handcrafted from five hundred separate parts, including red Italian burl, black ebony, horsehair, magnesium, aluminum, titanium, carbon fiber, parachute silk, and fine leather. Together, they cost more than the bellboy makes in a year. So the weed stink coming from the dragon box—probably the least of his worries.

Also, did they have to use horsehair and leather? Goddamn 3-D printers now work with over seven hundred materials.

Bo watches the bellboy depart, then passes Lion an oversized black envelope, thick rag weave and tied with brown string.

"Sir Richard asked that you review this before tomorrow's meeting."

Lion takes the box, the envelope, remembers to say thank you.

Out the front door and into the night, Bo ghosts. As he passes beneath a streetlight, Lion notices the bar code tattoo again, the silver outline of a question mark like twinkling fireworks.

Live the questions, said Rilke.

I cannot formulate the question that is my wonder, said Alan Watts.

Lion steps into the elevator, wondering how to resolve that conundrum. Then he wonders about his wondering. Then he gets it. Ghost Trainwreck, rumors confirmed: produces heavy pattern recognition. Significant em-trace potential.

T minus two minutes and a traction elevator from some slower decade. The gentle rise of the car, the centuries that pass along the way. Lion steps out into a skinny maze of hard corners, a standard New York hallway circa 19-something. Tells himself to get the key fob out, have it ready.

Even tired, he's good at following directions.

It's right, left, right, down a straight stretch, then the diamond brass plate on a white door reads 22. A wave of the fob, a click of the lock, a wave of exhaustion.

Sir Richard's envelope will have to wait.

"Execute," he says, stepping into the room, "execute fast unpack."

Suitcase in the closet, bathroom, bed, he tells himself, and in that order.

The bathroom walls are black-and-white tile, the bedroom cozy with high thread counts. Light switches are a convenient swat away. In the complete darkness and the fading middle C of a distant cabbie's horn, he almost has time for one final thought, a cold foreboding rising up from deep in his cortex—don't open that envelope—but he's asleep before it can register.

REAP A DESTINY

Down by the Seaside" in cheerful synth tones pulls him into consciousness at 5:00 A.M. The signal has been long encoded, so he's feet on the floor by the second stanza. *Sow an action and you reap a habit, sow a habit and you reap a character, sow a character and you reap a destiny.* Psychologist William James paraphrasing philosopher Aristotle, and the first thing he thinks about this morning.

Then his habits: out of bed, cross to phone, silence alarm. Box of coffee pods on a tall gray table and auto-choosing Indigo Smooth. The chrome lever opens the drop bay and, without having to think about it, he slots the pod, locks the arm, and hears a satisfying click. The machine hums to life. Two buttons start glowing, the luminescent choice of small cup versus large cup.

But it's not actually a choice. The machine makes midget espresso or double midget. He chooses the lie that is large cup and robo-slides a mug under the nozzle. Every step done by rote, like playing scales, and the reason, he figures, James cared so much about habit.

While the coffee brews, he jumps in the shower. Clean lines, brass fixtures, and enough space that he can yoga out his back under hot water. Tea rose shampoo and hands in prayer pose, twisting over bent knees. And rinse.

A quick towel, a run of the razor, and he's stepping into his straight-world uniform: black jeans, gray sweater. Arctic sprang for a room with a terrace, so even though it's still chilly, he carries his coffee, a pocket Moleskine, Sir Richard's envelope, and the dragon box out a sliding door and into the elements.

Two chaise lounges, micro-fir trees in square wooden troughs, and seven stories' worth of view.

He crosses to a thin glass table beside a low brick wall, slides out a chair and feels the sure grip of the Modo outdoor model adjust to his frame. Then he faces the dragon box and an actual decision. This time he rolls 75-25, mostly tobacco, just enough Trainwreck that he can ride the double shot of THC and caffeine, not enough to muddy him for later.

He sips his coffee, lights the joint, and savors the view. The double-shot hit of the first hit hits. His pattern recognition system springs to life and the view reminds him of something, then something else.

Now he's ready to work.

Picking up the envelope, he unwinds the string, but the envelope stays sealed. Then he sees it, hidden under the flap, a small square of shiny black plastic. Flexible e-screen that must react to oxygen. With the flap now open, it wakes and pulses. Canary-yellow fingerprint outline glows, fades to black, then canary outline. The creators must have Apple lineage—Lion can feel the intuition built in.

He puts his finger on the e-screen and a nano-scanner kicks to life. A zip of light, a tiny click, the envelope opens.

Exactly as expected, that Apple lineage at work.

Out slides a small stack of newspaper article reprints and a handful of photos. The articles are regular stock, but the photos feel thick.

Mesh electronics woven into the paper perhaps. The photos are also marked. Arctic's iceberg icon floats on the bottom right corner. Red Ice is their term, but it pulses hot pink, so Lion thinks Slushy dregs.

He glances through the stack quickly. All crime scene photos, by the looks of them. He'll look later. The clippings are the better place to start. His em-tracking machinery is driven by words more than images, but that's only his make and model. Empathy is related to intuition, and intuition is individually customized, tuned to dominant talents. Chefs need tastes, painters images. His experience is biblical: It starts with logos.

The clippings are in English, or maybe a translation AI made a pass. One from a newspaper in Dubai, one from Cape Town, a third from something New York local, *The Upstate Register.*

He starts in Dubai, six months back. A Lebanese zookeeper at a private sanctuary released all the animals in his care, climbed into a cage with a pair of baboons, and went to sleep. Before dawn, it was lions, tigers, and bears on the highway. The army was called in. A pixelated photo shows an Oboronprom Ka-52 Alligator helicopter airlifting a giraffe to safety, like Noah with coaxial rotors.

He's seen this image before. Picks up the photo stack he'd set aside and counts four shots down. There it is: same Ka-52, same giraffe. He plays a hunch and touches the Red Ice icon. The photo whirs to life, going close-up on the helicopter, the pilot in mirror shades and serious concentration. Finger tap to freeze, another to unlock. Sliding right on the giraffe provides a different focus: long neck in tight zoom.

Neat trick.

The next image is an overhead of an octagon-shaped viewing area. A raised central platform surrounded by eight glass walls fronting eight large cages, all big and empty. The next shot details the inside of the octagon. Different vantage point, but the same glass cages. At the center of the photo, a canary-yellow arrow appears, pointing to a dark wooden table surrounded by six cheap plastic chairs that sit in the middle of the central platform.

Lion taps a finger on the table. The arrow disappears and the photo zooms. Close-up of wood grain in high relief, and atop the grain: five lines of silver powder and a silver straw. Three faint lines, already inhaled, two left intact, each the same hue as a classic Airstream.

Same silver as Bo's tattoo.

A click in his brain as data bit finds data bit. Neurotransmitters dump into synapses, end result, more questions: Is this a Rilkean thing? A drug thing? An animal rights thing? Whatever thing it is, Arctic sure managed to dig up his backstory. Lion definitely understands why they want him for this job.

The South Africa article is about a family on safari: kids, grandkids, parents, grandparents, aunts, uncles, a clan of nearly eighteen. Without explanation, they departed camp in the middle of the night and were found the next morning, sleeping amid a pride of lions. Everyone makes it back to camp safely; no one can remember why they left.

Corresponding photo shows the safari camp, a picnic table painted fire-engine red in the center. Another yellow arrow, pointing at the picnic table. Tap for close-up. Same silver straw, same silver powder residue.

The final article is a detective story, told twenty-first-century style. Airplane records show Robert Walker, fifty-four, departing Dallas, landing at LaGuardia. A kid taking a selfie catches Walker in snakeskin boots and desert fatigues stepping off the plane in New York. A camera over baggage claim has him lifting a camo-colored duffel and black gun case into a luggage cart. Uber gets him curbside to his Hamptons residence. His alarm system confirms entry. Drone footage from who knows where reconfirms. Four minutes later, Alexa has him asking about a silver residue on a table in his study. Two days after, an anonymous 911 from an untraceable burner brings in the cops. They report the house empty, so the press reports Robert Walker MIA.

Something not quite right is the only thing Lion gets from the story. He takes another hit from the joint and tries again. Still can't put his finger on it.

And no follow-up article.

But he finds two corresponding photos in the stack. The first shows a tartan graveyard that must be Walker's study. Plaid wallpaper and mounted animal heads covering every inch. Lion sees a Lucite end table beneath a giant elk, an unzipped gun bag sitting beneath the table and a .300 Winchester Magnum visible through its acrylic surface. A familiar sheen on the tabletop.

He taps and zooms, bringing the tabletop into close-up. Now he sees what he already expects to see: silver straw, silver powder lines.

The second photo takes him a second. It's another shot of Walker's study, the lens pointed straight at the animal heads. Deer, antelope, gazelle, zebra, tiger, and then human, male, roughly midfifties. The missing Robert Walker? His head neatly mounted to oval-shaped mahogany, hanging on the wall like just another trophy.

Lion double-taps the image for the zoom, maybe hitting the mesh electronics a little too hard, maybe not yet believing what's he's seeing.

Close-up reveals a wide, pale forehead, a tight web of crow's-feet jutting off hazel eyes, and a receding prep school haircut from another decade. Walker's jaw seems clenched, his neck muscles bulging, and nothing below his neck but high-gloss dark wood.

Decapitation.

What the hell has he gotten himself into? The Red Ice icon pulses hot pink, just once, then fades to black. And he knows, in the same way the rain knows gravity, Arctic is what he's gotten himself into.

But he's not gonna think about it right now. His attention is fixed on the dark ovals of Walker's eyes. Something in those eyes, Lion will think later, something else he should have seen coming.

HUNTING THE HUNTERS

Holding the photo of Walker's head on the wall, Lion finds it takes a few minutes for the gruesome to pass.

Once it does, he notes a different sensation, a lack of sensation. He's still staring at the photo, but not feeling much of anything.

And not the way things normally work.

He tries holding the image at different distances: arm's length, close up. Tap to zoom, double tap for wide. Five more minutes pass and still nothing. Em-trace machinery failing to em, and the taste of ash in the back of his throat.

Joint residue, or does em-tracking failure really taste like ash?

Answer probably still unknown. Em-tracking is a fairly new addition to the human repertoire. Not surprising, Lion knows, because the idea of empathy itself only dates to the late eighteenth century. The notion was invented by psycho-physiologist Wilhelm Wundt to describe our ability to experience another's experience, and different, Wundt thought, from sympathy and compassion. Empathy is about the transmission of information; sympathy and compassion are reactions to that information.

Lion stares at the photo, tastes more ash. It's the first time he's seen a dead body on the job—but no other information is transmitting.

A couple of years after Wundt's invention, philosopher Theodor Lipps wonders why art affects us so strongly. Comes to see the act of viewing art as an act of co-creation. An artist has a primal emotion that becomes an original insight that births a work of art. Viewers tap that source code via viewing, as if the feeling that led to the original insight gets broadcast, and people with the right kind of radio can detect the signal. Tune the frequency correctly and the experience is shared experience, transmitted through an object and across time.

Lion relights the joint, trying to tune the frequency. He rearranges his body in the chair, feeling the Modo auto-adjust to his motion, like tiny hands holding his hips. And a soft breeze bouncing off tall buildings.

Needing a name for this process, Lipps borrows *einfuhlung,* German for "feeling into," from an 1873 aesthetics dissertation. This gets translated into English to become "empathy" in a 1909 textbook, but not before the poet Rainer Maria Rilke recognizes this experience as a superpower, calling it "my very greatest feeling, my world feeling, the indescribably swift, deep, timeless moments of this godlike *in-seeing.*"

Lion's talent is expanded in-seeing.

Rilke used empathy as a virus-scan for truth, his way to live the questions. Lion lives bigger questions. His empathy isn't individual; it's cultural. He can feel how cultures collide and blend, the Darwinian mash of memes, the winners and losers and what truths remain. He's like a lie detector for potential futures. An emotional prediction engine for how the we fractures, the us becomes them, and then back together again. And a useful skill for a certain type of company.

He gets paid in cash; sometimes in crypto.

But holding the photo of Robert Walker, he's not in-seeing much of anything. Pattern recognition system refusing to cooperate, or these stories lead nowhere. Not to a real future, or not one he can find.

Usually all he's paid for is yes or no.

It's a no.

Work done, he pushes back from the table and stands up, taking one last look at Robert Walker before he goes.

Still gruesome.

Still a no.

Then a thought: Someone expended a lot of effort to decapitate this man, took the time to taxidermy his head with something that looks like shellac, and a careful mounting job as well. Lion counts sixteen dead mammals on the wall beside Walker. Then he gets it.

He opens his Moleskine and makes a quick note.

Someone is hunting the hunters.

Reading the words, he feels it. The primal emotion that became the original insight that led to Robert Walker's head on a wall.

Which is how Lion knows: He would like to meet that someone, maybe shake his hand.

ON THE SPECTRUM

Still hours before he's due to meet Sir Richard. Into shorts and a T-shirt and taking the back staircase to the gym on the roof. A shiny glass box surrounded by a brick parapet and New York's skyline stretching out like a carpet.

Exercise dulls the emo-stim overload, pretty much a job requirement for any em-tracker. Lion does pull-ups and jump rope and more pull-ups. He does push-ups and rowing machine and more push-ups. Goblet squats to exhaustion, then finishes with whatever damage he can do with their limited supply of shiny chrome barbells. Can't anybody lift over fifty pounds anymore?

And another round of goblet squats.

Down the stairs and to his room, where he indulges in a second shower, then back into his straight-world uniform. The Moleskine with its single note goes into a black Burton sling-pack. A second-edition *Dune*, sunrise over Arrakis on the dust jacket, follows. Photos and articles slip into the envelope, a whirl of the fingerprint scanner locks it closed, and into the sling-pack as well. Then traction elevator to Dirty French for cage-free eggs and hash browns.

He takes a booth by the window, beneath a cantilevered mirror rimmed in vintage marquee lights. Less Vegas than vaudeville. Sling-pack beside place setting, he slides out his copy of *Dune*. He likes to reread the book before certain kinds of jobs. Frank Herbert being one of the first to spot how subcults meld, Arctic starting to feel like one of those jobs.

Opening the book, Lion finds a passage about Thufir Hawat, a Mentat for the ages. Herbert dreamed up the Mentat in like 1965. A human computer. A walking logic bomb. This was fifty years before Silicon Valley became a hotbed for a certain type of analytical mind. People on the spectrum. Historical outcasts, now prized for their whiz-bang math skills. Spectrum-ites get hired in droves, invited to parties and laid, many for the very first time. On the spectrum breeds with on the spectrum. Kids arrive with hyper-logical minds, or where, as-sumes Lion, we are today. But Lion knows what Herbert knew, a few more generations down this trail and we're into a different thing. A different species. Mentat.

Em-tracking, he figures, is the very opposite of the Mentat. Another doorway into the adjacent possible. More niche creation. More specia-tion. Down a different spectrum. Into a different thing.

A sip of coffee. Not as strong as Lion usually prefers, but he finds he doesn't mind. He reads a couple of paragraphs and tries to focus, but something outside the window keeps grabbing for his attention. Looks up to satisfy the urge. A scrolling screen atop a parked taxicab, its con-stant fluttering similar in effect to the dazzle of the airport. Once again, the motion tricking his life recognition machinery.

Lion thinks empathy is another way we have learned to recognize life. When the party ends and guests leave, the house doesn't just look empty. It feels empty. Absence of life gives off sensation. One possibility is mirror neurons, which are the habit machinery beneath empathy. In the presence of the living, we automatically mirror their behavior. In their absence, with nothing to mirror, this lack emotes a feeling, the null set of empathy. Presence or absence of aliveness, Lion believes, is one of the basic bits of information conveyed by empathy.

Out the window and across the street, a black flash. Bo and the shiny mobile pulling into a parking space. Lion checks the clock to be sure. Bo's twenty minutes early.

Dune is still beckoning, but Lion changes direction, picks up his phone and Googles Arctic. He's been to their site before, but the puzzle of this morning makes him want to see their client list. Product development, consulting, start-ups, nothing pharmaceutical, nothing animal rights, nothing that gives him a clue as to what he can't quite sense from those articles and photos.

Nothing that explains Robert Walker's head on the wall.

He glances back at Bo and thinks about the meeting he's about to attend.

"Arctic," he says aloud, wondering again what, exactly, he's gotten himself into.

Turning his attention back to his browser, he decides to find out. Loading Arctic's homepage auto-starts a video of Sir Richard. "The arc of the twentieth century can be traced by the failure of language," as Lion struggles to find PAUSE.

Nearby diners give him hard glares.

"Language crystallizes the nebulous," continues Sir Richard, his accent Middlesex posh with a faint trace of Cockney, "imparting form to the embryonic."

And still too loud.

Unable to find PAUSE, Lion gives up and powers down, tossing the finally quiet phone into his sling-pack in relief. Across the street, Bo steps out of the car to stretch his legs. The waiter brings a fresh carafe of coffee. Lion tries to turn back to his book but can no longer focus.

So sling-pack open again. Trading book for phone and, as the bitten fruit that means *on* begins to glow, Lion feels even more relief. Is there a word for the comforting emotions produced by the presence of technology?

As he's thinking about this his phone buzzes with incoming messages. A text from Lorenzo, which he decides to check later. A second, he doesn't recognize the number. *Possibly Sir Richard* reads the screen, and a stranger message: *Forgive myocardial. Meet Jenka.*

"Forgive myocardial" sounds as serious as a heart attack. "Jenka" means nothing to him.

Like most everything else this morning, this text makes little sense. Or little right now. So these facts get slotted, fodder for his pattern recognition system, fodder for later.

OUT OF THE DIRTY FRENCH, INTO THE SLAV

Turns out, "Forgive myocardial" is autocorrect for "Forgive my tardiness." Not sure how that happened, but maybe Sir Richard's right: The arc of the twentieth century is the failure of language.

Either way, the receptionist with ringlets of blonde and a proper Armani straight skirt assures him, Sir Richard will be late. She offers him a seat on a long, low couch made of red sequins. Like someone skinned a chorus girl.

Turns out to be more comfortable than it looks.

Jenka turns out to be a severe Slav with hair gel, a white Hermès double-breasted suit, a Black Label herringbone knit cashmere tie, and no socks. A male specimen, late-thirties variety, and appears to not like him one bit.

From his perch on the couch, all Lion gets is Slav in side view: cheekbones the size of supercolliders and the left half of a loose pompadour peeking around a corner. Something mumbled. Machinery kicks into gear: primary auditory cortex for signal decoding, Wernicke's area for basic meaning making. A millisecond later, Lion realizes what that something was: a fast hello with a heavy accent.

But before he can respond, Jenka gives him a quick follow-me wave of his hand and disappears back around the corner. Lion extracts himself from the chorus girl, re-slings his sling-pack, and starts after him. Makes it around the corner in time to see sockless ankles marching away from him, in silence, down a very long hallway. Only closed doors of sturdy oak and the watchful eyes of incandescent track lighting keeping Lion company.

Finally, Jenka opens a door at the end of the hall.

"We're in here."

Lion follows him through the entryway and is immediately blinded by the white. Like something out of NASA. White chairs, white table, clean whiteboards on all the walls. The ceiling, some fourteen feet above, a maze of pipes and plumbing, also painted shiny white.

Jenka takes a seat, pointing at another.

Lion slides out a hot-white task chair, like fluorescent baby powder, realizing he's been positioned at the opposite end of a repurposed Ping-Pong table—also in hot white—from Jenka. Eight feet between them and no one else in the room.

"We'll wait for Penelope," says Jenka, not bothering to look at Lion as he speaks.

So they wait. Neither checks his phone. Lion notices that with the white suit in the white room, Jenka is a kind of optical illusion. Depth of field impossible to gauge. Bets this is intentional.

"Who's Penelope?" he asks, eventually.

Jenka slow-pans to the left. "Pardon?"

"Penelope."

"Sorry. Severe jet lag, as you can probably tell. Penelope's bringing the coffee."

"Where were you?"

"Everywhere, I think. Kuala Lumpur last night."

Lion notices an oversized white grub in the corner. He prefers old New York, back before they understood beanbag chairs on the East Coast. Decides there's something not quite right about Jenka, and jet lag is only an excuse. Another thirty seconds of silence and Lion tires of waiting. "Pardon my ignorance," he says, "but who are you?"

Jenka smiles; Lion sees Soviet Bloc silver dental work. "You're asking about my crappy Moldovan childhood? My fake news start-up? How I helped put a real-life James Bond villain into power?"

"What do you do for Arctic?"

"Global director of creative oversight, in charge of the extra-special division."

Lion thinks this through and decides he has no idea what Jenka means, but he's willing to bet this is intentional too.

"I oversee our extra-*special* creatives."

Like that clears it up.

But this is a thing companies have been doing lately. Intentional obfuscation. An old subcultural affect deployed in the face of over-zealous scrutiny, like Bob Dylan in that Scorsese doc, spouting nonsense: "We all like motorcycles, to some degree." Decades later, with the omnipresence of social media and surveillance technology, obfuscation became a brand strategy for edgier brands. Arctic, via the medium of Jenka, is telling Lion something about Arctic.

"And back at you," says Jenka, his accent lending a hard edge to soft consonants. "What is it that you do for us?"

Lion leans forward, setting his elbows on the table, gray sleeves displacing white glow. Doesn't know what to make of Jenka just yet, but he's pretty sure that in Arctic's book em-trackers are found in the file marked SPECIAL CREATIVES. Seems like Jenka should know about him, especially with Arctic's penchant for research. More intentional obfuscation, or something else going on?

He counters with simple truth.

"I say yes or no."

Jenka nods, slowly, like something's been settled.

"I do that as well."

Then he reaches a hand beneath the table, slides open a hidden drawer, and extracts an envelope similar to the one Lion's been carrying. Same thick rag weave. Same double wrap to undo the string.

Jenka lifts the flap and sets his finger on the e-reader. "Like our nano-scanner?"

"Is it new?"

"There have been versions in Malaysia for three years. Sir Richard did a favor for a minister, got an early line on the Western market."

Lion catches the zip of light, hears the soft click. Then the door opens and in walks the missing Penelope. Red hair braided into higher-dimensional knots, full sleeves of ink bleeding through starched white button-down, and a tray with refreshments.

"Would you like coffee, sir?"

A slight tinge of an accent. English? Scottish? And dangerously attractive.

"Just black, please."

White saucer and white cup gets set on white table in front of him. Then she pours a second cup for Jenka, sets it down, and turns to depart. Lion spots a bar code tattoo on the back of her neck. It's the same one that Bo has, including the question mark. Just a soft twinkle, like dying sparklers on a jet-black night.

Do two tattoos a pattern make? Does Arctic have some sort of Rilkean connection?

But, before he can ask, Penelope's out the door, leaving as quickly as she came.

Jenka takes his with two sugars and two packets of powdered milk. The end result is more white. White coffee, white walls, white suit. Lion sips his coffee and savors its blackness.

Sliding a stack of photos out of the envelope, Jenka starts laying them out in a big square on the table. The same images Lion saw this morning, same Arctic icon pulsing in the bottom right corner.

"Mesh electronics in the paper," says Lion.

"Romanian." Not bothering to look up.

After finishing his arrangement, Jenka rises from his chair, rounds the Ping-Pong table, and comes to stand uncomfortably close to Lion. He points at the photos.

"So yes or no?"

Tamping down the slide-away impulse, Lion looks at the images again. Something definitely not right, though he still doesn't know what. But Jenka's too close for comfort, and Lion's never really had much interest in crime puzzles. And with Walker decapitated, definitely a crime puzzle.

"No."

Jenka gives him a serious look from inches away, then reaches two fingers inside his jacket and pulls a silver laser pointer from his breast pocket. Twists the tip and aims the beam at Walker's mounted head.

"You noticed?"

Lion pushes back his chair, trying to get a little distance from Jenka, knocking into one of the photos along the way. A shot from South Africa flutters toward his feet. Reaching down to grab it, he notices the word PONG engraved in diamonds on one of the table's legs. Talk about bling—must be a hundred gemstones in total.

"I noticed," he says, setting the photo back on the table.

"Any thoughts?"

"Gruesome," looking at the image of Walker's head once again. "And someone let Arctic into an active crime scene, or someone knows someone at the crime lab."

"True," says Jenka. "But not what I was asking."

Lion grabs his Moleskine out of his sling-pack, opens it, and reads the note he left himself. It hasn't changed since this morning.

"Someone's hunting the hunters," he says.

Jenka nods again, supercolliders retracting and a flash of Iron Curtain dental work. "And this doesn't interest you?"

"Doesn't really matter."

"Why?"

"I do cultural projection," he says, sliding his notebook back into his sling-pack. "Judging from the nano-scanner and the mesh electronics, Arctic does product development. Do these photos point toward a future product with appeal to an emerging culture is what matters."

"They don't?"

"Not that I can tell."

"How can you tell?"

Lion's never been a fan of this particular conversation, but the check Arctic's cutting is not small. "Shifting culture requires a confluence of inciting incidents. Something directional that leads to a tribal fracturing and reknitting. Often shows up in language first. In music. Fashion. It can feel a little like hope." He points at the images. "This doesn't feel like hope."

"So it's no."

Lion nods.

"You did some work for the Tyrell Corporation," says Jenka, "em-tracking early-stage cyborg evolution."

"I thought you didn't know who I was?"

"Also for Weyland-Yutani, that led to a new kind of body armor. And then in Sicily, a Mafia spin-off group, that crazy ICO, the hover-scooter, the arrests."

"I can't talk about it. Nondisclosures."

Jenka sighs, clicks the laser pointer off and returns it to his inside breast pocket. Stepping in front of Lion, he slides the sling-pack to a far corner of the table and begins restacking photos. A precision operation by the looks of it. Only after the nano-scanner whirs closed does he seem to remember that Lion is even in the room.

"Sir Richard will be here any moment."

He isn't following.

"It would be better if you told him yourself."

Lion can think of absolutely no reason it would be better, but it doesn't matter. Sir Richard isn't there in a moment. Or another. So good-bye to the white room and back down the long hall. Jenka stops him at the front door, a hand grabbing his elbow.

"You'll be available later? If Sir Richard desires to call?"

Lion almost yanks his arm away, but then he notices Penelope, standing at the edge of the waiting room, watching him. She has a look in her eyes he's seen before. He flashes on the look in Robert Walker's eyes. Regret? Remorse? And what about him would make her feel that way?

He doesn't know.

But before he can do anything about this puzzle, Penelope turns on her heel and disappears back down the hall, taking his question and her question mark tattoo along for the ride.

But Jenka is still there, still waiting for his answer.

Back to Bo and the shiny mobile and now working their way through Times Square traffic. Living-screen billboards the size of buildings make him think *Blade Runner*. Discover new life in the off-world colonies. What did Lorenzo say—without the voice-over it's just a movie about a psychopath with a cool gun.

This reminds him of the message he never checked.

Lion opens his sling-pack to retrieve his phone. Double-clicks the text, sees a familiar refrain: *There are mines over there, and mines over there, and watch out, those goddamn monkeys bite.*

Lorenzo's way of asking for contact.

Also kind of an SOS. When really tired, Lorenzo limits all his communications to *Apocalypse Now* quotes. More intentional obfuscation, though he maintains it was once a very practical form of communication.

The text is accompanied by a photo of the band playing a gig in what looks like Japan. Kanji neon over saloon-style bar, rhinestone cowboy hats on the patrons, sawdust on the floors.

So contact via Skype perhaps, an idea that makes him smile.

Lorenzo is a friend. And, at sixty-six, nearly thirty years older than Lion, though it's often hard to tell. Stuck on semi-permanent adolescent, also a cinephile and a conga player in a cow-punk blues band. The band does Robert Johnson through Social Distortion. Lorenzo does the older groupies.

Lion starts to plot out his afternoon. Food, nap, some Ghost Trainwreck and Skype with Lorenzo.

Inside, he can feel his stress levels level off.

The human brain does information acquisition, pattern recognition, and goal direction. Give the goal direction system a goal and you give the pattern recognition system a purpose and the information acquisition system a target. Cortisol levels drop. It's why, Lion believes, everyone needs a mission.

And this reminds him.

Types *I wanted a mission and, for my sins, they gave me one* into the text box. It's his *Apocalypse Now* response, code for "Give me a few hours before contact."

Message sent, Lion decides to leave himself a post-nap reminder to call Lorenzo. He reaches into his sling-pack for his notebook but can't seem to find it. Swats around for a while, then dumps the bag onto the seat beside him. Strands of loose tobacco slide into every available crevice; his copy of *Dune,* a couple of pens.

No notebook.

When did he see it last? The meeting? He remembers Jenka easing up next to him. He examines each pocket carefully. No Moleskine. He remembers Jenka stepping in front of him and sliding his sling-pack to the corner of the table. How long does it take to steal a notebook? Lion shakes the bag a few more times to be sure, triple-checks the pockets. Finds the Arctic envelope wedged into the designated laptop sleeve. Nothing more.

Why would Jenka steal his notebook?

None of it makes sense; all of it makes him twitchy. He tries telling himself that it was a new notebook, with only one note, and he can take the loss. When that fails, tells himself to take a breath. Doesn't help.

Walker's head mounted on the wall, the white-on-white room, the full creepiness of the day begins to register.

Pulse throb in his neck, levels spiking.

He hunts out the window for something to take his mind off the subject. Gray skies and gray buildings, pedestrians in auto-walk mode. And too depressing to be distracting.

He counters with the *Dune* mantra: "Fear is the mind-killer. Fear is the little-death that brings total obliteration. I will face my fear. I will permit it to pass over me and through me. Where the fear has gone there will be nothing. Only I will remain."

But it's no use. Adrenaline's pumping through his system, like fire ants crawling through his veins.

Out the window, an argument in front of an auto body shop, two men in stained coveralls, one threatening the other with a tire iron— or exactly how Lion feels about Jenka right now.

"We're going to need to make a stop," he tells Bo, through gritted teeth.

Sunglasses in the rearview. "Where would you like to go?"

"A place that sells Moleskines."

"The notebooks?"

Nods, brushing tobacco strands into his palm, squeezing for all he's worth.

"Union Square Barnes and Noble?"

"That'll work."

Bo takes a left at the light. Lion feels dread mixed with jet lag mixed with what the fuck.

THREE-INDIAN TUESDAY

A walk might calm him down.

Lion asks Bo to pull over, just a random block somewhere along East Seventeenth. The SUV glides to the curb with a floating sensation, almost like a boat docking. The door opens automatically the moment the rocking ceases, with reflexes too responsive to be a sign of life.

Rather a sign of not-life.

An auto-stair uncurls, a rail of nonslip synth-rubber in high-gloss black, and a low clunk as it locks into place.

"Half hour?" asks Bo.

"In front of the bookstore," says Lion, pointing into the distance.

His boots hit the stair, next the ground. The sure grip of asphalt below, gray skies threatening rain above.

Chasing the calm, he tells himself.

One step out of the vehicle and Lion starts to straighten up. Two steps and a sideways toss of his hand sends tobacco strands into a storm drain. Three steps and he's fully ambulatory, catching sight of a sky crane on a distant roof, like a giant robot resting its head on storm clouds.

Chasing the calm was the way he explained it, thinking of the Q&A session after that University of Chicago talk. Standing onstage with white-hot lights blinding him. All he could see was the edges of the room, and pin spots shining down on photographs of oversized floating heads. Twelve-foot-high images of Nobel-laureate alumni, their sentinel faces in black-and-white, hanging on all the walls. Michelson, with his brushfire mustache, for measuring the speed of light; Abrikosov, like a family doctor from the 1950s, for superconducting superfluids.

Lion doesn't remember the question, only his answer. Anxiety is the enemy of empathy. Fear makes us egocentric; egocentric makes us blind. An amygdala/prefrontal-cortex two-step that narrows the search parameters of the pattern recognition system. Pretty soon, as anxiety climbs too high, we lose our ability to find one another.

Chasing the calm wasn't his logos. The phrase first showed up at the early meet-ups, meant to describe an em-tracker's tool kit, a way to handle the heightened emotions. Lion is working his way through the kit. He tried the deep breathing, and the *Dune* mantra; now he chases the calm with long strides.

Halfway down the block, a pair of Uber autonomous taxis idle by the curb, the *U* in "Uber" pulsing pink from their side doors. Similar in color to the Red Ice icon, and meant as both a warning sign and a sign of life. Not your father's sign, either. A new species of habit machine: awake and aware, but not quite conscious. So the hot-pink *U* is a new kind of signifier, and one of the conditions placed on the New York test fleet rollout.

He read this somewhere, and recently.

Another glance reveals their Lidar eyes have evolved again. Less insectoid, more gunship, but still seeing all. Nearly four hundred million data points a second, and definitely capturing the data points of his set jaw and tight grimace.

The car sees emotions. Signals have been pre-programmed, down to the basement level, below Ekman's micro-expressions, getting to the core biophysical: heart rate variability, blood oxygen levels.

And all from pointing a laser at a tiny vein in the human forehead.

The car sees emotions, yet feels nothing. So morality too has to be pre-scripted into the code. Aim for garbage cans and not pedestrians; aim for solitary pedestrians rather than large groups. Empathy programmer, he's heard it called, someone's job now.

Lion walks on, a few blocks at a faster pace. Past a line of aluminum garbage cans and a series of well-kept brownstones, thinking about those Bolivian chemists and the last time he was in this area. They turned a top-flight walk-up into one of the better labs on the East Coast, slept in bunk beds, rarely slept. Lion counted stars in the sky one night, perched beside the toilet in their bathroom, high on something he couldn't pronounce.

Woke up there too. The stars turned out to be glow-in-the-dark paint splattered on ancient asbestos. The hangover turned out to be different than expected. Grapheme-colored synesthesia, heavy impact on vowels. The letter *A* a somber red. *E* a translucent lilac, clearly a happy letter. The catalyst a not fully described dopamine-acetylcholine interaction, or so the Bolivians had said.

He takes a left at the light, now able to make out the outline of Union Square in the distance, and quickens his pace. A thwack of high-density plastic as a skater sails the curb in front of him; defensive maneuvering arcs him into a tour bus unloading Bulgarians in matching purple tracksuits.

He crosses the street to avoid them, cutting into the square, passing a vendor selling vintage medical equipment on a folding table. An array of ivory-handled bone saws, cutting teeth made of silver, carefully laid out on a red velvet tablecloth.

Reminds him of another of those early em-tracker meet-ups. Red velvet chairs in a Victorian tearoom, and when was that? Definitely after the Rod of Correction story in Jamaica, smoking early attempts at Ghost Trainwreck on the front steps of Tuff Gong, and just a few days before his talent emerged. Past those initial rounds of neuro-probing, the brain scans at UCLA, his chance to meet other em-trackers for the first time. All of them trying to figure out what the hell was happening, one of them coming up with the idea for the get-togethers.

So more than a decade ago.

A quick left around a leafy hedge, and he sees the bronze statue of Gandhi with walking stick, a garland of orchids draped around his neck.

Someone says, "Get the Indian with the Indian."

Get the what?

Neck cranes left, then right. Then he notices: a tall Sioux in beaded elk-skin posing in front of Gandhi, talking to a Bengali woman in a red silk sari shooting video with her phone.

Data bit finds data bit. For the first time today, Lion cracks a smile.

The woman notices his expression. "It's three-Indian Tuesday," she says.

Another smile, seems to be clearing his head. Arctic with their research, Jenka with his notebook, that white-on-white room. Intentional intimidation meets intentional obfuscation, and one thing for sure: If he gets the chance, he's going to punch Jenka in the mouth.

Then he notices Gandhi again. Nonviolent salt maker in slowly oxidizing copper. So maybe he won't punch Jenka.

Nope.

Right in his Communist Bloc kisser.

Which is when he spots the Moleskines. Last thing he remembers is the Indians. Now he finds himself standing in front of a Moleskine notebook display. Clothbound volumes arranged in order of size. He looks around slowly. Hardbacks on bookshelves in every direction. People carrying lattes. Did he robo-walk into Barnes and Noble? No other explanation pops into his head, and another thing for sure: His habit machinery works just fine.

Lion grabs a Moleskine, going traditional black cover, blank pages. Sometimes he prefers graph paper, especially when drawing the vector diagrams needed to explain subcult melds to corporate types. He remembers the executive boardroom in the Grand Rama Tower, Bangkok, trying to explain to an East Asian mining consortium how the splatter-punk arm of the Mumbai Tantras would soon corner the market for 3-D-printed silver jewelry. "So the English Goths of the 1980s begat the American Emo movement of the early 2000s begat the Mumbai Tantras circa 2015. . . ."

But he's done with corporate types for the moment, so squelches the memory. And stays traditional: black cover, blank pages, empty of logos.

Notebook in hand, Lion glances back and forth, trying to remember which way he came in. Science and Science Fiction to the left: Psychology and Self-Help to the right.

He strides into Psychology, with a confidence he does not feel.

Book spines on either side. Titles he recalls from college, the weight of all the time that's passed between then and now catching him unexpectedly, and heavier than usual.

Still no exit in sight.

Lion decides to head left, stepping around a stack of paperbacks in the aisle. *The Collected Works of Charles Dickens,* an anniversary edition wrapped in cellophane, a sticker on the outside with black Bauhaus lettering: "We wear the chains we forge in life."

Two aisles later, he feels his phone buzz his pocket and stops walking to check the message. Possibly Sir Richard again and "Available for pinging?"

He doesn't know.

Hunting his answer on the shelves in front of him, Lion spots *Your Erroneous Zones, Your Erroneous Zones, Your Erroneous Zones*— Wayne Dyer in triplicate. He must have made his way into Self-Help. Also a huge blue book with white lettering: *Infinite Jest* by David Foster Wallace.

Definitely not Self-Help, but it gives him an idea.

Infinite Jest is Lorenzo's favorite novel, also his version of the I

Ching. When faced with uncertainty, he'd open it at random, searching for a sign in the text. "Yarrow casting for lit snobs," Lorenzo called it.

Lion slides the book off the shelf, snaps page 37 open. Sees "Year of the Trial-Size Dove Bar" in big, bold letters. The Year of the Trial-Size Dove Bar, he recalls, is Wallace's version of our near-term future, where the calendar itself is available for advertising sponsorship purposes. "Subsidized Time" is what Wallace called it, and fairly prophetic.

Not exactly the sign Lion was looking for, but he feels it anyway, that familiar tug, how he used to feel as a journalist on the front end of a story, that sense of a question forming: How the hell did Robert Walker's head end up on that wall?

And that tug again, not quite curiosity, more like gravity.

So yes, apparently, he's available for pinging.

Slides the book back onto the shelf and thumbs his response to Richard. The cheerful whoosh that means send and, finally, Lion spots the checkout counter in the distance.

Navigates without incident.

"Would you like to try our chocolate-covered crickets, sir?" as he hands his Moleskine to the clerk. Plastic rectangular name tag reads JOHN ANDERSON; face seems to be Korean exchange student. "Peruvian dark, eighty-eight percent cacao, knock your taste buds to Tunisia."

"Pardon?"

"Also a great protein snack."

Lion's not tracking.

"We also have *The Well-Hanged Man: The Unpublished Poems of Stephen King*. On sale for Easter."

Then he gets it: the dreaded up-sell.

"Does it look like I've forgotten how to shop?" he asks.

"Sir?"

"Do I appear to have choice amnesia?"

"I'm not . . ."

"Like I no longer know what I want?"

"The crickets are also on sale, sir," fumbles the clerk.

Lion glances out the front door, then back at Mr. Anderson.

"It's also three-Indian Tuesday," he says, "but I'll just take the notebook."

Lion finds the SUV out front, curbside, its hazards pulsing like a heartbeat. Slow and steady. Bo nowhere in sight. Then he spots him, straightening up beside the front right fender, polishing the headlights with what looks like actual deerskin.

Once again, Bo notices that he notices.

"Also lab grown," says Bo, tossing over the rag.

Lion snatches it out of the air. It's a different kind of soft, but with no haptic memory of deerskin, he has no actual grounds for comparison. "More tissue engineering?"

"Not my department," says Bo, "but yeah, animal friendly."

"Progress."

"Agreed," nods Bo. "You get everything you wanted?"

Tossing the rag back, Lion slips the notebook from his back pocket, wags it twice. "I did, thanks."

"Would you like to go back to the hotel?"

Nods.

The side door to the SUV glides open and Lion climbs inside. He settles into the seat, hearing that exhale again, like the upholstery is breathing. Also a sign that his ears have adjusted to the city, now able to find clear signal amid New York white noise.

Bo slips into the front seat and slides the car into traffic. Congestion in every direction. Buses, trucks, cars, cabs, and a heavyset woman in a corseted Victorian frock pedaling a ten-speed. A look of fierce determination and her hands iron-gripped on the handlebars.

Hunting a way out, Bo banks a smooth right turn, dodges two cars to get across three lanes, and a harder left. He drives halfway down the block and darts through a dark alley. Lion sees redbrick buildings on either side of the fenders, and a menacing slash of Cyrillic graffiti. But when they pop out the other side, the road in front of them is completely devoid of traffic.

Just a long asphalt ribbon the way its creator intended.

"I don't think I've ever seen an empty street in New York before," says Lion.

"Part of the service," replies Bo, with a smile.

"How did you know?"

Bo touches a finger to his right ear. "New Arctic tech. Subdermal implant. Waze mixed with satellite feeds."

"You're getting real-time traffic patterns?"

"Better. Predictive algorithms. I get traffic patterns two minutes before they appear."

Lion isn't sure he could take the constant chatter in his ear. "I'd go bonkers," he says.

"It's haptic. I have it set on small dog. Like being kissed by a pug. One lick for straight, two for right."

"A pug?"

"I'm used to it."

Before Lion can respond, Bo jerks the SUV quickly to the right, just missing two stockbrokers on electric longboards. Another second and it would have been pancaked pinstripes. So primal instinct or predictive algorithms?

"Nice move," says Lion.

Bo touches a finger to the rim of his Kangol.

Thinking about it a moment, Lion doesn't believe it matters anymore: Instincts and algorithms are becoming indistinguishable. Evolution, blind as a bat, still managed to design the human brain to handle peripherals. A white-tipped cane, a cochlear implant, whatever. The system is pre-prepared for the easy integration of external data feeds. But if Arctic's implant has the ability to spot stockbrokers from space? That's a level of high-res detail that only comes, Lion suspects, from tapping into military-grade feeds.

That might matter.

And not something he wants to forget.

He pulls his new Moleskine from his sling-pack, finds a pen, and slices a fingernail through the cellophane. Opening to the first page, he jots down a reminder: "Arctic. Someone knows someone." Then he recalls the Ghost Trainwreck, the lab-grown skin on the dragon box, and every other detail Sir Richard's researchers seem to have dug out of his past.

Starts a fresh line: "And someone did their homework."

He looks up as they slow for a red. Corner of Houston and something. To his right, a rusted Gremlin. To his left, a storefront selling forgotten game consoles alongside fresh produce A stack of red Japanese pears in a raw wooden crate next to a tower display of Xbox 360s, and a store clerk in a white-on-white suit. A suit exactly like Jenka's.

Then the light greens and he hears "Down by the Seaside" in cheerful synth.

Someone is calling.

"Lion Zorn," says a voice that sounds like Sir Richard on autoplay. "Great to meet you."

Not sounds like, actually is.

"Sir Richard?"

"Just Richard, please. I'm truly sorry I missed our meeting."

So this is what billionaires sound like on the phone. Different than expected. Same Queen's English consonants, much friendlier than the autoplay.

"Not much happened," says Lion.

Silence on the line and also unexpected. Could Richard really be thinking before he speaks?

"Your em-tracking system . . ." says Richard, then another pause, "I'm sorry, is 'system' the right term?"

"System is fine."

"So your em-tracking system did not detect a signal."

"No."

"If you will," says Richard, "I'd like the chance to change your mind."

"It doesn't really work like that," aiming for even tones. "It's a kind of gut instinct—just yes or no."

"Can I buy you dinner?"

"It won't change the no to a yes."

"Jenka," says Richard, "Jenka said you were intrigued."

Lion flashes on side-view pompadour and the sensation that is almost, but not quite, angry.

"Jenka stole my notebook," he says flatly.

"He mentioned that you had left it behind."

"Doubtful," says Lion.

"Penelope found it under the table. I can have someone drop it by your hotel, if you need it now, or I can bring it to dinner."

"You understand, crime isn't my thing."

"Says the reporter."

Lion feels pinpricks on his neck. Remembers the note he just left himself. Someone did their homework. Remembers the reason he left himself that note.

"Ex-reporter."

"There's a new Tibetan place on D. Heard it's great. Yak by Yang and Jake—so poly-tribe Tibetan, I suppose."

Which is when Lion feels the gravity again and knows, resistance is starting to fail. Somewhere between what does Tibetan food actually taste like and Arctic's check representing three months off his mortgage, easy. Plus, what would Lorenzo say: "Gravity, it's not just a good idea, it's the law."

"Could you meet me at the Ludlow instead?" says Lion, giving in, but feeling the edge of the countdown.

"Seven o'clock at the Messy French?"

Dirty French, thinks Lion, but leaves it alone.

"Seven o'clock is great."

Lion hangs up, slides the phone into his pack, and leans back into the seat. A second later . . . or what feels like a second later . . . he realizes they're pulling up in front of the Ludlow. How'd they get here so fast? A gap in his memory, like the time lost between Union Square and the bookstore. Not a comforting feeling, but one he's gotten used to.

The brain uses 25 percent of our energy at rest. Lion, with his information filters wide open, uses more. Makes him sleepy. Makes him lose time. Makes him forget anything without significant emotional salience. The downsides of em-tracking, like a North Star he never wanted.

Bo clicks on his blinker, slipping back into the exact same spot he occupied this morning. Directly across from the hotel.

The licking pug must be on the job.

A doorman he doesn't recognize, with a pompadour all his own. Shorn on the sides and bleached platinum on the top. The Thin White Duke model and more wedding cake ornament than hairstyle.

"Welcome back."

Across the threshold and into the lobby. In the daytime, the wood-paneled walls exude translucent ocher. In the distance, slashes of light from the atrium, catching dust motes midflight like insects in amber.

"Mr. Zorn?" calls the desk clerk.

Lion stops and turns.

"Yes?"

"A package came for you."

"A package?"

"I had it sent up."

He didn't order anything. Doesn't recall ordering anything. "What is it?"

"Don't know," with a shrug. "It was in a box this big." The clerk holds his fingers six inches apart. "I just signed for it."

"Do you remember who delivered it?"

"Woman, red hair, white shirt, early thirties." Touches the back of his neck. "A question mark tattoo here."

Lion realizes he's talking about Penelope, then realizes it's the same clerk from last night. Same lilting afro. Different skinny suit.

"You're working a double?"

A big smile. A phone. A couple of clicks.

The clerk holds out the screen, showing Lion a photo of flesh and cloth, a very small human wrapped in a very big blanket. "Have to keep her in diapers."

Everyone a story. Another thing Lorenzo had said, the night they met, smoking cigarettes on that Twin Peaks rooftop in San Francisco. Lorenzo pointing at the lights of the city in the distance, ten thousand fireflies and each one a life, each one with memories as thick as our own, everyone a story.

"Congratulations," says Lion.

"My angel."

But the thought of babies makes Lion weary. Not just babies. Also dust mites. Packages. It clicks into place: the countdown again. Emo-stim overload meets that vicious jet lag. T minus three minutes as he starts across the lobby.

"Have a pleasant afternoon, Mr. Zorn."

A little crowd when he gets to the elevator. A dreadlocked woman with a silver hoop through her eyebrow rides with him to five, the really big engagement ring stays on to eight, the Cleveland Browns jersey until nine. Has the car to himself after that.

Out of the elevator and down the hallway. Right, left, right. A déjà vu wave of exhaustion as he opens the door, gray skies pouting through a wall of windows as he steps inside. A freshly made bed, white linen and corners pulled hospital tight, calling his name.

On the bedside table, he sees the package that Penelope dropped off. A small white cardboard box with a white envelope on top of it. Red Ice icon on the bottom right corner of both. Not pulsing. Lifeless.

Yet, Lion suspects, no less dangerous.

But T minus one minute—so he'll wait to open them.

Blackout curtains bring the blackout.

In the darkness, he undresses quickly. Shoes and socks. Straight-world uniform slides to the floor, like a puddle of cloth. Leaves jeans and sweater where they fall, slips under covers. His head hits the pillow before T minus thirty seconds.

He doesn't dream. Just a deep hard sleep.

Waking, when it comes, comes easier than expected. Transitioning through the hypnogogic, and Lion feels like himself again, or some close facsimile.

Out of bed and into his habit. Slides the coffee pod into place, cocks the chrome arm, and chooses the lie that is large cup. He takes a shower while the coffee brews. Not a thought in his head.

The first thought arrives while toweling off: Is he late? Doesn't seem like he overslept, but walks into the bedroom to check the clock. Ninety minutes until dinner and more than enough time to stick to his plan. Ghost Trainwreck and Lorenzo, in that order.

Dragon box, new notebook, phone in one hand, coffee cup in the other. He crosses the room and reaches the curtains, but his hands are already occupied. Has to stack cup atop phone to slide them apart. A dicey moment as he blinks away the incoming light, but his auto-balancing program seems to be awake as well.

Not a drop spills.

Drapes parted, he opens the terrace door and steps outside. Skies of leaden gunmetal and buildings that match. Also strangely quiet, more white than noise, and maybe the reason for the wall of black plastic shingles behind the potted mini-firs. Some kind of sonic absorptive in the polymer.

This time he chooses one of the lounge chairs, but after sitting down and stretching out decides he doesn't want to be that comfortable. What would Lorenzo say: It never ends well, not for nations, not for individuals, this getting too comfortable with comfortable.

Lion stands up and carries his coffee, notebook, and phone over to the glass table. Auto-chair molds to his frame, back straight, feet on the floor. Exactly what was required. Fully conscious, fully lucid.

But not for long.

Lion opens the dragon box, this time deciding 50-50 seems about right. He crumples dank weed in with drier tobacco and scoops the pile into a rolling paper. Pushing the edges together, thumbs slide up, thumbs slide down, until this universal origami produces a tight cylinder.

He clicks his lighter with one hand, punches open the Skype app with the other. Hits the connect button. Inhales as it starts to ring, exhales as—but what time is it in Japan?

Hangs up a second later.

Google tells him it's 4:00 A.M. in Tokyo.

Awake? he texts Lorenzo instead.

Twenty seconds later, he hears his Skype ringing. Clicks the answer tab.

"You're awake," he says.

The screen pixilates for a second, then settles down. Lorenzo, seated at a hotel room desk, snaps into view. Broad shoulders, pale skin, five-day gray stubble coating heavy jowls. He's wearing aviator sunglasses, a straw cowboy hat, and some kind of kimono, red silk decorated with steampunk iconography. A qwerty keyboard made out of bronze, attached to a leather bracelet, attached to a bodice-clad woman. A man dressed in a top hat and tails, wearing a gas mask, carrying a copper telescope.

"I never went to bed," says Lorenzo.

"Have you been playing gigs in that?"

Slides back in his chair and raises a leg. Lion sees boxer shorts that match the kimono, bare bulgy knees and dusty brown shit-kickers worn with tube socks, white cotton with three red stripes.

"Boots and all," says Lorenzo, taking off his sunglasses and setting them down. Red-rimmed eyes, either lack of sleep or something actually wrong.

"Are you okay?" Lion asks.

"I used to think if I died in an evil place, then my soul wouldn't be able to make it to heaven. But now, fuck, I don't care where it goes as long as it ain't here."

More *Apocalypse Now*, also Lorenzo's usual gripe about long tours. And something mildly amphetamine in his voice, so the red eyes—it's probably just lack of sleep.

"How's Japan?"

"Been here for three weeks and I honestly can't tell you. Inscrutable. And lots of tea."

"But you're okay? I got your request for contact."

"Hank's being stingy with the drink tickets," says Lorenzo, lighting a cigarette with an ancient brass Zippo. "But what else is new. Other than that, I just wanted to see how you be."

"Fine," he robo-answers, then stops himself. "Though that may not be exactly true."

"You're in New York?"

Lion nods.

"What's going on?"

He talks Lorenzo through his day: Robert Walker's head on the wall, Arctic's predilection for research, his stolen notebook. Feels good to say it aloud, seems to neutralize the surreality. He finishes with his perplexing dinner plans with Sir Richard.

"Sounds like Japan," says Lorenzo, but not smiling. "Did you really see a guy's head on a wall?"

"A photo."

"That's a thing? Bad enough that I need Sinder to get a date, now we're into decapitation."

"Sinder?'

"Tinder for old farts," exhaling a thick cloud. "A head on a wall is not something you see every day."

"No."

"Think it's a new kind of subcult? French Revolution revivalists mixed with great white hunters?"

"Doesn't feel like it."

Lorenzo thinks about this a moment, "Are you still gonna take the job?"

"I took the job. Now it seems like they want me to take some other job."

The wind whips between buildings, sending a quiver through the green needles of the mini-fir. Lion hears a momentary hum from the black polymer, like someone choking off a scream.

"I thought all you do is say yes or no."

"I do," agrees Lion. "I did, at a meeting this morning. Tried to. But Sir Richard called afterward, and it sounds like they're still interested."

"He of the mighty checkbook," says Lorenzo. "You're getting paid, right?"

"I am. I definitely am."

"That's never a bad thing."

"Maybe," he says. "I don't know about this time."

"Because they did enough research to find out you smoke pot? Kemosabe, everyone smokes pot." But watching him carefully.

Lion takes a sip of coffee, catching the reflection of his right eye in the dark liquid. Fractal red lines on his cornea, the temporary tattoo of Ghost Trainwreck. Focuses back on Lorenzo. "You ever heard of an inhalant, a silver powder, like someone scraped a sparkler?"

"Party drug?"

"Possibly," considering the idea, "but it's a strange kind of party."

"What does it do?"

"Not sure, but here's the thing—it's got something to do with animals."

Lorenzo sits up straight. "Animals?"

"That's what I mean," says Lion. "Arctic seems to know a little too much about me."

Lorenzo picks up his sunglasses and twirls them back and forth between his fingers. Mirrored frames catch steampunk on red silk. Bodice-clad woman on the upswing, men with clock parts for eyes on the down.

"Let me ask around," he says finally.

"I'd appreciate it."

"No sweat, Kemosabe," pushing up the brim of his hat.

SWEAT, KEMOSABE, SWEAT

t's still early, so the Dirty French is only half full. Sir Richard is waiting for him at the left elbow of the bar. Lion expected a suit, something Savile Row in hard-edged navy. He gets early 2000s hip-hop instead. A throwback Ben Wallace jersey in faded Piston cerulean worn over a white T-shirt four sizes too big for him, saggy Sean John jeans tucked into unscuffed Timberlands, and a trucker's cap in sunshine orange.

Behind the bar, bottles of expensive liquor, and a mirror. Richard spots Lion's reflection in the glass and spins on his stool to face him. The same face Lion has seen in the tabloids. Sir Richard Receives Secret Technology from Aliens; Sir Richard's 48 Children by 48 Different Women. White teeth in even rows, eyes too shimmery blue for anyone's good, and I HAVE ISSUES printed on the brim of the trucker cap.

You can get through this, Lion tells himself.

"You must be Lion," says Sir Richard, extending a hand.

"I must," he says, extending a hand.

Firm grip meets firm grip. That ancient signal: Feel the flesh for yourself, I carry no weapons. Lion isn't so sure.

"Have a seat," says Richard, tapping the red leather of the stool beside him. Lion cops a squat and bellies up. Bartender in white tux with crimson bow tie wants to know what he wants.

"Ah-ha," says Richard, high tea accent turning two syllables into four, "the eternal question."

You can get through this, thinks Lion, then changes his mind and orders a Knob Creek.

"Rocks?" asks the bartender.

"Neat."

"A purist," says Richard, plucking his Ben Wallace, the jersey's fabric stretching out from his chest, fluttering back. "Pardon my peacocking. I caught a ride with Prince Shiz and he insisted on dressing me before I got on his plane."

Lion blinks.

Half-Louisiana Creole, half Jamaican, Prince Shiz is a Toaster throwback with KRS-1 leanings and Arabian-Zydeco rhythms. A poly-tribe superstar. *Preaching, Teaching, and Steaching* stayed number one for years; then after Shiz vanished—riding rumors that he went the way of the Tupac—stayed there for longer.

"I thought no one had seen him in years," says Lion.

"Three years, four months, and twenty-two days."

"That sounds oddly specific."

Richard sips champagne from a tall flute, peering at him through expensive stemware, deciding something. Decides.

"It was Arctic technology that helped him disappear."

"A cloak of invisibility?"

Teeth in rows again. "A new kind of scrubber. AI, of course, and capable of removing any hint of a person from very early in the data chain."

"How early?"

"The system targets the first echo of binary translation, the ones and zeros that comprise the foundational information. The AI works backward through the code, removing a zero here, a one there."

"To what end?"

Lion's drink arrives. Liquid in burnt sienna sloshing in heavy-bottomed glassware. Richard waits until the bartender is out of earshot to begin speaking again.

"Say a photo of Prince Shiz appears. In the original file, the image, once clear, becomes blurry. In any copy, enough corruption that the file is rejected. Essentially, it makes sharing information impossible."

Lion picks up his glass, trying to figure out if he's being lied to. Sharing of information being foundational to the internet. Sir Richard not striking him as the kind of man one would want in possession of a technology that can unhinge that foundation. "You're serious?"

"I'd wager you thought Shiz went the way of Tupac."

"I also heard he went Rilkean," watching closely for some kind of reaction, "back before they were even a myth."

"No," shaking his head firmly against it, "those rumors aren't true."

"Because you know Shiz?"

"Because I started those rumors." Another sip of champagne, another smile. "Actually, Jenka started them. He's very good."

"Why?"

"What do you know about the Rilkeans?"

"Deep subcult. One of the first poly-tribes. And a lot of whispers: hard-core environmentalists, serious consciousness hackers, bar code tattoos—which, I guess, considering Bo and Penelope, is now confirmed. But why start rumors about Shiz being a Rilkean?"

"Let's come back to that in a moment. I'd like to ask you something first. You were a journalist?"

Lion tastes his bourbon, midlevel octane burn in his throat as he swallows.

"It was a long time ago."

"Nabokov said the most interesting part of a writer's biography is the biography of his style. What was your style?"

Interrogative flattery, designed to slice to the heart of the ego without tripping alarm wires. Lion finds himself unable to resist. "I was a new New Journalist. A revivalist."

"Exactly," says Richard, snapping his fingers twice, the same beatnik clap that Jenka had used, "exactly what I thought."

Why, thinks Lion, why would you think that?

"I read you. The Rod of Correction piece. All that excitement in Jamaica."

"That was a long time ago."

"But I'm a fan of the genre. I make all my employees read *Slouching Towards Bethlehem*. So we have a connection, you and I."

He's a carnivore, thinks Lion, always remember he's a carnivore.

"Why that style?" asks Richard. "What was the attraction?"

"It's an approach to truth."

"Tell me."

"Journalism is supposed to be about hunting the truth. Objective truth. But coming out of the 1950s, there was a growing mistrust of this idea, especially among journalists."

"So Chomsky was right?"

"Not like that. No corporate overlords. Nothing that complicated."

"So what, then?"

"You call it the failure of language," says Lion, "which it sort of is. A winnowing of meaning. Reporter goes out and reports the facts. Then writes them up, choosing idea one and two, discarding three and four. Quote A over quote B. No malice, simply the process. Then editors make other choices. Discard this plotline, explore that tangent. Copy editors, managing editors, editor in chief. No one wants distortion, but choosing itself is the distortion. It creates a version of the truth, but it's definitely not objective."

"It's a story," says Richard, polishing off the final swallow of champagne, waving at the bartender for another glass.

"Yeah," says Lion. "So New Journalists fought back by inserting themselves into the story. They let you behind the curtain, replacing false objectivity with extreme subjectivity. You can get to know the storyteller and understand the why behind their choices."

"Thompson's paranoia in Vegas," says Richard. "Didion's detachment in San Francisco. You're saying this is a more honest form of storytelling?"

Lion nods. "An approach to the truth."

"Fantastic," snapping fingers again, once with the left hand, twice with the right. "Let's eat."

And no sooner does he say it, food starts arriving. Crimson bow tie setting down plates, covering the bar in cow parts and crustacean remains and something that might be asparagus. Richard diving in, scooping food into maw, masticating for all he's worth, swallow and repeat.

Lion tries the asparagus.

Richard swallows again. "I'd like you to go out to the crime scene."

"Pardon?"

"Walker's home. I've had it preserved as it was found. I'd like you to go there and see if it changes your mind."

Lion wonders what it takes to have a crime scene preserved, then wonders how he would feel seeing that decapitated head up close. Doesn't like either wondering one bit.

"I don't do crime."

"I know," nodding enthusiastically, "but go anyway."

How often do people turn down Sir Richard? A churn in his stomach. Not very often. Lion opts for the dodge. "Why did you have Jenka start rumors about Shiz being a Rilkean?"

Richard takes his trucker hat off and sets it on the bar. His shaggy black mane tumbles down to his shoulders and I HAVE ISSUES stares Lion in the face.

"Do you know what Arctic does?"

"Product development." Thinks about those Shiz rumors. "And guerrilla marketing."

The light in Richard's eyes seems to flatten. Some kind of line has been crossed. "Products are for the dead," he says, like he wants to spit. "Kodak did products. AOL did bloody products. They're a relic of the last century, a nostalgia. Products are a finite game. Arctic is always, always interested in the infinite game."

"Richard," carefully, "what infinite game?"

"Buckminster Fuller said don't try to change human behavior. It's a waste of time. Evolution doesn't mess around; the patterns are too deep. Fuller said go after the tools. Better tools lead to better people. Arctic doesn't develop products. We may cultivate them, occasionally, in our own particular way, but our business is change. Significant change."

Lion's gut broadcasts another warning, coming in Funktion-One loud and Harman Kardon clear.

"And the Rilkeans?"

"They might have a tool I was interested in cultivating."

"Might?"

"It was a hunch. I was trying to confirm it, but there was an issue."

"No one had ever seen a Rilkean."

"Not back then. And no web presence. I had Jenka go deep. No dark web presence."

Now he gets the purpose of the rumors. "You were trying to smoke them out."

Richard nods. "Shiz was the honey pot. I figured if the Rilkeans got a sudden rush of publicity it might stir things up. Might make them, even momentarily, visible." Lifts his fresh flute to his lips and takes a large gulp of champagne. "So now you know—will you visit the crime scene?"

In the early days of em-tracking, not long after the talent was first identified, there was talk of a felt-sense of the future that rises up so quickly that it completely blots out the present. Like an emotional time machine, past the event horizon, through the wormhole and gone. Not having had this experience, Lion assumed he might be immune. Now, he's not so sure.

"I'll sleep on it."

"I'll have Bo meet you here at nine o'clock. You'll be back before dinner. Or you can spend the night in Montauk."

And that tug again. Gravity. Pulling him in an unfamiliar direction. Also the sight of a carnivore winking and smiling at him.

So many teeth. So much gravity.

Lion dreams of William James. A simulacrum of sorts. Photos he's seen becoming animate, approaching. James in the Amazon, wearing cream-colored trousers, a dark wool waistcoat with cocobolo buttons and jacket to match. Oval sunglasses, gambler's top hat, paintbrush mustache, the works. The later James, Bandholz beard flecked with gray and houndstooth coat, lecturing at Harvard. James at a small table in the dining car, penning a letter to brother Henry while riding the midnight train to Edinburgh.

Dreams he's had before.

When Lion volunteered for the UCLA study, one of the first to use fMRI to examine em-trackers, they'd assigned him a therapist. Something about coordinating psychological profile with neuro-anatomical function. Fetu. Samoan, tribal tats, bald head, big laugh. He'd told Fetu about the dreams.

Fetu had called James his "secure base." Out of Bowlby's attachment theory. A safe haven, a place to return to in times of uncertainty. Fetu had a few variations on a theory.

Perhaps Lion felt a kinship with James. He'd read him first in college, before his major switched from psychology to pharmacology to history of science to journalism. James and his pioneering pragmatism, his multidisciplinary approach, his vastly open mind.

All of it left an impression.

Or a more subtle variation: Fetu called it his last truly happy period. Where he was just before he dipped too far into the history of science and discovered what scientists not named William James did to animals. Before he met the Animal Liberation Front. Before the arrests.

What does it matter now.

He shakes off the dream and sits up in bed. Blackout curtains still doing their job and what time is it?

His cell phone is on the nightstand, sitting atop the package Penelope dropped off, not charging, not happy.

Angry red battery bar and no clock available.

Not bothering to flip on a light, Lion grabs his phone and barefoots across the room to find his charger. On the table beside the coffeemaker, sharing the outlet. Pawing around in the darkness for the cord. A satisfying click as prong meets sleeve, the haptic marriage that means power to come.

Needing juice of his own, he grabs a coffee pod out of the wooden tray and slots it into the machine, the chrome arm, the full ritual. He decides to hold off on the shower. A break in routine and necessary, because, while he slept on it, he still doesn't have an answer for Arctic.

But he has a plan.

Lion dresses quickly, adding a few extra layers against the cold, then walks out to the terrace. The cup steaming in his hand and the city in stealth mode, before the waking, the traffic. When you can still see the skyline as imagination rendered visible, something someone thought up.

A lot of someones.

Lion tastes the coffee while tracking the red flash of taillights in the distance. A small sip. He wants the caffeine to prime focus but is try-ing to hold on to his alpha brain wave status for a little while longer. Beta waves are fast waves, the signature of a brain fully awake. Alpha is a few cycles per second slower, or where the brain hovers first thing in the morning. Also the gateway to the unconscious, if his old Psych 101 textbook is still to be trusted.

One more swallow, then he sets the cup on the table and sits down on the ground. A slight rearrangement of garments, feet in a half lotus, hands on his knees, eyes settle closed.

Slow and steady breaths.

Five seconds in and ten seconds out, five rounds. Six seconds in and twelve seconds out, five rounds. Working his way up to ten and twenty, following this with a long breath hold. As he closes in on ninety seconds, a total fuzz-out, graying of vision, detachment from emotions, no thought, no self, a clean wipe of the slate.

Exactly the party he came for.

Lion's a little wobbly when he opens his eyes, less so as he sheds a few layers. Gray jacket on chair, black hooded sweatshirt beside it, and into push-up position. Now for part two of his plan. Chest to ground and back up again. A set of fifty, then forty, then thirty, twenty, ten, five, three, one. Fast as he can. Lying on his back and staring at the sky between rounds, panting like a dog.

Lying there, he remembers Fetu telling him about the relationship between the empathic and the mnemonic. Overlapping skills, he'd said. To feel another's feelings, we need the brain to hunt for similar situa-tions from our own past, times when we felt then what the other is feeling now. Why the fMRI scans of em-trackers showed mirror neu-rons in overdrive, heavy hippocampal action, and extensive mnemonic networks, much more complex than controls. Why, when Lion recalls William James penning a letter to his brother Henry, he doesn't just have the episodic prowess to remember all the words, he has the em-phatic talent to find the emotion that preceded those words.

Dear Henry,
I have read your latest. And while I am still not certain why
you insist on so much not saying what you're saying, I will
SHOUTSHOUTSHOUT from the rooftops it is the greatest
work yet in this English language and I will chase down and
throttle with my cane anyone who dares say differently.
                              Your Brother, William

Then it comes: an overwhelming wash of brotherly love and loyalty, a sensation so strong Lion momentarily forgets himself. Instead, the future opens up inside of him. An expansive, room-to-breathe liberation and how he knows that even though the storybooks might not bother to tell this tale, the fealty felt by the brothers James was a force that shaped history.

Fetu had a theory here too: Em-trackers have a kind of eidetic somatic recall—like a photographic memory for emotions, a deadly accurate felt-sense of the past that allows them to find truth in the future.

Now he's awake.

Lion stands back up and walks back inside. Cell phone at 37 percent and clock reading 5:12 A.M.

He uses the phone's glow to track a light switch. An upward flip turns on a Zephyr salon hair dryer from the 1930s, repurposed as a chandelier. Named for the Greek god of the west wind, for America's love of speed and power, now casting its soft yellow glow from Flokati throw rug in one corner of the room to white marble bedside table in the other.

The bedside table where Penelope's package remains, unopened.

Box first, envelope second.

The box contains white tissue paper wrapped around his Moleskine. He flips through the pages, his single note, the rest looking unmolested. The envelope holds a square of white paper, thick rag weave and more mesh electronics. The Arctic icon sits in the bottom right corner. Now exposed to the air and fresh with oxygen, it winks pink, just once. There's also a short note:

> *Jenka says you dropped this on the floor at your meeting. He's lying, of course. XO Penelope.*

Then

> *P.S. If you want to go to the Hamptons, message me and Bo will pick you up.*

And a number.

XO Penelope? Not the message he'd been expecting. Did he accidentally make a friend? Or is this just another form of Arctic guerrilla marketing?

Lion heads for the shower, thinking this through. Flirting has to be the original form of guerrilla marketing, from back before markets even existed. But there were always suckers, he reminds himself.

Three minutes. Five minutes. He lets the hot water beat on his shoulders while steam layers the mirror. Then folds forward, pressing his fingers to the ground, letting the water pound his back for a while.

Toweling off, he knows before he knows, something's been decided. Just a tiny thrum of excitement. How he used to feel on the front end of a story, tracking curiosity to curiosity, that little rush when things start to come together. So he delays his flight and spends a day in the Hamptons and maybe his em-tracking system provides a new answer. Not likely. But he can't deny that he likes feeling like this.

He also knows Arctic's up to something. "Our business is change" still echoing in his ears. Absolutely a reason to say no.

Knows he's going to say yes.

Decision made, he doesn't bother to dither. Texts Penelope, asks her to double his day rate, and wants Bo there by nine. Also types: *XO Lion.*

Hits SEND and, immediately, regrets it.

Five uneasy minutes. Seven. Around nine he's had enough of himself, so grabs *Dune* from his pack—thinking, for the umpteenth time, that he might be the last man on earth to pack in paperbacks.

Even his mom Kindles.

Book in hand, he forces a sit-down on the couch. Muted aquamarine cushions and gold silk throw pillows and he still can't get comfortable. Gives up and opens the book.

For the next ten minutes, he tries to move words off page and into brain but keeps glancing at the phone. What is he, in the fifth grade? But he can't think of anything else.

Five minutes later, a titillation from the table. He grabs the phone and checks the screen.

Done, XO

And Bo is there by nine.

CLAPBOARD MODERN
ON A SIZABLE LOT

Driving out of the city and the licking pug says the Sunrise Highway is bumper to bumper, so Bo drops them down to the old Montauk. Two lanes for nearly a hundred miles and Lion dozes for much of the ride. He catches sights in snatches: West Islip, East Patchogue, state parks, surf clubs, vestigial saltboxes, past the walking dunes in East Montauk and nearing the seaside cliffs of Ditch Plains before they break inland. Captain Balfour Way, north for two miles, a sharp right and a long slice of gravel driveway, curving out of sight.

Acres of tall trees in every direction.

At the top of the driveway, Bo parks under a grandfather oak. Through the windshield, Lion can make out an oversized rectangular house wrapped in gray wooden shingles and white cottage trim.

Clapboard modern on a sizable lot.

"I'm going to walk the grounds," he says.

"Want company?"

Lion's em-tracking machinery works better on solo, and he says as much. Bo picks his copy of *Slouching Towards Bethlehem* off the dash, then slides the window down, just halfway. "Holla if you need me."

Getting out of the car, Lion has that sense of being watched, maybe from above, maybe from the trees. He looks around slowly, staring into the forest, but can't find the source.

Deciding to follow a gravel path that winds around the eastern side of the house, Lion passes a small front porch, an oval parking area, and a five-car garage. A cluster of white elms stands beyond, probably genetically tweaked to be disease resistant and part of the East Coast reintroduction program.

He also realizes his earlier assessment was off. The house only appears to be a long rectangle. His tour reveals three rectangles, each half the size of the previous, stacked in an offset row. White metal suspension porches hang off each, anchored to the house by steel guide wires, and casting long shadows across the lawn.

Lion walks the path once clockwise and once counterclockwise and for no reason he can think of beyond avoiding the sight of Walker's head for a little longer. And when was the last time he cased a crime scene?

Stepping around another corner, he remembers. That Slenderman job, about a decade back. Em-tracking his way back to the original Reddit poster, just a shy Millennial from Pasadena wanting what many shy Millennials from Pasadena want: to write a horror story and start a movement.

Along the way, Lion visited the site of the ritual, the stabbing. The woods in Waukesha, Wisconsin, in cold November. He found remnant crime tape attached to bare trees, the yellow plastic fading, but still the only color around for miles.

He knew then—Slenderman was just the beginning.

A few years later the press dubbed the phenomenon "emergent storytelling," a fictional tale written collectively by a nearly anonymous internet, then veering into reality—first via teenage girls and ritual sacrifice, then as an Amazon miniseries about that sacrifice. Some kind of meta-meta chain that only a Derridean would grok. Also a different approach to the truth, which might be why Lion saw it coming.

A third lap around the house to continue avoiding Walker's head for just a little while longer. It doesn't quite ease his unease. Lion can't shake the feeling that he's still being watched. He slow-pans around the forest. Stately elms and oaks, stories high, and then a dash of sherbet.

Not paranoia, after all.

About thirty feet away, a Mexican amber dragonfly with orange lace wings and garnet eyes perches on the lip of a leaf, watching him intensely. He gazes back for a moment. Glam rock colors meet prehistoric optical design, and usually not found east of Arizona.

"So what are you doing here?" Lion wants to know.

With no answer forthcoming, he glances back at the house, spotting a stairway that leads up to one of the suspension porches. By the time he looks back, the dragonfly has departed, the forest darker.

He crosses to the stairway and climbs up to peer in one of Robert Walker's windows. Floors of hard wood, walls painted flat gray, and a glassed-in fireplace surrounded by slender Italian couches. The gentle touch of an expensive decorator. What Lion doesn't see, scanning back and forth, is a trophy room chockablock with dead mammal heads, Walker's among them.

He tries the porch door but finds it locked. Back down the stairs and to the car. "Do you have the keys?" he asks, through the half-open window.

Bo opens the center console and takes out a pair of oversized keys, big and brassy, like they were made for a pirate chest. Also a small piece of Arctic stationery with an eight-digit number.

"Top lock," holding up a pirate key, "alarm code," holding up the stationery, "bottom lock," holding up the other.

Lion slides the set into his coat pocket, grabs his sling-pack from the backseat, and starts toward the house. Reaching the front door, he slips his pack off his shoulder, opens the lid, and removes the dragon box.

More than one way to case a crime scene.

Lion opens the box and removes a vial of Ghost Trainwreck. He rolls quickly, lights up, and looks for the door's lock.

Not where it should be.

Instead, he sees a small wooden panel, which opens to reveal a pair of gaping keyways. A click as he turns the first key, another panel slides open, a small keypad. Lion pulls the paper from his pocket and taps in the code. Then bottom key into bottom lock, and an industrial whirring as the front door slides left, sucked into a slot hidden in the jamb.

Stepping through the entrance, Lion finds himself in a wide hall, facing his reflection in an enormous mirror. He sees some older creature, jet-lagged eyes, hair at geometrically difficult angles from sleeping in the SUV.

Or maybe this is just what he looks like now.

Lion glances left and right. Left spills into a kitchen, right into a great room. He tries to think like a detective, but that doesn't even last a second. Not law enforcement material, he decides, hitting the joint.

Blowing smoke toward the kitchen, he heads toward the great room, remembering that New York is one of the final three states not to legalize marijuana, then wondering about Richard having to explain the smell to the police. Who's he kidding. Richard's not the type to bother explaining.

The great room is tall ceilings and sparse furnishings. A large brick fireplace. Coffee tables of African blackwood and couches in Cape Cod white. Three books on an end table. Lion picks them up one at a time. Photographs by Peter Beard, *Swahili for Dummies*, and a leather-bound collection of Hemingway's short stories with a bookmark marking two-thirds of the way through "The Short Happy Life of Francis Macomber."

Setting them down, he backtracks to the kitchen. Nothing out of place. A glass-fronted refrigerator: a cheese plate with prosciutto and olives visible on the central shelf, orange juice in slender white cartons on the top shelf, and ten small mason jars with salad dressing and folksy labels stacked on the side. So neat that it looks like someone was paid to arrange the food.

Lion takes a step closer, peering in. The vegetable drawers are empty. The cheese drawer holds a wedge of Parmesan. The freezer is all meat. One tall stack with more folksy labels. Venison, buffalo, kangaroo.

So food as a form of vanity.

Also, looking around the kitchen again, that expensive decorator. Probably, judging from the fresh bag in the trash bin, a housekeeper. But no food-trace of a girlfriend. No wife.

Robert Walker, Lion decides, was a bachelor.

He walks out of the kitchen and into the breakfast nook. Gray walls and wide windows peering into heavy forest. The only furnishing a square wooden table, empty save for a second set of pirate keys tossed absently at its center. Paper plane-ticket debris beneath them.

Nothing to see here.

He backs out of the room, but stops and glances at the table. Even Lion, with his throwback ways, doesn't use paper plane tickets anymore. Crosses over for a closer look. Not a ticket.

Unfolding the paper, Lion finds an itemized bill for the Twombly Hunting Ranch, Killeen, Texas. Four nights, five days: rooms at a thousand a night; twelve hundred in food and beverage; four thousand three hundred in poker chips; thirty-six thousand for two kills.

Itemized as well.

Twenty-two thousand for a black rhino; twelve thousand for an Iberian lynx. Taxidermy, mounting, and shipping included.

Lion feels sweat on his brow and a churn in his stomach. He knows it's more than a feeling. Spins around, trying to find a bathroom. Two doors against the far wall of the nook. The first discloses a well-stocked pantry, the second a stairway to the upstairs. A warning lurch and Lion realizes he doesn't have a clue where to puke in this house.

He backtracks instead, barely making the sink in time for a strong heave of partially digested Dirty French eggs and hash browns. Three or four follow-up heaves.

Lion was always an animal lover, but em-tracking deepened that bond. So now he deals with uncontrollable vomiting in the face of abject cruelty. An innate reaction, was how Fetu described it, a somatic rejection, the disgust response dialed up to eleven.

Resistance is useless.

Also one of the ways researchers first learned to identify em-trackers. The reigning theory says the retching is the by-product of a fundamental widening of spheres of empathy, past the color lines, gender lines, and out-group/in-group concerns. Beyond the border of species. The best among them can feel all the way around the planet, and those contest winners, the first em-trackers who got to ride Musk's rocket around the moon, claimed to be able to push it out to galactic levels.

Lion wipes puke from his mouth with a towel from a drawer, realizing he's still clutching the bill. He tosses it back on the table, knowing his initial instinct was right: Whoever beheaded Walker—Lion really would like to shake his hand.

He looks left, then right.

Which way to the decapitation?

From four feet away, Robert Walker's head looks like something from an old TV show. Neutral and nonviolent. Or as neutral and nonviolent as a decapitated head can be.

Four feet, Lion has also determined, is the critical distance necessary to blur the edges of his peripheral vision. From here, he can look at the head and not quite see the rest of the trophy room. A way to concentrate on the task at hand and ignore the pillage and plunder of Noah's Ark that surrounds him.

"Done puking," he tells Walker's head.

But there's still too much carnage in the peripheral. He takes a couple of deep breaths to steady his stomach, then lifts a Mongolian antelope off the wall. Hard to ignore those sad eyes and long face, nose like a twin-piped hot rod, eyebrows bushy and arched. A hard life on the Eurasian steppe, even before it was cut short.

Head in hand, Lion surveys the room. He realizes there's no foul stench. No scent of rotting flesh. Glancing at Walker's head, he notes the sheen of shellac, just like he'd seen in the picture. Walker wasn't just decapitated. Someone went to the trouble to preserve him. Someone with taxidermy skills. Gang related? A warning of some kind? He can't tell, so on with the survey.

Next up, tartan wallpaper. It isn't of the old school Scottish variety. More modern. Shimmering poly-fabric, light green on dark green stripes, highlights of sagebrush. The heads are a bigger problem. It's the eyes that bother him most. Avoidance the better choice. He flips the antelope facedown, a back plate made of teak, the price tag still attached.

$59.95 from BringTheWildlifeHome.com.

Walking the wildlife across the room, he sets it in a back corner, on the floor beside Walker's desk. He takes a moment at the desk. Opening the main drawer reveals a Montblanc Masterpiece with platinum nib, packages of ink refills, and nothing else. A side drawer holds a gold-plated Rolodex.

Subtle, thinks Lion, very subtle.

As he's departing the desk, he notices a flash of silver on the floor. Reaching down, he picks up a squat cylinder with a plastic screw top. Maybe some kind of pen holder? Lion doesn't know what to make of it, so sets the cylinder on the desk and goes back to de-heading the wall.

Dama gazelle, Amur leopard, white rhino, and now struggling with an unwieldy Cape buffalo. He tries stacking the buffalo on his pile but doesn't get the balance right. The head slips left, its sharp right horn poking through his jacket and snatching a whorl of wool from the sleeve of his sweater. Somehow, missed his flesh completely.

But then the head slips again.

In slow motion, Lion watches his jacket rip elbow to wrist. Move, says the voice in his head, move now. Spinning clockwise, he tries to free himself from the fabric. Happens with a hard snap. The recoil drives the point of the horn into the underside of his forearm. A sharp pain on impact. His flesh tears as the mount skids farther sideways, bouncing from leopard nose to gazelle horn to hard wood floor with a thump.

He clamps a hand around the wound, trying not to scream. Color drains out of his vision.

It takes a few minutes for it to come back. A few more for him to shake off the pain enough to glance at the cut. A deep slash by the looks of it, blood soaking his sweater at multiple locations. He re-clamps his hand and squints around the room, hunting for something to staunch the flow.

Dama gazelle, Amur leopard, Cape buffalo—nothing to sop blood.

Then it dawns on him. Dama, Amur, and Cape are all species on the endangered list. He glares at Walker's head.

"And just when I was starting to like you."

Lion unclamps his hand and pushes up his sleeve to check the damage. The jacket is shredded, the sweater ruined, the arm not much better. A long scimitar slash from wrist to elbow, thankfully not bone-deep.

Still bleeding, though.

He looks around again, needing something to press against the wound. Finds a second wall of tartan and carnage: bear, mountain lion, seven kinds of deer, desk, armchair, Winchester in gun bag. Finally, a zebra-hide pillow on a black leather couch.

Grabbing the pillow, he presses hide to cut and sits down on the couch to wait. He tastes puke in his mouth, his arm throbs. "I want hazard pay," he tells the head.

Then he remembers asking Penelope to double his day rate.

"I want more hazard pay."

It takes about ten minutes to calm the wound. When the throb dials down to semi-manageable, he turns his attention back to the almost empty wall. Beside Walker, only a stuffed African lion remains, perched on a heavy stone pedestal. Adult male. The irony not lost on him.

He looks from Walker to the lion and back again. Another endangered species, but, thinking it through, not everything Walker's slaughtered is on that list. The itemized bill Lion found on the kitchen table.

Black rhino and Iberian lynx are off the list. Now, they're on another list.

No más. No more. Extinct.

Glares at Walker.

"What the hell is wrong with you?"

But dead men tell no tales and, eventually, Lion pries himself out of the couch to finish the job. Crossing to the corner, he attempts to lift the lion, but it's got some heft and his bum arm can't get a grip. All he can manage is shoulder against mane and a four-foot slide across the hardwood floor.

Far enough to be out of his field of vision.

Contemplating the wall again, the only thing left to see is Robert Walker, dead center, tartan wallpaper, and the occasional nail where a head once hung. His stomach feels a little better.

Lion decides he wants the nausea all the way gone, but his joint got lost somewhere midpuke. It's dragon box and the familiar origami instead. He clicks his lighter, pulls smoke into his lungs, pushes off the floor, and walks over to look directly into the hazel of Walker's eyes.

Not what he was expecting.

From this close, the eyes don't look terrified or enraged. So Walker didn't fight the person who killed him? Not drugged, either. Too clear around the irises, not enough pupil dilation. So he was conscious when it happened? More than that. The emotion that Lion reads in Walker's eyes is the exact same emotion he noticed in the photos: remorse. Pure and deep. Lion is absolutely sure of it. Robert Walker died sorry about something.

Clicking into journalist mode, he grabs his notebook and lists all the species in the room. Adds the two from the bill in the kitchen. Then, beneath them, underlined: Robert Walker felt remorse.

He takes another drag and stares at the words, trying to find signal in noise. And then he feels it: a change in atmospheric pressure, space to breathe, a tingle of hope—and not sure where that's coming from.

He glances back at the wall, sees the prep school haircut and the ache of sorry in his eyes. Data bit finds data bit. If a man like Walker can feel remorse, maybe, just maybe, there's a little hope after all.

Since taking this job, it's the first future he can feel.

There's another sensation on top of that feeling, more like a lack of sensation, a gap. It's the sense that something's missing. Not an em-tracker's skill, a journalist's skill. But definitely missing.

But what?

Arctic's crime scene photos are still in his bag, the rag weave envelope wedged between padded sides of computer sleeve. He slides it out, flips it over, and lifts the flap. Oxygen-saturated plastic pulses, illuminating canary-yellow fingerprint. He puts his finger on the square. The flap, with a soft click, opens.

Sliding out the photos, he finds his answer. The end table with the silver straw and silver powder is absent from the room. Double-checks the images to be sure. Sees Lucite in close-up, five silver lines, two already inhaled, three thick with powder. And the table is supposed to rest on the far side of the black leather couch, near the buffalo head, atop a zebra-skin rug.

Lion puts the photos under his arm and walks over to the buffalo. Careful of the horns, he crouches down and slides the head out of the way. Wavy black and white stripes and four indentations in the fur—where an end table once sat.

He pinches the cherry on his joint, sets it on the ground, then triple-checks the photos. His hunch is confirmed. Lion opens his notebook and starts writing: Crime scene preserved, but end table missing. No silver powder, no silver straw. Stolen? Stolen by someone working for Sir Richard?

Lion glances around the room, the pile of animal heads, the now bare wall, the bloodstained zebra-hide pillow. He's made a mess but isn't going to bother to clean up. Let Sir Richard explain it to the cops. Then he remembers.

Sir Richard's not the type to explain.

NOT THE OPIATE OF THE MASSES

ion almost makes it all the way back to the truck before the adrenaline wears off.

Almost.

Exiting the house, he jostles his wound on the doorjamb. A sharp pain shoots wrist to elbow and the nausea comes back full force. Down the steps and onto the garden path on hazy autopilot. Bile rises in his throat, forcing him to stop and catch his breath about ten feet from the SUV.

"You look like you're going to puke," says Bo, watching him through the driver's side window.

"Done puking," through gritted teeth.

"You're bleeding."

He notices his sleeve is still pushed up, the cut clearly visible and starting to leak.

"Gored by a dead buffalo."

Bo reaches under the dash to push something. Lion hears a hard click and then a whisper from the rear of the truck. A hidden drawer slides out from beneath the back end, red metal sides, clear polyure-thane lid. He takes a step closer to get a better view. Beneath the lid, the shiny red nylon of a commercial first aid kit, the kind available at any camping supply store.

"I'm going to take a look," says Bo. Not a question.

He opens his door, climbs out, and walks to the back of the SUV. Out of the drawer comes the first aid kit. Out of the kit come a couple of sterile wipes and an oversized syringe, red plastic with a black cap. Bo wipes his hands with one of the wipes, unscrews the cap, and turns to face Lion.

"Put your pack down and give me your arm."

Lion bends over to set it on the lawn, wobbles as he stands back up, then extends his arm. Bo grips the syringe in his teeth and inspects the cut with clinical disinterest. Teasing apart the skin at the point of impact, probing, trying to see how deep it goes. A meticulous proce-dure. Lion gets the feeling he's done this before.

"You had training?"

"I'm an Eagle Scout."

"Uh-huh," he says, thinking about the bar code tattoo on the back of Bo's neck, "you're an Eagle Scout."

"Twenty-one merit badges. Seriously. Do you want to see me tie some knots?" Bo tears open the other wipe. "This will sting."

Then he rubs the cloth over the cut, sopping up blood, cleaning it thoroughly. Lion wobbles again but stays silent. Setting aside the wipe, Bo takes the syringe out of his mouth and passes it over.

"You're going to apply this to the cut. I'm gonna push the sides to-gether. It's gonna hurt."

Lion looks at him.

"Then it's going to stop hurting."

Bo wraps his hands around Lion's forearm and, using thumbs and palm heels, pushes the edges together. Lion grits his teeth.

"Put it on thick, an even line."

Depressing the plunger exudes a translucent yellow cream, like a wax-paper inchworm, flecked with shiny blue particles. He tries to slather the wound. The ache in his arm starts to burn, then turns cold, icy cold, searing. But soon the sensation vanishes completely, almost as quickly as it came. Instead, a warm glow in his toes, ankles, legs, spreading toward his chest and a smile on his face.

"It feels," says Lion, wide-eyed in surprise, "really, really good."

"Low-temperature superglue mixed with long-lasting fentanyl nano-crystals."

The cream has hardened into a tight seal, and he can't stop smiling.

"It's about five hundred times more potent than morphine," explains Bo. "You're gonna be pretty high, at least for the next few hours."

"What happens in a few hours?"

Bo grabs his sling-pack from the lawn and passes it over. "In a few hours, you're gonna want to smoke more of what's in that dragon box."

"Thanks," taking it back.

"Part of the service."

He lifts his arm. "And thanks."

"You're welcome."

Lion turns toward the SUV and waves at the back door. The sensor doesn't read, the door doesn't move.

He tries again.

"I think you have to get closer."

Lion double-takes. He's still standing in the middle of the lawn, ten feet from the SUV. So five hundred times more powerful than morphine and heavy impact on depth perception. He attempts a step closer, but his feet don't work like he remembers.

"Not . . ."

Not what? Open for business? Working? Lion can't recall what he was trying to say. Then it hits him.

"Not the opiate of the masses."

And a wobble.

"I got you."

Bo's hand on his elbow, steady until Lion's tucked into the back-seat.

"Back to the hotel?"

"Please."

Bo drops the car into gear and starts down the driveway. As they approach the street, Lion sees a flash of silver metal from a thicket of green. The mailbox, tucked between bushes. It reminds him of the silver container he found beneath the desk, the cylinder he thought was a pen holder.

Not a pen holder.

"We need to go back."

Bo looks at him in the rearview. "Fentanyl."

"Yeah?"

"Walking's not the best idea right now."

"Agreed, but it's important."

Bo nods and reverses back to the top of the driveway, parking under the same grandfather oak. He climbs out and steadies Lion up the path to the front porch. Pirate key into pirate lock, the panel slips open, the code, the other key. The door slides into itself, and both step inside.

Auto-whoosh as it closes behind them.

"Step away from the airlock, Bo."

"What?"

"*2001: A Space Odyssey.*"

"Fentanyl, my friend, just fentanyl."

Lion sees himself in the mirror again, worse than before—if that's even possible.

"Where are we going?" asks Bo. "I think I should steer."

The words seem to arrive at Lion's ears a few seconds late, so his experience is mouth moving without sound, like a Kung Fu classic with bad lip-synch. It takes him a second to crack the code, then decides Bo might be right.

"The trophy room. Off the hallway at the end of the great room and down the stairs."

Which they manage without incident.

Lion leaves Bo by the door and makes his way over to Walker's desk. He picks up the silver cylinder. Maybe three inches long and an inch wide. He unscrews the plastic lid and sees nothing inside.

"Tsunami?"

Lion looks up, sees Bo pointing at the pile of animal heads.

"Carnage," he agrees, then gestures toward Walker's head, "and this guy's an asshole." A twinge of guilt penetrates his opiate haze. "I'd clean it up, but I'll start puking again."

"That's true, huh? I heard about it on a podcast. Didn't know if it was just the guy they were interviewing or all em-trackers."

"I can puke again. It's like the licking pug—I'm used to it."

"Do what you came to do," says Bo, walking over to lift the buffalo head off the floor.

Lion looks back into the cylinder and notices it's not completely empty. There's a tiny wedge of crystal pinned to the bottom. He taps the container against his palm, dislodging flecks of silver powder, like miniature snowflakes made from tinfoil. Maybe enough for a mass spectrometer to analyze, which would be useful, he concludes, if he knew anyone with a mass spectrometer.

He turns his attention back to the container. The clear cap looks like half a bullet. An oversized bullet. Suddenly, he knows what he's holding. All that's missing is a disco beat and a silver spoon.

A snuff container.

A clatter beside him and Lion turns to see Bo failing to pick an antelope off the floor.

"Careful of the horns," he says.

Feeling a flash of heat against his palm, Lion glances down to see one side of the cylinder shiver. A bright white light that quickly fades, leaving behind a glittering question mark, like dying fireworks, visible for only a second. Lion wraps his palm around the container again. Moments later, he feels more heat, sees the flash again, and the shimmer.

He also notices a second pulse of light from inside the container, but it's gone before he can get a good look.

This time, when he wraps his palm around the cylinder, he stares down the barrel. It's the same shiver, but on the inside of the container, near the bottom. Hard to say, but definitely not a question mark.

More like writing. Short words in cursive script. A phrase? A name?

Carrying the container over to Walker's desk, Lion snaps on an Arteluce lamp, adjusting the shade until the light falls straight down the chamber. Smooth silver on all sides, and nothing more. To figure this out, he needs a jeweler's loupe, special tools, skills he doesn't have.

"Know a good jeweler?" he asks Bo.

"No." Thinking a moment. "Penelope would."

Lion slips the snuff vial into his pocket, then catches sight of his joint, on the floor beside the desk, where he left it. A little unsteady on the way down, but slots it between his lips on the first try and manages to stand back up. Bo glances his way at the click of his lighter.

A long inhale, a long exhale, holds the joint out. "Interested?"

"Ghost Trainwreck #69," says Bo, crossing the room and taking the joint. "My brother, of course I'm interested."

NOT A RILKEAN

Fentanyl and Ghost Trainwreck and Lion falls dead asleep before they're even out of Montauk. He's down for an hour and again does not dream. When he wakes, it's to a light drizzle, dark skies, and two lanes of empty freeway. Maybe east of East Quogue, but can't say for sure.

Back upright and his vision starts to clear. It seems like he's not quite as high as before, but does that acid-head test, checking the lines on his palm to see what's moving.

Yup, still high.

Despite his altered state, he feels like doing something. Grabs his Moleskine and a pen. Bo notices the movement, asks if he'd like a bottle of water, maybe some music.

"Music," he decides, "would be great."

"Do you have a preference?"

"Surprise me."

Bo clicks a button on the steering wheel. Lion hears the slow build of an Egyptian melody, dubstep stutter bass and a soft accordion wail, like King Tut got lost on the bayou. Hip-hop lyrics: "You thought I was dead; I was living the questions; just hidden from sight, Sir Richard's deception."

He knows that voice. "This is Shiz."

"Yeah," says Bo, "unreleased."

Lion listens to a few more verses, but already he has questions about Shiz living the questions. Richard said he started those Rilkean rumors—was he lying? Why would he lie about that? Then he considers another possibility, that Shiz became a Rilkean after Richard started those rumors. Fiction becoming fact, like Slenderman. Is this more emergent storytelling?

Too many questions to hold in his head.

Lion opens his notebook and starts listing puzzle pieces. Arctic, Shiz, the snuff container engraved with Rilkean symbols. All of them mean something to someone; none of them mean anything to him.

He can feel the edge of frustration poke through the fentanyl. An overload of questions that he can't answer. A grind in his teeth. Lorenzo would tell him to go get laid. Not really an option right now. He decides what he really needs is sustenance. And caffeine.

"Any chance we could stop for coffee, maybe a sandwich?"

Bo punches another button on the steering wheel and a razor screen rises from the middle of the dashboard, showing a map of the old Montauk Highway marked with restaurants. "There's Cajun takeout, pretty good too, if you can wait twenty minutes."

"I can wait."

They pass under a couple of traffic lights and through a couple of towns: interchangeable cute with the occasional strip mall, the way they do it in the Hamptons. The Prince Shiz track ends and the next one cues. Superfly trumpets mixed with Dre-era fuzz tones. Bo's head bobs a little harder and Lion glimpses the question mark tattoo on the back of his neck. He decides this is one question he might actually be able to answer.

"Bo," he asks, "are you a Rilkean? Is that a rude question?"

"My tattoo?"

"Yeah."

"Not rude, not a Rilkean," says Bo, taking off his cap and running a hand through his hair. "I used to wear it longer, to hide it."

"If you're not a Rilkean . . . ?"

"It's a long story."

"It's a long ride."

Bo glances at him in the rearview, sighs. "I met a woman with this same tattoo. I go to night school at NYU. She was in one of my classes, ended up in my study group. She had silver hair, the dyed kind, not the old kind."

"That's how you got the tattoo?"

"That's how I fell into things. And we were good together . . ."

"But?"

"But I'm Chinese. Really tight families. I decided I had to meet hers. She didn't say no; she said there were conditions and let's wait and see. It became a thing for me. Stupid, but things become things in relationships."

"Copy that," says Lion, nodding in agreement.

"In the end, she gave in, sort of. Her mother, brother, and her, we were all supposed to meet up at Hudson's, in the West Village. You'd like it—you can smoke there. Some kind of cigar bar with books and ashtrays everywhere. The last thing I remember was ordering a drink."

"The last thing you remember?"

"I woke up in a hotel in Tribeca with my neck burning."

"You got roofied?"

"And tattooed."

Shaking his head, "I have no idea how I'd feel if that happened to me."

"I'm still not sure how I feel about it."

"Did you go to the police?"

"She left me a note and a burner phone. It said the Rilkeans were her family now and the tattoo was their condition. If I still wanted to meet I should call her from that phone."

"You call?"

"Didn't call the police, didn't call her either. I drive limos and go to night school. I don't get tattooed to attend secret meetings."

Lion laughs. "Why didn't you have it removed?"

"Rilke knew what was up. Live the questions now. Perhaps you will gradually, without noticing it, one distant day, live right into the answer. What's truer than that? I kept the tattoo as a reminder. Plus," tapping a finger on the back of his neck, "the ladies love a good bar code."

Lion laughs again, then glances out the window. "Wha . . . ?"

Not possible.

He rubs his eyes. Still there: a Mexican amber dragonfly with orange lace wings and garnet compound eyes, watching him from less than five feet away.

Got to be the fentanyl.

He blinks hard. The dragonfly doesn't move. But it registers his blink, reacts quickly, banking left. As it turns, Lion notices a shiny red dot in the middle of its belly, the telltale sign of a Lidar laser, proof of not-quite-life winking at him across the lonely gray sky and then gone.

INTRODUCTION TO MILLENNIAL SEMIOTICS

Leroy's Phat Cat Cajun is a food truck at the back end of an asphalt parking lot, across from a decaying industrial warehouse. Sitting on a wooden bench beneath a tin roof, Lion drinks coffee and eats a fried green tomato sandwich. Having promised himself he wouldn't think about the dragonfly until after his meal, he's been staring into the warehouse's dirty windows, watching a pair of long-armed shelf-stocking robots go silently about their business.

But the robots don't distract, or not enough.

It's the details that don't stack. Insect drones have been around for a while, but that dragonfly was something new and very high end. Probably lab grown and military grade. Which leads him to an obvious question: Why would Arctic have him watched? It's got to be Arctic. No one else knew what he was doing or where he was going. And no one but them—at least no one he's met recently—has access to military-grade technology.

But Bo works for Arctic, and couldn't he just report back about

Lion's movements? For that matter, as of right now, Lion works for Arctic: Why not just ask him?

He finishes the sandwich and wipes remoulade from the corner of his mouth with his already ruined sleeve. The movement jostles his cut. The pain is there, subdued and distant, but only a matter of time before it comes for him again.

A long day. A long couple of days.

Thinking about his long couple of days, he decides that maybe it wasn't Arctic the firm deploying that dragonfly. Maybe just an employee of that firm. A pompadoured, notebook-swiping employee.

Of course it was Jenka.

A gust of wind sends ripples through puddles, and another realization follows his first: Lion's not even angry. What's a little more surveillance in an age of a little more surveillance? He takes another sip of coffee. All these puzzle pieces: A zookeeper who liberated a zoo, a family lying down with lions, a remorseful great white hunter. He's got to admit, what he's really feeling is intrigue.

Jenka and the dragonfly only thicken this plot.

But it might not matter. His journalism days are behind him. No longer does he get paid for the plot. Now, he's paid for saying yes or no—the sum total of his contractual obligations. His work in the world reduced to one-word responses. When, he wonders, did his life get so small?

No answer forthcoming, so he drops his plate in the recycling and starts back toward Bo. Halfway across the parking lot before he remembers his coffee, still sitting on the bench. Lion retraces his steps.

As he's reaching for the cup, the snuff container in his pocket bangs into his thigh and reminds him of the Rilkean engraving. Bo told him to eat quickly, wanting him back at the hotel before the fentanyl wore off. But—fingering the cylinder—there might be time for one extra stop.

He pulls out his cell, types a text to Penelope, asking for the name of a good jeweler in the city, one with engraving expertise. Does not hit SEND. This time it's not an XO issue. Standing there, he realizes he hasn't made up his mind about the snuff container. Does he divulge this information to Sir Richard? Old habits tell him to hoard the data, but current instinct says momentum matters most. Stay with the hot lead. True when chasing a story as a journalist; true when chasing the future as an em-tracker.

He sends the text.

By the time they're back on the highway, his pocket buzzes with a name and address: *Masta Ice, ask for Balthazar Jones, on Mercer.*

Lion passes on the information.

"We won't make it in time," says Bo.

Clock reads 4:41. He had no idea it was so late. Texts Penelope to find out what time the store closes; five minutes later, learns Balthazar will stay open for them.

"They're gonna keep the lights on for us," he says, then remembers. "You go to night school. I don't want to mess you up—you're not missing a class?"

"I'm only taking one this semester. Two hours every Monday. But thanks for asking."

"What's the class?"

"Introduction to Millennial Semiotics."

"Is that your major? Is that actually a major?"

"Not even a minor. It was Sir Richard's suggestion. Emoticons as a new class of oversignifying precision grammar. When I understand what the hell the professor is saying, it's kind of interesting."

The traffic starts to thicken as they close in on the city, the masses on the move, and increasingly claustrophobic as they edge into the Midtown Tunnel. Lion peers into the darkness ahead. He can feel weight in metric tons on all sides. Cars and trucks and concrete. Bo slides left and punches forward, weaving to the front of the pack. Through the windshield, Lion sees blackness, and the tunnel's only illumination, a series of dingy yellow lights, streaking by like rotting comets.

"Can I ask you something?"

It takes him a second to realize Bo's talking to him.

"Uh-huh."

"Why'd you take the animal heads off the wall? Was that about not throwing up or something else?"

Lion takes his time before answering, "You said you had a tight family."

"I do."

"Brothers and sisters? You're close?"

"Three sisters. And we're very close."

"Can you imagine what it would feel like if you saw their heads on a wall in someone's trophy room?"

Bo looks at him in the rearview, realizes he's serious. "I can't imagine."

"I know," says Lion, suddenly very tired, "that's exactly the problem."

THE DOUBLE TAP OF HOLY
EXCLAMATIONS

Heavy rain by the time they're pulling up to Masta Ice. Lion dashes out of the SUV and through the front door of the store. He finds himself dripping wet and standing inside a gray concrete rectangle polished to some hyper-sheen. Dramatic spot lighting and display cases from a different century. Ruby pendants inside vintage specimen jars, an array of gem-studded rings and grills under bell-shaped glass, diamond-encrusted watches inside oversized test tubes inside the open drawers of an ancient apothecary chest.

And not a soul in sight.

"Towel?"

Lion whips his head left and sees a ninja offering him a white hand towel. He blinks twice. Got to be the fentanyl.

Then realizes it's a sales clerk in a ninja outfit. Pageboy bangs, Asian eyes, and a jewel-handled katana slung across her back.

"Towel," she says again.

"Thank you," he says, taking it, wondering if today can get any stranger.

After sopping his hair and face, Lion looks back at the ninja. With the water out of his eyes, he notices living screens woven into her black knit top, displaying fight scenes from early-era Batman movies. The Dark Knight punching a bad guy in a bowler hat, KAPOW over left breast. Robin in short shorts with gold cape, BAMMO over her right.

"You're Lion Zorn," she says, a little breathless.

"Penelope called?"

"No. I mean yes. But you're really, really Lion Zorn."

People are rarely this excited to meet him.

"Balthazar does a little em-tracking on the side," she explains. "He's so-so-so to make your acquaintance . . ."

"Lion Zorn," booms behind him.

He jerks at the sound. Exaggerated startle response, worse when tired, worse when wounded, a kind of embodied paranoia common to em-trackers. Then he sees the source of the voice.

Out from behind the counter walks an extra-large black man in an extra-large smoking jacket. A black silk do-rag tied across his forehead, a black silk top hat worn over the rag. Diamond studs pierce each of his cheeks, and a living screen is built into the top hat, displaying gem-stones spelling out phrases: CHEW MY DRAWERS, in sapphires, currently visible.

So he was wrong: Today can get stranger.

"Balthazar Jones," says the man, extending his hand.

Hand shakes hand.

"You do a little em-tracking?" asks Lion, more puzzled than anything.

"Call me a fan of the genre."

"I didn't know the genre had fans."

"The Rod of Correction," says Balthazar, turning to face him directly. "Lion Zorn, em-tracker of the Rod of Correction."

That doesn't happen every day.

"Welcome to Masta Ice," continues Balthazar. "How may I be of service?"

"Would you mind. . . ." says Lion, reaching into his coat pocket for the cylinder, realizing he left it in the SUV. "Hold on a second."

He runs out the front door and into the sheeting rain. The truck's sensor notices his approach and slides open the back door, but it doesn't happen fast enough and Lion's getting drenched.

"Forgot this," he tells Bo, water sheeting down his face. He grabs his sling-pack off the seat and starts toward the store.

On his way, Lion pulls the snuff container from his pack. Clutching it in his hand, he shoulders open the door, steps inside and finds the ninja holding out another towel for him. THWACK on both breasts, the double tap of Holy Exclamations, Batman.

"Thank you."

He mops his hair and face a second time, sets the towel on the counter and holds up the snuff container. He closes his hand around it, then opens his palm when he feels the heat flash, gripping it with only his fingers so Balthazar can see the shiver of the question mark.

"The same thing happens on the inside of the container," says Lion. "It flashes down near the bottom. Might be some kind of writing, maybe. Do you think you could tell me what it says?"

Balthazar takes the container from him without saying a word. He crosses to the back of the store, steps behind the counter, and heads over to an old wooden desk. Lion and the ninja follow. Balthazar slides open a drawer and removes a pair of complicated goggles with steel rims, a small telescoping jeweler's loupe built into the right lens. His eyes disappear behind them. Lifts a hand to touch a switch and a single LED light glows hot white from the nose band. With the coat and top hat, the effect is pure steampunk, like an image last seen on Lorenzo's boxer shorts.

Turning the container over in his hands, Balthazar stares at it through the loupe. A minute passes. He takes the goggles off and fiddles with a dial. Then more staring. Next, he closes his palm around the cylinder, opening his hand in time to see the question mark shiver.

Repeats this twice.

Taking off the goggles, Balthazar slides over a chrome third hand from the corner of the desk. The hand appears to be of the traditional inanimate variety, but the alligator clips at its end slide outward automatically, extending their claw-toothed fingers to encircle the cylinder without being asked.

Out of a drawer comes a black velvet bag; out of the bag comes an assortment of skinny steel mirrors attached to steel chopsticks. Selecting one thin enough to slide inside the cylinder, Balthazar polishes it on the velvet, slides a small switch forward, and holds up the mirror so Lion can see the rim pulse pale blue.

"German optics," says Balthazar, "fine German optics."

Inserting the mirror into the cylinder with one hand, Balthazar holds the container in his other. Lion catches the flash through heavy fingers.

"It's taking a picture?" he asks.

"An extremely good picture," says Balthazar. "Image capture down to a millionth of a second, pixel count up the yin-yang."

Sliding the mirror out of the snuff container, Balthazar sets them both down on the desk. Placing the thumb and forefinger of his right hand on the top of the mirror and grabbing the other end of the chopstick with his left, he wiggles it slightly, breaking an invisible seal, then removes the mirror entirely.

Underneath, Lion sights the metallic circuitry of a mini thumb drive.

"Let's see what it says," says Balthazar, opening a desk drawer and removing a vintage iBook. A few seconds while it boots up; then Balthazar slips the drive into a port. A few more seconds until a folder icon pops onto the screen. A double click opens the file, another opens a photograph. The image shows the inside of the cylinder, silver sheen and bobbing white lights.

Balthazar pulls up a dropdown menu, selects SOFT FILL, and double-clicks. The image refocuses. The dazzle dims, heavy cursive script, maybe Arabic, becoming visible.

"Nice piece," says Balthazar. "GFP molecular engraving."

"What's that?" asks Lion.

"Stego."

"Still not following"

"Encrypted digital watermarking," explains Balthazar. "Information gets hidden in information, like a code inside the pixels. Only visible with the right kind of key. It's called steganography. Here," pointing at the cylinder, "they're using a similar technique, but done at the nano-level, with DNA as the information carrier. GFP is green fluorescent protein, in this case jellyfish genes woven into the atoms of the metal. The heat from your hand is the key."

"Awesome sauce," says the ninja.

Balthazar frowns. "Not in my store you don't."

"Retro-meme."

"Retro your ass back to So-Cal on the first flight. Didn't like it then, don't like it now. Awesome, by itself, is superlative aplenty."

"Is that Arabic?" interrupts Lion.

Balthazar fiddles with software; the image refocuses again and enlarges.

"Al-Andulus," says the ninja.

They both look at her.

"What? Khan Academy. I'm like-like-like three semesters shy of my graphic cert."

"Like-like-like?" thunders Balthazar. "Woman, I will sit on you until the grammar takes."

"What's Al-Andulus?" asks Lion.

"It's an old font," sayeth the ninja. "English, made to look like Arabic."

Pattern recognition system recalibrates. Now Lion can read the script. Three words, not a phrase.

Three words he knows very well.

"Muad'Dib," intones Balthazar, "Sietch Tabr."

"What's a Muad'Dib?" asks the ninja.

"The little mouse," says Lion. "Admired for its ability to survive in the desert. The little mouse that jumps."

He gets blank stares.

"From *Dune*."

More blank stares. No one reads the classics anymore.

He opens his sling-pack, takes out the book and shows it to them. "Twentieth century sci-fi. Muad'Dib is the name of the main character. He's human, but named for the jumping mouse. Sietch Tabr is a cave in the desert where he lives."

The ninja lifts the snuff container off the desk and looks at it closely. Batman decks the Joker. POW and ZAP in happy cartoon red and yellow.

"Any idea what it means?" she asks Lion.

"Herbert saw the mash-up coming. He dreamed up the first protopoly tribe, an Islamic-Zen hybrid. Muad'Dib was their leader. But no, I have no idea what it means." Looks at Balthazar. "Any idea where it comes from?"

"Not here," says Balthazar, "not what I do. I'm just a guy who encodes data in diamonds."

"I didn't know you could do that," says Lion.

"Imperfections store information. Any flaw in a diamond, at a structural level, it's actually a gap. A place a carbon atom is supposed to sit. When it's missing, nitrogen atoms slip in. Whenever there's a nitrogen atom positioned next to a carbon atom, you can trap electrons. If the vacant spot has an electron, it's a one. If the electron is missing, it's a zero."

"Neat trick."

"Expensive trick."

"How expensive?"

"About eighty grand for a single stone."

"Nice work if you can get it," says Lion.

"Interesting work as well. Turns out, diamonds don't just hold the ones and zeroes needed for binary code, they can also store both states at once."

"Quantum memory."

"Exactly," continues Balthazar. "And you don't need to supercool the stones. It works at room temperature. Completely stable. Never degrades, near-perfect data storage. Plus, a gem the size of a grain of rice can hold five terabytes of information. The only issue is fragility in the sequence. You can build an AI out of a thousand stones, but remove one, the whole thing collapses."

"Sounds pretty exotic."

"A handful of jewelers doing it in America, a couple overseas. But GPS engraving," pointing toward the snuff container, "is way more exotic. You still need a special kind of 3-D printer and, with the new laws, a tissue-engineering license."

"Hard to get?"

"It is here. In Asia, different story. But I could ask around."

"Quietly?"

"SON?" booms Balthazar. Lion jerks again. "It look like I do anything quietly?"

Now that you mention it.

"But discreet? Balthazar Jones can most definitely be discreet."

LIONS AND LAMBS

He's back at the Ludlow, where Bo must have dropped him after leaving Masta Ice. It's now morning, or some close approximation. He has no memory of getting into bed the night before, but that could be the fentanyl talking. But it's not talking anymore.

His arm, a steady throb.

Setting feet on floor, he tries standing up. It goes better than anticipated. He shuffles across the room to paw around in his suitcase for something to silence the ache. In a side pocket, he discovers two tablets of partially crumbled Naprosyn in a plastic single-pack. Bought by the dozen at a truck stop in Lubbock. That cowboy poetry job, emtracking to nowhere, the only future he found involving cheap whiskey and a relentless headache.

Lion dry-swallows the crumbs and heads for the shower.

Ten minutes later, straight-world uniform in tatters, Lion opts for option two: different pair of black jeans, different hooded gray sweater. He always buys duplicates, always packs duplicates, a lesson learned as a journalist, though, right now, he can't recall why.

Lion looks around for his phone and finds it on the floor beside the bed. Not sure what it's doing there. Checking the screen, he immediately understands how it ended up on the ground—perambulated off the nightstand. Phone set on vibrate, eight incoming texts. Two from Richard, three from Penelope, one from Jenka, one from Lorenzo, and his carrier, Tesla-Verizon, with exciting news about a new data plan.

Richard wants to know if his no became a yes, then wants to know about his arm, and if he would like a doctor sent over. Penelope follows up on the doctor in triplicate, no XOs this time. Jenka echoing the no becoming a yes, apparently not giving a shit about his arm. The last text is from Lorenzo, with news and another sign of the Apocalypse: *Weeks away and hundreds of miles up a river that snaked through the war like a circuit cable . . .*

He texts Lorenzo, telling him he's ready for contact. Texts Penelope back, declining the doctor, but remembering the rip in his jacket sleeve and asks about a tailor. Two minutes later a return from Penelope. *Gored by a dead buffalo? XO.*

An immediate follow-up. *P.S. I'll send a messenger over for the jacket.*

An immediate follow-up to the immediate follow-up. *If you're feeling up to it, Richard would like to take you to lunch. Yak by Yang and Jake at 1:30?*

He brews the lie that is large cup, contemplating what lunch with Richard might be like. Too fuzzy to contemplate. Texts back a request for dinner instead and, remembering what Bo said about the bar where he got roofied, asks for a restaurant in the West Village.

Then he carries his coffee out to the terrace. This time, no questions asked, he needs the lounge chair.

Supine, the view is partial skyline and rising mist, last night's rain drying off the pavement. The swirl brings his opiate fog back, violently. Five hundred times more powerful than morphine and the hangover to prove it. A sip of coffee helps the acoustics dial in. Hiss of air brakes, screech of tires, sounds of the city in waking mode. Must be later than he thought; later still, decides to check.

8:40 according to his phone.

Also another message. From Lorenzo: *Sietch Tabr, mon ami, holla at you in an hora.*

Sietch Tabr? Lorenzo doesn't typically quote *Dune,* but that's as far as Lion's brain can take him. His hangover is blunting his pattern recognition system and there's no use struggling. He leans back, stretches out his legs, and the next part is a little hazy. There might have been a knock on his door and a messenger from a tailor's shop.

Later still, a second cup of coffee and more lounge chair.

Halfway through that cup, the Naprosyn kicks in and the arm becomes a distant ache. Tries to get a read on his head. A couple cocks past half-cocked, but sobering fast. A walk might do some good. Maybe some food. On his way out the door, he sees the claim check from the tailor atop a low dresser.

So, good, that really happened.

He takes the traction elevator to the lobby and a left out of the hotel. The street is empty of people save for a dog walker and a pair of bloodhounds in the distance, tail-wagging their way around a corner. Lion works his way down the block, passing a street sweeper, a handful of taxis, and takes a right turn for the hell of it.

He likes getting a little lost in New York.

A left at the light, a few blocks, then a right. Halfway down that block, Lion finds a quiet coffee shop, a ceiling made of hammered tin, a display of bagels in a glass case and a copper-plated espresso machine beside it. A barista in a throwback rockabilly flannel over a T-shirt reading GRAVITY ALWAYS WINS wants to satisfy his breakfast desires.

Lion tells the clerk he desires an everything bagel, toasted, with vegan cream cheese.

While he's waiting for his food, his phone buzzes with a message from Penelope. Sir Richard agreeing to meet him for dinner instead. Seven thirty at Torah Toro, corner of Hudson and Horatio.

"Torah Toro?" he asks Gravity Always Wins.

"Yiddish-Asian fusion," handing him his bagel.

"That's a thing?"

"Intersectional cuisine? Brah, where you been?"

"You know," says Lion, taking his breakfast, "that's a very good question."

THE HORROR, HORROR BLUES

At a table by the window, Lion takes a tentative bite of his bagel. It smacks of salted cardboard—thanks, fentanyl—but a couple of swallows later he feels his blood sugar stabilize, and that normalizes his taste buds. Bagel becomes bagel again. A few minutes after that he feels awake enough to want a mission.

Checks his email instead. Been a little while, and he sees more messages than he can countenance this early in the day. Quick scan for anything work related, forwarding a Costa Rica engagement possibility to his agent, and then a feral curiosity about Sietch Tabr takes over his consciousness.

Double clicks his browser and brings up a search screen. The term unleashes *Dune* fandom on overdrive. He chooses a page at random. "Sietch: the Fremen word for community or village, typically a series of caves carved through the rocky outcroppings which are the dominant geological formations on the desert planet Arrakis. Sietch Tabr: the Fremen home of Muad'Dib, where he drank the water of life; where his transformation began."

"Where his transformation began?" Lion asks the air.

He clicks on the images tab. A full page to choose from, stills from a variety of *Dune* movies, also dozens of artist's renderings. Huge caverns, columns carved from sandstone, bloodred desert skies. Nothing here he doesn't already know. Nothing in the images to suggest a snuff container or a silver powder.

Maybe he does need more coffee.

Unfolding from the chair, he crosses to the counter and orders a triple-shot Americano. His phone starts to ring as he's paying.

Contact from Lorenzo.

Not wanting to be overheard, he takes his coffee and phone to a bench outside the front door before answering.

"Are you alright, Captain Willard?" says Lorenzo.

"What does it look like?" responds Lion, finishing the quote.

"It looks like your silver powder inhalant is strangely absent from the World Wide Web. Have you tried Googling this drug?"

"By typing new silver powder inhalant that makes you love animals into the search bar? Not yet."

"Sietch Tabr, remember that?"

"From *Dune*."

"Not anymore it's not. Sci-fi became sci-fact. That's what your silver powder's called."

Clicks into place. The engraving in the snuff container. But then he remembers what Lorenzo just said. "What do you mean absent from the web? I Googled Sietch Tabr and got lots of hits."

"Yeah, but find anything to snort? Any references to a drug?"

Come to think of it, "No."

"Nothing to find. Not anywhere. I figured if you're asking me about a new party drug, other people would be asking too. So I had a couple of conversations with a couple of search engines. Nada online." Lion hears the hard click of a Zippo, the soft suck of an inhale. "Doesn't make any sense, right?"

"Doesn't," he says, but feels a cold chill when he remembers what Richard said about hiding Shiz behind a new kind of scrubber.

"Which is when I called Hector and Ruiz, the brothers," says Lorenzo. "Remember them?"

"Did I meet them?"

"Yeah, you did, party in Seattle. They program pharmacy bots for the Gates Foundation or, I guess, what's left of the Gates Foundation."

"Vaguely," says Lion, recalling a high-ceiling loft, craft beer, chips and guac, and a couple of guys wearing pleated khaki.

"They'd heard of your drug. Hector had, at least. He told me it was called Sietch Tabr. I also called a couple other people. A few more had heard of it too. Which is kind of weird. Couple people I know have heard of the drug, you've heard of the drug. Makes me wonder why the internet hasn't heard."

"It's been scrubbed."

"You can't scrub everything," says Lorenzo. "Information gets what it wants, and it wants to be free."

A horn honk grabs for Lion's attention. Looking up, he sees gridlock has seeped into the city. Cars pass before him with the slow drip of an old faucet. A Datsun carrying two women in dashikis arguing, flashes of outrageous color through the windshield as arms move in anger. Then an Audi.

"Arctic can," says Lion.

"The people you're working for?"

"I think today's my last day, but yeah, they have an AI scrubber that corrupts at a foundational level. Makes sharing of information impossible."

"Last tango in cyberspace," says Lorenzo.

"I don't know that phrase."

"Cyberspace, the noosphere of the internet. William Gibson called it a 'shared consensual hallucination.' Shared being the critical part. No sharing, no communication; no communication, no cooperation; no cooperation, no empathy. Game over. An AI that makes sharing information impossible, as an em-tracker you should get this . . ."

"Last tango in cyberspace," says Lion, "the end of something radically new. Copy that."

An open-air bus passes by the bench, Japanese tourists wearing wireless headphones and VR glasses with opaque lenses, their heads pointed in the same direction. Like something out of *1984*.

"The people you called," asks Lion, "anyone mention Muad'Dib?"

"Hector quoted from the 'Collected Sayings of Muad'Dib.'"

"He did?" asks Lion. "Do you remember which one?"

"Give me a sec, I wrote it down in my Moleskine."

"One of the ones I gave you?" asks Lion; the notebooks were Lorenzo's birthday present last year. "Have you become a convert?"

"Completely. First class on the way over to Tokyo—which was a miracle. One of those private rooms and women in short skirts bringing me drinks in actual Waterford. Halfway through my second Walker Blue I realized that someone needs to turn *Apocalypse Now* into a blues opera. I filled a whole notebook."

"A blues opera?"

"*The Horror, Horror Blues*."

Groans. "Which Muad'Dib saying?"

"I'm still looking." Lion hears pages turning, cigarette smoking, more pages. "Got it: 'Greatness is a transitory experience. It is never consistent. It depends in part upon the myth-making imagination of humankind.'"

Lion finishes the stanza: "'The person who experiences greatness must have a feeling for the myth he is in.'"

"You know the quote?"

"Remember that University of Chicago talk I gave?"

"With the floating heads of intimidation on the walls?"

"That's the one. I had a variation on a slide. 'Em-tracking is a transitory experience. The person who experiences em-tracking must have a feeling for the myth he is in.' That's a little weird."

"We're way past weird. You learn anything about what Sietch Tabr actually does?"

Lion's been asking himself this same question. Has a small list. "Expands empathy, widens spheres of caring. Probably a serotonin thing, like MDMA, but I'm guessing."

"Not like MDMA. More basic. And I'm quoting Hector here: It opens information channels. You take in more data per second, pay more attention to that data, and find more patterns in it."

"Lot of drugs do that."

"Hector said you'd say that, but, okay, understand I have no idea what I'm talking about here, but something like Sietch Tabr expands your umwelt—which, turns out, is not some kind of vegetarian sandwich."

"True that," says Lion. "It's the world as perceived by a particular organism. Humans are visual. Dogs smell. Cats feel with whiskers. We all use the same information, but we end up in different realities because we have different information processing machinery."

"Sure," laughs Lorenzo, "absolutely. You get that I play bongos in a blues band, right?"

"Tell me about the umwelt."

"Hector says Sietch Tabr expands your umwelt. You ever heard of something called 'grandmother neurons'?"

"Neurons dedicated to extremely familiar images, promotes faster pattern recognition."

"Exactly," says Lorenzo. "According to Hector, Sietch Tabr finds the neurons used to recognize the other, the out-group, and turns them into a hypersensitive grandmother neuron network. The strange, the not-like-me, becomes the super-familiar. Plus it tweaks the senses. Hector knew this dude who tried it at a dog park—said he could smell time. Did you know dogs could smell time?"

"Yeah," says Lion, remembering a documentary, maybe on Animal Planet. "They sense it in fading scent trails."

"Well, dude said he started to smell time. Flipped his whole vegetarian sandwich upside down. Said it was like waking up on another planet. And that's not even the weird-weird part."

"Seriously, weird-weird?" says Lion, having ninja flashbacks.

"Nah, I mean two weirds. The drug changes how you smell, the thing you do with your nose, and it changes how you smell, your scent, the thing that other noses do to you. That's why it's called Sietch Tabr."

"You lost me."

"Remember how living in the cave changed Muad'Dib's scent? He started to smell like the cave, the spice. Sietch Tabr changes how you smell to animals. Something in it messes with pheromones, makes animals scent you as friend, not foe."

"Makes sense," says Lion, thinking about the family in South Africa lying down with lions.

"Is that why you're so interested in this? I mean, beyond all the obvious Lion shit."

"So interested?"

"I can hear it," says Lorenzo, "in your voice, same pit bull tone you used to get as a reporter, when the story you were digging into started digging back. You're not gonna get arrested again are you?"

"What's the obvious Lion shit? You mean beside the animals, the empathy, the weird drug, and the slammin' paycheck?"

"Yeah."

Lion thinks about it for a moment. "It leads somewhere. It didn't at first. Not when I took this job, but then I visited the crime scene. I don't know. It was a no, now it's a yes."

"You visited the crime scene—does that mean you saw that decapitated head?"

"Yeah. Trust me when I tell you it was worse in real life."

"Wait a minute," says Lorenzo. "Your no became yes? I thought that didn't happen."

"It's never happened before."

"So why now? That head screw you up? It would screw me up."

"Yeah," says Lion, remembering the look of remorse he saw in Walker's eyes. "Maybe that. Maybe worse."

I t used to be trendy Asian fusion," explains Jenka, ushering Lion down the long entrance hall of Torah Toro, beneath a silver flow-metal ceiling and walls decorated with oversized photographs of twentieth-century board games superimposed over Hubble Telescope images. "Now," continues Jenka, "it's trendy Asian Yiddish fusion."

They pass a twelve-foot-high photo of Mouse Trap, the original 1963 edition with the blue zigzag slide, overlaid atop the smoking columns of the Eagle Nebula. And around a corner.

The hallway opens into two stories of cavernous space, dark, gleaming, and thoroughly packed. Mostly corporate types holding oversized cocktail glasses. Strange lumps floating inside.

"You should try a wasabi matzo ball martini," shouts Jenka, trying to be heard above the din.

"A wasabi say what?"

Indicating the pale turds in martini glasses.

"I'll stick with bourbon."

For their night out, Jenka's traded in the white suit for a pink cotton dress shirt, French cuffs uncuffed and floppy as he leads Lion through the restaurant. They skirt a table of Hasidic power traders, blue suits and blue yarmulkes, arguing bond-yield retardation and collateralized debt obligations and other incomprehensibles. Another table filled with young women wearing birthday hats.

"Sir Richard's holding our spot," says Jenka, pointing toward a far corner of the restaurant.

Lion follows his finger across the room. Richard at a distant table, wearing a white button-down shirt, a black jacket, and the I HAVE IS-SUES trucker cap. It takes some maneuvering to get there.

They thread between a drunken debutante and a waiter carrying an enormous tray of gefilte fish wrapped in nori decorated with orange roe. Finally, Richard standing up to greet him.

"Lion," he says, before he's even reached the table, "what's the Turing test for tree consciousness?"

Blinks.

"Richard," says Jenka, his tone cheerfully diplomatic, "let him order a drink first."

"Ordered," passing over a Knob Creek neat. "What's the Turing test for tree consciousness? What kind of proof would it take to convince you?"

"The Turing test?" asks Lion, taking a seat, trying to shift his brain into a higher gear. "The how to tell an AI from a human thing?"

"Yes, but for trees."

"Are we not," says Jenka, his tone a little less diplomatic, "here to discuss business?"

Richard ignores him. "We know trees process information just as we do, with neurochemicals. Dopamine, serotonin. They have senses, take in data, integrate it, make decisions. Send out defense chemicals, which sounds like an automatic response, but trees also practice altruism, form memories, and you can knock them out with a human anesthetic. So how would you test for tree consciousness? How would you know?"

"Why," snaps Jenka, "would anybody care?"

"We care," says Richard, fixing the Slav with his too-blue eyes, "because trees are what's next."

"What's next?" asks Lion.

"Three hundred years ago we decide owning other people was a bad idea. Two hundred years ago and women should vote. Then black people want to be free. Then the LGTB variety pack and a hundred different gender pronouns. Then animals. Switzerland grants basic rights to great apes. No-kill shelters in most major cities. Hopefully in-vitro meat replaces ranching. So maybe the animals are still next, but whatever, it's never over. We'll fight another battle over whether robots and AIs are conscious and deserving of rights, just like we'll fight the same fight over trees and plants. And it might very well be turtles all the way down."

"I don't know this expression," says Jenka, resigned to his fate.

"An infinite regress," explains Lion, trying to recall the details. "A philosopher, Bertrand Russell, I think, was lecturing about how the earth orbits the sun and the sun orbits the galaxy. This old woman stood up and called him a liar and said: 'Everyone knows the world is a flat plate supported on the back of a giant tortoise.' So Russell asked the woman what the tortoise was standing on. 'You're very clever, young man,' she said, 'but it's turtles all the way down.'"

"Patterns inside of patterns inside of patterns," says Jenka, glaring at Richard. "Why didn't you say so."

Lion takes a sip of bourbon and waits.

Richard continues: "Lots of people believe consciousness is a fundamental property of the universe, like space and time. If that's the case, then it is turtles all the way down. We'll have this debate about our microbiome. About rocks and atoms and quarks. Until we have Gaia consciousness, there will always be an us-them divide, always a next frontier for empathy—isn't that right, Lion?"

Said it better than I could, is what Lion's thinking, and finds himself uncomfortable with this fact. Like Richard's invaded his territory.

Might not even be personal. Entirely possible that Gaia consciousness has become the new mega-rich-guy thing, like the billionaires who used to become libertarian sea-steaders.

Another possibility: This could be a well-calculated, well-disguised up-sell, an Arctic ploy like Penelope's flirting. Guerrilla-guerrilla marketing. Lion decides to proceed slowly. "I'm not sure about the conscious universe part," he says, "but em-tracking is like that; it's the experience of cultural empathy. That's a new frontier. It's empathy in a direction we didn't even know we could feel."

"Bloody exactly-exactly," says Richard, doing that finger-snapping clap again, I HAVE ISSUES bobbing to the beatnik beat.

"I'm not sure about the Turing test for trees either," Lion continues, "but whatever it is, it's probably going to require empathy."

"Why?" Jenka wants to know, his eyes narrowing. "The test Alan Turing designed was about how an AI would fool a human into thinking the AI was human. That's deception, not empathy. Why would tree consciousness require empathy?"

"It's an interface problem," Lion explains. "The point where two systems meet—that's an interface. The web browser Mosaic was an interface for the internet, an easy way for people to communicate with the new tech. AIs were designed by humans, with human-centric interfaces. Trees weren't. They communicate mostly by pheromones. Dogs, with their incredible noses, speak tree. But not us, not at any conscious level. Our umwelt is different. If your umwelt is different, then empathy has to be your interface."

"I agree," says Richard. "I also agree that the Turing test for tree consciousness is, for now, inscrutable." He leans closer, speaking in a conspiratorial stage whisper: "But I do know what the proof would look like."

The whisper works. Lion feels curiosity grow. Humans, he thinks, such simple toys.

Jenka bites first. "What would it look like?"

"Like hyperactive grandmother neurons," says Richard.

So this is what this conversation is actually about.

"Sietch Tabr," Lion says flatly, looking closely at both of them, watching for any change in expression.

Jenka smirks. Richard does that subject-switching thing he does. "Your no became a yes. Can you tell me why?"

Lion notices that the picture on the wall behind Richard is the Horsehead Nebula with a Monopoly board superimposed over it. Park Place landing on the snout of that cosmic stallion. So who is going to own the Horsehead Nebula? Probably, he realizes, somebody like Richard.

"Can you tell me why you stole the end table covered with powder?" asks Lion, choosing to counter with a different question.

Jenka smirks again. "Borrowed."

"And for good reason," says Richard, sliding an ornate envelope out of a briefcase. Rag weave paper and Red Ice icon. Lifting the flap, Richard places his finger on the nano-scanner. A zip of light and the flap opens. He slides out a piece of paper, blank.

"A white piece of paper?"

"We'll get to this in a minute," tapping the paper, subject switching again. "Tell me why the no became a yes."

"You know it doesn't work like that," says Lion. "All I get is a sense of the future. A little room to breathe, like a way forward."

"But you visited the Walker residence and felt that way forward?"

Nods.

"Humor us—extrapolate, please, if you can."

"Humans," he says, looking from Jenka to Richard, "are clannish, insular, happy to divide into teams and tribes. Rich, poor, class, color, nation, species, whatever. These splits lead to predictable outcomes. Empathy, though, bridges the divide. As a result, it leads to more interesting futures. Less predictable, more hopeful. That's what I got from the crime scene. A little sense of hope. But does any of that matter to Arctic? Does it lead to new products and profits?" Hands spread wide. "Open question."

"Yes," says Richard, "yes, I think that too, which is why it will make a great medicine."

"A medicine?" Now confused.

Richard puffs up in his chair, tosses the trucker cap to the table with a soft flourish, and flips over the paper. Reveals a new icon, blue ice this time, an iceberg in its natural shade. Also two words: Arctic Pharmaceuticals.

"You're going into pharmaceuticals?"

Proudly, "Yes."

"A new branch of Arctic," crows Jenka, clearly happy to be back to business.

"To treat what?"

"We start with autism," says Jenka, ticking them off on his fingers, "Asperger's. Soon, social phobias, anxiety. The markets will be significant."

"You want to turn Sietch Tabr into a social phobia drug?" But in a way that doesn't even seem particularly screwed up, it makes sense. They turned MDMA into an anti-anxiety drug. Why not Sietch Tabr? And he's right, Arctic Pharmaceuticals will make bank. For the first time since taking this job, Lion actually feels a sense of relief.

"That's what this has been about all along?"

Richard nods, but a hitch in the motion. "There does seem to be one small issue. We can't get the compounding right. We saw the market potential early, almost as soon as rumors about the drug surfaced, hired the best chemists. Couldn't get there. We heard about the Robert Walker incident and decided to get, shall we say, a tad more aggressive in our approach."

"You borrowed a sample from the crime scene, is what you mean?"

Jenka jumping in: "A month now, the best chemists mass-speccing it from every angle. There's something we can't identify. A mystery."

"We'd like your assistance in solving this mystery," adds Richard.

"Way outside my lane," says Lion, yet can't help but wonder, "What would I do?"

"You would help us find someone."

He raises an eyebrow.

"Muad'Dib," continues Richard, then, turning to Jenka, "Show him."

Jenka reaches into his shirt pocket, fingers disappearing behind pink cloth, reappearing with an Amex Centurion, the black neon issue. You could buy an aircraft carrier with that piece of plastic. Lion has never seen one up close. Jenka taps a finger on the raised letters of the nameplate. Two words: Judah Zorn.

"You would have our full resources behind you," explains Richard. "And a place to start."

"Who's Muad'Dib?" asks Lion. "Unless you're talking about the protagonist in *Dune*."

Richard smiles, putting too many teeth on display. "I'm talking about the leader of the Rilkeans."

"The Rilkeans don't have a leader. They're entirely nonhierarchical."

"When they emerged, yes. Leaderless, rudderless, poetry geeks of all stripes. But they had a shared interest in consciousness-hacking pharmaceuticals. Muad'Dib became their leader by being the master chemist, the one who created Sietch Tabr. He gave them a better way to live the questions."

"And soon to be our third partner in Arctic Pharmaceuticals," adds Jenka.

"The Rilkeans are deep subcult," says Lion. "They don't strike me as the Big Pharma kind."

Jenka snarls, "As your great American poet David Mamet once said, 'everyone needs money—that's why they call it money.'"

"You can leave the negotiations up to us," adds Richard. "We just want you to find Muad'Dib, get him to agree to a meeting. We'll take it from there."

"I'm an em-tracker."

"Lion," says Richard, in his mellifluous best, "you are many things.

An excellent reporter. An animal rights advocate willing to get arrested for the cause. A man with a deep interest in consciousness-changing compounds. You are perfect for the job."

"Why not ask Penelope? I saw the tattoo. She's a Rilkean."

"Not a Rilkean," says Richard, cryptically. "And she doesn't have your particular skills."

"What skills?"

"She's not an em-tracker."

"I'm still not following."

"The way to find Muad'Dib is through Prince Shiz," Richard explains. "Unfortunately, despite the fact that Shiz hired us to aid in his disappearance, he's not interested in disclosing Dib's location to a man of my persuasion."

"Your persuasion?"

"Rich," snipes Jenka. "Shiz is half Jamaican. Thinks money is from Babylon. All he does is quote Marley: 'Possessions make you rich? I don't have that type of richness. My richness is life.' But he's a big fan of yours, Lion Zorn, em-tracker of the Rod of Correction."

"I didn't think em-trackers had fans," he says, both stalling and knowing, because of Balthazar, this isn't exactly true.

"Shiz is a fan," says Jenka. "He's just so-so-so to meet you."

"Let's eat," says Richard, suddenly adopting diplomatic tones. "We can certainly let you ponder over a meal."

Jenka nods, resigned. "Of course."

Richard pushes a button to his left and a small lens rises from the center of the table, projecting a holographic menu they all can read. Dragon roll borscht in a challah bowl. The words in luminous baby-blue chalk dust, hovering in the empty space between them.

"One question," says Lion, fixing Jenka with a hard glare. "What the fuck's up with the dragonfly?"

"Dragonfly?" both Jenka and Richard say in unison, and with what might be genuine surprise.

"The one that followed me."

"What dragonfly?" asks Jenka again, amping toward befuddlement.

Humans are able to fake many emotions, but not the so-called distressed quartet of anger, fear, sadness, and surprise. Feeling these feelings, Lion knows, requires the simultaneous contraction of antagonistic facial muscles. Surprise tugs eyebrows upward while knitting foreheads together, for example, and this collusion lifts up the inner corners of the eyes. Totally involuntary, very hard to fake.

Lion looks at them. Foreheads knit, inner eyes up. They honestly have no idea what he's talking about.

"Never mind," he says. "Forget about it. Let's eat."

L ion leaves them at the table. He has little desire for chocolate-covered matzo-mochi, telling them to enjoy dessert without him, telling them he might or might not be interested in tracking down Muad'Dib.

"I'll let you know in the morning."

On his way out, at the tail end of the entrance hall, he notices one final picture, smaller than the rest: Earth, from a great distance, a sun-beamed speck amid the vastness of deep space, with a chess board and a handful of pieces overlaid atop the image. Lion studies the arrangement.

Check in four moves.

And through the door.

Outside, he finds the weather has cleared. Dry skies and warm air. He sees Bo and the shiny mobile, parked at the curb, but it's a pleasant evening and he doesn't want the ride. Also doesn't want to tell Bo where he's going.

"I think I'm gonna walk back to the hotel," he says.

"A good thirty minutes," says Bo. "You sure?"

"No," says Lion, "not in a long time. But yes on the walk."

"Roger that," says Bo, starting toward the driver's side door.

Lion stops him. "Can I ask you something?"

"I already told you—not a Rilkean."

"Not you," says Lion, glancing at the front door of Torah Toro, checking to make sure Richard and Jenka are still inside. "What about Penelope? Is she a Rilkean?"

"It's a different thing. But also not a Rilkean."

"What kind of a different thing?"

Bo hesitates, uncomfortable with this line of inquiry. "Might not be my place to say."

"Understood," says Lion. "Sorry I asked."

"Then again," says Bo, the slightest hint of a smirk visible along the edges of his mouth, "got any more of that Ghost Trainwreck?"

Lion pats down his jacket, front left, front right, remembers he'd placed a joint in his inside pocket. Reaches in, removes it, then realizes he'd rolled 50-50, "Mind a little tobacco?"

"Beggar," says Bo, "not a chooser." Then he points at the restaurant. "But can we move it away from the spot where my boss is having dinner?"

"Take a stroll," says Lion, striding off.

Bo falls in beside him. Lion waits until they're down the block and around a corner before lighting the joint.

"If you ask Penelope about the tattoo," Bo explains, "she'll tell you that she saw it and liked it. That it was—what do you call it, the thing I learned about in class: meme contagion."

"And it wasn't?" passing over the joint.

Bo sucks in a lungful, starts talking mid-exhale. "Do you know what her original job title was?"

"I thought she was Jenka's exec assistant."

"Now," says Bo, passing the joint back, "but that's punishment. Her original job was in extra-specials. She was Chief of Rilkean Relations."

"And the tattoo?"

"I drive people around," he shrugs, "people say things. I hear things. Not my fault."

Lion is about to hit the joint but stops, feeling a familiar unfamiliar feeling, like he's being watched again. Same vibe he felt at Walker's house. The dragonfly, back for round two?

He glances down the block.

Formerly light industrial, now two-story lofts in sunshine colors. Completely wrong in New York—a city he always sees in black-and-white—but not the source of his concern.

"What's wrong?" asks Bo.

Lion can't decide.

"Dunno," he says. "Tell me what you heard."

"Richard made her get the tattoo; it was one of his hiring conditions."

"Seriously," says Lion, shaking his head. "How'd she end up working for Jenka?"

"Again, hearsay, but apparently she sucked at her first job."

"Which was?"

"The general gist was find the Rilkeans for Richard. And she didn't find any. Well, that's not entirely true. She found me."

"Where did she find you?"

"At NYU, actually. I came out of class and Penelope was standing there. She asked me if I wanted a job."

"You did?"

"You've noticed Arctic's proclivity for research?"

Lion waves the spliff. "Ghost Trainwreck #69, tissue-engineered dragon box, em-tracker of the Rod of Correction. Yeah, you could say I've noticed."

"What their research showed was that I was broke. On fumes and rice for dinner. I was desperate for the job."

"But you're not a Rilkean."

"Turns out, no."

Out of the corner of his eye, Lion spots a motorcyclist in a black full-face helmet and head-to-toe riding leathers, idling in the middle of the road. Watching them in his side-view mirror, is what Lion thinks—but perhaps it's nothing—as the rider kicks the bike into gear and vanishes around a corner. He turns his attention back to Bo. "How come that fact didn't show up in Arctic's research?"

"That I wasn't a Rilkean? That mine was just your typical boy-meets-girl, boy-gets-drugged-kidnapped-and-tattooed story?"

"Yeah."

"Stupidity."

"Arctic doesn't strike me as stupid."

"Not them, me. The woman, Sarah, that's her name, the silver-haired kidnapper, I was really into her. Even after everything that happened, I was kind of hoping for—" Shrugs. "I don't know what I was hoping for."

"But you didn't call her?" asks Lion, passing the joint back to Bo.

"Did you miss the part about her being in a psycho-cult that brands new members?"

"Yet?"

"Yet, okay, I entertained the idea of calling her. Which is why Arctic's research never turned anything up. I didn't tell anyone. I couldn't. Figured if I told anyone, I'd also have to tell my mother. Chinese, right? Like I said, tight families. Plus, my mom's Dick Tracy. Even if I didn't tell her, she'd have dug the truth outta my friends or my sisters."

"And can't introduce Sarah to Mom, if Mom knows Sarah's crazy."

Bo snaps his fingers twice. "Exactly, exactly."

"Don't tell me you do that too?"

"Meme contagion," says Bo, smiling.

"What does this have to do with Penelope?"

"Since I was the only Rilkean she ever found and I wasn't actually in the club, Penelope became Jenka's assistant and Arctic took a . . . a different approach."

"Different how?" asks Lion, looking up and down the street again.

Something still not quite right or residual dragonfly paranoia made worse by the recent application of Ghost Trainwreck—he can't quite tell.

"Again," says Bo, "could just be chatter. But something about Jenka starting Rilkean rumors about Shiz."

"The honeypot."

"The what?"

"Not important," says Lion, brushing away the question with a wave of his hand. "Go on."

"Nowhere to go. That's about all I know. But want to hear something ironic? Penelope looks a little like Sarah. I didn't notice it until she got the tattoo, but afterwards, there's something similar." Bo stops walking. "Now can I ask you something? That podcast I heard. The guy talked about em-trackers having a higher than usual suicide rate."

"Emo-stim overload," says Lion.

"Uh-huh," says Bo. "He said that. Also said there was more to it, a kind of loneliness that comes from knowing, pretty much upon meeting someone, exactly how that relationship will play out."

"Yeah," says Lion, noticing they've rounded the block and are now back in front of Torah Toro. "It's a little more complicated in real life, but the basics are right."

"More complicated?"

"The loneliness for sure . . ." Trying to find the right words. "Humans are social mammals, hardwired to seek attention. As an em-tracker, if I really pay attention to someone, to them, it feels like we're really close. Like we go way back. To me, they still feel like a total stranger, but to them, we're lifelong friends."

"Sounds like an unfair advantage on a first date."

"Only fun for a while is my point," says Lion.

Bo touches his earlobe and the shiny mobile hums to life. Headlights wink up, driver's door cracks open. Must be a sensor built into the licking-pug implant.

"You still walking?" he wants to know.

Lion nods.

"Am I driving you to the airport tomorrow?"

He hadn't thought that far ahead. "Maybe."

"Then maybe I'll see you tomorrow. Good night, Lion."

"Night, Bo."

With that, Bo taps the rim of his cap in a farewell salute, climbs into the SUV, and pulls away from the curb. Lion looks up and down the street again. No Richard or Jenka or source of his unease. No one but the restaurant's doorman, a solemn rabbinical student with a peach-fuzz beard.

Lion walks over to him, "You know where Hudson's is?"

A hand lifts to rub the peach fuzz. "The cigar place?"

"Yeah." Thinking to himself: the cigar place where Bo got kidnapped. "The one with the big ashtrays."

The doorman points down the road. "Ten blocks up, a couple east."

Lion sets off, thunk of boots on pavement, whoosh of cars on asphalt, and down the street. He nearly makes the corner before he realizes that Penelope's old job title . . . If he says yes to Richard, doesn't he, de facto, become Chief of Rilkean Relations? And when was the last time he had an actual job title?

Good question.

It takes him a while to figure it out, eventually settling on his last journalism assignment. Technically, an embedded reporter joining an Animal Liberation Front raid on a National Institutes of Health primate lab, but the judge threw that distinction out after he was caught on camera releasing a family of rhesus monkeys from their cages. It was the last straw for Lion's editor, his four arrests in six months having totally destroyed any pretense of objective reporting. The tabloids had already gotten hold of the story; his prominent byline had become a problem. His writer-at-large status was revoked. His last title lost.

"Lion Zorn," he says aloud, "Chief of Rilkean Relations."

So maybe his life isn't so small after all.

THE CAT EYE OPEN SOURCE
PROJECT

A few blocks from Hudson's, nearing the corner of Gansevoort and Greenwich, Lion spots the motorcycle again. Same black riding leathers, same black bike. Down the block and tucked in between a delivery van and an ancient Tesla roadster. A good hiding spot. It would have kept the rider totally invisible except for the helmet's visor catching the moonlight for a momentary starburst and nabbing his attention.

Pretending not to notice, Lion ambles over to a storefront. One of those 3-D-printed confectionaries, Cosmic Chocolates, according to the sign. He feigns interest in five tiers of a dark-truffle-blend wedding cake sculpted to resemble the Gates of Mordor, complete with an army of orcs hidden behind the casements. Really just checking out the motorcyclist in the reflection.

Still there.

He feels it then, the lengthening of gargoyle shadows, the incoming creep of paranoia.

Strolling onward, he stays close to the storefront windows so he can use the occasional reflection to keep an eye on things. The angles are wrong from the front plate of a newsstand, but a mirror hanging in the window of the upscale furniture shop reveals the motorcycle hasn't moved.

Idling by the van, the helmet's visor pointed in his direction, the dark shield of the faceplate staring after him.

Could be a coincidence. Could be a lot of things.

Lion tries to think of the things it could be. By now, he's not putting anything past Arctic, but Richard and Jenka both looked genuinely surprised to hear about the drone dragonfly. And if they're not the ones following him, then who?

He has absolutely no idea.

Another glance into a storefront window, another glimpse of the rider in the reflection. The tilt of the head, the cant of the visor, Lion can tell, he's definitely being watched.

His heart rate picks up and pattern recognition system kicks into gear, pawing the databanks for appropriate ass-saving information. Then he remembers—this is not the first time he's been followed. Fifteen years ago, when the Animal Liberation Front story first broke, one of the tabloids put a tail on him. Also when he learned that the CIA teaches agents to bore tails to death. Go slow. Don't do anything interesting. Make cover stops, pausing at places with absolutely no meaning to disguise true intentions.

But the map is not the territory.

Before he can stop himself, Lion picks up his pace, then picks it up again. Not bothering with storefront reflections, he whips his head around and sees the motorcyclist slipping into the street, moving impossibly slow. Creeping down the middle of the road, sizing him up.

Adrenaline washes over him. Drop-down menu in his mind offers fight, flee, or freeze as available options. Autonomous nervous system selects flight, and so much for disguising true intentions. He cuts hard left into an alley in full sprint mode. Boots bashing pavement and arms pumping wildly for a couple hundred feet before a wash of anger makes him pull up short and whirl around.

The alley's empty save for blowing trash.

Did he imagine it?

Twitchy legs make walking difficult. Takes him too long to get out of the alley. But nothing happens along the way. He makes it onto a side street; the buildings are brownstones on diets, impossibly thin, made from very old brick. To his right, one of those all-night road crews slicing into concrete with a water-cooled laser. Mist rising, air shimmering, and a spotlight drone hovering over the whole operation, the halogen shine of its million candle-watts blinding his eyes.

Lion blinks against the glare, lifting an arm as a shield, using the motion to cover a backward glance.

Nothing to see.

He turns around and surveys the whole street.

Still, nothing.

But his heart is pumping and his legs are trembling and the paranoia feels here to stay. A couple of deep breaths to steady himself. When this fails, he tries the Herbert mantra. Fear is the mind-killer.

That seems to help.

Feeling a little more under control, Lion starts walking again. This brings the return of rational thought and the rise of the questions. What the hell, for starters. Did that actually happen? What would Lorenzo say: "You understand, Captain, that this mission does not exist, nor will it ever exist."

Perhaps there's a different truth at work.

As much as Lion doesn't like admitting it, this week has been more fun than last week. And the week before. And the week before that. Something inside him is starting to wake up. It's entirely possible that Lorenzo would have chosen a different retort: "Disneyland. Fuck, man, this is better than Disneyland."

Lion smiles at the thought, walking past the tail end of the work crew on the right, the storefront of a syn-bio hacker space on the left. A scrolling screen embedded in the lab's window advertises a Saturday afternoon meet-up for the Cat Eye Open Source Project. Lion knows about the Project. Another emerging poly-tribe, hard-core Silicon Valley strain of the bio-hacking movement crossed with hard-core Eastern European strain of the vampire movement—the former in it for the science puzzle, the latter looking for DNA tweaks that will give them actual cat eyes.

And spreading.

Richard said that animals are next and he might be right, but staring in the storefront, Lion suspects synthetic biology might intercede. The tech makes human-animal hybridization available to anyone who wants to learn a little code. Hybridization, he figures, is destined to become one of the ways this generation out-rebels the last generation. How we went from long-haired hippie freaks to pierced punk rockers to omnisexual teenagers taking hormones. This time no different. Won't be long before injections are available at every tattoo parlor, just the next step for the body-mod crowd.

But, he also suspects, the trend will likely produce an ugly prejudice, a keep-humans-pure backlash, another hatred we didn't know we had until its hostility was fully upon us.

Thinking about this, Lion makes it two-thirds of the way down the street before suspicion sneaks back into his evening. He slows his pace as he reaches an old pickup truck with extra-wide side mirrors, parked by the side of the road. Casually stopping beside the truck, he removes his tobacco pouch from his pocket. Rolls a cigarette while watching the mirror.

The reflection reveals nothing. There's no one chasing him.

He leaves the truck and makes his way to the corner, finding the street suddenly crowded, the way it happens in New York. A small swarm of people waiting for the light. Lion stops a few feet away, smoking his cigarette, watching for anyone looking in his direction, any sign of the motorcycle.

Nobody glances his way. The street stays empty. But the fear, the fear stays with him.

BETTER THAN DISNEYLAND

I t takes ten minutes to backtrack to the corner of Hudson and Horatio, then a quick dart across the street and Lion strolls up to the front
entrance of Hudson's. A pair of burgundy velvet ropes attached to polished brass stanchions rest in the middle of the sidewalk, a rectangular awning above, a doorman in a suit beneath.

"Good evening, sir," he says, not bothering to scan Lion's ID.

"Evening."

A last look around the street and he walks inside. Like stepping back
in time. Panels of dark oak, walls of books, and the dense fog of cigar
smoke everywhere. A couple of steps forward and the smoke lifts
enough that he can see the rest of the room: a long and narrow rectangle with a gleaming hardwood bar stretching down the left side, a
row of wooden small tables down the right, and a pair of black curtains revealing a small VIP seating area in the back. Lion looks past
the curtains and sees a trio of blockchain billionaires, familiar from
an article he read somewhere, and an older Japanese man sitting knee

to knee with a very attractive young blonde who—you never know— just might be his niece.

Spotting a couple of empty seats toward the end of the bar, Lion takes one, sets his sling-pack on another. Cocktail napkin slides into place in front of him. Bartender from another era. A tie. A jacket. "Good evening, sir."

"Please," he says, "just Lion."

"Lion?"

"It's better than sir."

"That it is, sir," but smiling. "Roberto. It's nice to meet you, Lion. Cocktail?"

"I was thinking whiskey."

"Anything specific?"

Now it's his turn to smile. Lion reaches into his pocket and pulls out the Amex Centurion card, which he'd taken possession of at dinner, telling them he'd give it back if he decided not to take the job, not telling them he had other ideas. He lays it on the bar, knowing exactly how much this tab will annoy Jenka.

"Surprise me."

Roberto looks from card to Lion. "How big of a surprise?"

He taps the card with his forefinger. "Very big."

As Roberto goes about choosing, Lion looks around the room. Despite his hopes, Hudson's really doesn't seem like a Rilkean hangout. The vibe is more Rat Pack than subcult. Another slow pan, this time zeroing in on the backs of people's necks. No one seems to be sporting a bar code tattoo. Also, while there's clearly a back door somewhere, he sees only one exit, up near the front of the room. Highly visible from pretty much everywhere. Nothing about the place explains why Sarah chose it as the spot to abduct Bo.

Lion opens his sling-pack, removing his well-thumbed copy of *Dune*, which he sets on the bar with a conspicuous thump. A tumbler appears beside it, a slosh of amber inside.

"Yamazaki single malt," says the bartender, "the forty-year variety."

"Thank you," says Lion, picking up his copy of *Dune*, tapping the spine against his palm a couple of times to draw in Roberto's attention, then using the book to point at the whiskey. "Would you like to join me?" Smiling, "I'm buying."

Roberto nods once, then opens a menu to the whiskey page. He places his finger on a price. *Yamazaki, 40 yr. $305.*

"You sure?"

Lion looks at the price, looks back at Roberto. "Definitely. I'm still buying. Celebrating, in fact."

He scans the room once more, fifteen patrons by his quick count. Here goes nothing. Waving *Dune* above his head like a signal flag, Lion raises his voice above the music. "I just got promoted. So I'm buying all you fine people a Yamazaki."

Heads turn. A handful of nods, a chorus of thank-yous. A couple of African businessmen puffing Montecristos raise their glasses. Lion hates the attention but tries on his big-smile disguise, making sure to keep the book lifted and visible for just that extra couple of seconds.

"Celebrating," says Roberto, lining rocks glasses up on the bar, filling them carefully.

Lion takes a sip of his drink and cracks open *Dune*. "The concept of progress acts as a protective mechanism to shield us from the terrors of the future," reads a familiar refrain. The collected sayings of Muad'Dib, and not much else going on.

Lion waits. Time passes. A handful of patrons come by to thank him. He makes sure to make *Dune* a part of every conversation, watching for any sign of recognition. A number of people are familiar, but no other signs forthcoming.

He orders another drink, deciding to give it another half hour. Maybe he just blew four thousand of Arctic's dollars on nothing. Well, the expense will annoy the shit out of Jenka.

That's something.

His drink arrives. He takes a sip, noticing a trio of circular water stains on the bar, a sign that someone else sat here. Probably a lot of someones, a whole stack of lives piled onto one stool, all trying to feel a little less for a little while.

This reminds him of an empathy-expansion exercise Fetu used to have him run. Zero in on some detail in the environment: a blade of grass, a mark in the wood of a park bench, and work backward. Feel through all the lives—plant, animal, human—that colluded to produce this particular history. The mouse that ate the seed that shat the tree that begat the wood that became the bench. The craftsman who built the bench, the workers who installed it, the lonely teenager who carved his initials, the angry attendant who tried to sand them out—but Lion's too amped up to play that game.

Yet little else happens in the next half hour. The Africans leave; a couple of college students in Plushy drag pop their heads in. Furry rabbit and something that resembles a hedgehog on steroids. But not their kind of scene, so gone almost as soon as they appear.

Lion smokes another cigarette, finishes his drink, and decides to give up. He's only getting older sitting here. Uber app on his phone. Car ordered. "Roberto," he calls to the bartender, "can you close me out?"

His math wasn't that far off. $3,985. Of course, with Arctic picking up the tab, he tips 35 percent.

Sliding off the stool, Lion walks toward the exit. A couple of heads nod in his direction. A woman who looks like Betty Boop after a bar fight; a man beside her in Western garb sporting a black eye. Lion had heard rumors about a Fight Club revivalist movement; this might be confirmation, but not the kind of proof he was after this evening. Apparently, his hunch was wrong. Hudson's isn't a Rilkean hangout.

He's five feet from the door when the young blond "niece" stops him with a hand on his wrist.

"Thanks for the drink, Lion Zorn," she says.

Steady eye contact. Something familiar about her gaze.

"You're welcome," but it's not coming to him. "I'm sorry—do we know each other?"

Shakes her head no.

"How do you know my name?"

She twirls her finger through her hair, and Lion realizes she's wearing a wig. He catches sight of a few errant strands of her real hair, dyed silver and jutting out from behind her ear.

"Sarah?" he asks. "Is your name Sarah?"

The woman squeezes his wrist, just once, and then a sly smile as she strides quickly away. As she heads out the door, Lion catches sight of a bar code tattoo on the back of her neck.

"Sarah," he calls again, but she doesn't turn.

Trying to follow her out of the bar, Lion bumps into her companion, the older Japanese man, who has suddenly stumbled in front of him, possibly drunk, definitely blocking his way.

"Very sorry," the man mumbles.

Lion tries to step around him, but the companion steps with him, wobbles again, then grabs his sleeve in an attempt to stay upright. Precious seconds pass before Lion can untangle their limbs and head out the door. By the time he makes it into the street, there's only a taxi pulling away in the distance and steam pouring out of manhole covers.

No sign of Sarah.

He looks back at the Japanese man, wondering if this was somehow planned, but he's disappeared.

"Did you have a good time?" the doorman wants to know.

Lion glances right, then left. Still no sign of him. No sign of her. And the motorcycle, nowhere in sight.

"Fuck, man, it was better than Disneyland."

THE OTHER SIDE
OF THE OTHER SIDE

Lion wakes to sunshine through the Ludlow windows. A rectangle of shivering blue sky and brighter than he's used to.

He must have forgotten to close the blinds.

Sitting up slowly, the room swims a little, a few inches left, as if the furniture were on rollers. One too many whiskeys the night before. Determines to fight his hangover with exercise. Then he remembers Arctic waiting for his decision. And the fact that he was definitely followed by a dragonfly, and maybe followed by a motorcyclist.

Makes the hangover worse.

Stretching his arms above his head, Lion chews on the idea that his being followed might not have anything to do with him. Arctic Pharmaceuticals is the kind of play that would attract unwelcome attention. Everyone from business reporters to business rivals would want to be in the know.

He climbs out of bed and starts to make coffee, recalculating probabilities as Indigo Smooth percolates. If Arctic heard Sietch Tabr rumors, other companies probably heard as well. Richard isn't the only tycoon crafty enough to see commercial possibilities in the drug. Or steal a sample. So maybe Walker's mounted head has nothing to do with animals or Rilkeans; maybe it's about business after all. A severe way of warning off the competition.

That's more crazy than Lion's prepared to handle.

An outside opinion might be useful. Texts Lorenzo to see if he's awake and starts pulling on workout clothes. As he moves his jacket out of the way, the snuff container falls out of a pocket. He picks it up, stares down the tube and waits for the flash. Now that he knows what to look for, he can make out Muad'Dib's name. It reminds him of a monogram. And if it's a monogram, then this container might belong to Muad'Dib. Does this mean that the man Arctic wants him to find is actually the murderer of Robert Walker?

And that really should be way more crazy than Lion's prepared to handle.

The sensible thing would be to thank-you-no-thank-you Sir Richard, pick up his already large check, and head home. But the fact that Muad'Dib murdered Robert Walker—damn if that doesn't make Lion want to track him down that much more.

No return text from Lorenzo, so he puts a to-go lid on his coffee cup and carries it down the hall to the elevator. The car crawls, as usual. Somewhere between floors 18 and 19, he decides to turn down the job, then changes his mind by 22. Walking into the gym, he realizes it's already settled. Sits down on the rowing machine and texts Penelope.

I'm in. Please set up the meeting with Shiz.

He rows for twenty minutes, alone in the room. That ends when a stern woman in a bright blue tracksuit with the flag of Switzerland embroidered on her left sleeve stomps in, slides on a pair of nonslip AR glasses, and unleashes five rounds of frustration on a punching bag in the corner. Whatever she's seeing on the other side of those glasses—could be an onslaught of Tibetan demons or a parade of ex-husbands—reminds him of something William James once said: "Each mind keeps its own thoughts to itself."

Decamping from the rowing machine, he unfurls a yoga mat and works through his push-up protocol and a series of stretches. Moving from the backward arch of camel pose into the forward fold of child's pose when Penelope texts back, waits until he's flattened into pigeon pose before checking the screen.

Can you leave for San Francisco this evening?

Replies in the affirmative, then pigeon on the other side.

Coming out of corpse pose, he's got a response.

Flight's at 4:00. Newark. Bo will be there at 1:30. I'll meet you at the airport.

An attached document reveals he's first class on Jamaica Air. Despite himself, he grins. More Arctic research at work. Of course it's Jamaica Air. The very product he predicted on his first official job as an em-tracker, the root of the Rod of Correction. Checks the icon parade below the ticket to see if further suspicions are correct, noting a small circle with a baby crawling inside and a red line through the infant, another showing a familiar three-pronged leaf, no red line. The signifiers signify: a child-free and pot-friendly flight.

Sliding his phone back into his pocket, Lion wonders why Penelope's meeting him at the airport. Decides he'll find out soon enough and double-times the back stairs to his room for a shower.

Toweling off, he catches sight of himself in the mirror. The circles under his eyes have expanded their colonization mission and are beginning to resemble the outline of the state of Florida. Walking into the bedroom, he notices the sprawled bedcovers seem to resemble California. Pattern recognition system stuck on national geography perhaps.

Gets dressed, calculating in his head. If he's leaving for the airport in a few hours to meet Shiz, definitely enough time to review the Arctic folder once again.

And drink more coffee.

After waiting for the lie that is large cup to finish brewing, Lion carries his coffee, phone, and sling-pack out to the table on the terrace.

Removing the Arctic envelope, he pages through the stack of articles until he finds the story about the zookeeper in Dubai.

Decides to start there.

Reading it again, it dawns on Lion that freeing wild animals has to be a crime in Dubai. And crime stories always generate more press. He combs the article for the zookeeper's name: Nassir Tabbara, then picks up his phone, clicks open a browser window, and types "Tabbara, zookeeper, Dubai," into a search engine.

Dozens of offerings dated to the incident, too many to sift.

Narrows search parameters, focusing on stories written about the aftermath. A three-month-old piece from the *International Herald Tribune* tells him Tabbara was arrested and taken to the lockdown ward of a local hospital for medical and psychological evaluation. Nothing unusual there. But a follow-up article from a few days later shows that someone broke Tabbara out of the hospital, stole his blood work and deleted his records.

That's unusual.

Playing a hunch, Lion grabs the article from South Africa. He scans it for the name of the family that found themselves sleeping with lions. Taylor. And the last graph contains the detail he's hunting: The Taylors were taken to Mandela Memorial for medical care.

Follow-up article from the *Zulu Independent*, the last free voice in South Africa, contains a telling detail: Two weeks after the Taylors were admitted to Mandela Memorial, a break-in occurred. Biological samples destroyed, computer records deleted. Lion takes a sip of coffee and stares into the middle distance, trying to think this through.

Arctic's not responsible for the break-ins; of that, he's almost certain. If they were, Richard would have deployed the AI scrubber, removing any news of the events from the web. The fact that these stories exist seems to be more proof of a second player involved. But that's as far as his thoughts take him.

He turns his attention back to the articles, grabbing the Robert Walker story next. The papers reported him missing, so he wasn't taken to a hospital. No medical records to steal. And the shellacking of his head, plus whatever other chemicals were pumped into it for preservation, would pretty much obliterate anything an autopsy could discover.

But still, those twin robberies? Up to now, Lion had been thinking they were unrelated incidents. The by-product of Sietch Tabr starting to transition from a Rilkean sacrament to a street drug. But these missing medical records tell a different story. Someone wanted to know what Sietch Tabr did to unsuspecting strangers. Someone went to a lot of trouble to find out.

Was this a Tuskegee-style drug trial?

It makes sick sense. If Lion were testing the compound, his first go would be on an unsuspecting friendly. An animal lover. Someone like a zookeeper. Second test on an animal-friendly group: the Taylors on safari. Were other trials run that he doesn't know about? And if Arctic's not responsible, could it be the Rilkeans?

His thoughts are interrupted by the ringing of his cell.

"Are my methods unsound?" says Lorenzo, when he answers.

"I don't see any method at all, sir," like putting on a favorite shirt. "So you're still in Japan?"

"Tonight's our last night."

"End of the tour?"

"We have four days off, two weeks in Kuala Lumpur, then we're done."

Lion flashes on Jenka in the white room telling him he'd flown in from Kuala Lumpur. "How good's your connect in KL?"

"Hank and the club owner go way back. It's why we're staying two weeks. How come?"

Lion brings up a search engine and types in Arctic. The website loads and he finds the last name he never got. "Jenka Kalchik," spelling both words out.

"The guy who stole your notebook?"

"Yeah. But the day before he stole my notebook, he was in Kuala Lumpur. I was wondering why."

"Know anything beyond the fact that he was there?"

Lion searches Arctic's page for partners in Malaysia. Doesn't find corporate interests in the region. What he does notice, after clicking the link for "recent mergers and acquisitions," is a preponderance of net media—bloggers, podcasters, and virtual-casters—all with deep ties to the healthcare and human performance industry. Must be three dozen of them, and most appear to be newly formed partnerships. Yet none of this helps with his current problem.

Then he starts laughing.

"Kemosabe," says Lorenzo, "did you need me to ask Hank something?

"Never mind Hank. Didn't you sleep with that woman from American Express? The head Centurion concierge."

"Charlotte Brontë."

"Really?"

"No relation."

"How'd you leave things?"

"We bumped into each other in an elevator in Hong Kong, like two months ago. Then we spent the night bumping into each other in her suite."

"Didn't she tell you every card came with a GPS tracker?" says Lion, getting up from the table and crossing to the railing to look out over the city. A dozen passenger pigeons mill on a nearby roof, their red breasts giving them away, New York's much lauded de-extinction program in full swing. Lion remembers the advertisements: See Central Park as it once was.

"Uh-huh," says Lorenzo.

"If Jenka was in Malaysia for Arctic, I'm pretty sure he brought an Amex Centurion with him. Think Charlotte would tell you where it went?"

"No, nope, absolutely not. But it can't hurt to ask."

"I'd owe you."

"No worries, I have a few days off and Charlotte's still in Hong Kong. Maybe she wants to bump into me some more. How come you want to know?"

Lion brings him up to speed: Arctic Pharmaceuticals, his decision to meet Shiz, his Tuskegee-style drug trial suspicions. Quiet on the line when he's done. He waits out the silence looking at the passenger pigeons.

"If the Rilkeans were running tests," says Lorenzo eventually, "how'd they do it? How'd they get them to take the drug?"

Lion picks up the stack of photos and thumbs through them, remnant Yamazaki-hangover finding him as he does. That swimming sensation again, tinged with an unfamiliar loneliness. He wonders if Japanese whiskey brings Japanese hangovers, as if the bad dreams of a society could be disguised as a good time, bottled and sold.

"Kemosabe?"

Refocuses. "None of the photos show signs of a struggle, but a gun would solve that problem."

"True, but why bother? If it was me, I'd tell 'em it was a new drug with a killer high. Some coke-Viagra mix that won't melt your ticker. Seriously, we send men into space, but nobody can figure out how I can keep my dick hard while on gak?"

Lion snorts. "The zookeeper, maybe, but the Taylor family on vacation?"

"You've met my family. Wouldn't even have to ask twice."

"Walker doesn't fit. He what? Liked the drug so much he cut his own head off and used a taxidermy robot to mount it on the wall?"

Lion hears the soft tap of fingers on bongos, "Down by the Crossroads" in three-four time and what Lorenzo does when concentrating.

"From this point on," says Lorenzo, "I want you to text me from wherever you end up. Send me locations and times. Where you are, when you show, when you split. Best I can do from here."

"I don't think it's that kind of thing."

"You're not em-tracking the Rod of Correction. This isn't product development. This is some guy's head on a wall. Plus, you find futures for other people, that's the job."

"Yeah?"

"But they've always been other people's futures."

"Uh-huh."

"This time," says Lorenzo, "the animals, the empathy. This time you found a future that includes you."

Lion glances back at the pigeons. Sees a flicker he didn't notice before. Remembers that the de-extinction program was a failed effort, realizes that what he's actually looking at is a light-vert. An AR projection of an almost. The bad dreams of a society disguised as a good time.

and I wan welcum I and I to dem friendly skies," says a dreadlocked first class steward in a dapper blue suit, colonial-ironic brass buttons, and red, yellow, and green piping up the side.

"Thank you," says Penelope, who, Lion learned upon arriving at the airport, will be accompanying him to San Francisco. "Shiz needs me to identify you as you when we get there" was her only explanation.

Then she led him through the terminal in silence. Form-fitting black dress, black leggings, her elegant braid of red hair.

The steward leads them to a pair of side-by-side first class suites, like something out of *The Jetsons*. Bubble domes, seats as big as couches, doors that close completely. Like a futuristic hotel with wings, back before we discovered the future doesn't look like we thought it would look.

"Flown Jamaica Air before?" the steward asks Penelope, his heavy patois suddenly melting away.

"My first time," she tells him.

"Smart glasses to the left of the console," pointing with exceptionally long fingers. "Ganja menu on the screen. Edibles and combustibles. Please wait until the sign turns off before ya fiyah up." Long fingers point to a small overhead sign.

Lion looks up and sees a snow-cone-sized joint with a red line through it. The very symbol he suggested.

Is it déjà vu if it actually happened?

"The Eye-N-Eye VR app responds to touch," continues the steward. "Controller to the right of your seat, beside the vaporizer."

"Any suggestions?" asks Lion.

The steward thinks for a second, his dreads hanging over his eyes, his hand rising to his chin, like some poly-tribe remake of the Lincoln Memorial. "Goat Shit with the nose cone view, give thanks."

"Yes-I," replies Lion.

The steward lifts an eyebrow. "If I and I need anyting," pointing to a button on the armrest, icon showing a megaphone, "hit de holla button."

Then he's off to help other passengers.

Lion, seated across the aisle from Penelope, removes his Moleskine from his sling-pack, uncaps a pen, and turns to face her.

"Tell me about Prince Shiz."

Penelope reaches across the aisle and takes the pen out of his hand, recaps it, and passes it back. Reaching beneath her seat, she lifts a small black backpack. Out of the top compartment comes another Arctic envelope. Passes it over. "Full biography. Plus everything the scrubber caught, before it got erased."

"Arctic research at work."

"I've culled anything that mentions the Rilkeans. You'll find those articles at the back of the packet."

A cocktail robot dispersing bottles of Red Stripe and platters of ackee and salt fish slow-steps down the aisle. An Atlas Skinny, the older humanoid model, its white chestplate embossed with an Asiatic lion wearing a gold crown and holding a long scepter. The Lion of Judah, his namesake.

Lion grabs a beer.

"I and I?" asks Penelope, after the bot departs, "what does that mean?"

"One consciousness. I and I means you and me. It means we're all in this together."

"Do you think that's true?" she asks, smiling at him. "Do you think we're all in this together?"

"Know why this flight is child-free?"

Penelope glances up and down the aisle. "It's brilliant. No screaming kids to deal with. I'm amazed it took them this long to figure it out."

"That's marketing."

"Cannabis-friendly, so adults only?"

"True," says Lion, "but a legal issue. It's child-free because the Rastas reversed their position on procreation. Go back a few decades and most Jamaicans believed birth-control was some rass thought up by the white man to keep the black man down."

"What changed?"

Lion points down the aisle at the chestplate of the serving robot, "*Panthera leo persica.*"

"Isn't that an Atlas skinny?"

"Not the robot. The Asiatic lion. Population explosion in India. Deforestation, habitat fragmentation, poaching. The Asiatic lion got listed as endangered on the Red List, and the Rastas are big on symbolism."

"The Lion of Judah?"

Nods. "The Rastas used to be fierce opponents of birth control, but the red-listing made them reverse their position."

"To what?"

"If we're all in this together, that has to include animals, plants, and ecosystems. The Rastas take that responsibility seriously. The web of life isn't a metaphor. They reversed their position because having children is pretty much the single worst thing you can do for the environment."

"That's why Jamaica Air is child-free?"

Nods again.

She reaches across the aisle, lifts the Red Stripe out of his hand, and takes a sip. Something about the presumed intimacy in the gesture that Lion appreciates. Then again, a little like the XOs in her texts, it's hard to tell with Penelope—what is genuine emotion and what is business strategy.

The modern condition.

"If everyone on the planet stopped having kids for five years," she says, working a fingernail under the Red Stripe label, starting to tease it away from the bottle, "population would drop by a billion."

"I didn't know that."

He takes the beer back, the label now hanging half-off, like a sagging flag from some forgotten nation. Takes a sip. Passes it back.

She uses the bottle to point toward the envelope. "It's in your packet. The Five Year Ban."

"Which is?"

"One of Muad'Dib's major teachings." Something in her tone. Pride? Where would that be coming from? "It's a grassroots movement among Rilkeans. A temporary moratorium on childbirth."

"Five years?"

Her turn to nod. "The time frame needed for that population drop. Muad'Dib believes it would give the environment a chance to recover and our technology a chance to catch up to the problem."

A deep rumble like a waking dragon as the plane starts to taxi down the runway. Acceleration.

"What do you think?" asks Lion, after they're airborne.

"Nobody's forcing anyone to do anything. It's just people making up their own minds. I find it noble."

"A kindred spirit," then turns the envelope over in his hand. "Will Shiz tell us where Muad'Dib is?"

"I've only met him once."

"And?"

"And he wanted to sleep with me." A curious smile. "He was really polite about it. A little regal."

"Would my lady like to accompany me to the bedroom?"

"Something like that."

"You slept with Shiz, that's useful. Do you think he'll tell us?"

Penelope reaches across the aisle and squeezes his arm.

"I didn't sleep with him, and I don't think he's going to tell us." Brushing her thumb back and forth across his wrist. "But he might tell you, Lion Zorn, em-tracker of the Rod of Correction."

ROCKY MOUNTAIN HIGH

Somewhere over Ohio, the Atlas Skinny slides by with another tray of drinks. The motion tickles his life recognition machinery, but Lion doesn't bother to look up. He tries to remember when he stopped noticing the robots. When they moved from science fiction to science fact to everyday scenery. He wonders if there's any measure for this, some way to track how long it takes the pattern recognition system to inculcate imagination as just another form of information. The march of progress, though he also wonders if this is true.

In the pod beside him, Penelope has fallen asleep, her sleeves pushed up slightly, revealing a conspiracy of ravens. Conspiracy is the collective noun used to describe the birds, Lion knows, like a murder of crows or a crash of rhinos. He also knows, in older dictionaries, a group of ravens is sometimes called an unkindness. And her skin beneath, a milky shade micro-dotted with pale freckles.

Somewhere over Kansas, he realizes he's having difficulty not watching Penelope sleep. Time to take his mind off the problem. For a moment, he considers the envelope beside him, then remembers the landscape below him. Decides on the latter. Lion dials up the nose cone view on the Eye-N-Eye VR, finds Goat Shit on the ganja menu and places his order. From the beverage screen, he chooses an Americano, black, with one, no two, extra shots.

A few minutes later, there's a knock on his cabin door. Lion depresses a button on his armrest and slides the entranceway open. The dreadlocked steward steps into the room, holding a tall white coffee cup in his left hand and a silver tinfoil swan in his right. The coffee cup is decorated with some kind of cartoon, the swan the kind of thing his parents used to bring home from nice restaurants, before 3-D-printing leftover containers became the thing.

Lion takes both and thanks the steward, who starts out of the door, but stops and turns. "You're Lion Zorn—em-tracker of the Rod?"

"Yeah," cautiously.

"Big up for mi Bredren," says the steward. "Before Lion Zorn preach Jamaica Air, I-man haffi Mechanical Turk. Mash up a dread."

"Mechanical Turk?" he asks.

"Geo-tagging port-o-potties for Babylon funds. Nah way for dem free to livity."

Lion laughs.

The steward presses his hands to his heart and bows slightly from the waist, his dreadlocks waterfalling forward. Then out the door and gone.

Unrolling the silver swan, Lion finds a small gray tub containing the Goat Shit. A couple of aromatic nugs, dark green, with the occasional purple highlight. Setting those aside, he picks up the coffee cup and studies the cartoon.

In the foreground, a cadre of heavyset birds hanging out on a beach, reading books and playing chess. In the background, a tall wooden ship filled with conquistadors. A caption near the bottom: "Unbeknownst to most ornithologists, the dodo was actually a very advanced species, living alone quite peacefully until, in the seventeenth century, it was annihilated by men, rats, and dogs. As usual."

Nah way for dem free to livity, thinks Lion.

Setting the cup aside, he fires up the vaporizer and watches the Goat Shit reduce to ash. Three hits later, he slides on the smart glasses and launches the nose cone view. Like the jump to light speed. In an instant, he's catapulted from the minor claustrophobia of his first class cabin to the massive agoraphobia of the nose of the plane, like he's been transformed into some kind of Boeing hood ornament. And that still-eerie teleportation sensation—another feeling we had no idea we felt until the virtual came along.

The camera must be 3-D panoramic, mounted on the very tip of the plane. The view is spectacular in every direction. Massive cumulus castles dead ahead and craggy mountains below, like gargantuan alligator teeth.

"Welcum dem realz Rocky Mountain high," booms in his head.

Lion yanks off the glasses and looks at their stems. Sees a dot matrix of slender holes drilled into the plastic. Nano-Bluetooth speaker with deep cortical throw capacity. He felt that one down by his brain stem.

Mutes the audio and hits the vaporizer again. Glasses back on. The enormous vista arrives a second later, and with it the free-floating sensation that is virtual antigravity. He's flying again, a line of text floating in his lower left peripheral providing the details: "Rocky Mountains, 32,106 feet."

Peering straight down, Lion sees granite spires that date back to the Cenozoic. If Sir Richard's right, and rocks themselves are conscious, what stories these rocks could tell. Then through a thick cloud and out again.

He rides the nose cone into Nevada, his reverie broken by a knock on his door. The dread-steward with an offer of a hot towel. "Iron bird in San Francisco in thirty-five," he says.

Lion slides the smart glasses back into their holder and buries his face in the towel. Inhaling eucalyptus, he decides that there's enough flight time left to get a little work done.

Arctic envelope and Moleskine notebook, both open on his lap.

From the envelope, he slides out the packet on Shiz and starts reading from the top. The first article is standard biographical fare, much of which Lion's familiar with. Rasta father, Creole mother, born poor in New Orleans, raised poor in Kingston. An early aptitude for music and science becomes a string of first place wins at regional then national then international science fairs that get him a full-ride scholarship to Oxford. Then a detail Lion didn't know before: Shiz studied environmental science.

He makes a note in his Moleskine.

After three semesters at Oxford, Shiz dropped out to focus on his music. Made his bones in the early days of YouTube VR, riding the platform rise for all it was worth. Most famous for his poly-tribe sound and dread-trances, routinely getting so lost in the music, clapping his hands so hard, by show's end they'd be rubbed raw and bleeding furiously.

Lion glances at the accompanying photo. Shiz onstage in Amsterdam: his throwback dread-hawk with short stalks dyed a bright baby blue, eyes closed, and hands frozen midclap. Tarantinos of blood flying off of them.

He takes another sip and turns his attention to the next article. This one drills into Shiz's time at Oxford, including a second-semester freshman-year class schedule. Lion glances at it: Early 21st Century Nihilism: Gaga Through Trump; Genetic Correlates of Acoustics, a graduate-level seminar in the Music Department; Michael Soule and the Mechanics of the Sixth Great Extinction; and a History of Eco-Empathy: Edward Abbey, Rise of the Animal Liberation Front, and the Rilkean Solution.

Rise of the Animal Liberation Front?

He glances back at the stack of articles and sure enough, Penelope's included a reading syllabus for all of Shiz's classes. He runs his finger down the list until he finds Eco-Empathy, and beneath: "Rise of the Animal Liberation Front," a five-part report for the *Times* by a certain Judah Zorn.

He stares at the syllabus.

Lion's early reporting on the movement won a couple of journalism prizes, so he's not that surprised to find his articles, but it does raise the question of why Shiz wants to meet him.

He finds no answers in the next few stories, skips ahead, hunting for details of Shiz's Rilkean conversion. Discovers a half-page photo, a close-up snapshot of the back of Shiz's neck showing white scars above a bar code tattoo. The accompanying article describes the tale Richard had told him, but from the inside out. How Shiz noticed stories about him becoming a Rilkean showing up online and grew curious about the movement. The more he learned, the more their message resonated. Then a conversation at a bar in New York pushed him over. Lion reads a few more sentences and blinks.

Rereads the graph.

Shiz was out for drinks at a bar in the West Village when he saw a woman with the question mark tattoo from across the room, approached her, and struck up a conversation. Doesn't remember the name of the bar, does remember the woman's name: Sarah.

Lion flashes on silver hair peeking out from beneath a blond wig. "Thanks for the drink, Lion Zorn."

Bo's Sarah. His Sarah. And the uncomfortable whirl of his brain interrupted by a quiet whoosh beside him. In preparation for landing, the door to Penelope's cabin has slid open.

He sees her, hair unbraided for the first time, smiling in his direction. If he didn't know better, he might assume she was genuinely pleased to see him.

The plane touches down, bounces twice on tarmac, and taxis down the runway. Iron bird in San Francisco.

A SHEEP DOG ON A SHORT CHAIN

Walking out of Terminal One, heading toward daylight, and Penelope stops dead in her tracks.

"Rhechan fel ci defaid ar jaen gwta," she snarls.

"What?"

Staring straight ahead, jaw clenched. "Rhechan fel ci defaid ar jaen gwta."

"What language is that?"

"Welsh," turning to look at him. "It means farting like a sheepdog on a short chain. It's an expression," pointing out the glass doors, "of unpleasant surprise."

Lion follows her finger, sees the airport in busy mode. Hordes of androgynous people being trailed by hordes of autonomous luggage. He can hear the commercial in his head: "Roll, roll, rolls itself, gently through the terminal."

Beyond that, a line of Uber autonomous taxis purring against a distant curb, a decrepit yellow Toyota and a bright pink Hummer stretch limo, festive with streamers, toilet paper, and other wedding ornamentation.

He has no idea why she's so pissed off.

Then he spots it. On the passenger door of the limo, the outline of a heart, drawn in what appears to be whipped cream. Written inside of it: LION + PENELOPE = FOREVER.

So this is what dumbfounded feels like.

"Tongue ma fart-box ya cunty wankstain," her voice quivering with what sounds like actual violence.

Stays dumbfounded.

"That one's Scottish," she says. "It means Jenka's a wankstain who can lick my Irish arse."

"Jenka?" He starts laughing. "Seriously?"

A dark flash in her eyes.

"Wankstain?" he repeats, still laughing.

Penelope pivots on her right leg and snaps out her fist. A lightning-quick right cross catches Lion's shoulder. The blow rocks him forward and he stutter-steps to stay upright, accidentally kicking a dark gray autonomous suitcase, which sways, then skitters sideways.

"What the hell is wrong with you?" he says, trying to right himself.

"Sorry," she says, reaching for him.

He sidesteps her hand, rubbing his shoulder, staring at her.

"I really am sorry."

She really does, he notices, look sorry.

"Who taught you to punch like that?"

"My therapist." Shrugs. "Misdirected anger—it's an ongoing issue. She suggested Krav Maga."

"Yeah," still rubbing his shoulder, "tell her it worked."

The inside of the limo is worse than the outside. A lighted lime-green pathway down the center of the aisle, glowing pink bar to the left, purple love seats shaped like giant lips to the right. The ceiling is a disco wash of colors.

Jenka went all out.

Lion plops down on purple lips. Penelope sits a couch away. The Hummer glides into traffic with as much dexterity as an oil tanker.

"Four Seasons, please," she tells their driver.

"The Four Seasons?" he says, suddenly a little queasy.

Penelope slides into professional mode. "Arctic has a relationship."

"Isn't there a different relationship?"

"What's wrong with the Four Seasons?"

Wondering how he's going to explain this one. "Posh freaks me out. People wearing watches freak me out."

"Watches?"

He takes her phone out of her hand, pushes the home button, and the time, in oversized digits, fills the screen. Points at the numbers. "Every phone comes with a clock, yet we still coat our wrists with baubles for the sake of the signifier. 'I Have,' the sign says. 'You Have Not.'"

She smiles at him, then asks, "Didn't you just fly first class?"

"Sista," Lion says, passing her back the phone, "no-ting Babylon about I and I friendly skies."

They pull onto the freeway and straight into traffic. Crawling up the 101 in thirty feet of hot-pink limo and stares from all sides. Penelope texting furiously, the cuffs of her sleeves flopping as she types. She slides the cloth up to her elbows, revealing bracelets of tattoos beneath: cursive script wrapping her wrists and the ravens again, like oversized black commas soaring up her arms. From one couch away, he can't read the words, but the birds translate just fine.

Knows there's a reason for this—but it's not coming to him.

"I'm trying to set up our meeting with Shiz," says Penelope, glancing up from her phone.

"I thought it was all set."

"The meeting is set, not the time of the meeting. Shiz keeps odd hours."

Then head down and texting again.

He glances back at the ravens and it clicks. A story Fetu had told him about environmental philosopher Paul Shepard's "Pleistocene paradigm," the idea that our eons of sustained contact with the natural world played a significant role in the evolution of the human brain. Animals were humankind's initial grounds for comparison, our earliest metaphors, and remain fundamental to how we see the world. Why Shepard once said, "We learned to think in animals," and why we still say things like "he's as big as a gorilla" or "she's as fierce as a lion."

Also, he thinks, watching Penelope's arm, why we can recognize the outline of a bird from across a room and can't read writing. Words are too recent an imprinting. Animals, though, are part of our ancient grammar, prehistorically embedded in the brain.

The limo slides over a lane, down an exit ramp, and into the city. Traffic is worse. It takes ten minutes to churn six blocks to the Four Seasons. As they edge into the driveway, Lion counts town cars and limousines. An old journalist habit. Three autonomous, four human-chauffeured, and one giant pink stretch.

Snorts.

Penelope looks up from her phone, quizzically.

"The pink limo," he explains. "I didn't think Jenka had it in him."

"Don't make that mistake."

"Which one?"

A stern look. "Underestimating Jenka."

Then the valet opens the door, notices the whipped cream heart, and congratulates them on their nuptials. "Not another word," says Penelope, stepping out of the limo and into his face.

And inside the hotel.

The lobby is boardroom chic, dark wood paneling and geometric art. Marble floors and high ceilings. Crossing beneath a long skylight, a ribbon of sunlight catches the back of Penelope's neck, illuminating, for an instant, the question mark.

Something about the sight bothers him.

Then it comes to him. The origin story Bo had told: Richard forcing her to get the tattoo. Tongue ma fart-box Penelope doesn't really seem the force-able type. Doesn't exactly know what type she is.

A desk clerk in a dark suit behind a tall teak counter welcomes them to the Four Seasons. "Did you iris-scan your reservation?" he wants to know.

Penelope shakes her head no, taking an Amex Centurion out of her wallet and sliding it across the counter.

"We're old-fashioned."

The clerk needs to go into the back to run the card.

After he's gone, Lion asks: "Old-fashioned?"

"Glutch."

"Is that more Welsh?

"'Glitch,'" she explains, "with a *u* instead of an *i*. A collective started in Lithuania. They figured out how to hijack the camera in your phone and make it scan your eyeball whenever you take a selfie. Over time, enough selfies, enough detail, you can hack an eye-scanner." Shrugs. "They're our partners, but Richard prefers to be careful."

The clerk returns, sliding a pair of key cards in their direction.

"We have you in adjoining Superior Executive Superior Suites," and without a hint of irony.

RESIDUAL GOAT SHIT

Five minutes later, Lion slides the key into the lock and steps inside his hotel room. Beige and tan on nearly every available surface. Midcentury modern desk and chair. Living screen covering nearly one wall. Suitcase in closet, pocket detritus on table, and as far as his habit machinery can take him.

What the hell was he doing?

He looks around again, spotting the expanse of white linen and plump pillows in the other room. California king with hospital corners. There's a buzzing in his pocket. It's the twitch that means text. A note from Penelope. The meeting with Shiz is set, 1:17 A.M.

Odd hours, alright.

The clock on his phone tells him that 1:17 A.M. is six hours away. He changes into his workout clothes and heads to the hotel gym. Fifty minutes of yoga, then push-ups until he crumbles, then more yoga.

Afterward, Lion stops in the lobby café for a sandwich before heading back up to his room. Kicks off shoes, plops down on the bed, and starts to check messages on phone. He changes his mind.

It's going to be a long night: A nap might do some good.

Rolls into comforter and nods into the land of nod. Two hours later, a buzzing wakes him. Deep in his head, a hard rattling between his ears, like a brain-quake.

"Shit."

Incoming text—he'd fallen asleep on his phone.

He sits up in bed, notices the room's completely dark and where is he? Waits for his eyes to adjust.

Hotel room, San Francisco.

And the heavy thump, thump of someone knocking on his door.

"Hold on," he calls, setting his phone down and getting out of bed. But when he opens the door, the hallway is empty. Just a long plush carpet bereft of souls.

Thump, thump.

Coming from behind him, he realizes, the door to the adjoining suite.

"Wanna get dinner?" asks Penelope, once he gets it open. She's changed out of her dress and into a pair of jeans, a black T-shirt, and an army jacket. "We've got three hours until we meet Shiz."

He does fuzzy math in his head. Which means he's been asleep for over an hour. Looking around the room—that would explain the darkness.

A small lamp on the table to his left. He clicks it on.

"Dinner?" she asks again.

"I need to shower first," and heads toward the bathroom.

"Lobby bar, ten thirty," she calls after him.

Ten minutes later, Lion's dressed and downstairs. Black boots, black denim, black hoodie. Passing a matronly woman on her phone, he remembers the text he has yet to check, the one that woke him from his nap. He parks himself on the armrest of a cream-colored couch and digs his cell out of his sling-pack.

Two texts, actually.

The first from Lorenzo: *We R GO for Operation Charlotte,* and an emoji: a pair of rainbow-colored unicorns, one mounting the other from behind.

The second text is from Balthazar Jones. *Call a brother back. I found your engraver.*

Lion had totally forgotten about the jeweler. Checks the time. Ten minutes before he's supposed to meet Penelope, almost 1:00 A.M. in New York. Balthazar does not strike him as the early to bed type.

He slides off the armrest and into the chair and calls a brother back.

Rings once, rings twice. "Good evening, Lion Zorn," booms in his ear before the third ring starts.

"Hello, Balthazar."

"Are you still in New York?"

"I just left."

In the background, echoing through the phone, a female voice, the sounds of a ninja: "Is that Lion? Tell him I say hey-hey."

"Woman," snarls Balthazar, "you're a travesty of diction."

"Tell her I say hey-hey back," says Lion.

"I will do no such thing—but I did track down your engraver."

"Where is he? Or is he a she?"

"He's a he. And he moves around a lot, so I don't have a location. But I've got a name, if that helps."

"It helps."

"Tajik Tabbara."

Did not expect that.

"Lion?"

"Can you repeat the name, please?"

"Tajik Tabbara."

"Spelled how?" Digging his Moleskine out of his pocket and checking his notes. Sure enough, Nassir Tabbara, the Lebanese zookeeper. And their last names are spelled the same.

"There's a little more," says Balthazar.

"Hold up a sec."

Lion grabs a pen from his pocket, pins his notebook between his hand and his left knee, writes down *Tajik Tabbara* and a short reminder—*find out if Nassir is related.*

"Okay, ready."

"GFP engraving, as I told you, it's pretty rare. You need specialized equipment. I checked to see which labs were capable of pulling it off."

"Are there a lot of them?" Making another note: *possible lab locations*. Draws a line under it.

"Not many. Because of the legalities, all are in Asia. Two in Tokyo, one in Malaysia, couple in Shenzhen. When Tabbara made the engraving, it had to be in one of those places."

"That's useful," says Lion. Then it dawns on him. "That lab in Malaysia, do you know where, exactly, in Malaysia?"

"Got it right here," says Balthazar. "Kuala Lumpur."

There's that city again.

"Thanks, man, that really helps."

Lion puts his phone back into his pocket, and his notebook back inside his sling-pack, thinking it could be coincidence. Digs out his phone again. A search tells him Tabbara is a common Lebanese last name. And, certainly, Kuala Lumpur is the same city that Jenka just visited, but it's a big city.

Still . . .

Looking up, Lion realizes he's sitting across from a marble pedestal displaying a miniature sculpture version of Picasso's *Guernica*—must have been 3-D printed—in what looks like green glass. Lit from below, the demonic bull, the braying horse, the suffering of the innocent.

BETWEEN THE SIGNIFIER
AND THE SIGNIFIED

The bar at the Four Seasons looks like a British men's club from a bygone century. Dark wood walls, white Victorian ceiling, dim lighting. Penelope is seated at a mahogany rail, her back to him. She's removed her army jacket, and her black T-shirt has a slender slit down the back. Pale skin decorated with dark tattoos. Lion sees a line of text. Can't read the writing, but her flesh—that translates just fine.

More Arctic guerrilla marketing?

"Good evening," sliding onto the barstool beside her.

She looks up from her drink, her eyes very green and far away.

"Good evening," says Penelope, then noticing the look in his eyes. "You okay?"

"Yeah," he says, nodding.

"Jet lag?"

"A little. The Goat Shit didn't help. Plus," sliding up his sleeve, showing her the slice, "I was recently gored by a dead buffalo."

His cut a long scab up his arm.

Penelope slides her drink his way. "Low-tech pain reliever," she says. "It's working for me."

Lion takes a sip. Tastes tequila and lime over ice. And then a bartender standing in front of him. An older Filipino man wearing a black vest, black tie, and black-framed Buddy Holly glasses. Lion points at the tequila. "I'll have what she's having."

"Including the steak?"

Lion grimaces. "Steak?"

Penelope smiles. "It's why we're at the Four Seasons."

He's not following.

"They're the first hotel to exclusively serve cultured beef," she says. "Steak from stem cells, all lab grown. Totally animal-friendly. Richard thought you would like it."

"Neiman Ranch," the bartender tells him, "cultivated just for the Four Seasons."

"Richard's right," says Lion.

He wonders if he can stomach the taste of faux-beef, decides to find out. And a side of fries.

Afterward, Lion asks and Penelope tells. A little about her past, Irish American parents, born in Seattle, raised in Wales, then her parents went through a messy divorce, Scotland, Dublin, back to Seattle. "We moved around a lot." Shrugs. "Single mother raising two kids."

"You have a brother or a sister?"

"Sister." Something about the way she says it catches Lion's attention; something else tells him not to ask. But Penelope changes the subject before he can decide. "What about you?"

"We stayed put." He takes a sip of his drink, changes the subject again. "What does your tattoo say?"

Holding up her arms, displaying bracelets of cursive script and explosions of crows. "Which one?"

Lion points at her upper back and the line of text he almost saw.

"'Between the signifier and the signified: Rises.'"

It's a Tweet-Ku. No, Twaiku. Seventeen syllables tucked neatly into 140 characters.

"Benny what's-his-name," says Lion, "the Twitter poet they gave that prize to?"

"Aren't you a journalist?"

"Ex-journalist. They kicked me out."

"And you wonder why." Smirking at him. "Benny what's-his-name is Benny what's-her-name. Benny Takayama is a she. And that prize was a Pulitzer."

"Yeah," smiling, "I know. But why that poem?"

"The gap before the brain makes meaning out of language, when things haven't been completely decided. It moves me." She touches his arm. "Have you ever been in love?"

Sonya comes to mind. Seemed like the perfect hippie-chick-next-door type, yet carrying a pair of heavy-duty bolt cutters the day they met. Lion asked about the bolt cutters, and she'd agreed to show him, not tell him. A long ride in her crappy Ford, blaring *Straight Outta Compton* and driving straight into Compton. Sonya used the bolt cutters to liberate three large pit bulls from three tiny cages, passing him one of the leashes and telling him to run. His first experience busting up a dog-fighting ring and his introduction to the Animal Liberation Front.

"Maybe," he says. "I was definitely in something."

"Did it last long?"

"Long enough to get me arrested." Another swallow of tequila. "Why?"

"When you met her, that first conversation, she said something, you said something, and something changed. Between the signifier and the signified: Rises. And, in your case, got you arrested."

Blinks. "What are we talking about?"

"Dunno," she says, touching his arm again.

Their steaks arrive. Penelope orders another drink. Lion delays tasting the faux-meat a little while by doing a fast recompute. Tattooed with Twaiku poetry, yet works for Jenka. Between the signifier and the signified—something doesn't stack.

"Richard makes everyone who works for Arctic study semiotics," she says, somehow reading his mind. "He thinks the failure of the twentieth century is—"

"I've heard," says Lion, "the failure of language."

"It's a creative destruction. Out of that failure comes culture. Out of culture comes desire. Out of desire come products."

"Is that Sir Richard's motto?"

"More of his business strategy," with a look in her eyes that reminds him of the look in Walker's eyes. Regret. Remorse. And what's that about? But Lion decides to head in another direction.

"Does Arctic have a Malaysian division?" he asks. "Kuala Lumpur specifically. Anyone you work with there? Do you have branches or clients?"

"No," she says. "But Jenka was just there on a talent run."

"A talent run?"

"Prospecting special creatives. Richard likes to collect talent. Jenka likes it when the talent can make us money. These are not always the same thing."

"And there's talent in Kuala Lumpur?"

"Two virtual worlds designers, probably a couple of meetings I don't know about."

Lion would like to know about those meetings, especially if one of them involved an engraver named Tabbara. But Penelope works for Jenka and he doesn't want Jenka knowing about this particular curiosity. Decides not to press.

"Where are we meeting Shiz?" he asks instead.

Before she can answer, the bartender arrives with her drink and their check. Lion reaches for it, but Penelope takes it out of his hands. "It's on Arctic." She signs her name and passes it back.

"I'm sorry," she says afterward, "what were you asking?"

"Where are we meeting Shiz?"

"Private terminal out by the airport." Shakes her head. "He won't tell me which one."

"So how are we supposed to find him?"

"Uber to the corner of Cargo and Field and ask the driver to blink the headlights twice."

She's not joking.

"Very cloak and dagger," he says, laughing.

"Very Shiz," she adds, digging into her steak.

He can't delay any longer. It's been a decade since he's tasted flesh, but faux-flesh isn't that different. And he was always one for a good hamburger. He chews slowly, wondering if this is another empathy-expansion exercise, wondering if Penelope feels it too.

They finish their meal in silence. He watches the bartender polish bottles with a white hand towel. After their plates have been cleared away, Lion stands up and helps Penelope into her coat.

"Thank you," she says, then extends her arm and looks at him. "You with me?"

He loops his arm through hers, and they walk out of the bar, through the lobby and into the cool of the night. For a good hundred yards he feels her gravity and pretends the pull is his to feel—because, well, you never know.

THAT RANGE WEE SHITE

Cargo and Field, empty and industrial. A nearly forgotten corner of San Francisco running between airport and freeway, featuring warehouses, an all-night coffee shop serving the graveyard shift, and an autonomous forklift carrying two wooden crates across a distant parking lot.

Not a soul in sight.

From the backseat of an Uber X, Lion looks for signs of Shiz and struggles to breathe. Heavy new-car scent being pumped in via a slender pink ionizer plugged into the dash, barely covering up the fading remnants of Chinese food.

Lowers his window another few inches.

Out the crack, he sees a sky like an ink stain, three lonely poplar trees, and a battleship-sized car park.

"You want me wait more time?" asks Kumar, their Uber driver. Midsixties, dark-skinned, bald in all the wrong places.

"Flash your lights again," suggests Lion.

"Don't," says Penelope, "it's a game. The rules are flash your lights twice and wait. We flashed twice, now we wait."

"Lady," says Kumar, "I don't want your dirty drug business near my new-car-smelling car."

"We're not here on dirty drug business," explains Penelope, for the third time.

"I only wish we were here on dirty drug business," sighs Lion, lowering the window a little farther.

"One minute," says Kumar, "I am going, going, gone. If you are still waiting, you are still waiting outside of my car."

Lion looks back out the window. The empty streets, the dark night, no longer certain this was a good idea.

"We're meeting friends," says Penelope, "getting out of your car, and tipping you a hundred dollars."

She holds up the bill.

Kumar sucks his teeth. "And what that get me? Ten grande, quad, nonfat, one-pump, no-whip mochas? God's truth, my wife make plenty good mocha at home. Keep your hundred dollars. Let me grow old with my wife and her mocha that tastes like sheep shit."

Second time today Lion's heard mention of sheep—what are the odds?

"You can have both," says Penelope.

"Lady," snaps Kumar, pointing through the windshield at two stories of electrified steel mesh and razor wire. "That's airport property. Bad people want to do bad things, and the American government, like the thousand eyes of Varuna, always watching. Spy drones, spy satellites, spy everything. Your dirty drug business going to send me to jail time."

"No one's going to jail time," says Lion.

"I want jail time, I could've stayed in India. My country is very, very happy to do this for Kumar."

A sharp knock on the side door. Lion startles, feels his pulse rate spike. Outside the window, two female shapes. Takes a breath. Whatever is going to happen next is actually happening now.

"Here they are," says Penelope, dropping the hundred in Kumar's lap and opening her door.

Lion squares his shoulders and follows her out. The shapes cohere into twins. Two identical women who both seem to have stepped straight out of Black Power central casting circa 1975. Afros and army jackets. Like someone cloned Angela Davis.

"Apologies for the subterfuge," says one of the women, waving a slender hand in a circle. "It's a maze around here. Our hangar's hard to find."

"I'm Kali," says the other. "This is Shiva."

Clicks.

"You sang backup on 'More Human than Human,'" says Lion, "the White Zombie cover on *Preaching, Teaching, and Steaching*. That haunting Creole chorus, over the xylophone solo."

Both women beam.

"It's really nice to meet you."

Research and flattery, classic journalist weapons, feels pretty good to dust them off again.

"We're this way," says Kali, or is it Shiva—they really must be identical twins.

Across an empty parking lot, around a half block of industrial storage, through a gate, then another. On the far side of the second gate, they cross a long alley between two rusty warehouses and out into a manicured courtyard.

The baritone growl of large dogs freezes Lion in his tracks.

Two small guard robots, essentially Lidar sensors and loudspeakers mounted on wheels, pincer in from either side. They're armed. Lion sees the electric crackle of Tasers mounted behind chrome grills aimed in his direction.

"Um . . . ," he says.

"For fuck's sake," snaps Penelope, glaring at the afro twins.

Kali steps forward and palms a scanner plate behind the Lidar sensor on guard dog one. White light whoosh and instant silence. The 'bots must be networked, Lion thinks, as they spin around and begin to move away simultaneously.

Looking past them, he realizes they're standing in front of an oval of saw grass, and beyond that, the hulking shadow of Exec-Jets, like a partially deflated zeppelin airship being attacked by giant glass shards from outer space.

Private aircraft terminal chic.

Must be 24/7. Wide glass doors and lights on in the lobby. The doors retract and an armed guard, human this time, strides into view.

"Just us," calls Kali.

The guard waves, and they skirt left, around the zeppelin and down another alley and into the shadow of a gigantic aircraft hangar. Four-story bay doors shut tight. Hidden in a far corner, a red awning over a small entranceway.

"We're this way," says Shiva.

Stepping inside the hangar, Lion sees a football field of mirror-polished concrete. One large jet in the center and two Ehang 184 autonomous drone taxis, like oversized quadcopters, in a far corner. Pretty Lights blasts from invisible speakers, making Lion think about candy-flipping back in high school.

"Welcome to the Bay of Shiz," shouts Kali, over the music.

Closer in, he realizes he recognizes the plane: an Airbus ACJneo, the panoramic model, with huge plate glass windows wrapping the upper third of the aircraft. The interior is caramel-colored calf leather and done by that sports car maker. Ferrari. No. Pagani. Lion knows this because Lorenzo flew to a gig in Hawaii in one and wouldn't stop talking about it. Made him look at pictures.

Kali and Shiva lead them across the gray sea. In the light, clearly visible below their afros, Lion spots bar code neck tattoos. A few more steps and the twins stop beside a yellow aircraft maintenance ladder that leads up to an open door in the side of the Airbus. They take up posts on either side of the ladder, something hard and military in their countenances that Lion didn't notice before.

Clear as day now.

And the hip-side bulges under their army jackets, which he couldn't see outside, also clear as day.

"I don't do guns," says Lion, no longer walking.

Penelope shouts over the music, "What?"

"They're strapped," pointing at the bulges. "I'm out."

She glances at both women, takes another couple of steps closer to the ladder, and shouts up toward the plane. "Shiz, ya fuckin' bampot—get your arse out here."

The music stops. A wall of African muscle fills the plane's door, like a shadow against a shadow. Lion sees only the whites of his eyes and a bald head. Not Shiz.

"Luther," says Penelope, pleasantly, "the twisted sisters are armed."

"I don't make the rules," says Luther.

"I don't care who makes the bloody rules. Tell that radge wee shite to lose the weapons."

Luther ducks back inside the plane, comes back about thirty seconds later. "Shiz says protocol. The Bene Gesserit stay strapped."

Lion blinks. The Bene Gesserit? Lethal sisterhood from Dune, protectors of Muad'Dib?

Penelope does not blink. Before anyone can react, she ninja-slides beside Shiva, traps her right arm with her left hand, de-holsters the gun with her right. Points the Ruger straight at Kali. "No," she says, still pleasant, "as a matter of fact, they do not stay strapped."

Luther clucks his tongue, stares at her for a second, and ducks back inside the plane.

Down on the concrete, nobody moves.

He comes back a minute later. "Shiz says come on up. You can bring the guns with you."

Penelope turns to Kali. "Slowly, just your fingertips."

Kali removes a matching Ruger, passing it over. Penelope slips it into her waistband, the other into her pocket. Starts up the stairs. Four steps up, calls over her shoulder to Lion, "You with me?"

"Your therapist suggested Krav Maga?"

Penelope winks at him and disappears inside the plane. Luther follows. Lion stands there.

"Go on, sugar," says Shiva. "You're down. Shiz is down to meet you."

LET THEM EAT CRACK

ion's eyes take a second to adjust to the dark of the plane. So spray paint and sandalwood incense, those scents hit first. The interior of the cabin is awash in them. And a hissing sound, coming from somewhere in the back.

As his eyes adjust, he can make out a small candelabra resting on the floor in the corner. Eight slender tapers with long wicks, and the only light in the room besides a tiny reading lamp above Luther, who, having seated himself near the side door of the plane, pages through the *Sunday Times,* in the single remaining caramel-colored calf leather chair. The rest of the furniture is missing. The floor covered in thick plastic tarps. The walls covered in—what the hell is he looking at?

Directly in front of him, a six-foot black rat standing on its hind legs, holding an umbrella in one hand, a briefcase in the other, wearing a striped tie and a clip-on name tag. Dollar bills leak out of the briefcase, a couple floating away. Beside the rat, in large, bloodred block letters: LET THEM EAT CRACK.

Data bit doesn't find data bit.

But it percolates. Crack not as split, break, or fracture. Crack, the drug, from back in the day. Cocaine coated with something evil and baked. Mandatory minimums, three-strike laws, and everyone in jail— kept the prison-industrial complex filthy with lucre. Now he gets it. Let them eat crack.

Graffiti. Cranes his neck around the interior. Similar graffiti everywhere.

Technicolor hieroglyphs coat nearly every inch of the plane's walls, from the bottom of their curve to the lower edge of the upper windows. That explains the spray-paint smell.

And those windows? Lorenzo wasn't kidding about the panoramic view. Lion feels like he's in a glass-bottomed boat, but inverted. The plane's roof is nearly all windows, a mosaic of dark glass ovals in different sizes. The smallest five feet long, the largest stretching over fifteen. A sea of eyes, like Varuna, always watching.

He walks a few steps onto the plastic and can't help but recall all the movies he's seen where the bad guys lay down drop cloths before they shoot the good guys, so the blood splatter doesn't ruin their expensive interiors.

Okay, not going to think that thought anymore.

He squints around the main cabin again. About thirty feet long and twelve wide, though it felt much bigger when he first stepped inside.

No sign of Penelope. Or Shiz either.

Lion glances back at Luther, who remains hidden behind the newspaper. So he's supposed to do what now?

Not a clue.

He crosses over to the candelabra. Eight candles in total, and doesn't look heavy. He picks it up and walks over to the wall to his left to get a better look. The first image he sees has the same black-and-white stencil style as the rat, but human this time. A life-sized punk rocker, male, early twenties, spiked mohawk, head bowed, hands in the pockets of his shabby overcoat, more block text: THIS REVOLUTION IS FOR DISPLAY PURPOSES ONLY.

Lion takes a few steps to his left, reaching the next piece. A black-and-white stencil of a leopard running directly toward him, adult female, life-sized, captured midstride and full power. Behind the cat, lying on a flatbed truck, a giant bar code has been rendered to look like a jail cell. The code's stripes turning into the bars of the cage. There's a pronounced bend in a few of those bars, the spot where the leopard pried the cage apart and went hell's bells toward freedom.

Lion recognizes the image.

Leopard and Barcode. An anti-commodification-of-nature protest, a statement about animal liberation. That explains where he's seen it before. Sonya. Animal Liberation Sonya. She had a poster of it framed on the wall of her crappy Hollywood apartment. He remembers lying in her bed, sweaty and naked, staring at it as she fell asleep in his arms.

Hanky? Panky? No, Banky—that's the name of the artist.

He looks at the bar code cum jail cell again. The Rilkean bar code tattoo—could this be the source? Some Banky-Rilkean connection trickling up through the poly-tribe? Not Banky. Banksy—that's the name of the artist.

Lion glances to his left, sees more graffiti: a black boy in a white T-shirt, sideways baseball cap and a gas mask. Block text reads: IF AT FIRST YOU DON'T SUCCEED—CALL AN AIRSTRIKE.

Another Banksy. Lion's seen this one before as well. Same book. Same Sonya. The book was sitting on her coffee table the day he was fired, the day before they started shouting, the day before the day before they'd broken it for good. Buried beneath a pile of whiskey bottles, cigarette butts, and small blue pills crushed into lines of powder.

A bitter memory that he didn't even know he had.

Makes him want a cigarette, but he doesn't know if he can smoke in here. Surveying the room, he doesn't see an ashtray. Does spot, on the floor by his feet, a break in the plastic and another image beneath, sprayed onto the carpet. Pulls the tarp back and crouches down to get a closer look.

A small robot standing on a busy city street corner, looking around. I SEE HUMANS BUT NO HUMANITY.

Lion stands back up and twirls slowly, holding the candelabra at arm's length, his eyes finally focused enough to take in the whole of the visage. Wall-to-wall and floor-to-ceiling, the entire plane is coated with Banksy.

"Luther," he can't help himself, "your ride is freakin' dope."

"Affirmative," says Luther, dropping the newspaper to peer over the top. "Shiz can spray."

And back behind the paper.

SHUT YOUR MOUTH WHEN YOU TALK TO ME

A door opens toward the rear of the plane, splashing soft light into the cabin. Lion sees Penelope in silhouette, walking toward him, from what appears to be a small bedroom. He does a quick gun scan. Hard to tell in the dim, but her hands are empty and nothing seems to be tucked into her waistband.

And behind her, filling the doorframe, Prince Shiz.

Fame in the room, rock-star wattage, a dopamine push to which no social mammals are immune. It's the by-product of the ruthlessness of evolution and the critical importance of status to survival. Lion feels the jolt but stays silent.

Shiz steps into the cabin, taller than he looks in photos, full lips, wide nose, chocolate skin, in a black crushed-velvet jumpsuit flecked with paint and a Vietnam-era gas mask, wedged high on his forehead, forcing the blue ropes of his dread-hawk to spike at strange angles.

"Lion Zorn," says Luther, from behind his paper, "please meet Prince Shiz."

"Luther," says Penelope, arms crossed, leaning up against a wall, "you're biting my rhymes."

"Affirmative," says Luther.

Shiz takes a step toward Lion, spreading his arms out wide. "'Sup, my brother," his accent poly-tribe complicated. Oxford phonetics, flavored with island spices, mashed up with street New York. "Been a long time coming."

"Good to meet you."

Bro shake, bro hug, Shiz still holding on. "Long time coming," he says again, thumping his fist once against Lion's back.

So he's not just saying, *he's saying.*

"Long time?" asks Lion.

Shiz releases the hug and takes a step back. The world's first poly-tribe superstar and also a good five inches taller than Lion.

Nine inches if you add the mohawk.

"I and I," says Shiz, Rasta-izing his syllables, "have Bredren in common."

"We do?"

"Actually," taking a can of spray paint out of his hip pocket and flat-spinning it in his palm, "Sistren. I think you knew her as Sonya."

An elevator drop, slices right through the dopamine.

"Animal Liberation Sonya?"

"Who got you arrested Sonya," says Shiz, spinning the can again. "Who almost got me arrested Sonya. Buck wild. That woman is treacherous."

Lion hadn't thought about Sonya in years and now thrice in one night? And Shiz knew her too? Is his past hunting him, for reasons unclear?

"Sonya," says Shiz, gesturing around the plane with the can of paint, "introduced me to Banksy."

"Me too," says Lion.

"Not me," says Luther, still behind his paper.

Shiz nods solemnly, setting the paint can on the floor by his feet. "That's her contribution. She introduced the Rilkeans to Banksy."

"Sonya's a Rilkean?" But Lion finds he's not surprised. "How is she?"

"No," with a sad shake of his head, "Sonya's not a Rilkean."

But before he can ask, Shiz slips the gas mask off his head and arcs it into a corner with a flourish, dips a hand into the chest pocket of his coveralls and produces a legit Rasta joint.

"Lion Zorn, em-tracker of the Rod of Correction, Bredren, wa gwaan, care to fiyah up?"

Penelope walks over to join them. "Bredren," she says.

They both look at her.

"What. The fuck. Is a Rod of Correction?"

THE ROD OF CORRECTION

nnerstand history?" Shiz asks Penelope, unzipping the upper half of
his jumpsuit, revealing a white-ribbed tank top and wiry black muscles. "Overstand Jamaica?" Tying the jumpsuit's arms around his waist.
"Overstand?"

"Chew mah banger," says Penelope, "I overstand former British col-
ony, major exports include reggae, bauxite, sugar, coffee," lifting her
hand to point at the joint, "and weed."

Shiz lights up the spliff, taking a Rasta-sized hit from his Rasta-
sized joint.

"Fiyah up the wayback machine to overstand the Rod of Correction," he says, pumping smoke out between his consonants. "Back to
1972, Jamaica's been free from colonial oppression for a decade, but,"
wagging a long finger in the air, "no-ting change. Shantytown just a
pretty word for people living in garbage. Hugh Shearer was in power.
Conservative, Jamaica Labour Party." Shiz takes another hit, passes it
to Lion. "But '72 was an election year and 'ere come Michael Manley, the challenger—democratic socialist man of Jah people singing his

Redemption Song. And rude-bwoy smart," tapping the shaved side of his head, "decides to court dem Rasta vote."

Penelope doesn't get it.

"Dread-I knows poly-tricks are just con-man with con-plan," says Shiz. "Chant down Babylon."

Penelope turns to face Lion. "Translation?"

"The Rastas don't vote. Not ever. They think politics are Babylon. Manley changed all that," shrugs, "and that changed everything."

"How?"

"He visited Haile Selassie in Ethiopia," says Shiz, pointing at Lion, "the OG Lion of Judah."

"My mom saw the face of Jesus in her toast," says Luther, finally setting down his paper.

They all look at him.

"I'm just saying, Selassie starved his own people. Big leap to call him the second coming."

"Marcus Garvey prophesied a black king in Africa," says Lion. "Selassie fit the bill."

"Or," says Luther, "smoke enough ganja, anything means anything."

"Jah Rastafari," says Shiz, upping the volume, "King of Kings, Lord of Lords, ruler of the tribe of Solomon for twenty-five hundred years, Selassie I."

"Absolutely," says Luther. "They locked the dude in his palace. When the coup came, they locked the God Emperor up with his butler and left him to rot. Tells you everything you need to know."

"At the end of Manley's trip," says Shiz, ignoring him, "Selassie gave him a walking stick."

"Selassie gave that to everyone," says Luther, "his parting gift, 'Thank you for coming to Ethiopia, here, have a stick.'"

Not a stick, thinks Lion, a staff, from the Ethiopian Imperial Navy.

"Manley gets back to Jamaica," continues Shiz, "tells people Selassie has bestowed upon him the Rod of Correction. From the Bible, the actual rod Solomon used to beat down foolishness; Manley gwan use it to beat back corruption, lift up Jah people."

"Starved Jah people," says Luther, going back to his paper. "And someone pass me that joint."

Penelope walks it over.

"Manley holds rallies in the Blue Mountains," Shiz continues. "Dreads rain down. Weeping, bowing before the Rod, dem waiting in line for days to kiss it. Manley turns it into his campaign slogan: 'Lick 'em, lick 'em, with the Rod of Correction.'"

"And this worked?" asks Penelope.

"Rastas ate it up," says Shiz, "and Hugh Shearer knows, if he want stay in power, the I-Rod is trouble." Lifts his hands up, palms open. "But how ya fight Jah symbol?"

"Steal the Rod?" asks Luther, still behind the paper.

"Exactly," says Shiz, snapping his fingers twice, the same beatnik clap that infected Arctic. "Labor send badman to rob Manley the challenger. Dem steal the I-Rod, and Manley man steal it back. Then there's two Rods—the Rod of Correction versus the Stick of Deception. In Jah end," spreading his hands wide, "downpressor man, where you gwan run to?

"So Manley won?" asks Penelope.

Shiz jabs his left foot forward, nicking the bottom edge of the paint can. It flips straight up into the air and lands in his hand. "In a landslide."

Penelope turns to face Lion. "And you found this thing?"

"The story before the story that got me fired," he says. "I was in Jamaica writing about the forty-year anniversary of Bob Marley's death and the cultural impact of reggae. How it became the foundation for both hip-hop and punk, proto-poly-tribe stuff."

Shiz loses interest in the conversation the moment Shiz stops talking. Eyes wandering around the room. Either typical rock-star ADD or the Prince is more stoned than suspected.

"I was talking to some Rasta elders," explains Lion, "and they told me about the Rod of Correction. Shiz was right, it changed everything."

"How does a walking stick change everything?" asks Penelope.

Before he can answer, Shiz says, "I'll be right back," and stomps out of the room.

Lion watches him go. Seems to be moving in slow motion. Maybe Lion's more stoned than suspected.

"Lion?" she says, snapping him back.

"Between the signifier and the signified: Rises," he says. "It's a classic example."

"Her tattoo?" asks Shiz, coming back into the room a moment later, a bottle of beer in one hand and a small silver box in the other. Interesting, thinks Lion, that Shiz knows about Penelope's tattoo.

Then Shiz opens the box.

More interesting, what's inside.

Thirty-six white capsules, in six neatly spaced rows of six.

"Bredren," says Shiz, holding out the box, "celebration in Zion."

"Celebration?" asks Lion.

"Glad you asked," says Shiz, smiling broadly. "My suggestion: We take Molly, remove our outerwear, and see what happens."

Looks from Lion to Penelope.

"Shut your mouth when you talk to me, Shiz," says Penelope. "I told you already, we're not shaggin'."

Then she reaches into the box, removes a couple of capsules, chases one down with a swig of Shiz's beer, hands the other to Lion.

"But Lion Zorn," she says, shrugging off her army jacket and letting it fall to the floor, "em-tracker of the Rod of Correction."

"Affirmative," he says.

"You I might shag."

"Here we go again," says Luther, still behind his paper.

THE ORIGINAL REDEMPTION SONG

Penelope, Lion concludes, has the entirety of a T. S. Eliot poem tattooed on her left leg. Black ink broken into seventeen stanzas. Starting out "We are the hollow men," on the meat of her calf; rising toward "This is the way the world ends," on the crest of her ass.

Shiz and Luther and the Black Power twins are elsewhere. Lion and Penelope are naked, afloat in Shiz's waterbed, awash in chemically induced serotonin and more feral, postcoital chemistry. They're staring up at a million gently rotating points of light, the whole of the cosmos projected onto the cabin's roof.

Like bathing in intergalactic space.

Beneath that sky, Lion's been using the light of his phone to slowly read his way across Penelope's skin. It's the only light in the room save for the galaxies above and the glimmering below. Under them, the bed's platform is a queen-sized aquarium, black-light lit and populated by translucent jellyfish robots in pinks and purples, mechanical innards visible through their bells. Like steampunk in Day-Glo, their slow pulse jet propulsion refracted in mirrors that stripe the bottom half of the room's walls.

"Come here," she says softly, patting the spot beside her.

Shiz has navy-blue sheets that seem to writhe in the light. Could be nano-particles sewn into the weave. Could be the drugs. Molly does something to the eyes, but unearthing one semester of advanced psychopharmacology so many semesters later? While his own psychopharmacology is retarded? Retracted? What's the politically correct opposite of advanced?

"Ya range wee shite, come here and pet my head."

So yeah, retarded works.

He slides up next to her. Kisses her. Gets a little lost. "You wanted something," he says, remembering.

"Pet my hair," then, sometime later: "Moved you how?"

"What?"

Penelope tries to sit up, which takes some maneuvering. An elbow prop, pale leg darting out of navy sheet and held akimbo for balance, finally upright, the sheet falling into her lap, the chrome barbells piercing her nipples catch the glimmer of Andromeda as it passes by overhead.

"The Rod of Correction," she says. "You never told me why it moved you."

"I don't know that I can."

"We're naked."

A line of Hebrew text slants from her right hip and onto her belly. The letters, he decides, look angry.

"Lion?"

"Yup," snapping back, "we're naked."

"Now's when you're supposed to tell me."

"No," he says, sitting up beside her, setting his phone on the bedside table, "not like that. Not sure how to work my mouth."

But he does, suddenly, remember how MDMA affects vision. Dampens down our ability to perceive negative emotions. The Morphed

Facial Recognition Task; Reading the Mind in the Eyes Test, that's how we know what we know. The filtering even works with memories. It's harder to recall negative experiences on MDMA, and the ones recalled are blunted.

Then Lion recalls a negative, not blunted. Blurts, "Where are the guns?" and louder than intended.

"Which guns?"

"The ones you took from Kali and Shiva."

"Safe," touching his shoulder, "safe, baby."

"No," he says, suddenly a lot more sober than he feels, "not safe."

"Shhh," tracing a line on his chest, "locked in the safe. In the recording studio. Shiz barely remembers the combination sober," runs her hands through his hair, "no way he can figure it out now."

Now he gets it. Safe and safe. He's safe-safe. Laughs, thinking about Balthazar's ninja—and Penelope's fingers like ghosts dancing on his skull.

Lion floats off with her touch.

"Moved you why?" she asks again, reeling him back.

"Jamaica, in '72, wasn't some cargo cult backwater. People could read. There were major industries. Lots of contact with the outside world. But the whole country gets turned upside down because of a hoax built on a myth resting on a fable sitting on a fairy tale? The Rod, Selassie's deity status, Marcus Garvey's Back to Africa prophecies, the entire Rasta religion."

"It's the ultimate arbitrary signifier stack," she says.

"Yeah," nodding in agreement, "but the voodoo worked. It changed culture. Anyway, I had to see the Rod for myself."

"It's still around?"

"Bob Marley," he says.

"What about him?"

"Got shot in '76, splits from Trench Town for London and smuggles out the Rod. Chris Blackwell, Island Records founder, ends up with it. Like three decades later, a cleaning woman finds it in Blackwell's basement, and someone, one of his kids maybe, sends it back to the last surviving Wailer." Shrugs. "Turned out to be the cousin of the cousin of the dread who told me the story. He brought me to see it."

"I think your mouth works just fine," says Penelope, almost kissing him, pulling gently back. "So then what happened?"

"I had . . ." What had Fetu called it? That trauma studies loanword? "An inciting incident."

"I-Lion was I-cited by the I-Rod?" In near perfect patois.

Smiles at her. "I thought you didn't speak Rasta."

"I and I a quick study."

"I was I-cited," he says, riding a serotonin pulse deeper into her arms. "Some em-trackers see colors, or hear words. I get the feels. I picked up the Rod and *bam*: I felt what that first Rasta felt. How society didn't give a fuck about him so he wouldn't give a fuck right back. One righteous, punk rock decision, the original Redemption Song, turning powerlessness into power. And how reggae carried that decision through time and space."

Two loud bangs on the door and it opens wide. Luther, skin as dark as coal, muscles stacked atop of muscles, and wearing a bright yellow rubber-ducky pool float around his waist, strolls in.

"Luther," says Penelope, "are we going swimming?"

"Lady," he says, not smiling, "what gives you that idea?"

Then laughs.

"We're in the studio, laying down tracks, come join," and he's gone. The door being swallowed by the Horsehead Nebula as it closes.

Hazy, long pause.

"That happened?" asks Lion, eventually.

"Luther, rubber ducky?"

"Affirmative."

"Affirmative."

"You have pretty eyes."

"Focus."

"What was I saying?"

"Reggae."

"The word is an insult," says Lion. "Did you know that? It's an up-town way of saying ragga, which is just a rude word for ragamuffin, which is what the rich in Jamaica used to call the poor."

A crowded galaxy whirls overhead; Lion pauses for a moment to watch before continuing.

"But the music gives Jamaica's poor a voice. Then comes punk, basically exported Jamaican ska on speed, which gives voice to a different poor. White and poor. And hip-hop, which was Jamaican toasting from way back, proto-reggae, gives voice to black and poor. All that music, it's an empathy drug. Like Sietch Tabr before Sietch Tabr. Or Molly before Molly, if that makes any sense. And where are my cigarettes?"

"Clothes, pile on the floor, sort of makes sense."

Lion leans left over the bed, swats through the pile until he fishes tobacco and lighter from his coat pocket. Getting back into the bed afterward, that part taking some effort.

"Empathy is the brain's way of answering a question," he says, fumbling out a rolling paper, spilling tobacco all over the bed, coordination iffy. "Whenever we encounter anything living, the brain asks a series of 'is this thing like me or not like me' questions. Does this thing look like me? Smell like me? Move like me? Talk like me? Make meaning like me?"

His fingers seem to be made of some alien material, still unable to roll that cigarette.

"If it's like me, maybe I can fuck it. Or cooperate with it. If it's not like me, maybe I need to kill it, or run away. 'Like me or not like me,' for every conscious organism in the world, that's the question. Emotions are answers. Empathy is just a bunch of yes-like-me answers bundled into one clear signal."

"Yes, let me," she says, taking the tobacco out of his hands and quickly rolling a cigarette.

Lights it, passes it back.

"Yes, thank you." Inhales and smiles. "Christ, smoking on drugs, that's one goddamn thing God definitely got right."

"That's how you became an em-tracker," she says, "you touched the Rod?"

"As far as origin stories go," taking another drag of the cigarette, exhaling, "mine's lame. All I did was tell a couple Rasta elders that the Rod had some juice left, and maybe they should do something useful with it."

"Like what?"

Shrugs. "Make it the symbol of the world's first pot-friendly airline or something."

"The very first time an em-tracker got paid to be an em-tracker," says Penelope. "Lion Zorn, empathy-preneur."

"I didn't think you knew the story."

"Jenka runs extra-specials," she says, touching her fingers to his face, "I research extra-specials."

"I thought you were hired muscle."

"I am," she says, smiling, her fingers tracing the side of his jaw, "muscle and research. I and I contain multitudes."

Her touch seems to precipitate some deep shift in his system. Is he coming down?

No, going up.

Must be hitting her too. Teeth-grind, and eyes like pinballs. Sexy, wild green pinballs floating in a sea of clover.

Jesus is he fucked up.

Shivers, sweats, and a memory of Shiz, in satin underwear, offering them a second hit of Molly and when was that?

But the question gets lost in the blast of the blastoff, and the feeling of his soul being sucked up, one molecule at a time, through Penelope's fingers.

BETWEEN JAH ROCK
AND JAH HARD PLACE

They're gone for minutes, hours, or weeks. Probably all three. Penelope says something to him, a whisper he watches more than hears. Her lips moving, sound traveling, going somewhere.

Does he answer?

Maybe he's dreaming, maybe it's later, maybe they made a decision of some kind. Which is when he notices, he's vertical. Out of bed and moving forward and amazed that his limbs actually remember this part. Amazed, come to think of it, that he has limbs at all.

He tries to get his bearings.

It's a little hard to say, but they seem to be oozing through the intergalactic space of the bedroom and into the candlelight flicker of the recording studio. Smaller than the bedroom, a lot smaller than the main cabin. There's a candelabra on an end table in one corner, just about the only light in the room, and illuminating fresh spray paint on the walls. Looks like, well, not another Banksy.

It's a cartoon image Lion's seen somewhere before. A small, furry creature with an oversized brush mustache, standing on a tree stump.

Text as well: "Unless someone like you cares a whole awful lot, nothing is going to get better. It's not."

Not a chance that data bit finds data bit.

But Lion's eyes are starting to gain ground on the situation. In a mirror beside the not-Banksy, he catches his reflection. He appears shirtless, barefoot, and wearing baggy Detroit Pistons sweatpants that he must have borrowed from Shiz. Penelope is wrapped around him. Underwear, army jacket, and possibly nothing else. They seem to be swaying slightly, some kind of pitch-and-yaw problem.

Looking left of the mirror is when he realizes.

"Not sure what to do now," he whispers to Penelope. "You didn't say anything about there being other people here."

"Bloody hell," she whispers back, folding deeper into him, knocking him backward. Pitch goes left, yaw goes right.

"Between Jah rock and Jah hard place," intones Shiz, starting to come into focus, on a small stool in a corner of the room. He's sitting at a keyboard, near a tall stack of electronics, wearing navy-blue satin boxers, a black-and-gray-checked topcoat, and paint-splattered combat boots.

"You two are a shit-show, alright," says Luther, slapping congas from a spot beside Shiz. He's traded in the rubber ducky for a black silk robe. Dark skin, dark robe, dark room—making him nearly invisible.

Then Lion spots the twins, deep in the cushions of a long black couch, just past Shiz. Kali in camo-colored lace and a white headband with IRONIC printed across its middle. Shiva has on a cutoff pair of army shorts and a living-display bra, C-cups animated with the same furry creature as the graffiti on the wall.

Shiz hits a key on the keyboard. Funky Outkast bass licks rise over Luther's slow drum swat and some kind of Cuban rhythm. Coming out of surround-sound speakers.

"I rap for the trees," raps Shiz, "for the trees have no tongues."

Shiva, from her perch on the couch, shimmies her C-cups, bringing up another image: same furry creature, standing in a forest of slender trees, their foliage starburst explosions in pinks, yellows, and purples.

"Shiz is turning the Lorax into a rap opera," explains Kali, pointing at the bra. "I'm designing the wardrobe."

The Lorax—that's the image on the wall. Another wobble.

"How you guys doing over there?" asks Luther. "Just an opinion, but the couch could be safer."

"The Lorax?" asks Lion, unable to peel himself off the wall. "A rap opera?"

"Next phase," says Shiz, "coming out of Banksy, trying to learn to channel Seuss. Adding more poly to the poly-tribe."

Lion knows channeling is a Rilkean idea. Extreme empathy exercise, an archetypal embodiment practice, sort of like method acting. Becoming the other's art in order to become the other, another way to live the questions.

Shiz spins on his stool, putting his back to the keyboard, turning to face Lion directly, "Lion Zorn," he says, adding a little island spice to his pronunciation, "gwan tell I and I why you wanted to reason?"

Couldn't be a worse time to try to reason, thinks Lion, which, he suspects, might be exactly why Shiz wants to do so now. He takes an unsteady step forward, limbs not working properly. Penelope comes to his rescue, walking them over to the couch, pulling him down beside her. He lands in a heap, her arms slide around his torso, legs wrap his waist, drawing him closer.

"Muad'Dib," says Lion, struggling to not get lost in Penelope's touch, "I'm trying to find him."

"Difficult man to find," says Shiz, toying with the keyboard, a little stride piano riff dancing out of the speakers. "Is it you who's looking? Or your employer?"

"You talked to Penelope?"

Shiz shrugs. "All she told me is she met you through Sir Richard. But I know a ting or two about Sir Richard. And now I know a ting or two about Lion Zorn. I don't see me Bredren chillin'. Two tings and two tings together—you're working for him."

"Deductive logic," says Luther.

"I'm not sure who I'm trying to find Muad'Dib for," Lion says. "I told Richard I'd locate him, have a conversation. I didn't say anything about what I'd do next. Right now, I just want to chat."

Lion also wants a smoke. Looking around, he seems to recall his cigarettes are still in the bedroom.

"About?" asks Shiz.

"About Sietch Tabr and . . . ," trying to find the right language, "his agenda."

"Big word for this time of night," says Luther.

"I think it's morning," says Kali.

"It's got connotations," Luther continues, nodding toward Shiz. "I think my man needs to understand those connotations."

A lonely sensation, full body, a warning shot across the bow—the drugs are starting to fade. Not vanishing completely, just dropping him down a level.

"Lion?" asks Shiz.

"Sorry," he says. "It's still a little . . . inchoate."

"Another big word," says Luther.

"Gentlemen," says Kali, pointing at Luther and Shiz, patting the couch. "Man's inchoate, bring it in."

Luther settles on the far end of the sofa. A land grab, his large frame taking up most of the remaining space. Kali shifts toward him, leans back against his chest, and pats her lap, which Shiz half-occupies. Legs extend, arms rearrange.

"Better," says Kali.

"Inchoate?" asks Shiz.

"How do you feel right now?" asks Lion.

"Little high," says Shiz.

"Lot high," says Luther.

"A little on the edge of the comedown," adds Penelope, "like it's starting to sneak up on me."

Slow nods all around. The motion activates Shiva's display bra, bringing up another image: the Lorax in sherbet colors, standing on a tree stump, looking pissed.

"The drop, right?" says Lion. "How the drugs wear off and leave that pit of lonely. Cause you know you're going to miss this . . . ," gesturing at the body sprawl on the couch. "This oneness. Molly extends the boundary of self, so when it retracts, feels like a part of you has gone missing."

Shiva massages Luther's scalp. Shiz, he notices, is actually paying attention.

"Ironic," Lion continues. "We ache for this feeling, but it's everywhere. Booze, drugs, sex, sport, art, prayer, music, meditation, virtual reality. Kids, hyperventilating, spinning in circles, feel oneness. Why William James called it the basic lesson of expanded consciousness—just tweak a few knobs and levers in the brain and *bam*. So the drop, the comedown, it's not that we miss oneness once it's gone; it's that we suddenly can't feel what we actually know is there. Phantom limb syndrome for the soul."

"Lion Zorn," says Shiz. "Preaching, steaching, and teaching."

"Em-tracking," he says, "feels like that, not at a personal level, at a cultural level. Like the drop never quite ends. That's why I want to talk to Muad'Dib. Follow out Sietch Tabr, and that's a future that feels different."

"Different how?" asks Shiz, unwinding an arm to scratch his dreads. "Less lonely?"

"Maybe. More promising. More dangerous. I honestly can't tell. That's why I want to talk to him."

Shiz becomes silent, glances at Luther. A long pause before Luther nods. Shiz nods back before turning to face Lion again. "Muad'Dib's going to space. Low earth orbit. He's on the next Virgin Galactic flight to the Bigelow Space Hotel. Wants to experience the overview effect."

"The what effect?" asks Kali.

"Edgar Mitchell," explains Luther. "Sixth man on the moon. Looked back at the earth and realized every molecule in his body was exactly like every molecule in the solar system. All manufactured in the same star factories. Mitchell experienced oneness as a result, but what he'd discovered is that it's not just a sensation. It's physics, the actual geological history of our universe. He called it the overview effect."

"Yes-I Lion Zorn," says Shiz. "Two days from now, you can find Muad'Dib at Spaceport America, Truth or Consequences, New Mexico."

"I can get you there by tomorrow," adds Penelope.

"They finally got that place open?" says Lion. "I thought Virgin was flying out of Zimbabwe, Zanzibar, one of those Z places . . ." Then he looks at Penelope, suddenly realizing, "You're not coming?"

She holds up her phone, the light too bright for the room. "Text from Jenka," giving Lion a squeeze. "He needs me back in New York by tomorrow. I'm out later today."

Lion feels a surprising jolt of sadness. Discovers he really doesn't want her to leave, then discovers he doesn't know what to do with this discovery. Putting it out of his mind, he tries to focus on Shiz. "How do I find Muad'Dib once I'm in Truth or Consequences?"

"He finds you," says Luther.

Lion doesn't like the sound of that, but something in Luther's tone tells him there are no other options.

"Set it up," he says finally, unwinding himself from the pile and standing up.

"You're leaving?" asks Kali.

"To take a piss and find my cigarettes."

"Can you bring beers?" asks Shiva.

"In the fridge," adds Shiz, "by the leopard painting."

"Smokes, piss, beers, coming right up," and walks out of the room.

MEXICAN AMBER REDUX

Lion makes his way through Shiz's bedroom, the ghost dusting of the Milky Way rotating overhead as he crosses to the bathroom. Walks inside and does not bother with the light. Navigating by the sound of the stream alone, completes the next portion of his mission without a hitch.

Locating the refrigerator, that turns out to be trickier.

The candles have all gone dark, and there are no other lights in the main cabin. As he walks into the room, Lion's foot lands on something soft, nearly sliding out from under him. A pair of pants, maybe a bra. Falling on his ass, he decides, is not an experience he's currently interested in having.

Crouching down on hands and knees, Lion crawls across the plastic tarp lining the main cabin until he finds the definitive curve of the plane's far wall, just the faintest braille of a welding seam at their nexus. Flicks his lighter and sees the stenciled leopard where Shiz said it would be, just above him now, a muscular shadow pawing away from a jail cell.

He stares at it, thinking of Sonya and how strange that she was the one to teach the Rilkeans about Banksy. Even for an em-tracker, Lion knows, back-tracing a meme to its original point of emergence is a rare occurrence. He inspects the bar code more closely, thinking of the years between then and now. The lighter is burning his fingers. Lion releases the flame, watching it sputter and go dark.

Keeping his hands on the wall, he slides left until he bumps into the cold metal of the refrigerator. Hand slapping his way to the handle, he opens the door to bright white light and the scent of industrial chemistry. Two four-packs of Guinness cans and nothing else inside.

Grabbing both, he cradles the stack in his arm and hip-checks the door closed. Pitch black again. Like someone extinguished an angel.

Turning slowly around, Lion starts across the room, sweeping his path with his foot before committing to the step. And again. Finally making it back to the bedroom, he finds the Milky Way still hovering above, rotated slightly. He sets the beers down on the bed to look around for his tobacco pouch.

On the nightstand, where he left it, but he's out of rolling papers.

Taps his pockets for a spare pack. Maybe in his sling-pack, on the floor, beside Penelope's backpack. He crouches down beside his bag and undoes the drawstring. The aquarium lights up beside him, a swarm of jellyfish robots reacting to his presence beside the tank, bells glowing pink and purple.

In the fluorescence, he notices that the zipper on Penelope's backpack is open, a piece of bright orange lace visible inside. Spare underwear perhaps.

Turning his attention back to his sling-pack, Lion paws around a bit until he uncovers a pack of rolling papers tucked in an inside pocket. Pulling them free, he realizes: Not underwear.

Too rigid for underwear.

Lion glances toward the recording studio door, making sure he's still alone. He tugs the zipper open a little more. The orange lace isn't lace at all. It's an insect wing attached to a dragonfly drone. A bright orange insect wing. Mexican amber—just like the one that followed him around Robert Walker's house.

A cold prickle runs up his spine, and the feeling of being frozen in place. All he can think of is how he felt about Penelope moments ago versus how he feels now. He tries to shake off that feeling. Lifting the drone from the bag, Lion runs a finger over its thorax. Lab-grown synth-flesh roughly the same texture as the dragon box. He flips it over, knowing what he's going to see before he sees it. Exactly as remembered: a tiny Lidar sensor in the middle of the insect's abdomen. Not much more than a micro-scale LED light. Turned off now, its bulb the color of dark, pooled blood.

REROUTING

Hard to measure how much time passes while Lion crouches, motionless beside the bed, holding the drone in his fingers. Long enough that the jellyfish robots have lost interest, swimming off to another corner of the aquarium, the tank now dark, the only light left the pale glow of the Oort Cloud traveling across the ceiling.

His brain keeps replaying the same questions. Was Penelope using the dragonfly to spy on him for Arctic? Does not compute. Richard knew where he was and where he was going. But, if not Arctic, who?

And repeat.

From the other room, he hears Shiz calling his name. That snaps him back.

Time to act, Zorn.

He shoves the dragonfly into Penelope's pack, yanks the zipper closed, and slides the bag into the corner. Stands up, trying to get his bearings. He was on a mission. Cigarettes, beer, both sitting on the bed. Grabbing them, he takes a step toward the recording studio and stops. The rest of the evening? Facing Penelope now? Management of this particular phase of the operation uncertain.

A couple of deep breaths and he walks the rest of the way into the recording studio. Shiz and Luther are at the keyboard, playing blue notes. Comedown conversation in piecemeal mode. A thought. A pause. Maybe a response. Lion sits back down on the couch, distributes beers, and takes Penelope's hand. Like nothing happened. Except his eyes, pegged hard to the Lorax on the far wall.

After an appropriate interlude, he unclasps Penelope, gives her thigh a squeeze, and bids them good night. "Totally shattered," he says, telling the absolute truth while pushing up from the couch. "Can I take the bed?"

"Yours," says Shiz, who stands up to give him a hug. "Be careful, Lion Zorn," he whispers. "Keep this up, you might find what you're looking for."

Luther salutes.

"Night, sugar," say Kali and Shiva in unison.

"I'll be there in a second," says Penelope, kissing his forehead softly.

The trip from recording studio to bedroom seems to stretch on for a very long time, but once Lion gets under the covers, the crash comes quickly. Doesn't so much fall asleep as fade to black.

And when he wakes, he wakes alone.

Not just in the waterbed—in the entire plane. Maybe the entire warehouse. He can feel it. The absence of life; the null set of empathy.

Getting out of bed, Lion walks into the main cabin to check. Skylights built into the roof of the plane are blue with daylight, revealing nothing. Bedroom, bathroom, recording studio, main cabin again, even the cockpit—all completely empty.

Out the door and down the steps for a quick look at the warehouse, his bare feet slapping the yellow metal of the ladder with a series of flat thwacks, the sound echoing off faraway walls. Cold concrete beneath his flesh when feet hit the floor. Glancing back and forth, sees no one.

The place is empty.

Feeling very uneasy, Lion walks around the plane and over to the Ehang 184s in the corner. Black carbon-fiber bodies, white cabins made of reinforced composites, and nobody in either cockpit. Another glance around the warehouse.

It's a ghost town, alright.

Lion puts his hands on his hips and sweeps his eyes back and forth across the concrete sea. Vision not quite adjusted to daylight displaying blotches of color more than stable images. But through the haze, one clear thought rises: He doesn't want to be here anymore.

Not for one second.

Slipping into a higher gear, Lion climbs back up the steps of the plane and crosses toward the bedroom. Atop his sling-pack, he finds a plane ticket and a note from Penelope, telling him that something came up and Shiz and Luther had to run to a meeting and she had to run to New York. Can't wait to see him when he gets back to the city, XO.

Staring at the XO, quivering at his stupidity. More guerrilla marketing.

Lion shoves the note in his pocket and gets out of Shiz's sweatpants, crossing over to his own clothes. It takes a small struggle for him to get into his straight-world uniform, limbs not quite working as remembered. Finally dressed, he grabs his sling-pack and strides through the main cabin one last time, stepping over the Banksy on the floor, the lonely robot: I SEE HUMANS BUT NO HUMANITY.

"Affirmative," he tells the robot, and heads toward the door.

Down the ladder, across the concrete sea, and banging out the entranceway. Daylight pours into the world, the midafternoon sun and much too bright. Lion lifts a hand to shield his eyes and digs into his sling-pack with the other. Notebook, copy of *Dune*, tobacco pouch. A short prayer of gratitude when he finds his sunglasses in an inside pocket.

Silver wire-frame aviators.

After putting them on, he surveys right and left. The warehouse standing sentinel and no one else in sight.

Lion doesn't know where to go. He decides on a tight alley across from him, not much bigger than shoulder width and buildings on either side. A left turn and another alley, trying to reverse the route they took the night before. He expects to get lost along the way, but surprises himself, popping out near the main entrance of Exec-Jets.

In front of him, he sees an oval of saw grass, an armed guard standing just inside the main glass doors of the terminal, and a black Uber autonomous taxi idling by the curb. Another prayer of gratitude when he realizes that the only conversation required to get him from here to hotel is with a robot.

"The Four Seasons, please," getting into the cab.

They pull away from the curb, take a left at the corner, and drive the speed limit down the long winding road that leads to the freeway on-ramp. He feels acceleration as they merge into traffic, then an even glide as they find their lane. Smooth sailing from there.

The rest of the trip stays uneventful, save for the anger, confusion, betrayal, rage, shame—Lion can't decide how he feels about Penelope.

"But not good," he says aloud.

"Rerouting," says the car's AI, "the Good Hotel."

"No," snaps Lion, "not rerouting. The Four Seasons Hotel."

"Rerouting," says the AI, "the Four Seasons Hotel."

"Fuck you," says Lion.

"Rerouting."

And eventually, mercifully, back to the hotel.

YOU CAN'T GO INTO SPACE
WITHOUT FRACTIONS

He can't find his key. The door is where he remembered, the floor hasn't changed, but his key, which Lion is sure he slipped into his wallet before leaving to meet Penelope, is not where he left it. A search of his pockets, an inspection of his sling-pack, neither discloses a way into his hotel room. Neuro-electrical signals run the wires. Did he misplace it? Move it? Did Penelope steal it? Grinding his molars, Lion stalks down the hall toward the elevators.

The front desk prints him another copy. He fidgets while he waits. Fidgets in the elevator. By the time he makes it back to his room, he's pretty certain it was Penelope who stole his key. And combined with the residual MDMA twitchiness, this leaves him too wound to be useful.

But tries to fake it.

Sitting down on the edge of the bed, Lion goes through the motions of checking his email. That charade doesn't last a message. He drops his phone, lies back on the covers, and stares at the ceiling, running his hands along pillowcases made from high-thread-count Egyptian cotton. Soft and cool to the touch, but no match for brain on fire.

It doesn't take long before he's out of bed and pacing the carpet, a low-shag variety, gray-on-gray diamond pattern flattening beneath his feet. Maybe he should call Lorenzo?

Maybe he should calm down first.

Not, he concludes, going to happen on its own.

Lion changes into his workout clothes, takes the elevator to the fourth floor, and finds the fitness center, a well-lit rectangle lined with faux-wood rubber matting. Free weights line one wall; cardio stations line another. He sees an older-model rowing machine in the back corner and unearths an old punk playlist on his phone. Rise Against rising in his ears and pulling for all he's worth.

Takes a half hour for his twitchiness to subside. Another forty-five minutes lifting weights and there's space to think—though he doesn't know what to think. Penelope spying on him for whom?

No answer forthcoming.

Heading for the exit, Lion grabs a banana from a bowl beside the door. He peels it as he walks back to the elevator, takes a first bite while he waits. The MDMA had him grinding his teeth and now his jaw aches. Drops the rest of the fruit into a silver trash can long before the car arrives.

Back in his room, after a long shower, Lion tries to figure out what he wants to do next. Does he head to New Mexico? Between the dragonfly drone and his missing room key, the chances that Muad'Dib will actually be at the Spaceport? Even if he can't trust Penelope, what about Shiz?

His earlier instinct was correct: call Lorenzo for advice.

On speed dial. But the call goes straight to voicemail, and he doesn't feel like leaving a message. Instead, he decides to review the crime scene photos one more time—a long shot, but he has no other ideas forthcoming.

Carrying his sling-pack over to a rolltop desk, Lion opens the lid and finds the plane ticket Penelope left for him. I and I friendly skies from San Francisco to Albuquerque, then a Virgin America charter for the short hop down to Truth or Consequences, New Mexico. He leaves tomorrow morning.

Which is when the phone starts to ring.

"You can't travel in space," says Lorenzo, when he answers, "you can't go out into space, you know . . . with fractions. What are you going to land on? One-quarter? Three-eighths?"

"Funny that you should mention that," says Lion.

"Fractions?"

"Space."

And he fills Lorenzo in on the happenings of the past forty-eight hours, his evening with Shiz, his discovery of the drone, and the supposed meeting with Muad'Dib at Spaceport America.

"Penelope was the one spying on you?" asks Lorenzo afterward. "I didn't see that coming."

"When I went to visit Walker's house, for sure. On the motorcycle, when I was back in New York City, maybe, maybe not. But I can't figure out for whom. Can't be Arctic. A second player? A rival pharmaceutical company? Something else entirely? You get what I'm saying here?"

"Let's table those questions," says Lorenzo. "You gonna quit?"

"Fuck no," with a vehemence that surprises him.

"Okay. So your first job is to find Muad'Dib. Shiz said he's gonna be at the Spaceport."

"If he's not there already."

"Any chance that Shiz and Penelope are working together?"

"It's possible. Why?"

"Well," says Lorenzo, "if they're working together, not sure if I would trust the info about the Spaceport. If they're not working together . . ."

"Yeah," he says.

"But you're still going?"

"I guess, technically, you're right, my assignment was track down Muad'Dib and arrange a meeting with Sir Richard. The trail leads to

New Mexico, and that . . . ," thinking it through, "should mean I'm going."

"Should?"

"Let me ask you something. The snuff container I found had Muad'Dib's name engraved into it, like a monogram on a shirt. Would you lend a monogrammed shirt to a friend?"

"You ever met a bongo player with a monogrammed shirt?"

"But it's unlikely, right?"

"Unlikely," says Lorenzo.

"Which places Muad'Dib at Walker's house during the murder, at least."

"And pretty high on the suspect list."

"So I'm heading into a meeting with a killer, or a friend of a killer."

"Which isn't—"

Lion cuts him off. "But if I don't talk to Muad'Dib? I don't know. Sietch Tabr, even Penelope, I can't get a bead on where this leads."

"Unusual for an em-tracker."

"Which is why I want to have that conversation."

"Do you want me to come with you?" asks Lorenzo.

"Pardon?"

"I could get on a flight tonight. The band will understand. Hank will be pissed, but whatever, family emergency, he'll get over it."

"I don't think there's time. Plus . . . ," with a conviction he doesn't quite feel, "pretty sure I got this."

"But just that. Go to the Spaceport, find Muad'Dib, have your conversation, preferably in a well-lit public area, arrange the meeting with Arctic, get paid, and head home. Penelope spied on you with a drone. My advice—never see her again."

Lion thinks about this for a moment. "Maybe."

"Christ," says Lorenzo, "you want to see her again."

"Say that's true," but then he remembers what Bo said about not telling his mother about Sarah, even after she had him roofied and tattooed. "No, that's too crazy, even for me. You're right. I go to the Spaceport, have a talk, arrange a meeting, and be done with it."

"Safest play, Kemosabe."

"So I'm heading for Truth or Consequences."

"Aren't we all," says Lorenzo, "aren't we all."

TRUTH OR CONSEQUENCES, HERE WE COME

From above, coming in for a landing, the main terminal of Space-port America looks like someone parked the *Starship Enterprise* in the middle of a desert, coated it in dust, and dotted it with blue lights. Also, a little arachnoid.

Touchdown on runway two, taxi to the terminal.

Out the window, Lion sees undulations in his field of vision, heat shimmers rising from the baked soil of the high desert. He lifts his gaze up to take in the larger view: an empty blue sky, scrub brush, sandy plains, and the shadows of jagged mountains in the distance. Like the land that time forgot.

And now, a gateway to outer space.

Stepping out of the cabin, he's greeted by the midday sun and a searing heat. The breath being sucked from his lungs. It only lasts as long as it takes to walk down the ladder and across thirty feet of tarmac and into the terminal, but long enough to make him sweat.

Inside an aluminum-clad holding area, Lion dabs his brow with his sleeve and looks around. Oversized doorway to his starboard. He walks through it and into a large hallway, sleek and modern, with a twinge of Western rustic. Arched ceilings and couches made of faux-cowhide. To his left, a rectangular window peering toward a pair of forty-foot-high steel curtain doors modeled, a wall-mounted scrolling screen tells him, on NASA's blast-shielded launch control center from the early Apollo days. To his right, the Spaceport's main hangar visible through another rectangular window. On the other side of the glass, he sees the bullet-shaped frame of *SpaceShipTwo* and the larger, more recent upgrade, *SpaceShipSix*—both named, another screen tells him, not for the iteration of the spacecraft, but rather for its passenger carrying capacity.

Then down a hallway and into the terminal itself.

A squat stadium. High white walls, beige stone floors, and the building's front, a giant window of glass looking out onto the New Mexico desert. The light reads early afternoon, but you could have fooled him.

A cup of coffee might help.

He looks around, seeing an octet of gates serving standard terrestrial travel, then a long wall separating the extra-terrestrial wing. On the wall, there are photographs of astronauts and aircraft designers, and a framed advertisement for the Bigelow Space Hotel, back when it was still just three inflatable pods ringed by solar panels.

Lion takes a step closer to get a better look. A cutaway reveals the interior of the main pod: a woman in a wedding dress, a man in a tuxedo. They stand on a starship bridge not much bigger than a phone booth, surrounded by the whole of the galaxy. GET HITCHED IN SPACE.

And in the corner, thankfully, a caffeine dealer.

Lion orders a triple-shot Americano and carries it over to a small chrome table in a miniature food court. The chairs are gunmetal curves atop steel bases. They don't look, in any way, comfortable.

Seated, the experience is worse than advertised. He shifts his weight, sips his coffee and slow-scans the terminal. First thing he notices is heavy muscle. Young, fit, and not your standard airport fare. Private contractors, by the looks of them.

And a lot of them.

Lion remembers an attempted bombing, like two years back. The Islamic Brotherhood took the initial blame, but it turned out to be a crazed Amazon fan who wanted Bezos to defeat Branson in the race to become the first legitimate space tourism outfit.

He counts maybe a hundred-plus people in the room, maybe a hundred and fifty if you include security. East Asians and West Texans dominate, what seems to be a healthy group of each. Also a dusty conglomerate of New Mexicans off a commuter flight, sunbaked skin and long-distance stares. No one, at least no one he can see, has a bar code tattoo.

It dawns on him that what he's actually doing is scanning the Spaceport for signs of Muad'Dib, which leads to another realization: He has no idea what Muad'Dib actually looks like. Also, come to think of it, what his real name might be. Or if he even has a bar code tattoo.

Way to journalism, Lion Zorn.

He finishes his coffee, drops the cup into a recycling bin, and walks toward the glass wall. Moving out the terminal's main doors is like walking into a sauna. And now what?

He spots a taxi stand a half block to his left. A single yellow cab idles at the curb. It's the old-fashioned kind, still burning gasoline, piloted by an actual human. Cowboy hat, plaid shirt, black Wayfarer sunglasses. "Adonde va, amigo?"

Lion doesn't actually know.

Penelope's note says she booked him into the Space Ace, which his phone tells him is the latest installment in the Ace franchise and conveniently located seven miles away, on the way to the town of Truth or Consequences. But does he trust Penelope?

Apparently not.

He opts to change those plans. Untraceable is what he wants to be, at least for a little while.

"I need a bank," says Lion.

"Closest one is Truth or Consequences."

"Truth or Consequences, here we come," says Lion, no pun intended.

The trip takes about a half hour. A long stretch of desert and then, in the distance, the town rising up to greet them. A white church steeple, adobe buildings, also, like the landscape, untouched by time.

Or sort of.

They stop at three banks before Lion finds one with actual human tellers. He doesn't want to leave an electronic trail. No credit cards, cell phone calls, or ATM transactions. Nothing anyone can actually track. Not that he knows a damn thing about how not to leave an electronic trail.

Taking a thousand dollars out of his account, he pays cash for the cab ride and more cash for two nights at the Holiday Inn. His room is on the third floor, and the elevator takes too long.

But it gives him time to think.

Before the doors open, he's got the semblance of a plan. Luther said Muad'Dib would find him, so Lion decides to believe him, at least for the next few hours. Right now, he wants to reread the file on Shiz that Penelope assembled. He's less interested in the actual articles, more interested in why she might have selected them. Could be that he's been coming at this from the wrong direction. The dragonfly drone, the whatever the hell happened in San Francisco. Maybe this isn't about Penelope spying on him, wanting to know where he's been. Maybe this is about where he's going.

Maybe she's been trying to steer.

SPACE ACE, POR FAVOR

Early evening when he gives up on the Shiz file. He tosses it aside, absently, thinking it doesn't explain anything. That's not entirely true. When Shiz was younger, a journalist from the *Tokyo Sun* claimed, he had a fondness for boy bands. That explains something. Just not the something that needs explaining.

Either way, if Penelope chose these specific articles for a particular reason, it's not coming to him. Em-tracking machinery failing to em, and his head hurts from trying.

He gets up from his chair and looks around the room, noting the décor for the first time. Some kind of brown hashtag pattern for carpet, walls made of mauve. The bathroom is beachside chic. Baby-blue tile, white towels in a neat stack. He considers a shower but decides to splash cold water on his face instead. Turning on the faucet, Lion notices the Holiday Inn logo imprinted in the soap and realizes his hotel choice might be a problem.

If Penelope did her job, then she told Shiz where Lion is staying. If

Shiz did his job, then he passed that information along to Muad'Dib. Is Muad'Dib hunting Lion in the wrong locale?

Time to visit the Space Ace.

Back in the bedroom, Lion pulls on his boots, texts Lorenzo to let him know he'd arrived in New Mexico and is heading to the Space Ace, then remembers his decision to stay off the radar—cellular paranoia still with him—and does not hit SEND.

Instead, he sets down his phone and notices his copy of *Dune*. It must have slid out of the pack when he grabbed the file. This reminds him of waving the book around Hudson's. Might be worth another shot at the Space Ace. Might be enough to catch Muad'Dib's attention.

Maybe, if he's even there.

Out the door and down the hall and the slow elevator. A courtesy pot in the hotel's lobby gives him an okay cup of coffee and, still not trusting the anonymity of apps, he asks the desk clerk to call him a cab.

"You're a cab," says the clerk.

"Funny," says Lion.

He walks out of the hotel to wait. The day's heat has faded, leaving a mild night and the sound of crickets in the distance. Behind the parking lot, he sees the faded remnants of an old BMX track, mostly overgrown with weeds, except for a single straightaway of raked dirt and a solitary tire track running down its center.

Glancing around, he doesn't see anyone with a bicycle. But he does notice the same yellow taxi pulling up in front of him. Same driver too. Same shirt, same hat. No sunglasses this time, revealing eyes, dark and weary.

"Adonde va?" as he climbs inside.

"Space Ace, por favor."

As they pull out of the parking lot, Lion's phone grabs a signal from the ether and buzzes with an incoming text from Jenka: *Where are you? Is Penelope still with you? Sir Richard wants a sit rep, ping me ASAP.*

So hotel-swapping worked? He smiles at the possibility that he slipped Arctic's radar, if only for the moment. And the fact that Jenka thinks Penelope is still with him? Didn't Jenka call her back to New York? Didn't she go back to New York? That's interesting too, in a way he can't quite figure.

He glances out the window. A moonlit desert, a wide sky, and a sudden flash of silver. A lone jackrabbit, bounding off through the sagebrush. Then he looks back at the text.

What time is it in New York?

A little after 6:14 P.M. here in New Mexico—converting Mountain Standard to Eastern Standard—makes it 8:14 there. Early enough that he could call Jenka back, but his desire to avoid Arctic's radar exceeds his interest in whatever Jenka might tell him about Penelope's whereabouts.

So no sit rep for now.

THE PROBLEM IS VIBE

The Space Ace is a dimly lit anachronism. Victorian gas lamps illuminate walls of repurposed aluminum siding, and Shaker-style furniture patched up with Grunge-era flannel filling the lobby. Lion spends two hours at a wooden table in the bar, reading *Dune*, not exactly waving it around with the same Hudson's verve, but enough to get him noticed.

So far, no one's noticed.

Glancing right and left, he takes in long, low couches in soft grays and blues, a small crowd beyond. Apparently, some kind of historical reenactment biker convention. Everyone in sight has a beard and a Budweiser. Black leather vests with archaic gang patches. Names he recognizes only from old movies and conversations with Lorenzo about playing in bars behind chicken wire for audiences who wore these vests. And no sign of Muad'Dib.

He needs a better plan.

Lion pulls out his Moleskine and decides to try to order his objectives. First priority: locate Muad'Dib. Underlines it twice. But—chewing on his pen cap—not much he can do about that one. Muad'Dib is supposed to find him and not the other way around. And, he knows, if that's going to happen, there are only two locations that make sense: the Space Ace or the Spaceport.

The problem with the Space Ace is vibe.

Everything in sight is commoditized hipster. More poly-tribe light. The Rilkeans are legit subcult. Oil and water. Also too many ifs. If Penelope told Shiz; if Shiz told 'Dib. Plus, Penelope he no longer trusts, and, seriously, when has depending on rock stars been part of any sane plan?

A graybeard carrying Budweisers swings past his table. He eyes the color of stone and two front teeth missing. Since dental regrowth stem cell kits are available via Facebook ads, he knows this has to be a fashion choice. The patch on the back of the biker's vest another choice. REAPERS written across the top, BALTIMORE across the bottom, and dead center, a skeleton in a purple cloak, hood up, fists extended, letters tattooed on bony knuckles. GAME OVER clearly visible.

The issues with the Spaceport are equally vexing. Heavy security deters excessive loitering, so doubtful he can spend the next two days in their lobby. But when is Muad'Dib's actual flight to space? Doesn't know.

Turns out, the Space Ace has been designed with such questions in mind. There's a QR code etched into the top of his table and a little brass plaque beside it, reading SPACEPORT 411.

Using his phone to scan the code brings up an information menu. He selects "flight schedule." If Muad'Dib is on the next shuttle out . . . reading his way down the page . . . the launch is the following evening.

Which gives him less than twenty-four hours to find Lion.

But Lion seems to recall some kind of pre-flight quarantine requirement. A quick search partially confirms his suspicions: Astronauts are supposed to arrive early for their flight, but it doesn't say how early.

He takes a sip of bourbon and considers his options. He could text Penelope and pretend he knows nothing about her not flying back to

New York and ask what to do next. Or he could text Penelope and ask her why she didn't fly back to New York. Or he could text Penelope and ask her why she's such a lying . . . Think like a reporter, Zorn, not like a twelve-year-old.

A sharp crack behind him. Lion whips around, smashing his arm into the table. Impact dead center. The same spot where the buffalo horn hit. A searing pain from forearm to elbow, a low groan, and the sight of a large tan suitcase rocking on its side, having flopped off a bell-boy's luggage trolley.

"You alright, honey?" his waitress wants to know.

He's fine, thank you, though still rubbing his arm.

Another sip of bourbon, hearing Penelope's voice in his head: "Low-tech pain reliever." And then another idea: He could text Jenka and see if he could get Muad'Dib's real name. If he had that, and a peak at the Virgin Galactic flight manifest, he'd at least know if loitering at the Spaceport was worth the hassle. But not wanting to text Jenka, he realizes he could just start with the flight manifest itself—which is when the semblance of a plan starts to coalesce.

Dropping a twenty on the table for his drink, Lion stands up and walks over to the waitress. "Question," he says, after catching her attention. "When's the last flight in or out of the Spaceport?"

"A red-eye from New York that shows up," she glances at her watch, "in a couple hours. After that, they shut 'er down for the night."

"Good to know," says Lion, "thank you."

He finds the same taxi waiting for him in front of the hotel, a swirl of gasoline exhaust fumes giving it away.

"Back to the Holiday Inn, sir?" once he climbs inside.

"Lion," he says, "please call me Lion."

"Ricardo," says the driver.

"Not the Holiday Inn, Ricardo. I need to make a stop first."

SPACE JAIL

The Spaceport at night, a curved concrete shadow and a floating ring of blue lights above it—got to be the upper rim of the main terminal—surrounded by the blackness of the desert sky. The overall effect is less futuristic than anachronistic, the spaceport not as a burgeoning hub of intergalactic travel, rather as the remnants of some long-departed civilization, an advanced society rumored to have unlocked the secrets to the stars and vanished.

The taxi stops out front, and Ricardo turns to face him. "Do you want me to wait?"

At this time of night, without the apps on his phone to lean on, this taxi may be the only game in town. Or the only game that takes him back to town. Lion hedges his bet, paying for the fare and taking an extra hundred out of his wallet. Operating entirely with a playbook drawn from cinematic scenes of espionage, he tears the bill in half, passes one stub to Ricardo, and tells him he can have the rest if he's still here when Lion returns.

"Seriously, man?" Taking half the bill, "Seen too many James Bond movies?"

"Yeah," thinking it through, "that's exactly what happened."

Out of the cab and through the front doors and the main room is more crowded than expected. A small clan of Prada-clad Euro-males have colonized the food court; a large Nigerian contingent occupies a four-pack of couches just inside the glass doors. Wives in bright-colored prints, husbands in double-breasted gangster.

"Numbah six," says one of the men, beaming, "I have suffehed for you, numbah six."

Walking farther inside the terminal, he spots an ancient Indian woman in a blue spaceport jumpsuit pushing a mop, trailed by a single toddler in a hand-sewn dress, filling out a coloring book. A couple more steps and Lion starts to waver. It's been over a decade since he's dusted off this skillset, though he can still remember his editor's first pep talk on the subject: "Be a journalist, Zorn. Don't give a hoot how. Get me some goddamn confirmation."

Get me some goddamn confirmation gets him moving again. Past the Nigerians and across the lobby, then around a corner to the Virgin Galactic side of the terminal. Technically, it's his first time in the extra-terrestrial wing, though it has the same cowboy modern flavor as the terrestrial version: sweeping ceilings, stone floors, the occasional bleached-white bull skull beside photographs of space commerce luminaries.

Also, lighter security, thankfully, and probably due to the late hour.

Lion notices a scrolling screen mounted on a wall displaying astronaut requirements and processes. Walks over to take a closer look. A three-day offsite training held prior to launch teaches passengers emergency space response basics and the ins-and-outs of macro and micro gravity management. Also, all passengers must undergo a forty-eight-hour quarantine, held here at the terminal. A safety measure meant to ensure no one carries unwanted germs into space.

As if humans themselves aren't the real unwanted germs is his first thought. "Shit" is his second.

That safety measure guarantees that if Muad'Dib is on the next flight out, he's already ensconced in quarantine. A metallic taste in the back of his mouth, like molars biting foil.

"Shit," he says again.

He flashes on Shiz telling him about Muad'Dib—did he know about the quarantine? Did he lie? And what now?

Lion scrolls down the page, looking for return flights. Finds what he needs a few paragraphs later: the Bigelow Space Hotel Deluxe Package—a three-day stay. Today's Monday. Three days makes Thursday. But he's getting ahead of himself. This decision is only relevant if Muad'Dib is actually on the next flight out.

He takes a deep breath, leaves the scrolling screen and crosses over to the Virgin Galactic counter, a long black marble monolith, like a ship's prow, and piloted by a solitary captain: a silver-haired Japanese man in a handsome pin-striped suit.

"Excuse me," says Lion, aiming for a worried tone. "I think my brother is on the next flight out. If he is, I know he's already in quarantine. Would it be possible for me to leave him a note?"

"I can see by your garb," says the agent, prim, proper, solid eye contact, "you are familiar with our ways."

Lion glances down. Black jeans, black boots, and a black T-shirt. "My garb?"

"It is the prophecy," he says, nodding slowly.

"Pardon?"

"It has been written."

"Wha . . . ?"

"I am just freakin' with you, man," says the agent, suddenly grinning. "Welcome to Virgin Galactic. How can I be of assistance?"

"My brother," says Lion, deciding to start again. "Last Thursday was his fortieth birthday. Our parents bought him a ticket to space. I just want to leave him a note before he departs. Wish him a safe trip, tell him to make it back home in one piece."

"I do not like what you're implying," says the agent, suddenly serious again. "Our safety record is spotless."

"We had an argument," sighs Lion. "I drove all night from Denver. It was stupid. But he's going to space, and it's space, right—anything could happen."

"Zero accidents on the job," glaring at him. "We have made outer space as smooth as a baby's bottom."

"So anything can't happen?"

Still glaring. "As safe as Mount Rushmore."

"Okay," says Lion, not sure what to do next.

"But what am I?" says the agent, snapping his cuffs out, "a barbarian? Of course you can leave him a note."

This is not going, not in any way, like he imagined.

"He's half Moroccan," tries Lion. "I'm not sure which passport he's traveling under. Can we check two names?"

"No sweat off my buttocks," punching a few keys on his keyboard and bringing up a new screen. "What names?"

"Either Mike Dib or, if it's the other passport, Muad'Dib," spelling it out for him.

"Hmmm," says the clerk, staring at the screen, clicking a few more keys. "I had a Maude Dib."

"Maude?"

"Is your brother perhaps a woman?"

"Pardon?"

"No matter," shaking his head. "The reservation was canceled two days ago." He points toward the Nigerians on the couches. "I believe one of those gentlemen got the sixth seat."

"That can't be true," says Lion, trying to edge around the counter to see the screen for himself.

"Sir?" Pointing at the floor. "Don't step beyond the line."

Lion looks down and sees nothing.

"I don't want to have to have you arrested."

"I just want to make sure we're talking about the right person."

"You don't want to go to space jail."

"Space jail?"

"Still freakin' you," he says, another smile. "I can't have you arrested for stepping over this line. There's no line. What are we, in Singapore?"

Turning the screen toward Lion, the agent taps his finger on a line of text, highlighted in red.

"See Maude Dib, right here? Canceled. Like the prophecy told us."

"Prophecy?"

"Freakin' you," he says again.

But now able to see the screen: CANCELED, in neat block text.

"Thanks for the freakin'," says Lion, rapping two knuckles on the counter before walking away with his jaw clenched and mind reeling.

ON AN OTHERWISE LONELY NIGHT

The last shuttle must have departed.

By the time he makes it back to the terrestrial wing, the Nigerians in double-breasted gangster are gone, as are the Prada-clad Euro-males. The terminal, save for the cleaning woman and her child, is all but empty.

Nothing but the deep-space echo of his boots bouncing off the cold stone floor.

Angling toward the doors, he passes a photograph of aerospace designer Burt Rutan standing beside his creation, *SpaceShipOne,* pale hands tucked in denim pockets, his gaze focused on the white stars painted on the craft's bullet-shaped nose; then out into the night.

And that gas-powered taxicab, the one with the driver who has half a hundred-dollar bill—doesn't appear to be anywhere in sight.

Lion glances back and forth. No cabs. No cars. Just a full moon, an inky sky, and a long road disappearing into the distance. If he doesn't want to turn on his phone—and until he knows what the hell is going on, he really doesn't want to turn on his phone—should he start walking?

The Space Ace is maybe seven miles away. The Holiday Inn almost forty.

But he's awake. Strangely, wide awake. Maybe it's the juice of his admittedly low-grade scam percolating through his system; maybe it's residual ire at Penelope still with him. Either way, sleep is not coming soon and seven miles is what? Fifteen minutes a mile average walking speed. An hour and a half to the Space Ace. He does, after all, still have that reservation.

"Screw it," he says, charging off the sidewalk and onto the street before he can change his mind.

Then he changes his mind, charges back.

Yanking his tobacco out of his sling-pack, Lion tries to roll a cigarette. But his fingers are too angry. The paper tears, the tobacco spills, and he crushes both into a ball and flicks it away in disgust.

A second later, he picks up the ball and tosses it in the trash can.

Another paper, another pinch of tobacco, a second attempt. This one sticks. As he's reaching for his lighter, there's a flash of headlights in the distance. Lion peers hopefully into the darkness—as if peering hopefully into the darkness ever produced the desired results.

A yellow maintenance truck turns into the driveway, its flatbed weighed down by tall metallic bottles shaped like oversized bowling pins. N_2O printed on their sides. Nitrous oxide, used as a rocket fuel additive, remembering his one semester of chemistry, because its atomic bonds shatter easily and produce excess oxygen. Also a psychedelic, used by William James in his early experiments with consciousness. Interesting, in a way Lion doesn't entirely understand, that the same compound accelerates explorations of both inner space and outer space.

Astronauts and psychonauts, both getting high on the same supply.

"If this is some kind of sign," he whispers to the darkness, the truck, the memory of William James, but no answers coming. Instead, he takes a long drag off his cigarette and starts walking.

Does the road rise up to meet him?

Not for the first few miles. His thoughts are a rampage, obliterating the scenery. No scrub-brush shadows lining the road, no mountains like craggy witch's teeth blotting out the horizon, nothing but the voice in his head for rotten company.

Even the *Dune* mantra, not worth a damn.

Eventually, one foot in front of the other does the job. A couple of miles in and he feels his vortex begin to shift. Perception returns in waves. He realizes there's a desert around him, a sky above him, and a little more space in his head to think. What a strange week. What a strange night. He hears the Virgin Galactic agent telling him he's going to space jail, and this almost cracks him up, but what it really does is make him want to tell Penelope about it. That one smarts.

"Arctic guerrilla marketing," he says to no one in particular, "playing for keeps."

But this thought makes him reconsider Penelope's actual skillset: rock solid on the research tip, legitimate ass-kicking chops, and a perfectly executed seduction. Noncommittal flirtation sets the trap. Banter that becomes curiosity, because everyone has an ego, to bait it. Inquiry into his love life—or, really, any extra-personal question works—to accelerate rapport and spring the jaws. Right out of the playbook.

Step by goddamn step.

Plus, picking him over the rock star for a night of Get Naked on Ecstasy, 'cause that happens.

Whatever else is true, he realizes Penelope's had some training. Lion learned most of what he knows about seduction from being a journalist, but there are other options. Industrial spy, clandestine services. None good.

Jenka's assistant, alright.

But this tells him three things. First, he's way the fuck in over his head. Second, no way this is simply about launching Arctic Pharmaceuticals and a new kind of social phobia drug. Third, did he mention, way the fuck over his head.

Keep walking, he tells himself. It's late, and there are miles to go, but he feels it, the hard drop back into reality. He's been played.

Like a piano.

The darkness around him encroaches, and an icy chill in the air. It's just the moon going behind a cloud. He tells himself again, it's just the moon going behind a cloud.

Twenty seconds later, the moon resurfaces, bouncing white lunar glow off refractive black asphalt and illuminating the world. Lion finds his limbs have stopped working. Frozen. A completely involuntary re-action to what? Then it registers. Directly in front of him, less than ten feet away, a coyote, adult male, German-shepherd big.

Lion gapes: gray-brown coat still winter thick, ears up, tail down, light orange diamond patches surrounding bright orange eyes.

Staring back at him.

Goosebumps on his skin, flutter in his gut, but then his training kicks in.

"Good evening," crouching down, averting his gaze, dangling out a loose, sniff-able fist.

The coyote takes a few steps toward him. Lion stays still, keeps talking softly. He feels a warm wind blow in from the south, his heart flux inside of him. Eventually, he lifts up his gaze. Eye contact between apex predators tends to produce instant adrenaline.

Not in this case.

The coyote stands there, holding the contact, letting Lion know he knows. Two travelers sharing a lonely road on an otherwise lonely night, a little empathy among the brethren, an actual not-quite-human connection.

Not what Penelope's selling, or Richard's preaching. The real, raw deal. Perhaps it's the sensation that Sietch Tabr can surface—now there's a thought.

Lion holds the eye contact for another thirty seconds, then stands up and starts walking again. The coyote falls in beside him. Time seems to slow down. The stars shine a little brighter. And out of the corner of his eye, the glisten of fur.

They continue that way for about a half mile, primate and canid, and then, headlights over a rise in the distance.

The coyote stops, nudges Lion's thigh with his snout, and nods once. Lion nods back.

Then the animal peels off the road and into the desert, and Lion watches him melt into shadow, then darkness, then gone, thinking about what Fetu had once said, "Sit at the table long enough, pay enough attention, eventually the universe will let you peek at its cards."

"You're talking about em-tracking?" Lion had asked.

"Something like that."

In the moonlight, the headlights coalesce into a taxicab, slowing beside him, the window dropping. Ricardo, his driver, bug-eyed. "What are you doing, man? I went for gas. There's real shit out here. Chupacabras, wolves, coming for your soul."

"We can only hope," says Lion, getting into the cab.

He opens his eyes to a wedge of light through cheap Holiday Inn curtains. Too bright. And "Down by the Seaside" in cheerful synth tones.

So it's not the light from the curtains, it's the ringing of his cell, that's why he's awake.

He untangles himself from the sheets, crosses the hotel room, and grabs for the phone. "Hello?"

"I'm here a week now, waiting for a mission, getting softer."

"Lorenzo," says Lion.

"Good to hear your voice."

"Back at you."

"Where are you?"

Lion looks down at the carpet, mustard with blobs of black-light purple, like the glow from Shiz's robo-aquarium. "It's a good question."

And he tries to answer it, filling Lorenzo in on the further adventures of Lion Zorn: the trip to Spaceport America, the potential double-cross, the missing Muad'Dib, the coyote that walked him home. "Then there's Penelope . . . ," he says in conclusion.

"I told you to forget about her."

"You did," said Lion. "Didn't seem to take."

"I've been there," says Lorenzo. "Colleen. Stacy. Ambergris. Who names their daughter Ambergris anyway? Amber I get, but 'gris' is a little too Haitian voodoo stripper for me. So—any idea what you're going to do?"

"Honestly, I don't have a clue."

"You could come visit me in Kuala Lampur. It's swampy hot and you can't walk on the grass."

"The grass? Why?"

"Snakes in the grass here."

"Huh?"

"Cobras. Literally. Snakes in the grass. Possibly two snakes."

"What are you talking about?"

"Charlotte," says Lorenzo. "Turns out Charlotte's about to quit her job at American Express and is pretty pissed at her boss."

"She let you peak at Jenka's credit card records?"

"For the time he was in Malaysia, where he dropped thirty grand at a place called Allah Bling."

"Allah Bling?"

"That's what I said, but I asked around. It's Islamic hip-hop jewelry, really high end. Lots of ice. But that's all they sell. From your description of Jenka, anal retentive, uptight white-suit guy, doesn't feel like his kind of gear."

"No," says Lion, "doesn't sound like it."

"Also, guy who runs it, his crew, heavy cats. He's this gangster artist type. Master jeweler, does some kind of nano-engraving, synthetic biology something or other. Also, from what I hear, likes to shoot people."

Lion crosses over to a pale blue club chair by the window, sits down. "Did you say nano-engraving?"

"Yeah."

"You get this guy's name?"

"The jeweler, yeah, I got his name. The hard way."

"How's that?"

"I was in the store, checking shit out, when this little big Malay dude with a red silk shirt unbuttoned halfway down his chest steps right up to me, says: 'Hey man, you read the sign?'"

"The sign?" asks Lion.

"Once again, that's what I said. What he said was, 'The one that says this is Tajik Tabbara's joint, and Tajik don't commerce with fat white dudes.'"

"Tajik Tabbara?"

"You know the name?"

"Remember the silver snuff container I found, the one with Muad'Dib's name inside? The engraver: Tajik Tabbara." Thinking about it a moment. "I'd like to talk to him."

"Not if you don't want to get shot."

"Or," says Lion, thinking of Jenka dropping thirty grand on bling he won't bling, "maybe all you have to do is spend enough money on jewelry."

Lion gets out of the chair, crosses to his sling-pack on the dresser, and tugs open the zippered compartment to make sure he's got his passport. Another old journalism habit, always traveling with it, because you never know. Also, tucked behind the passport, a skinny black vial. He'd given the dragon box back to Bo, but not before tucking a joint in here in case of emergency.

"Could work," says Lorenzo, "if you happen to have a spare thirty large."

Lion glances at the joint. Not yet an emergency. He glances at his wallet. About five hundred dollars left. But then he notices Arctic's Amex card.

"How many more days you staying in Kuala Lumpur?" he asks Lorenzo.

"Another week."

Lion brings up a travel site on his phone, checks a couple of things. "The night after tomorrow," he says.

"Uh-huh."

"Assume your dance card is full."

"What are you thinking?"

"I'm thinking the little big Malay dude was pretty judgmental. Did you tell him it was baby fat and you'd grow out of it?"

GOT TO SEE A MAN ABOUT
SOME BABY FAT

The bank, the one with the human tellers, is about five blocks down the road from the Holiday Inn. He gets there a few minutes before 9:00 A.M. While waiting for the manager to unlock the doors, Lion notices a shop selling pre-paid phones across the street. The shop solves his second problem. Actually, now that he's thinking about it, he should solve his second problem first.

He crosses the street, buys a pre-paid phone, and carries it out of the store and onto the sidewalk. Pulling out his own cell, he hunts through his texts until he finds one from Sir Richard. Reads off the phone number, punches it into the burner cell, and hears it start to ring.

"Yes?" says Richard.

"Shit," says Lion; the last thing he'd been expecting was the billionaire to answer.

"Pardon?"

"Richard, it's Lion."

A pause. "Where are you? Jenka says you vanished on him, Penelope too."

"Penelope?"

"We haven't heard from her in days."

"I don't know where she is. The last time I saw her was in San Francisco. She said she was heading back to New York."

"She's not in New York." Then he does that subject-shift thing again. "Did you meet Shiz? Where are you now?"

Lion glances at his phone, wondering how long it would take Richard to trace the call, wondering if Richard even has that capability. Decides he doesn't know, so decides to almost tell the truth.

"Met Shiz, in New Mexico, chasing a lead."

"Have you found Muad'Dib?"

"No," hesitates, "but I found a clue. I may need to take a little cash advance on the Arctic credit card to explore it further."

"You can't just use the card?"

"It's not that kind of transaction."

Silence on the line. "Where in New Mexico?"

Lion looks around, sees a sign that says WELCOME TO TRUTH OR CONSEQUENCES, hanging across Main Street. "I'm in Albuquerque, but I'm about to split and will be out of cell range for a few more days. I should be back in New York before the weekend, Monday latest. I can tell you about it in person."

"I'd rather you tell me about it right now."

"I'm sure you would," trying to think on his feet, "but I've got to see a man about some baby fat."

Not exactly what he had in mind.

"Baby fat?"

"I'll explain everything when I see you," he says. "Can you authorize that cash advance."

"Authorized."

"Thanks. Gotta go. Bye."

Lion hangs up, takes the battery out of the burner, throws the parts in separate trash cans, and walks into the bank.

A short line.

He stares at photos on the wall of Truth or Consequences from by-gone eras. Wide streets, a skinny church made from white adobe, pinion trees taller than houses. Then it's his turn. The teller informs him that the cash advance limit on the Amex is enough to purchase a small island nation. But he can't exactly fly into Malaysia with fifty large. Settles on nine thousand dollars, just under what he's legally required to report upon entering most countries.

After leaving the bank, Lion recrosses the street and buys another burner phone. He dials a number he knows by heart.

"Hello?"

"Lorenzo, it's me."

"What's with the new number?"

"I'm trying to stay off familiar channels."

"You just talked to me on a familiar channel."

"I wasn't thinking. Question, is Charlotte still around?"

"In Malaysia, yeah."

"She hasn't quit her job yet, has she?"

"Left Amex? No, she's waiting until after she gets her year-end bonus."

"Great," says Lion, "I need another favor, actually two." Thinking about it a little more, "Maybe four."

And then he fills Lorenzo in on what he wants, hangs up, and for the second time in thirty minutes breaks a phone apart and deposits the pieces in separate trash cans. It takes another ten minutes to hike back to the hotel, five more to repack and head down to the front desk to check out. Afterward, Lion asks the clerk if he can call him a cab.

"You're a cab."

"Funny."

While he waits out front, Lion digs the joint out of his sling-pack. He's got almost twenty-four hours of nonstop air travel in front of him. Clicks his lighter.

Sounds like an emergency to him.

LOOKING FOR THE SHIT

Lion's first impression of Kuala Lumpur is traffic. By the airport, on the freeway, in the city. And now, an accident blocking the lane where they're supposed to turn for the hotel. Looks like a Proton Saga executing a guillotine choke on a Honda Jazz, and two Malaysian men spitting insults at each other across crumpled hoods. His driver, an elderly Indian in a black linen Nehru, has been furnishing a running translation.

"Belacan, valiangkati," he says, "Tricky in English. It means 'shrimp paste who stands and watches while others work.'"

"Shrimp paste?"

"Maratel ooki," he says, ignoring Lion's question. "Easy one. Tree fucker."

"People do that here?"

"Ju tou mo lo—brainless pig head."

It takes ten minutes to edge around the accident. His driver stays on Jalan Sultan Ismail for a few more blocks, then takes a left onto

Jalan Raja something, and a right into a short maze of impossibly narrow side streets, the names of which go by too quickly for Lion to catch. He sees laundry strung up on makeshift clotheslines between neighboring apartment complexes that look one Richter hiccup away from total collapse. One thing for sure, between the chaos of the city and the relentless jet lag, he's glad he asked Lorenzo for favor number one: Find him a driver in Kuala Lumpur who is discreet, takes cash, and will pick him up at the airport.

The second favor involved finding him a hotel, one where he wouldn't have to officially check in. Passport control will still have him landing in Kuala Lumpur—who knows if Jenka can drum up that bit of information—but it's a big city, easy to get lost in, and if he's not officially registered at a hotel, his ruse might be enough to keep him off Arctic's radar.

The driver screeches to a halt in front of a twelve-story gray building, its main entranceway up a short flight of concrete steps and beneath a curved awning made from bamboo. The Kuala Lumpur Journal, a boutique hotel, adjacent to a throng of kebab kiosks lining a small park. It's the same hotel Lorenzo's been staying at. With Hank's connection to the owner, wasn't a problem getting him a reservation under the band's name.

The lobby is eclectic art deco: blue cloth chairs surrounding low tables made of wood, brightly colored plastic radios tucked into little nooks, a shiny black marble floor. To his right, a white neon sign reads EAT WELL, TRAVEL OFTEN. To his left, a long black wall decorated with eighteen miniature barber poles, their stripes rotating beneath silver end caps and looking more like tired lava lamps than anything advertising a haircut.

The third favor, the desk clerk informs him, is waiting for him when he checks in. Thank you, Charlotte. It's an oversized bank envelope containing thirty thousand dollars, a sum advanced to him on the Arctic Amex, delivered to the hotel by messenger, and hopefully large enough to bribe Tajik Tabbara. Lion can't be certain. The only thing he knows about Malaysian gangsters was gleaned from the appropriately named *KL Gangster,* which he watched on the flight over. Shirtless men, oiled up and wielding long knives. Also how he learned that the oil isn't just decorative. It makes the combatant harder to grab, a street-fighting tactic disguised as a cheap cinematic effect—though, usually, it's the other way round.

The desk clerk points him toward the elevators, but he mishears the directions and finds himself dragging his carry-on up an iron spiral staircase, painted orange, and clunking with every step. He tops out one floor up, at the Shack, a rooftop beer garden, now closed. Bright yellow chairs stacked atop distressed wooden tables. Apparently also where the band has been playing, because Lion sees a makeshift stage in a far corner.

A wave of fatigue when he realizes his mistake. T minus one minute. Back down the stairs and across the lobby to the elevators, and by the time he makes it to his room, sheep are counting him.

No time for the fast unpack.

Blurry visuals as he heads for the bed. Pale bamboo paneling on the walls, floor and desk. Covering nearly an entire wall, an enormous black-and-white photograph of dark men in white tunics crossing a city street. And the bed itself, thankfully, which executes a guillotine choke of its own the second he touches down.

Hours later, he tries to get up. Hours and hours later, he actually succeeds.

With a little help. A pounding on his door yanks him out of his slumber, snarling, "What the fuck," upon opening it.

"First of the Ninth was an old cavalry division that had cashed in their horses for choppers and gone tear-assing around 'Nam looking for the shit."

Lorenzo. Brown Carhartt work pants, brown cowboy shirt, brown cowboy boots, smiling.

"Good to see you, man," says Lion, stepping out into the hallway to wrap him up in a bear hug.

"Get dressed," says Lorenzo midsqueeze. "I've got to play a gig in like two hours. If you hurry, we can get stinking drunk first."

Lion looks down. He has no memory of undressing before he got into bed. But he does, now that he takes in the view, appear to be standing in the hotel's hallway wearing nothing but his underwear.

"Jesus," he says, "I think I need to be conscious before I can get unconscious."

"That flight doesn't fuck around."

"No," stepping back into the room to slide into jeans and a T-shirt, "it does not."

"Not to worry," says Lorenzo, reaching into the long pocket of his work pants, coming back with a vial of this, a vial of that, a couple of joints, a pile of reds, blues, and something that looks like Mickey Mouse cryopreserved in Jell-O. "I've got supplies."

"Shut the damn door," says Lion. "Are you insane? Isn't all of that a capital crime in this country? I heard the pilot announce that upon landing. On the plane, man, on the damn plane, they warned us that you get killed for that shit over here."

"They did," says Lorenzo. "Standard practice. But, seriously, when in history did fear of death ever come between a man and his drugs?"

"Fair point," says Lion, plucking a joint from Lorenzo's hand, shoving it between his lips, and looking around for his lighter.

"Jesus, man, not in here. Are you fucking insane? Don't you know what happens to druggies in Malaysia?"

orenzo leads him down the hallway to the elevators. Fast drop to the ground floor. On the way through the lobby, Lion sees a series of wrought-iron railway trellises hanging from the ceiling, three in a row beside the check-in counter. He didn't notice them before. And back up the orange spiral staircase to the rooftop beer garden.

Emerging into the open air, Lion feels a wave of Asian city noise wash over him. It's different from American city noise, though he couldn't say how exactly.

The bar is bustling. A multinational array of coeds drinking cans of Tiger beer and smoking Mild Seven cigarettes interspersed with cocktail waitresses wearing early Pan Am stewardess costumes in their distinctive baby blue, though updated with some kind of liquid metal woven through the fabric. Also, those little round hats.

They make it through the crowd and around the side of the stage, to a cordoned-off area, hidden behind a square of white curtains. "They built us a greenroom," says Lorenzo, pushing through a break in the drapes. "It's probably the safest spot in town to light that joint."

Lion follows Lorenzo through. He'd been hoping for a quiet place to talk shop and smoke up, a toehold in the firmament from which he could reel in the part of his soul that doesn't understand transatlantic travel and maybe sort through his feelings about Penelope. What he gets is the entire band, Hank Mudd and the K-Holes, splayed out on couches and chairs. Sherlock and Scheherazade, the brother-and-sister duo responsible for rhythm guitar and keyboards respectively, sitting with their backs to him on a red leather deco couch, talking to Luke on horns and Kevin on drums, both in matching red leather armchairs. Luke doesn't notice their arrival, but Kevin, skinny and dark-skinned, in a fedora and an old hobo suit, tips his hat to Lion.

"Evening, Kevin," he calls.

Everyone turns to look at him.

Hank, lead guitarist and vocals, his red hair combed into a rocka-billy pompadour and wearing blue jeans, a studded belt, and a skin-tight black motorcycle jacket, actually a scooter jacket, as Lion sees a Vespa patch over his right breast, walks over and gives him a hug. Surprising too, as Hank and Lion have not always seen eye-to-eye. Actually, rarely have they seen eye-to-anything. Hank's a bow hunter, of the persuasion that killing animals is just fine if it takes skill. "You fucking sadist" is how Lion typically counters. But, hopefully, not tonight. So he returns the hug.

"Haven't seen you since?" says Hank, as they pull apart.

"Alabama," says Lion.

"No, Venice," says Lorenzo.

"When did we play Italy?" asks Sherlock.

"California," says Lorenzo, "Dog-Town. Gig on the pier. Remember the pink-haired Japanese girl?"

"Yeah, yeah, yeah," says Sherlock.

"Yeah, yeah, you stared at her so much you got two bars behind on 'Stormy Monday,'" scowls Hank. "It was fuckin' Wednesday by the time you caught up."

"Bygones be bygones," says Lorenzo, walking over to the parapet, gazing at the nighttime traffic. He clicks his Zippo. A crackle as he lights the joint. Passes it to Lion. Beers follow. A couple of women follow the beers.

Hank is chatting up a Vietnamese runway model. Sherlock talks to a new species of poly-tribe: rainbow leather bodice, tartan bondage pants, ghost-white goth makeup, Shiz-style red dread-hawk, and hundreds of miniature stars shaved into the side of her head, each with a tiny gem gleaming back from its center. Implants? Glued on? Hard to tell.

And so goes the evening, at least for a while.

Before things get too hazy on account of the jet lag, the shots of tequila Lorenzo made them do together, and the couple of beers Lion drank on his own, he decides to drill down into the details of Operation Tajik Tabbara.

"How far away is Allah Bling?"

"The store's sort of tucked back behind Merdeka Square," explains Lorenzo, "near the Bird Park. You've got to check out the park. Two words, 'rhinoceros hornbill,' like the bird walked right out of a DMT trip."

"What time do they open?"

"The bird park? Ten A.M., I think, maybe earlier."

"Not the park. Allah Bling."

"Noon," says Lorenzo, "but I did a little recon. Malaysian gangsters like to sleep in. Sometimes things don't get going until one."

"I can sleep in too."

"Sleep as long as you want. Tajik's a night owl. Usually his crew opens up for him. If you want to find Tajik at the shop, he doesn't show up until four. If we get out of here by two, we can check out the birds and still get there before he arrives."

"Didn't you get tossed out the last time you visited that store?"

Shoulders back, spine straight, chest out: "I am Lorenzo Boldacci, son of Alessandro and Margarette Boldacci, and I will not be fat-shamed by little big thugs in red satin. Nor will I truck with an argument, Lion Zorn, I'm coming."

"Figured, but don't blame me if you get shot."

Lorenzo shakes loose a couple of Marlboro Reds from a soft pack, passes one over, keeps the second. Zippo click and flick.

"How you doing otherwise?" After their smokes are lit.

"You know."

"The girl's still on your mind."

"Oh no, she's definitely a woman. But yeah, a little on my mind. Also, other things."

"Like?"

"Like Arctic told me they wanted a meeting with Muad'Dib to discuss turning Sietch Tabr into an autism drug. But the shit that's gone down—seems too surreal for a Big Pharma play."

"Better living through chemistry, Kemosabe. Big Pharma's pretty surreal."

"Maybe you're right."

"Maybe I'm not. Say you're right. Say this is about something bigger than an autism drug. Bigger how? If you had access to a drug that expands empathy—what would you do with it?"

Lion nods toward Hank. "I'd be tempted to put it in the water supply."

"Agreed," says Lorenzo, a shadow passing across his face, "but from what you said, Arctic's all about the money. Where's the money in dumping an empathy drug into the water supply?"

"Don't know," taking a drag on his cigarette.

"Maybe it's the wrong question. Maybe it's not the before, it's the after. Putting Sietch Tabr in the water supply would seriously shift culture, so where's the money in that shift?"

"I hadn't thought of that."

"And?"

"And that pisses me off," says Lion. "You'd think, being an em-tracker, predicting future revenue streams is sort of my thing."

"But there's a woman on your mind."

Lion sighs in agreement.

"Gentlemen," Lorenzo calls to the rest of the band, "we're gonna open with the heartbreak set. Our friend requires the medicine."

Nods all around, except from Hank, who has had a couple of drinks, which makes him mean, which means he's got something to say: "Em-tracking, isn't that like perpetual heartbreak?"

"Shut it, Hank," snaps Lorenzo, not wanting the same argument.

Lion appreciates the gesture, but he knows Hank's prejudice is an ancient one, human superiority, dominion over the beasts, and so fundamentally deep in our thinking that rarely do we notice.

He crushes his cigarette into an ashtray.

Small favors: Hank lets it go, and the band heads toward the stage. Lion moves from standing in the greenroom to sitting in the beer garden. They kick off with a country-punk version of Joy Division's "Love Will Tear Us Apart" into a couple of twangy Social Distortion numbers, "99 to Life" and "Ball and Chain," and then one of his favorites, "Goddamn Lonely Love" by the Drive-By Truckers. A sentiment, reaching for his third beer, he currently appreciates.

Snatching his glass a little too quickly, Lion sloshes liquid onto the table. The spill is heading for his lap. As he grabs for a napkin, something by the spiral staircase grabs for his attention. An attractive woman? A bit of waitress commotion? Then it snaps into focus: a little big guy in a red satin shirt, staring at him while talking on his cell.

Lion starts to get to his feet, but the man notices him move, hangs up the phone, and heads down the stairs before he's vertical.

"What the hell?" asking the air, beer dripping onto his pants.

Easy, Zorn. Got to be a ton of guys in Malaysia with red satin shirts. He wipes up the beer, but the paranoia doesn't clean so easily.

No longer does he feel safe in the crowd.

Threading his way back through the tables, Lion trades the exposure of the beer garden for the enclosure of the greenroom, now empty save for the poly-tribe woman with the glittering stars.

"You're Lion," she says, giving him a quick wave as he enters. "I'm Changchang."

Chinese, his first guess, under all the makeup. "Nice to meet you."

"I heard what Hank said, you're an em-tracker?"

"Uh-huh."

"Never met one before." Toying with a vape-pen shaped like a nuclear submarine. "What's it like?"

Once again, he doesn't know how to answer, tries: "You ever met a cow?"

"No," she says, giving him a weird look, like meeting an em-tracker is not exactly like what she thought it would be.

"You should," says Lion. "Pretty amazing animals. They form life-long friendships, hold grudges against anyone who treats them badly, cry tears, just like us, when they mourn their dead or are separated from loved ones. And they're about as smart as a five-year-old human."

"No way-way."

"Way-way," he says, but not smiling. "When I walk through your world," gesturing around the room, "you're wearing a leather bodice, those are red leather couches, and my best friend Lorenzo," nodding toward the band, "is wearing leather cowboy boots. You see style. I see what you see, but I also feel what a cow feels, the sadness, the cruelty, there isn't exactly a word for it."

She takes a big hit off the nuclear sub, exhales a mushroom cloud. "That sounds, 'xing ten' is the word in Chinese."

"Xing ten?"

"It's the heartache that comes from watching those you love in terrible pain."

Sipping his beer, "That sounds about right."

Down in the park, the vendors are packing it in for the night, feeding leftovers to a pack of street dogs who have assembled for the ritual.

"The harder part is knowing where it leads," he explains.

She raises an eyebrow.

"Cows are emblematic. We're in the middle of the Sixth Great Extinction. Species die-off rates a thousand times greater than normal. All this human superiority, where has it led? We've fractured the web of life. Ecosystem services are shutting down. Scientists tell us we've got about two generations left before the slide becomes irreversible."

"That's some seriously dark shit."

"Moo," says Lion, suddenly too sad and too drunk to do anything but head straight for bed.

THE BIGGEST NOTHING
IN HISTORY

Awakened by the hotel phone, Lion discovers his hangover is not nearly as bad as he'd imagined it would be. Then the phone rings a second time and he changes his mind. Like someone wrapped thunderclouds around his forehead. It takes until the third ring before he actually locates the receiver.

"Uh-huh?"

It's the front desk telling him a package has arrived. The fourth favor, the last one he needed from Lorenzo, and right on schedule. Call Masta Ice and ask Balthazar Jones to overnight the snuff container he'd originally found under Walker's desk to his hotel in Malaysia.

"Sir?"

He glances at the clock, tells the clerk he'll be down in an hour, and goes back to sleep. Three hours later, he actually manages to make it to the front desk. While the clerk retrieves his package from the back room, he texts Lorenzo, telling him he's down in the lobby.

"Here you are, sir," says the clerk, passing over a small black box, MASTA ICE printed on the side.

Lion takes the box, thanks the clerk, and walks over to an armchair. He opens the package, lifts out the snuff container, and deposits it in his sling-pack. There's a short note beneath: *Brother, I know you asked me to be discreet, but Arctic throws me a lot of work. Jenka called. I had to tell him about Tajik Tabbara. Thought you should know.*

"Crap."

He tries to figure out how much that matters, but before he can decide, Lorenzo, in a cowboy hat, jeans, and dusty shit-kickers, and Changchang, now free of pancake makeup, saunter into the lobby.

"You are fighting for the biggest nothing in history," says Lorenzo, passing him a cup of coffee.

"Talking about Arctic?"

"*Apocalypse Now.*"

"Same thing," taking the coffee.

"Hiya, Lion," says Changchang, then, swatting Lorenzo's butt, "See ya, tiger," and then across the lobby and out the front door.

Lion looks at Lorenzo, says nothing. Lorenzo looks at Lion, says nothing back. Both sip their coffees.

"Bird Park?" asks Lorenzo, after a while. "Rhinoceros hornbill?"

"I have no idea what those words mean."

"But you will," starting toward the front doors. "Mind a walk? We can grab some grub along the way."

Lion falls in beside him. "Sweat off my hangover, puke up some Malaysian street food, why not?"

"You forgot meet a gangster."

"I think we already met." Lion fills him in on the red satin shirt from the night before.

"So what," asks Lorenzo, "he tracked me back to the hotel after he threw me out of Allah Bling?"

"Dunno. When I saw him, he was staring at me."

"Nobody knows you're here."

"Yeah," says Lion, "and the way I heard it, it was a lone gunman."

From a vendor outside the hotel, Lorenzo buys a couple of falafels.

They eat and stroll. A main thoroughfare, suburban colonial with a sprinkle of Miami Beach, gives way to a warren of side streets dotted with soot-stained high-rises. A couple more blocks and the side streets open up again, becoming a red-bricked sidewalk surrounding a Moorish castle like a moat. Intricate archways, a trilogy of domed spires, turrets in beige brick. Lorenzo says something about the sultan who once owned the castle, but Lion is only half-listening. The other half is wondering about why Jenka called Masta Ice and worrying about why Penelope vanished.

Too many maybes in the mix.

"You armed?" he asks, interrupting Lorenzo's monologue.

"You ain't digging the sultan story?"

"Are you?"

"I've got my dad's Ka-Bar tucked in my boot. No idea what to do with it, but a crazy fat white dude in a cowboy hat with a knife, if they've seen enough Westerns . . ." Shrugs.

They pass a sun-cracked tennis court and a weedy soccer pitch, both empty and surrounded by tall wire fences. A few blocks later and the fences become tall and wooden. They reach the edge of the KL Bird Park. Lorenzo pays their admission in local currency. Lion sees over-sized bills in cartoon colors.

And through the main gate.

Looking around, Lion's caught off guard by the size of the park, like someone planted a rainforest in the center of a city, though, of course, it was the other way round.

"This place is huge," he says.

"Eighty acres, like two hundred species of birds."

As if on cue, a pair of peacocks walks past them, while a half dozen parakeets ruckus it up in a nearby tree. Above everything, a thin mesh netting.

They walk in silence, a gray asphalt path threading between tall trees, until Lion hears a noise above him and double-takes. A large black bird, a long white beak, zebra-striped tail feathers, and, atop its head and nearly as large, a curved orange horn.

"What," pointing, "is that?"

Lorenzo tracks Lion's finger to an overhead branch. "The reason we came."

"A rhinoceros hornbill? I get the name now."

"The casque," says Lorenzo, gesturing to the horn. "It's prehistoric. Hornbills descend from hadrosaurids."

"That's a lineage nearly sixty million years old."

"If you say so."

Lion sips his coffee and stares at the hornbill.

"I can tell you," adds Lorenzo, "the bird is red-listed. Without parks like this, it'd be gone in a generation."

"Are you trying to make me feel better?"

"Yeah, Changchang told me you kind of landed on her. Something about cows and not liking my boots."

"I guess I did."

"But I heard you, back when you mentioned my boots the first time, that show in Venice."

"Yeah?"

"These are new boots. Lab-grown leather."

"They look like your old boots."

"Because I tied 'em to my truck and dragged them up gravel roads for a few miles."

"You're so punk rock."

"Stuck in my ways."

Then the hornbill flies out of the tree and lands by Lion's feet. He glances up at him, with a look like they've met before, and he's a little miffed that Lion doesn't remember.

White eyes, dark pupils, and holding his gaze.

ALLAH BLING

The front entrance to Allah Bling in the distance: an ornate Moroccan door beneath a curved white awning. It's tucked down a side street, beside a bank and a former government building that's since been partitioned into an open-air café and a high-end electronics store. As they pass the store, Lion notices a tall stack of Sega Genesis Classics beside crates of lychees. Rugged red skin, hiding flesh white and sweet. Reminds him of the fruit-and-video-game-console display he saw in New York. Those Xbox 360s and Asian pears piled up near the corner of Houston and something. Could this be some new poly-tribe thing? A first ripple showing up as nothing more than an odd pairing of wares?

A couple of bangers on mopeds drives slowly past them, bandanas across their foreheads, leather jackets. They park their bikes by the curb. One heads down the block, another into Allah Bling.

Lion points at the store, "Looks like they're open for business."

"Open for something," says Lorenzo, but he's not smiling.

They approach the edge of the awning slowly, feeling not exactly comfortable with their decision. A few feet from the front entrance, Lion decides to restate the obvious. "I'm not sure this beach is safe to surf."

"I'm sure," says Lorenzo. "It's definitely not safe to surf."

"You could wait here."

"I could," says Lorenzo, stepping past him, under the awning and into the shop.

Lion shakes his head and follows.

Two steps inside and the Nag Champa hits high in the nostrils and musky sweet. Persian carpets, tribal shields, and dim lighting. A long glass counter displays bejeweled chains; a tall glass bookcase holds shiny watches. Across the back wall, Lion recognizes the name of God spelled out in Arabic script—gold letters packed with gems—and behind it, spray-painted on the wall itself, a balaclava-wearing, Kalashnikov-toting "freedom fighter," with an iced-out Rilkean bar code tattoo clearly visible.

"Doesn't make sense," he tells Lorenzo, his voice barely a whisper.

"What doesn't?"

"The Rilkeans aren't violent," says Lion, pointing at the mural, "or Islamic—"

But before he can finish that thought, a wiry Middle Eastern man in his early thirties struts out of the back room. Pencil-thin mustache, white wraparound sunglasses, white old-school Puma tracksuit, and something herky-jerky in his demeanor.

"That's him," whispers Lorenzo.

Lion takes a step toward the counter. "Tajik?"

"Yo, yo," says the man, spreading his arms out wide, his pupils pin-balling. "What is the up, sex-ee. Gonna slay all the Lisa in da hizzy with da Allah Bling."

Beside him, Lorenzo mutters something, maybe "Gotta be fucking kidding me."

"Yo," says Lion, deciding to play along. "You may not remember. I'm Kevin Clark. Your brother introduced us, in Dubai."

"My brother?" says Tajik, jab-stepping toward them, his mustache twitching, something speedy in his eyes. "Got beef?"

Lion takes a step back.

"Guy's gakked to the gills," whispers Lorenzo.

Tajik pounds a fist on the counter. "Wanna get smashed?"

Angel dust? Injectable crystal? Not good, thinks Lion, not good at all.

"No beef," he says.

"What you think, bro? Think you VIP? Gonna be RIP." A mad grin displays a neat row of teeth filed canine sharp, diamond studs embedded in the front pair. "Bro, 'course you're VIP. Welcome to Allah Bling. How you know my bro?"

"You're Tajik Tabbara?" says Lion, still attempting casual. "Your brother is Nassir?"

As he's speaking, Lion notices movement behind him. Risks a quick glance. And does not like what he sees.

While he was focused on Tajik, the moped riding banger and the guy from the hotel bar, the little big dude with the red satin shirt, must have slipped into the room and taken up flanking positions in the back corners of the store.

"My brother is Nassir," says Tajik, dropping out of MTV gangster and into something colder and less cinematic. "And I'm Tajik." His hand darts under the counter and comes back out with a gun. "But you're not Kevin Clark."

To his left, there's a glint of chrome. Red satin shirt producing a combat shotgun, and pointing it directly at them.

"What you are," says Tajik, "Lion Zorn, is F-U-C to the T. Fuct. Do you know that expression. From the 1990s. Fuct."

"I like your plan," says Lorenzo. "I think it has tremendous potential."

"All we're looking for is information," says Lion, holding up his hands, trying for reasonable.

Tajik starts to laugh, not really a human sound. "But that's not what Jenka's looking for."

Lion blinks.

Tajik sets his gun on the counter and removes a small glass vial from his left pants pocket. "You know," he says, "my Malay brothers," nodding toward the red satin shirt, unscrewing the top of the vial and lifting free an eyedropper, "don't always appreciate the Chinese. I disagree on that point. I'll tell you why. Research. Great learning culture. Gangsters, too often, get hung up on tradition. Not the Chinese. The Tong, they have a market research division. A combat science arm. Know what they learned?"

A drop of translucent blue liquid in each eye.

"To anyone with a lick of street sense," continues Tajik, "nothing, nothing is more nerve-wracking, attention-grabbing than a meth head." The flutter in his eyes vanishes; his pupils return to normal. "Artificially induced nystagmus with one drop, complete remission with two. Did you catch the mustache twitch? I'm very proud of that. Took me six months to perfect. And, in exchange," tapping a finger against the vial, "the Tong paid for my lab."

"Jenka is Tong?" asks Lion, incredulous.

"No," says Tajik, picking his gun back up and shoving it into Lion's left eye, "he just pays well."

A starburst of black fills his vision, followed by a crack of pain. Deep in his skull. He tries to back up, but something's in his way. Squinting with his good eye, he sees an array of platinum chains in a squat glass case directly behind him, blocking his retreat. He's managed to wedge himself tight.

"Kamal," says Tajik, "do the honors."

Red satin shirt crosses over to Lion and yanks his sling-pack off his shoulder, undoes the buckles and dumps its contents onto the counter. Moleskine, *Dune*, snuff container. A harder shake knocks free the bank envelope with its thirty grand and sends strands of tobacco everywhere.

"Jenka messed up," continues Tajik, absently brushing tobacco from his tracksuit with one hand, pressing the gun harder into Lion's eye socket with the other. "In your first meeting. Told you he'd come from KL. He knew, sooner or later, you'd find me and put it together."

"So you've been waiting for me?" says Lion, hearing the unsteadiness in his voice.

"Jenka asked us to keep an eye out," cackles Tajik, shoving the gun into his socket even harder. "What he didn't know, not until recently, is that you've been carrying around what he wanted all along."

Lion spins his head sideways, dislodging the barrel, feeling the pain dial down a notch. Tajik makes a sucking sound with his teeth, then casually sets the gun on the counter and picks up the snuff container. "Haven't seen this in like seven years."

The pain in his skull recedes, but his cornea still burns and tears are blurring his vision. Through the haze, Lion semi-watches Tajik carry the snuff container over to a small workbench. He grabs a jeweler's magnifying glass attached to an accordion arm.

Pulling the magnifying glass toward him, Tajik clicks on a ring light before closing his hand around the container. Pale amber glow illuminating slender silver cylinder. A second later, opening his hand, the container pulses again, revealing an engraving on the cylinder's exterior—not one Lion's ever seen before.

Chemistry notations, a formula of some kind, and not winking out.

"Sietch Tabr," says Tajik, flashing teeth.

It takes Lion a moment, but then he gets it: "The formula?"

"The formula."

"It's been there all along?"

"Not all along," says Tajik. "I did the engraving on the inside, the signature, and put the electric potential sensors in the cap. This," pointing at the chemistry notations, "was added much later."

"Sensors?" asks Lorenzo, taking a quiet step forward. "Reading what?"

"Brainwaves," says Tajik. "EEG at a distance. It's keyed on suppressed mu waves."

"Suppressed what?" asks Lorenzo, another quiet step.

"It's one of the signatures of empathy," says Lion, maybe a little too quickly, trying to distract attention from Lorenzo. "When your mirror neurons fire, mu waves are suppressed." He looks back at Tajik. "So that's another thing Sietch Tabr does—it alters mirror-neuron firing patterns?"

"Not right away, but repeated use does. When anyone who has tried the drug a number of times holds the cylinder, the sensors activate and it brings up the formula."

"So that's a prototype?" asks Lorenzo, another casual step forward.

"He moves again," says Tajik, talking to Kamal, pointing to Lorenzo, "shoot him in the knees."

"Who added the engraving on the outside?" asks Lion, definitely a little too quickly.

Tajik ignores his question, tossing the snuff container to the moped rider. "Get this to the courier."

In one seamless motion, the rider plucks the cylinder out of the air, drops it into his messenger bag, and heads out the door.

"And yes," says Tajik, "it's a prototype."

"So what's this really about?" asks Lion. "Corporate espionage? Industrial sabotage? Clearly, the autism drug line Jenka fed me is bullshit."

"You really don't know?" says Tajik, baring pointy teeth.

Lion really doesn't.

"Patents," says Tajik. "Patents first, revolution second."

"I don't get it. Why are you working with Jenka? With Arctic? I thought you were a Rilkean."

"Turns out being a Rilkean is not quite as profitable as being an ex-Rilkean." Then Tajik says something else, sounds a little like "punk-ass Luther," but before the words are out of his mouth, the front door of the shop bangs open. Followed by the piercing whine of hinges under high strain. Lion spins and sees a storm of red hair blowing in—wearing a familiar army jacket.

"Tajik!" shouts Penelope. "You jobby-flavored fart lozenge."

Tajik drops the snuff container and reaches for his gun. Penelope doesn't pause. She keeps marching toward the counter, her left hand grabbing the bottom of her T-shirt, yanking it upward. Black lace bra catches everyone's attention.

Also why Kamal never saw the Taser in her other hand.

She fires. Her aim is true. Next second, Kamal does the drop-and-twitch. The shotgun skittering across the floor. Second after that, Tajik gets treated to a variation of the same move Penelope used on Shiva.

Or was it Kali?

Either way, before he can react, Penelope snaps out her fist, catching Tajik in the throat with one hand, then jumping over the counter and twisting the gun out of his hand with the other.

Does not quite go as planned.

Tajik drops the gun, but as he does, there's a tremendous bang. Misfire. And the sight of God's name exploding, launching a shrapnel of gemstones in every direction. Before Lion can duck, he takes a diamond to his forehead. His head snaps back and he can feel his flesh rip. Penelope shouts something, but his ears are ringing so he can't hear the words.

Sees Lorenzo pointing at the door, sees Penelope shouting again.

Then the adrenaline hits full force, snapping him into action. Lion grabs his sling-pack with one hand, sweeps its contents off the counter and into the bag with the other. He spins away and tries to take a step toward the door, but before he can execute, a freight train barrels through his liver. Lorenzo has wrapped him up in his arms and is now bull-rushing him through the door. His wrist smacks something on the way out and the dead buffalo cut springs to life. Bleeding again, but not his major concern. It's the blood pouring out of the cut on his brow that's the bigger issue. Seeping into his eyes, blurring his vision.

"Run," shouts Lorenzo, as soon as they're outside.

He does as told.

Hazy images of café denizens staring at them as they sprint past the electronics store and down the block. Lorenzo thundering beside him. Then around the corner and down another side street. For a moment, Lion thinks he sees Penelope running with him.

Does she wink? Maybe she winks.

A few more blocks at a fast pace before Lorenzo starts coughing and slows to a halt. Lion pulls up beside him, panting hard. It takes a few seconds to catch his breath, then he uses the bottom of his T-shirt to wipe his eyes. When Lion can see again he realizes they've run back to the edge of the Bird Park. Penelope is gone. Lorenzo looks like he's about to puke. No one seems to be chasing them.

"Fuck me," he says, taking tobacco out of sling-pack, attempting to roll a cigarette. Not working properly. His hands are shaking. Lion walks over to the wooden fence and leans up against it to calm down.

"That was—"

But a noise like a homesick foghorn drowns out his words.

Coming from above.

He looks up.

Sitting just beneath the mesh netting that encloses the Bird Park, perched high on a tree branch: a rhinoceros hornbill, white eyes, dark pupils, and definitely holding his gaze.

BE WATER, MY FRIEND

Lorenzo buys a chilled can of soursop soda from a street vendor, which Lion presses against his eye as they walk. The end result is vision more distorted than before. Also, the can appears to be decorated with a cheerful Triceratops wearing a tutu, a tiara, and a bra stuffed with leaves. Dino-drag, Lion recalls, started as a Japanese fetish, exported as a crossover anime, and really weird in close-up.

A block later a mirror hanging in a furniture showroom confirms his suspicions: cornea scratched, a lightning bolt of red amid a sea of white. Also a gash on his brow, not very deep, but face wounds tend to bleed a lot—which explains the looks he's been getting from strangers.

Above them, the late afternoon monsoon is moving in, darkening the sky to the color of an amethyst bruise. They're about six blocks east of the Bird Park, approaching the red-bricked sidewalk surrounding the sultan's castle, trying to piece together whatever it was that just happened.

"I thought Penelope worked for Arctic?" asks Lorenzo.

"Uh-huh," says Lion.

"And Jenka works for Arctic?"

"Uh-huh."

"And, technically, you work for Arctic?"

"Uh-huh."

"So?"

"So."

And down another block.

The traffic has gone from bad to worse. Gridlock, horns, and the silver flash of mopeds splitting lanes. Lion finds the sight of mopeds is producing an unconscious startle response. Like seeing shark fins in the ocean. A jerk-and-wince two-step that's drawing even more looks from strangers.

He knows the response is a bit of prehistoric habit code buried deep in the amygdala. Overexpressed in em-trackers, something else he remembers learning from Fetu. Also remembers the same thing happened the last time he had a gun pointed at him. When Sonya got him arrested.

Except that time, the stimulus wasn't mopeds. It was Maglites—what he'd been clubbed with while busting a rhesus out of jail, seconds before he hit the ground, monkey skittering across the floor and cop drawing his gun. The last image seared into his data banks. Though, thinking it through, Lion decides the difference between a cop shoving a gun in your face and a thug shoving a gun in your face cannot be measured by any technology currently available on earth.

"Good thing," notes Lorenzo, "they don't see Scottish breasts very often in a Muslim country."

"Allah be praised."

And down another block.

"Patents," says Lion, as they round another corner, coming onto a wide boulevard. Droves of knock-off vendors lining the sidewalk. "Tajik said this was about patents."

"And revolution."

"Yeah," pausing by a stack of Louis Vuitton purses, "but patents first."

"So," says Lorenzo, "Muad'Dib didn't patent Sietch Tabr?"

"For the Rilkeans, it's a sacrament, right? Sietch Tabr. It's their way to live the questions. That doesn't seem like the kind of thing Muad'Dib could patent, even if he wanted to."

"So Tajik stole the formula for Jenka—which means he does what? Gets the patent first?"

"Even if Arctic gets the patent, how does that become revolution? An autism drug, I can see. But an uprising?"

Lorenzo stops to light a cigarette, "You said things had gotten too surreal for this to be a Big Pharma play."

"Can I have one of those?" asks Lion.

Lorenzo passes him a cigarette. He digs his lighter out of his pocket and takes a healthy inhale. "I don't know," Lion says on the exhale. "Did you see which way Penelope went?"

"No."

"Me either," which, he decides, irks him more than it should.

Lorenzo notices the irk and stops walking. "Kemosabe, I know I told you to forget about her."

"Uh-huh."

"Don't listen to me."

"Don't listen to you? What about Ambergris? The voodoo stripper. You made a speech."

"I did. I changed my mind."

"You're backing down?"

"I see you," says Lorenzo. "You sleep more than anyone I know; you smoke more pot than anyone I know."

"Says the man with the psychedelic pharmacy in his pocket."

"I got holding duties. Long tour, and I'm the only one who won't go on a bender and do all our supplies. We're not talking me, though, we're talking you. The sleep, the weed, the need to damp it down. I get it. I wouldn't want to feel what you have to feel. But you're exhausted from everything it takes to be an em-tracker. So a woman who can wake you up—that's got to be interesting, right?"

"Yeah," says Lion, "when someone's not shoving a gun in my eye, definitely interesting."

They start walking again. The fake Louis Vuitton handbags become fake Chanel handbags, tall stacks arrayed on wobbly tables being sold by vendors in faux-Prada.

"So," asks Lorenzo, inspecting a Lucite Lego Clutch Classic, like a see-through lunchbox for some swank third grader, "did we learn anything today that's gonna help you find Muad'Dib?"

"Rule number one: No guns."

"Good rule."

"Not a choice. Blows my system out. I walked away when it happened with Sonya, walking away now."

"Did you sign a contract?" asks Lorenzo, setting down the clutch.

"Yeah," says Lion, "but Arctic's got their formula and I got thirty thousand of their dollars. I'm going to fly back to New York and brief Richard, which I'm contractually obligated to do, then I'm going to punch Jenka in the mouth, which I'm morally obligated to do. Then Zorn out."

Around another corner.

The wide boulevard is gone, replaced by a narrow lane wedged between anonymous mirror-clad high-rises throwing long shadows. Too dark for Lion's comfort.

"Are we lost?" he asks.

"Just wait . . ."

Lorenzo leads him down the block. The lane widens suddenly, the sea of buildings parting to reveal a miniature village tucked between skyscrapers. Tiny Japanese-style row houses, mochi ice cream shops, and directly in front of them: Bang-Bang-Bang, a store specializing in robot toys, sci-fi paraphernalia, and the full back catalog of *Mondo 2000*. In the window, a life-sized Bruce Lee doll standing dead center, complete with black gi and Jeet Kune Do patch over his left breast.

Lion takes a step closer and the doll turns to face him. He must have tripped a sensor. Silky smooth motion, cutting-edge animatronics, and the voice a perfect match for the genuine article: "I said empty your mind. Be formless, shapeless, like water. You put water into a cup, and it becomes the cup. You put water into a bottle, it becomes the bottle. You put water into a teapot, it becomes the teapot. Water can flow, or it can crash. Be water, my friend."

"Copy that," says Lion.

"Check it out," calls Lorenzo, "it's a Voight-Kampff machine."

He turns to see Lorenzo holding a do-it-yourself kit of some kind. A photo on the cover of what looks like a Polaroid camera attached to a small screen attached to an accordion.

"A what?"

"From *Blade Runner*," explains Lorenzo, "the Voight-Kampff machine. It measures empathy."

Like the electric potential sensors Tajik built into the snuff container, thinks Lion, smarting at the memory.

"It's how you tell replicants from real people," Lorenzo continues. "It's the original proof-of-life detector."

To his other side, a couple of teenagers have walked up to the window. They must have tripped the same sensor.

"My style," says Bruce, "you can call it the art of fighting without fighting."

Lion feels like he's been doing the opposite: the art of fighting is fighting. But Lorenzo's not wrong—Penelope definitely has his attention.

Then a moped sharks by to his left. He flinches again, breaking the sensor's beam once more.

"Do not pray for an easy life," says Bruce. "Pray you can endure a difficult one."

THE BENE GESSERIT STAY STRAPPED

The sight of their hotel arrives with a rumble of thunder, a crack of lightning, and the afternoon monsoon, coming down in sheets. The sky has become a thick layer the color of split-pea soup. Gutters spring to life. Cigarette butts, red candy wrappers, crushed beer cans, swept away in an instant.

That last block takes a while.

Dripping wet, they trudge through the front doors of the KL Journal, finding the hotel has erected an emergency dry-off station just inside. A slender table made from polished chrome, a stack of towels, and a thickset chambermaid shyly distributing them, as if looking at wet guests were a kind of taboo.

"Thanks," says Lion, taking two towels, passing one to Lorenzo, thinking about the last time he was handed a towel, the ninja in New York, and how very long ago that feels.

A gust of wind rattles the front door.

"I'm about as useful as a steering wheel on a mule," says Lorenzo, wiping himself off and dropping the drenched article into a hamper.

"Me too," says Lion, patting the towel against his soaked jeans to no avail, "pretty crushed."

"If it stops raining and they open the beer garden, I'm onstage in a couple of hours."

"Unless Tajik sends henchmen to kill me in my sleep, I'm on a plane tomorrow."

"I didn't think about that—he knows where we're staying."

"I thought about it," says Lion, dropping his towel into the hamper. "I don't think it'll happen. He didn't want to kill us, at least I don't think so. Tajik got what he wanted from me. Penelope, though, her he probably wants to kill."

"Yeah," agrees Lorenzo, "but if he's not coming for me, then I'm coming for room service, a shower, and a nap." He points toward the spiral staircase, "You'll find me later at the Shack?"

"Of course."

"Then I'm out," striding away. "Gonna make sure our equipment isn't sitting in the rain."

Lion watches Lorenzo start up the orange metal stairs before crossing to the elevator. The doors are sliding closed as he arrives. A split-second decision, spinning sideways and slipping through. On the other side, he finds himself alone in the car save for a stately brunette in an evening gown, a long leather glove, and a small snowy owl perched atop it.

Pure white feathers on head and breast, black flecks on crown and tail, and those ever-inquisitive yellow eyes.

But not this time.

Unlike the coyote, unlike the hornbill, the owl ignores him, completely. Not even an errant blink in his direction. This chills Lion, maybe more than anything else that happened today.

"Do you like my owl?" asks the woman.

"Usually animals like me," he says, and then it clicks. "It's not real, is it?"

"No," slight shake of her head, "animatronic."

"Expensive?"

"Very."

"It looks real."

"And before the operation," she says, smiling, "I looked like Johnny Cash."

Stepping out of the elevator, he's shaky in the hallway. Key in lock, clothes on floor, and into the bathroom to inspect his eye in the mirror. Not the full-bloodshot cyclops he'd imagined, more like a razor-thin scar on the right side of his right cornea.

When he slips off his jacket, his arm tells a different story.

The dead-buffalo cut had sprung back to life. Banging into the doorway when Lorenzo bull-rushed him out of Allah Bling. And now, semi-coagulated blood in a thick line from elbow to wrist.

The hot water helps, the blood coming off in the shower. Close inspection afterward and it doesn't appear to be much of a problem. The cut is closing on its own, but he should probably dress it. He wonders if he can have the front desk send up gauze bandages, maybe some codeine. He doesn't wonder for long. The thought of having to have a conversation, with the desk clerk, with whomever delivers the bandages, unbearable.

A wave of exhaustion threatens to pull him under. He wraps a towel around the wound and walks into the bedroom. Cool sheets and, once he clicks off the light, total darkness.

But sleep doesn't come.

He can feel his thoughts starting to race. Adrenaline memories flood in: Tajik's moustache twitch, the gun mashed against his cornea, the red satin shirt, jaw clenched, eyes bulging with electricity, as Penelope hit him with the taser. Lion can feel himself wishing for the unconsciousness that seemed, only moments ago, his certain fate.

Seconds later, maybe minutes, could it be an hour? There's a steady knocking on his door. Some kind of twilight fog seeping through his brain as he tries to make sense of sound. Did he ring the front desk to order bandages? Pretty sure he didn't place that call. Could it be Lorenzo? Tajik? What about Penelope?

Now he's awake.

Lion sits up and clicks on the light. The knocking continues. Getting out of bed, he looks around for a weapon. Doesn't even see a heavy object. A pen? If it's Tajik, he could stab him in the eye with a pen. Fitting justice. But he doesn't even see a pen.

Lion settles on a '50s-era Bakelite handset from the hotel phone, unclipping the cord from the base and carrying the receiver toward the door. A decent heft, possibly enough to knock someone out, definitely enough to break a nose.

No peephole. What kind of hotel room door doesn't have a peephole?

Lion grabs hold of the handle and turns it slowly, feeling the lock disengage. Then he whips open the door, holding the receiver high above his head like a war club. A flash of green, a familiar army jacket.

But not Penelope wearing it.

Standing in his doorway, it's the woman from Hudson Bar and Books. Blond wig gone, silver hair now visible.

"Sarah?" he asks, totally confused.

"Bloody hell," she says, a Scottish accent Lion definitely doesn't remember from the bar, pointing at his crotch, "yer tadger's out the windae."

He glances down. His tadger is, in fact, out the windae. He'd forgotten he got undressed.

And why does this keep happening?

"An what," she continues, poking a finger toward the receiver, "g'wan mash me? Well, git on with it, laddy."

He lowers the receiver, trying, if only for a moment, to cover his crotch, but the results are even more ridiculous.

"Fuck it," he says, chucking the handset onto the bed and walking back into the room. "Come in, if you're coming."

"Get dressed," she says, stepping into the room and closing the door behind her. "My sister's waiting for us on the roof."

"Your sister?" he asks, pulling on his jeans. But then a shiver down his spine as the details stack: the army jacket, the Scottish brogue, the resemblance—data bit finds data bit, alright. That ratchet-click of certainty makes him feel . . . not quite the detective. More like a sucker.

"You're Penelope's sister," no longer a question.

"My twin," she says.

Lion flashes on the Black Power twins, Shiva and Kali, and hears Luther's boom: "The Bene Gesserit stay strapped."

Son-of-a-bitch.

"You're both Rilkeans," he says. "The sisterhood. You're . . ."

"Guardians of Muad'Dib," explains Sarah. "Now get dressed."

A FUTURE IN MEAT PACKING

The heavy rain has subsided into a misty drizzle, leaving the roof of the KL Journal shrouded in fog. The ground is covered in puddles. Lion can hear the hum of conversation, wafting up from the beer garden, like ten stories below him now.

A few steps out of the elevator and the scene starts to coalesce. A rooftop pool deck surrounded by a metal railing. The view over the edge is cumulus towers of water vapor and the wet twinkle of the city at night, occasionally visible in their midst.

Inside the railing, a rectangular infinity pool, lit from below and surrounded by a checkerboard of black, white, and gray tile. Beyond the tile, along a far edge, there's an elevated wooden deck striped by a trio of long wooden picnic tables. And in the back corner, a tent made of clear poly-something, maybe twelve feet square and streaked with rain.

"We're this way," says Sarah, leading him across the tile and toward the tent.

Approaching the plastic wall, Lion sees candle-flicker and two shadows, one large, one small. Another step closer and the shadows firm up. The smaller one crystallizes into Penelope. The large one looks like someone reading a newspaper. Then Sarah opens the main flap.

Through the slit, Lion can make out a low acrylic table flanked by couches. A glass bowl filled with water sits in the table's center, and a half-dozen candles float on the surface. In their flicker, Lion sees Penelope wearing a pair of faded blue jeans, combat boots, and an old Sisters of Mercy concert shirt. He sees the newspaper is written in a language he doesn't speak. Cyrillic? Bhutanese? Then the paper folds in half and you've got to be freaking me . . .

"Luther?"

"Good evening, Lion."

"What are you doing here?" But as soon as he asks the question he knows the answer. "You're not Shiz's bodyguard—you're Muad'Dib."

"Sit down," says Luther, nodding toward a chair. "Want a drink? We've got a little bit to discuss."

Information goes whirring around his head, his brain trying to process everything he's learned in the past ten minutes. Sarah is Penelope's sister, and they're both Rilkeans. And Luther is Muad'Dib. Booze is definitely not going to help him process any of this.

"Got coffee?" he asks.

Luther nods toward Sarah, who disappears behind a back flap in the tent. Penelope walks over to him, kisses him softly on the cheek, whispers, "Nice to see you again, darling."

"You as well, darling," he says, surprised by how little effort it takes to play along.

Sarah reappears with a silver pot of coffee and four white mugs. Pours and distributes. Lion carries his cup past Luther and over to a tall table in the back corner of the tent, beside a brick wall. Sees a stairwell doorway to his left. A quick exit if he needs it, and with the wall, no one can sneak up on him.

"I'm listening," he says, starting to roll a cigarette.

"I grew up in Louisiana," begins Luther, "did you know that?"

"How would I know that? Don't you deploy an AI scrubber to keep the Rilkeans out of the news?"

"Actually," says Luther, "we don't."

"Doubtful," he says.

Luther shakes his head. "Why would I lie?"

"Jenka's the numpty fud using the scrubber," snaps Sarah. "He's the one been keeping the Rilkeans a secret."

"Jenka?"

"I grew up in Louisiana," repeats Luther, this time with an eyebrow raised toward Lion.

"Whatever, man, tell your damn story."

"We started out a big family. No money, but my father was a tough bastard. A grinder, if you remember the term. He worked in a slaughterhouse, no choice really, it was just about the only gig in town. Got his first job at sixteen, running the bolt gun on the killing floor." Luther turns his hand into a gun, puts his finger to his temple and pulls the trigger. "By eighteen, he'd balled up to foreman. Then Katrina. Our house collapsed, my mother drowned, and without her, Dad was lost."

Lion was in grade school during Katrina, but remembers the images. An elderly woman in a tattered nightgown on the roof of a chicken coop. Remembers thinking that the phrase "natural disaster" didn't quite cover it.

Luther takes a sip of coffee and keeps talking. "It happened slowly, then quickly. He started snorting oxy. My sister joined him. Dad overdosed when I was twelve. My brother went to jail. Somebody had to keep the lights on."

A gust of wind rattles the tent flaps. Lion glances out through the slit, seeing a police car, sirenless but with lights whirling, slashing down a distant street.

"I showed up at the slaughterhouse when I was fifteen." Luther shrugs, his massive shoulders rumbling beneath black cloth. "I don't know what I was thinking, maybe I could walk into my father's old job. The floor manager nearly fell over laughing when I tried. But he knew my father, and ducked union rules. Put me on nights and week-ends so I could stay in school. I started where my dad started, on the killing floor, running the bolt gun."

"So you're a killer?" Lion says, aiming for a journalist's detachment.

Luther glares at him.

"That's the moral of this story?"

"If I was you," says Luther, "what I'd want to know is why Arctic hired you, why Penelope drone-stalked you, and why Tajik shoved a gun in your eye."

"Drone-stalked—that's one way to put it."

"Have some manners: You should thank Penelope; she did save your ass earlier today."

"And I've seen his ass," adds Sarah, her Scottish accent melting into So-Cal valley. "It's like cute-cute."

Everyone stares at her.

"Just making nice-nice," she says with a wink.

"What's Katrina got to do with the Rilkeans?" asks Lion.

"I'm trying to tell you where this started," says Luther. "I'm trying to explain that you've been in this for a lot longer than you think you've been in this."

This catches his attention.

"Two decades ago, two trends were showing up in slaughterhouses. The first was the more humane treatment of animals. Later on, you were part of that movement."

"Sonya," says Lion. "The Animal Liberation Front."

Luther nods. "All of you became the sharp end of that stick. The dull end was a woman named Temple Grandin—famous for trying to make slaughterhouses more humane. You remember her?"

"The world needs all kinds of minds, she said that, right?"

Luther nods again. "She did. In fact, she actually said it to me once."

Penelope walks over to his table, picks up his pouch of tobacco, and asks, wordlessly, if he minds. He doesn't mind. In fact, he realizes, he actually likes that she almost didn't bother to ask.

"Toward the end of her life," continues Luther, "Grandin was hired by the slaughterhouse where I worked. Ownership wanted her there, management could give a shit. They assigned her to me. I was the lowest guy on the totem pole, but I had a mind for science. And I got to know her. Grandin was on the spectrum. Completely nonverbal and incredibly detail oriented. She thought in pictures, which is also how cows think. It gave her a way in, a way to learn the language."

"She spoke to the animals," says Lion. "I saw the documentary."

"She taught me how to speak cow. It's just pattern recognition, like every other language. And I practiced. That's what changed everything."

"Changed it how?"

"Words are just bits of information, but language is the full code. It's wired into every stage of meaning-making, from basic emotions all the way up to abstract thought. Once you can speak a language, you can feel in that language. It's automatic. It creates empathy."

A puzzle piece slots into place. "After Grandin taught you to speak cow," says Lion, "you couldn't kill 'em anymore."

One of the floating candles reaches the end of its life, flickers once, then fades to black.

"Exactly," says Luther.

"So this is why the Rilkeans got into animal welfare?"

"No, not the Rilkeans," says Luther. "They didn't start out with leaders. It was more of a hacker collective. Deep experimentalists. We lived for living the questions, and empathy, according to Rilke, is the best way to run that experiment. The animal rights agenda was just a by-product."

Lion hears the "we." So Luther started out just another Rilkean? But he asks a different question, "By-product of what?"

"I'm telling you where Sietch Tabr came from," says Luther. "Like I said, there were two trends sweeping the slaughterhouse biz. The first was Grandin's goal—make the killing more humane. The second was synthetic biology. Grow steak from stem cells, no more killing. Everyone knew this was the future. The slaughterhouse where I worked, the owners hired an in-vitro meat expert, a woman from California who brought in a tissue-engineering squad. And if Temple Grandin pissed off management, the syn-bio team drove them totally nuts. Between them and the slaughter bots, gonna be no jobs left for the brothers."

"But," says Lion.

"But I needed the money, and I was sick of the killing. I volunteered to be the go-between, between the biologists and the rest of 'em."

"You learned synthetic biology in a slaughterhouse?"

Luther nods.

"And Sietch Tabr?"

"The intersection of these two trends, courtesy of Lion Zorn."

"How?"

"Back when you were a reporter, one of your early articles on animal welfare. It was called 'In the Beginning Was the Word'. Know what I'm talking about?"

Lion nods. He remembers that article, remembers writing it perched on Sonya's old couch.

"You said that 'empathy,' the word, the term, showed up in the late eighteenth century. And you said the word worked, when nothing else did. Religion has been trying to get people to treat each other fairly for eons, with little success. Yet, ten years after the word 'empathy' enters our language, slavery has been abolished most everywhere, the women's rights movement gets started, and animal welfare isn't far behind."

"Language crystallizes the nebulous," says Lion, quoting Richard.

"That's what happened to me," agrees Luther. "Grandin taught me to speak cow. I learned the language and it produced empathy. A fuck ton of empathy."

"Bet it changed your relationship to animals," says Lion.

"And I wanted to change others. But the whole process took too long, took too much effort. The only way I could get other people to feel what I was feeling was to teach them the language. But it's too slow, the Sixth Great Extinction, fifty percent of all mammals gone by the end of this century . . . ," shaking his head, "there just wasn't enough time."

"I get that," says Lion, thinking back to his conversation with Changchang on the roof of the Shack—and was that only last night?

"By then," says Luther, "I'd gotten busy. Darknet psychopharmacology tutorials, some Howard University online classes, and the synbio I picked up at the slaughterhouse—put it all together and I found a way to bypass the language learning process entirely. That's one of the things Sietch Tabr does: It creates new connections between the limbic system and the language centers. Makes you feel like you speak another's language—even if you don't. It was your article that gave me the recipe."

It takes him a second to take this in. Then it registers. "You tested my recipe on civilians," says Lion. "Tajik's brother, Nassir."

"There was no other way. We had to test it on the unsuspecting. But Tajik and Nassir are hard-core psychonauts. Wasn't unusual for one of them to dose the other without telling him first. After Tajik joined the Rilkeans, after we decided we needed to test Sietch Tabr on outsiders—Nassir did drugs, was a zookeeper—he was about as low risk a choice as we could make."

"What about the South Africans? Was that low risk?"

"The family on safari? Those are Sarah and Penelope's people. Ask either of them, they're a junk show."

"They do love their mind-altering substances," Sarah explains.

"No one forced them to do anything they wouldn't have done just about any Saturday night," adds Penelope.

"And you should hear Aunt Karyn prattle," says Sarah. "Waking up with lions, just about the best experience of her life."

"What about Walker?" asks Lion. "Was having his head cut off one of the best experiences of his life?"

"Walker," says Luther, shaking his head sadly, "that's when shit got seriously sideways."

ion feels an odd dislocation. There's a part of him that's still pay-ing attention, but something in Luther's delivery, too languid, like a lullaby, making him tired. There's another part of him that's pretty sure he's still napping, convinced that this is all a dream.

Unfortunately, that part is not very convincing, so he's not exactly buying it.

"Lion?"

"Yeah, sorry, I'm . . ."

But he doesn't really know what he is.

"Give me a second," he says, getting up, crossing over to the tent flap, suddenly wanting fresh air. Pushing it open, he realizes the rain has stopped completely and a thin fog is rising off the city. Warm on his cheeks. And the faint strains of Hank Mudd and the K-Holes. Must have been dry enough to open the beer garden.

An old Nick Cave song? No, actually, Blind Willie Johnson.

Walking out of the tent and over to the roof's far railing, he stares out at the nightscape of Malaysia, seeing the sea of lights, thinking about Lorenzo, thinking every one of those lights a story, a complete life, with memories as thick as his own.

And suddenly, Penelope standing beside him.

"Interested?" she says, passing him a joint.

He stares at the joint. Tries not to stare at her. Eventually realizing she was asking him a question.

"No," he says, declining her offer, "I'm good."

They stand in silence for a few moments. Lion hears the closing notes of "Dark Was the Night, Cold Was the Ground," the dying fade of guitar twang as Hank turns the tune into a dirge.

"We need your help," she says eventually. "What Richard's doing—it's not the way."

Turning toward her, "what is Richard doing?"

"There are only two ways to bring change, fast and slow. That's what this is about. Jenka, Richard, Arctic, they want fast. Revolution. We want slow. Actual, legitimate, lasting culture shift."

"I'm not following."

"Arctic has the formula?" asks Penelope.

"Yeah, Tajik got it. Gave the snuff container to the moped guy to give to a courier."

"I saw him leave. My choice was go after him or save your ass."

"Thank you for saving my ass," he says. "And the snuff container?"

"By now," with a sigh, "Jenka probably has it. Or he will tomorrow morning. He's been stockpiling AI power for just this moment. By late afternoon, he'll have mutated the formula and patented every conceivable variation."

"High-speed patenting," says Lion.

Penelope nods.

He'd heard about this. Couple of techies got the idea from the high-speed-trading scandal on Wall Street. Catching patent applications midstream, grabbing the data right off the wires, then using a monster AI to play out all possible variations. The original patent remains untouched, but everything around it, all the downstream spin-off technology, gets absorbed and locked up by the interloper. "But why?"

"No one cares about the patents. It's what the patents set in motion. It's the off-label use of Sietch Tabr that interests Richard. You did your homework—did you notice Arctic's investment pattern, heavy media acquisitions? All the life-hacking bloggers, quantified self-podcasters, healthcare virtual casters on the payroll?"

"Yeah," he says, "and I remember you're on the payroll as well."

"Double agent," she says with a wink.

"So when you slept with me, were you working for Arctic or the Rilkeans?"

Penelope gives him a look but lets it pass.

"Off-label uses," he says, "what does that mean?"

"Remember Ritalin?"

"The ADHD drug. Crystal meth by a different name."

"It spread like a virus. All off-label. Some neuro-hacker figures out that Ritalin works as a study aid. Helps focus. It's bloody speed, of course it helps focus. Within a year, four out of five college kids have tried it. Spreads to Wall Street, Silicon Valley, to Main Street, into high schools, grade schools, like wildfire."

A scrolling-screen billboard on a distant rooftop, hidden behind the clouds, showing muted flashes of scenes too fuzzy to decode.

"All Arctic has to do," continues Penelope, "is announce a new autism drug in the pipeline and every net-caster on their payroll is going to start talking about its off-label high-performance benefits. They've got a warehouse of 3-D chem-printers and an entire underground distribution network. It's all set up. Sietch Tabr's gonna go wide, nearly overnight. That's what we're trying to avoid."

"A drug that expands empathy?" he asks. "Why would the Rilkeans, why would anyone, want to avoid that?"

"Won't work," says Luther, walking up behind them.

Lion turns, sees a large shadow stepping toward him. "What won't work?"

"High-speed revolution, especially if it's about consciousness."

"Why?"

"Tim Leary. He thought LSD was gonna be the next Malcolm X. More power to the people. But people weren't ready. The collateral damage, the drug war, one outta eight brothers go to jail, research outlawed for fifty years. MDMA in the '90s, same deal. Molly is a little bit Sietch Tabr, similar receptor sites, both serotonin agonists. What happened there? The man. Outlawed. Criminalized. Ravers thought they could change the world one glow-stick at a time, but the world doesn't want that kind of change."

"If millions of people start having revelatory experiences," says Penelope, "communing with the animals, seeing the issue from the other side, imagine the rift. All the people who haven't had those experiences. The backlash."

"Maybe," says Lion.

"But why risk it?" asks Luther. "Two decades back, we killed a hundred million animals a year for hide and fur. Forget food, we're just talking fashion. Syn-bio, stem cells, now we got options. But if the mood shifts? If we push too hard? Richard wants it like FedEx, he wants his change overnight. But you know why Rilke said you need to live the questions?"

Lion realizes he's actually asking. "Yeah," he says. "Live the questions now. Perhaps you will then, gradually, without noticing it, one distant day, live right into the answer."

"Not just wisdom," says Luther, "that's evolution. It's the way we evolved to change. Slowly, in fits and starts. Hit the turbo-boost? Rilke dropped that knowledge too: 'Do not seek the answers, which cannot be given you because you would not be able to live them.'"

"And you've got what?" asks Lion, "a slow growth alternative?"

"We had, you mean," says Penelope, "before Tajik stole the only copy of the formula."

"How could that be the only copy?"

"Timing," says Luther, shaking his head, "horrible timing."

"There were hundreds of versions developed," explains Penelope. "Dozens tested. But Arctic's scrubber erased everything. It found our database about the same time Luther finished the engraving on the snuff container."

The billboard flashes again, on that distant rooftop. More of the fog has burned off and Lion can see the image now: reptilian skin, dark green, and the glint of sharp canines. What the hell is he looking at?

"A week from now, " says Luther, "every Rilkean who has been through the ceremony was going to get a container. Just like you saw at Tajik's. With the formula."

"How's that any different?" asks Lion. "It'll still get out there."

"Slower path. Spreads the same change, but within the confines of a tradition. That matters. Historically, the revolutions in consciousness that have worked, they've been anchored by ritual, draped in religion, in tradition."

"You mean the ritual stabilizes the change?" asks Lion.

Luther nods. "More importantly, stabilizes the language surrounding the change."

"Like the Rastas," says Penelope.

"For one example," continues Luther. "There are many," leaning his big frame against the railing. "Remember DMT. It's ten times the ride of LSD. It scared people back in the 1960s. Think about that—a drug too radical for the hippies. But reintroduced it in the twenty-first century, wrapped up in the language of Amazonian shamanism, in their tradition, people could suddenly absorb the ride. They could be changed by it, not unmoored. The spiritual context, it stabilizes the experience. Suddenly, housewives from Iowa were heading to Peru. For Sietch Tabr, the Rilkeans have been trying to provide those rituals, that language, that stability."

It suddenly clicks, the puzzle finally snapping together. "But Richard, the scrubber, they've managed to keep you quiet."

"That's why Penelope was assigned to Arctic," explains Luther.

"She's been trying to locate the server running the scrubber and the hackers running the server."

"I sort of found the hackers," she says. "Jenka's got them buried in Russia. Arrested and moved to a private wing of a private prison. All voluntary, of course. Everyone is being extremely well compensated for this inconvenience and blah, blah, blah. But," her voice taking on funereal tones, "try to find anyone in the Russian prison system, especially when someone like Jenka, his skills, resources, is trying to keep them hidden."

"What about the server?" he asks.

"Pong," says Penelope.

"Pong?"

"That's the name of the AI. Jenka says it's from an old Atari game. The first video arcade blockbuster. The three billion hours a week people spend playing video games, Pong started that. Jenka's got a whole rap about Atari being behind the biggest drug launch in history. Says the only scam that comes close was the drug companies peddling oxy like aspirin."

Pong? The name reminds Lion of something. Before it comes to him, Sarah walks out of the tent carrying the water bowl with the candles. Their flicker catches the silver in her hair, like a drop of mercury pouring its way across the patio.

She sets the bowl down on a table and walks over to stand beside Penelope. The Bene Gesserit, thinks Lion, which reminds him: "So the Rilkean traditions, the tattoos, the *Dune* references. That's what, artifice?"

"Is and isn't," says Luther. "We did what religions do to stabilize a mystery. We borrowed, liberally. Religions are always poly-tribe. The Rastas got Kali weed from the Indians, dietary laws from the Old Testament, blended in Marcus Garvey, Haile Selassie, whatever they liked. So our religion is based on Rainer Maria Rilke, Frank Herbert, and Temple Grandin, so what? So we built spiritual rituals around

Sietch Tabr to stabilize the experience. And Robert Walker—I guess we learned what happens without that stability."

In the candlelight flicker, Lion sees Sarah wince.

"We knew," continues Luther, "even if we built rituals around Sietch Tabr, it was going to leak. Eventually someone like Walker, someone who felt completely superior to animals, would try it. We needed to know ahead of time."

"We were as gentle about it as possible," says Sarah.

"His head ended up on the wall."

"It did," says Luther. "At his request, it did."

An odd feeling, not one he's used to having, then he realizes: his jaw dropping open.

"The plan," says Luther, "man, the plan was simple. I showed up with a gun, forced him to snort Sietch Tabr, then brought in Sarah and swear to God, a half dozen puppies and kittens. Talk about a conversion experience. Walker was giddy. Like Aunt Karyn. But we screwed up."

"The dosage?" asks Lion.

"No, we had that right. What we forgot was that hunters, even assholes like Walker, have to learn to speak animal to be any good. Walker was good. He already knew the language. Our normal dose hit him like a train. Pushed him way over and we didn't notice."

"Pish-lickin' bampot," Penelope and Sarah say, simultaneously. Must be that twin thing.

"Everything was going well," continues Luther. "I went to piss. One of the kittens distracted Sarah."

"For a second," she says.

"But," says Luther, not happy about it, "long enough for Walker to grab his rifle and shoot himself."

Lion feels that swimming sensation again, as if the world were suddenly heading left, on roller skates. "He shot himself?"

"Out of remorse. He was aiming for his heart, missed. He was still bleeding out. I think that's when I lost the snuff container. Don't really know. The only thing clear was that the very thing I was trying to prevent—now I'd caused it."

"His head on the wall?"

"Walker's dying wish," says Luther, clearly struggling with the memory. "He wanted every other hunter to know the truth, wanted to show his remorse to the world. It was his last request, and I was responsible for his death. At the time, under the circumstances, I felt I had to honor it. At least I'd worked in a slaughterhouse. It made the hard part, not easier, but a little familiar."

A suicide? Walker's head on the wall was a suicide?

Lion sits down on the ground, his back leaning against the railing. He feels puddle water hit the back of his legs but doesn't care. Penelope sits beside him. Luther as well. There's nothing left to say. Just the soft hum of the city in sleep mode and the K-Holes doing a laconic version of an old Misfits song.

"Prime directive," sings Hank, "exterminate the whole human race."

Then it dawns on him. There is something to say. One final something.

"So, Luther," Lion asks, taking Penelope's hand in his. "What is it, exactly, that I can do for the Rilkeans?"

SOME DAY THIS WAR'S GONNA END

Luther answers his question. Not a terrible answer as far as these things go, but the countdown again, coming in for a fierce landing. Lion doesn't have the energy to think about it. Doesn't have the energy to think about anything—especially Sonya. Animal Liberation Sonya, got him arrested Sonya, and now, if Luther is to be believed, married to his old editor Sonya.

Yeah, definitely does not want to think about Sonya right now.

Sarah pulls him out of his head. "You alright, sport?"

Not in the slightest.

He struggles to his feet and has a memory of saying something to Luther. Maybe I'll consider it. Maybe not. His eye throbs, his flight out leaves the next morning, and right now, all he wants to do is to say a quick good-bye to Lorenzo and crawl into bed.

"Penelope's coming with you," says Luther. "For protection."

"I think I'm good."

"I think Tajik's crazy."

"It's not open for discussion," adds Penelope, getting to her feet, extending a hand toward Lion.

He's past the point of argument. Instead, he lets her help him up and starts toward the elevators, his left boot landing in a puddle. Hesitates before taking another step, a question pushing up through the fog. "How'd she end up with Carl?"

"Who?" says Luther.

"My old editor, Carl. How'd Sonya end up married to him?"

"When you got arrested, Carl didn't just want to fire you. Dude was pissed—he wanted to leave your ass in jail."

"That much I know."

The billboard on that distant roof finally pokes all the way through the clouds, its four-story screen displaying dinosaurs holding martini glasses. A decade as an em-tracker and still no way to decode Malaysian advertising. One thing he can decode—the feeling of Penelope taking his hand once more.

"What you may not know," says Luther, "Sonya convinced him to bail you out."

"He never told me . . ."

"It's how you got sprung," continues Luther, "how they met. Not sure when they started dating, or ended up married. But Carl's moved up. He's a boss." Lion sees Luther purse his lips, a tiny hesitation. "Editor in chief. Runs the whole Sunday magazine."

Lion doesn't know what to say to this. There isn't a word for the nostalgia one feels for the life that one did not get to live, but that's what he's feeling. A light rain begins to fall, and the billboard, in the distance, proudly displays velociraptors holding piña coladas.

"Might as well tell him," says Penelope, the dinosaurs swallowed by a fire-belching explosion, same color as her hair.

"Tell me what?"

"Sonya works with him," says Luther. "Carl's right hand. She's an executive editor."

Blinks.

"Look at the bright side," says Sarah. "Sonya's an executive editor. It's why we know that any story you wrote about us would get published."

He got fired. Carl got the girl. Sonya got promoted. He knows this information is going to come for him. Not now. Later, when he's falling asleep, or folding laundry, some unsuspecting plebeian task, brushing his teeth, and after that, well, he might just start drinking.

Then he realizes what Sarah just said. "You talked to her?"

"Shiz did," explains Luther. "He has the relationship."

Penelope gives his hand a tight squeeze. Either she's trying to make him feel better or the Rilkeans are still running their guerrilla marketing campaign. Then another thought: It's been a long time since anyone gave his hand a squeeze because they wanted him to feel better.

"I'll give you my answer tomorrow, maybe the next day." Then he starts toward the elevator again.

"Godspeed" is Luther's farewell.

"Good-bye" from Sarah.

Penelope drops his hand and falls in one step behind him. Through another puddle and skirting around the infinity pool and the rain, falling down again. He notices she's moved up beside him, starting to shake out her limbs, just a slight shiver, like a cat preparing to pounce.

But the elevator is empty. No threat in sight.

They step aboard in silence. Lion senses her body heat beside him but feels too many other things to do anything about it. He punches the button for the Shack's deck instead. The doors start to close. The last thing he sees before they shut tight is Sarah, gently reaching out her left hand to stroke Luther's cheek. It's too private a gesture, and something inside of Lion feels embarrassed for having seen it.

They ride ten floors down in silence. He feels oddly shy and keeps his eyes glued to the numbers. The sensation of slowing, and then the elevator's doors slide open, revealing the beer garden abustle and the K-Holes between sets.

Lion glances around. Definitely a healthy crowd, well-ornamented coeds with a smattering of poly-tribe. He notices Hank in the corner by the bar, talking to the same Vietnamese runway model he'd seen the night before. Notices Lorenzo standing beside them, a beer in one hand, a cigarette in another, a look on his face that reminds him of the look on his face.

The rest of the band is nowhere in sight.

"I'll be back in a minute," he tells Penelope, stepping toward the bar. She starts to walk with him, but Lion stops her with two fingers on her right hip. Rilkean guerrilla marketing—still a possibility. Other things.

"Alone, please."

Not wanting to deal with Hank, he leaves Penelope and angles through the crowd until he's about twenty feet away from Lorenzo, directly in his line of sight. Eye contact. Waves him over.

It takes a moment. On his way, Lorenzo has to pause for a poly-triber in a pair of fuzzy white pants and a fuzzy white coat, a series of living screens built into the jacket's sleeves. His left arm displays wooden crates filled with morphing fruit. Kumquats become Asian pears. The right sleeve shows stacks of old video games. Sonic the Hedgehog being masterfully played on a Sega Mega Drive transmogrifying into Space Invaders on an Atari Flashback 6.

The Atari Flashback brings up another flashback. Actually two. The first is the fruit-and-classic-video-game combo that he'd seen on the streets of New York, again on the streets of Kuala Lumpur, and now, a third time, here in the bar. Definitely a new kind of subcult trend.

The second flashback is more insistent. The Atari console reminds him of Pong, that other Atari game. Also Jenka's name for the AI scrubber. Pong. Data bit finds data bit and a full-body twitch, like he's mainlined electricity in the megawatt range.

"Son of a bitch."

But before he has time to do anything with his realization, Lorenzo appears in front of him.

"Someday this war's gonna end."

For the first time since he started looking for Muad'Dib, a viable way forward has begun to form in his head. Not a plan. Too risky. Way too dumb. But more than he had just moments ago. "Sooner than you think," says Lion, wrapping his friend up in a hug, "sooner than you think."

Lorenzo pulls slightly back from the embrace. "How do you figure?"

Lion doesn't reply immediately, and he doesn't break their hug. Instead, he spins Lorenzo slightly, turning them both around until he has eyes on Penelope.

Standing where he left her, not looking in their direction.

"I need another favor," says Lion, leaning in closer so he can whisper.

"You want me to call Charlotte again?"

"Yes, and," he says, doing quick math in his head. New York is ten hours behind Kuala Lumpur. "When do you play your last set?"

"I'm cashed," says Lorenzo, extinguishing his cigarette in a nearly empty martini glass. "Hank's hungover. With the rain, we're thinking short and sweet and calling it. Done in maybe an hour."

"When you finish," he says, "I need you to phone Charlotte."

"Uh-huh."

"And I need you to bribe a jeweler."

"Tajik?"

"No."

"Don't know if I can deal with that asshole twice in one day."

"Not Tajik."

Then Lion lays out his plan and pulls Lorenzo in for one final squeeze before starting toward the elevator.

"Kemosabe," Lorenzo calls after him.

Stops and looks back.

"You sure?"

"No, brother," says Lion, "not in a long time."

MINUS THE GOAT SHIT

On Arctic's dime, Lion flies Cathay Pacific, first class KL to NYC, with a refueling stop in Dubai. Flight attendants in snappy red outfits and another private cabin to himself. Minus the Goat Shit and the Eye-and-Eye VR, it's not all that different from Air Jamaica's cabin. Maybe a darker version of faux-mahogany and a slightly smaller flat screen.

Takeoff is a blur. Despite his hopes, he'd gotten little sleep the night before. Tossed and turned for hours on end. Now he feels . . . well, is it jet lag if it happens in a jet?

Needing to remedy this, Lion locates the recline toggle amid three dozen other switches and buttons that populate a cabin-control remote complicated enough to run a nuclear power plant. He turns the seat into a bed and crashes hard for some indeterminate time. Could be hours or days. Weeks are not entirely out of the question.

And where is he again?

That question opens the floodgates. Before he has time to reconsider, his brain jumps to light speed. The night before and all its permutations.

Not quite ready to deal with the influx, he keeps his eyes shut tight and tries to pretend it's a temporary interlude in an otherwise fine nap.

"You're asleep," he says to himself, that ancient prayer.

After leaving Lorenzo, he'd gone to his hotel room. Penelope accompanied him along the way but stopped at the door. He needed to get some sleep, she'd told him, and she needed to take care of a few things.

But not much sleep after that.

Then, like now, his brain was spinning. Not the typical hyper-agitation of emo-stim overload, more like em-tracking machinery in stunned mode. Not able to process the future he's feeling. A blank spot on his map.

Kept him up most of the night.

Now, he realizes, he's starting to get a little twitchy. Chase the calm, he tells himself. Taking his own advice, Lion runs through a breathing exercise and the *Dune* mantra. First lying down and then, after those attempts fail and he swats around in the dark until he finds the toggle that turns the bed into a chair, sitting up.

No dice.

Giving in, he flicks on a small light and surveys the uber-remote until he finds the call button. Cathay Pacific first class does not screw around. Instant stewardess. Same snappy red outfit, long white gloves that he didn't notice before.

"Bourbon?" he asks. "Is there a list somewhere?"

The stewardess extends a finger and clicks on his flat screen, runs through a couple of menus until arriving at a long list of whiskeys and scotches. Arctic's still paying the freight, so he orders expensive and Japanese. Something he's never heard of and can't quite pronounce.

"Right away, sir," and strides down the aisle.

Back in a minute with his drink and a tray of salted nuts. Lion takes his glass, takes a healthy swallow, and holds it up. He glances at the stewardess. "Please come see me again soon."

And she does.

But two drinks don't help. His brain refuses to calm. He doesn't want any more booze. Doesn't want to risk a hangover upon landing. Eventually, he realizes the way out is through.

Export the data.

He unearths his pack from a cleft beside his seat and digs out his Moleskine. Decides to order what he learned the night before. According to Luther, until the Robert Walker incident, this really had been about an autism drug. Arctic Pharmaceuticals started out legit. Even Jenka deploying the AI scrubber to erase the Rilkeans was nothing beyond standard industrial espionage, at least at first.

Walker's suicide changed things.

"When you cased the house," Luther had asked, "did you notice anything missing?"

"Sietch Tabr. In the photos I got, there were three lines left on an end table. But when I searched the house, the table was missing. Richard told me they stole it for research."

"Of a type. Richard and Jenka both wanted to try the drug. That's what happened, what changed, their conversion experience."

"That was the genesis of their . . . ," trying to find the language, "off-label distribution plan?"

Luther nodded. "Bloggers and podcasters were already on the payroll, part of the prep for launching Arctic Pharmaceuticals. But they had a problem. They could try the drug, but they couldn't synthesize it. For the tests, I customized Sietch Tabr, a hack against hacks, like the syn-bio version of a sleeper worm. When Arctic tried to reverse-engineer the compound, the molecules scrambled themselves."

"So even though they had a sample," said Lion, "they still needed the formula." Then it clicked. "That's why they hired me."

"Sort of."

"It's my fault," said Penelope, a look on her face that he recognized. The same look she'd given him on the day they'd met, standing at the edge of Arctic's waiting room. Regret. Remorse. The same remorse he'd seen in Walker's eyes. "Jenka was starting to get suspicious of me," she continued. "Since I was in charge of Arctic research—I needed to give him something."

Lion had been that something.

"She told Richard that Muad'Dib felt a great kinship with em-trackers," explained Luther, "especially an em-tracker named Lion Zorn. Told him about you, your work, that you could probably penetrate the Rilkeans."

"But why?"

"Because we couldn't find the scrubber," she said with a shrug, "we'd lost the formula, and we knew about you. If I could get you on the inside at Arctic, being an em-tracker, you might be able to dig up something I couldn't."

"I'd read your early animal liberation articles," said Luther. "Shiz knew the Rod of Correction stuff. We thought we might be able to trust you. But . . ."

"We had to be sure," added Penelope.

"That's why you followed me?"

"Yes."

"Sure of what?"

Penelope thumped his chest just then, two knuckles knocking on his breast bone.

"Your heart," Luther had said, and with gravitas.

So that was how all this started.

Lion glances down at his Moleskine and realizes he's not really taking notes. Or drawing up a list. More of a vector diagram, schematics for some extra-complicated heist. But he feels calmer.

Draining the last of his bourbon, Lion goes back to work. Writes: *snuff container.* Underlines it once. Draws an arrow to another quadrant. Writes out what he remembers.

After the suicide and the . . . searching for the right word, settles on "taxidermy" . . . Luther and Sarah had gotten out of Walker's house as fast as possible. By the time they'd realized the snuff container was missing, Arctic had swooped in and closed the scene. Tight as a drum, apparently.

Until Lion arrived, there had been significant attention from the cops and patrols of armed guards. Heavy blokes hired by Jenka, according to Penelope, and no way to get back in the house.

Something wasn't tracking.

"I found the snuff container under the desk," he'd said, "Not like it was hidden."

Luther confirmed, "That sounds about right."

"If Arctic searched the scene, they would have noticed it."

Indeed, they had noticed it. Jenka made the discovery. But this was before he'd tried Sietch Tabr, so the sensors in the container's cap didn't read changes in his mirror neuron function, because there hadn't been any changes, not yet. Jenka saw Muad'Dib's name, but not the formula. Still, you never know, so the container actually left the crime scene in his pocket.

"Once Arctic decided to bring you in," Luther had explained, "Jenka had it put back."

Remembering this now, Lion's scalp prickles. It's a reprise sensation. Happened the night before as well, when he first heard the story. A kind of kinesthetic haunting that will be with him for a while. Jenka had the snuff container put back because he knew that Lion would find it and that it would lead him to the Rilkeans.

He'd been played.

Not just by Penelope. By pretty much everyone involved. From the beginning and like a fiddle.

After that, everything snowballed.

"The problem . . . ," Luther had grinned just then, the image stuck in Lion's memory because it was the first time he'd seen that particular expression on that particular face, "you were better at your job than anyone expected. Us, Arctic, no one realized you had the snuff container until it was too late. When we figured that out, taking Molly. . . ."

A wider grin, Cheshire in nature.

Penelope told him the rest. "It was an easy way to search your luggage."

"But you'd left the container with Balthazar," continued Luther. "By the time we figured that out, Balthazar had shipped it to Malaysia. You pretty much know the rest."

Or almost.

They'd left him at the airplane hangar to search his hotel room, sent him on that trip to the spaceport to buy a little time, then tracked him to Malaysia through Balthazar. "That man is exceptionally bribable," Penelope had said—which, Lion realizes now, must have planted the seed that grew into his plan.

Luther had a different plan. More of a request. Since Arctic's play was already in motion, Sietch Tabr was going to break wide. Luther felt the best countermove was to get the Rilkean side of the story out.

"What about the scrubber?"

"Only combs new media. Online, virtual, ethereal. There are other ways to get a story out."

Other ways, old-fashioned ways. Traditional media. Thus Luther's final request: Tell the Rilkeans' side of the story by writing an article for Carl, his old editor. Shiz had talked to Sonya and she'd agreed to make sure it saw print. Thought it was a fitting full-circle ending to the saga.

So here he is, some twenty hours later, and still no answer.

He lifts up his window shade and glances outside. It's daylight out there. He closes the blinds again. Daylight no more.

He'd love another crack at being a journalist; they had that part right. But telling the Rilkean side of the story would require breaking just about every term in his nondisclosure agreement with Arctic. Jenka would seethe. Richard could litigate. Lawsuits, headaches, plus it's unlikely he'd ever work as an em-tracker again.

But the other option sucked.

Luther was right, Sietch Tabr was too big a shift to happen quickly.

There'd be a backlash. Animal drug cult stories swamping the airwaves. More Robert Walker–like incidents. If ravers dying of dehydration turned the tide against MDMA, he can't imagine what heads mounted on walls might provoke.

Not good.

He closes his eyes and reviews his third choice, the plan he's already set in motion. Hopefully Lorenzo's done his part by now. All he needs to do is visit a jeweler and set up a meeting with Jenka and . . .

"We're landing, sir."

"Wha . . . ," blinking about, he sees the stewardess in the door to his cabin.

"Sorry to wake you. Cabin doors must be open for landing."

He must have, finally, fallen asleep.

SCURVIES

ustoms at JFK Airport. Four million travelers a year, reads a scrolling screen in the arrivals lounge, greeting him as he steps off the airplane. He strolls down a long hallway surrounded by glass walls and a living carpet, red nap with flecks of white, and bright green arrows lighting up beneath his feet as he walks.

Humans, he thinks, just point and watch them go.

As he goes, his cell phone buzzes. Proof of life from his left hip pocket. Pulling it out, he finds two voicemails.

Stops walking to listen.

One message from Richard demanding a meeting, another from Jenka re-demanding Richard's demand for a meeting. After what went down with Tajik, Jenka's call catches him by surprise, bringing up a powerful sense memory, the feeling of a Glock nine being shoved into his eye socket.

He shudders, involuntarily.

A woman in head-to-toe Gucci catches his reaction, staring at him. This only adds to his unease.

The issue, he knows, isn't actually Jenka. Or the memory of Tajik. Or not right now. Right now, the issue is the thirty grand he has tucked in an envelope and wedged inside an old pair of Salomon trail runners at the bottom of his suitcase. He debated bringing the cash back from Malaysia—breaking US monetary import restrictions is not the kind of trouble he'd have an easy time getting out of—but knows, before tomorrow is over, if his plan has any chance, he's going to need the money.

Plus, thirty large is thirty large.

The Gucci woman has disappeared, but Lion hasn't moved. He glances toward the ceiling, tracking two different eye-in-the-sky domes and knowing there are more cameras he can't spot. With all of them pointed in his direction, just standing here can't appear natural.

Not wanting to arouse suspicion, he starts walking. Glances back at his phone. Notices two texts from Lorenzo.

Stops walking again.

The first says *80K, 10 am tomorrow, 89 Jane*; the second, *"Talked to C, go for launch."*

At least that's done. His sense of relief gets him moving. Down the glass hallway, in step with the center mass of disembarking passengers. He passes a picture window framing the rest of the international terminal. Coats, scarves, hats; the weather must have turned cold since he left. Then another hallway, branching left, right, up, down—they certainly don't make this easy.

Another green arrow points them through a short tunnel aquarium. Technicolor fish on all sides, coral reefs like stacked incandescent brains, the full undersea explosion. He'd read about this: a new kind of face-reading technology. For anyone walking through the aquarium tunnel, the darting fish, the immersive panorama, provide enough irresistible distraction that masking expressions and hiding emotions becomes nearly impossible. Deception defeated by proof of life.

Clearing the aquarium, he steps into a room the size of a football field. A complicated stanchion maze, heavily armed guards and a big sign: WELCOME TO AMERICA.

Passport control.

Security protocols have changed since the last time he went through customs, he notices, reading through a list of new procedures from a living screen on the wall. One thing remains constant: Ten thousand dollars is still the legal limit for import. Any additional funds must be declared.

His suitcase feels heavy, a bead of sweat forming between his shoulder blades.

Twitchier than he'd like, Lion looks for a short line. Waits his turn at an eye-scanning terminal painted the dull beige of a dying moth, behind a family from someplace flat. Ohio, his first guess, possibly Indiana.

The bead of sweat still there.

But he clears the eye scanner no problem—then gets randomly selected for an entrance interview.

Threat levels rev. He does his best to conceal the reaction, knowing the eyes-in-the-sky are feeding his micro-expressions to a security AI running statistical emo-algorithms, probably a nano-sniffer scenting the air as well. Hunting excess sweat, irregular pheromones, DNA for all he knows.

A sign hanging from the ceiling directs him to the yellow lane, where he queues up behind an couple of elderly European backpackers, carrying walking sticks and sober expressions. Waits for what feels like an entirely inappropriate length of time. Then it's his turn.

He steps up to a small glass stall, like an old-fashioned tollbooth. A heavyset black woman peers back at him from the other side, standing beside a long table. Midsixties, official attire that hasn't fit her in years, a small American flag pinned to her lapel.

He passes over his passport, sets his bags on the table.

"Coming from?" she asks, looking him up and down.

"Malaysia."

"Purpose of trip?"

"Visiting a friend."

A long pause as she rifles through his passport. Then a hard-edged glare. "Are you a Scurvy? Bringing fruit into the country?"

"Fruit?"

"Pears, kumquats, the like."

"No."

"Are you certain?"

"Yes," says Lion, confused. "What's a Scurvy?"

Her grim look becomes a bureaucratic scowl. "Anything to declare?"

"No."

She opens the top of his sling-pack, sliding the contents onto the table. Notebook lands with a thud. Tobacco flakes. The copy of *Dune*. He has a sinking feeling. If things keep going like this, no way she won't find the money.

But the sight of *Dune* stops her.

She picks it up, holding the book in her hands a little too tightly, staring at the cover with some faraway sadness sweeping across her eyes.

"*Dune,*" she whispers.

He nods, not sure what to say.

She stares at the cover for what feels like a very long time, finally looking up at him.

"It was my son's favorite book."

Lion notes the use of the past tense, feels his em-tracking machinery whirl to life. Signals traveling nerve fibers become neurochemicals bridging synaptic clefts. That's how he finds the future he needs.

A way forward.

He hesitates, knowing if he plays this card he'll be violating an old rule, a decision made early, a promise to never use empathy as a weapon, a promise he's about to break.

"Was?" he asks, making direct eye contact, already knowing the answer. "Does he have a new favorite book?"

"Afghanistan," she says, clutching *Dune*. "That war seems like a long time ago. Not for me. I think about him all the time. You know what I think about—how he died so far away. In a very foreign place. Carter, that was his name, even when he was little, didn't like sleeping over at friend's houses. He liked to be near his mother. And I think of him getting shot, so far away, in a place where he didn't know anyone. He would have wanted his mother then."

"Keep it," he says. "If it reminds you of him, you should keep it."

"Really?"

"Please."

She smiles at him then, the light coming back on in her eyes, "You've seen them—the Scurvies."

"I have?"

"Just didn't know it. They're everywhere right now, why I had to ask. Extreme gamers, dressed up in white-on-white clothing. Into old consoles. Sega, Atari. And fruit. We get a lot of them coming from Malaysia, trying to smuggle in exotic fruit."

The puzzle slots together. The street displays he saw everywhere, outside of Allah Bling, corner of Houston and something. The poly-triber from the night before, Jenka's white-on-white suit, even Pong—that old Atari game. One question remains: "Why are they called Scurvies?"

"That's what they go by," says the woman. "I didn't make it up. We got a memo," pawing through a stack of papers to her left, finding an official-looking letter. "'Cause of the fruit stuff. Some biodiversity thing, clamping down on the import of exotics."

"What's the fruit about?"

She wags the letter. "Not getting scurvy. I guess gamers forget to eat. The fruit started out as some kind of reminder. After those kids died in Korea, it became a thing, a whatchamacallit, a subcult."

"Scurvies," he says.

She nods, stamps his passport and slides it back. Starts to slide the book back, but he stops her.

"Seriously, you should keep it."

Hesitates, takes the book, and breaks into another smile. "Thank you."

"You're welcome."

"Welcome to America, honey. You have a blessed day."

BROTHER, CAN I BORROW YOUR NINJA?

He assumes Arctic knows of his arrival. With their surveillance capabilities, Jenka probably got an alert the moment Lion cleared customs at JFK. Decides to be as cautious as possible, eschewing the ease of an Uber for the anonymity of a traditional yellow.

Not as easy as suspected.

It takes a half hour to find a cabbie willing to accept cash to keep things off the meter. A tall Ethiopian in a psychedelic dashiki, internet radio tuned to an English-language broadcast of camel racing in Libya. Lion remembers hearing about this: The next-generation robo-jockeys controlling the camels are neural-laced with human jockeys controlling the robots, an entirely new form of slavery, or just the way we live now.

Lion asks to be dropped at the Soho Grand, then offers an extra fifty bucks for the privilege of borrowing the driver's phone.

"My friend," says the driver, catching his eyes in the rearview, "how illegal?"

"No," says Lion, trying for convincing, "nothing like that. I just lost my cell."

"Sure you did."

"Say I didn't."

"Then I'll ask again—how illegal?"

"Not illegal."

"How dangerous?"

"For you, not at all."

"Make it a hundred."

"No can do, my friend," says Lion. "I don't need it that bad."

"Sadly," he says, passing over the phone, "I do."

It's an ancient iPhone, once gold in color, now faded to sweat-stained yellow. Lion texts Jenka and Richard, apologizing for the gap in communication, explaining he was now borrowing a stranger's cell, claiming his own phone had been stolen along the way, closing with noon the next day as when he'll arrive at Arctic for their meeting. He gives them no other options.

"Thanks, man," he says, passing the phone back to the driver and glancing out the window. It must have rained recently, puddles on the streets, and the early evening air crystalline in every direction.

But traffic still crawls.

Forty-five minutes later, he exits curbside, beneath the long shadow of the Soho Grand. Setting his sling-pack on the sidewalk, he undoes the drawstring and digs around inside until his cabbie has taken a left at the corner. When taillights fade from view, Lion straightens up, re-slings his pack, and starts to tow his suitcase down the street.

Five blocks later, he finds the Truth, one in a new series of Joie de Vivre boutique hotels that have sprung up lately. Sprightly numbers with the impossible geometries of 3-D-printed facades. Gaudí 2.0. Each branch in the hotel chain is named after core Millennial values, Lion knows, because he was peripherally involved in the marketing plan.

One of his more forgettable em-tracking jobs.

Lion was the one who pointed out that naming hotels after Millennial values—the Truth, the Purpose, the Community—now that his generation had reached the age where the luxury of billboard ethics had been derailed by the verities of life, might be lucrative. "Aspirational nostalgia," he dubbed it.

But he misses the Ludlow.

His room at the Truth comes in two flavors, traditional and augmented. Traditional includes a robo-fish aquarium embedded into one wall, another holds a pink neon sign, displaying a long line of bubble text. A quote from Dr. Martin Luther King: "I believe that unarmed truth and unconditional love will have the final word in reality."

Lion considers this for a moment. Decides things didn't work out too well for Dr. King. Then again, he also thinks, when have truth and love ever produced the desired results.

Augmented is cheaper. It means the hotel has leased virtual space to outside companies for advertising purposes. Put on a pair of its private-label smart glasses and the room becomes a series of living billboards. The desk clerk said the longer he wears the glasses, the less his room costs.

Lion turns the glasses over in his hands. Little round John Lennon frames with nano-projectors lining the rims, like marching, gold-plated ants. He tries them for a few seconds. The bedspread sells shaving cream, the robo-fish peddle a lime-green liquor, the King quote animates, tastefully, asking for nonprofit donations. But there's too much scrolling, winking and blinking. Overloads the life recognition machinery.

He takes them off a few seconds later.

Lion drops the glasses on his nightstand and heads into the bathroom. Teeth brush, toilet flush, it's still early but his habit machinery seems to be running bedtime routines.

The countdown again, apparently. But didn't he just sleep on the plane? How tired he is, of being tired.

Back in the bedroom, a thorough investigation reveals there's no easy way to turn off the MLK sign. Lion gives up and goes to sleep in its neon-pink twilight, an old T-shirt draped over his eyes. Dreams in pink as well, which leaves him feeling cartoonish upon waking in the morning.

Caffeine his first priority.

Lion finds a Ludlow-identical coffeemaker on an end table, cocks the chrome arm, and chooses the lie that is large cup. Then a long shower.

Silver snake jets extend from the wall as he turns on the water, seventeen by his count. An LED light built into each. So the liquid needle streams form a crisscrossing laser show in the stall, and actually dazzling.

Lion realizes this may have been another of his suggestions: "Millennials have short attention spans," he'd told the hotel execs at that meeting. "Treat them to art in places they don't expect it—like the shower."

After toweling off, he downs the coffee in a few gulps and climbs into his straight-world uniform. Grabbing his sling-pack from the bedside table, he punches into the hallway and heads for the elevator. Out the front door of the hotel before 9:00 A.M. The map on his phone finds a bank three blocks away. Boots on the ground get him there just after opening.

A light rain, the bank's windows tinted black and water streaked. He ducks through a gold-plated entranceway, a bas-relief engraved with the Code of Hammurabi, making no sense at all.

There's no line to get to a teller, though Lion's request requires the attention of a branch manager. He taps Arctic's Amex on the counter as he waits.

The manager arrives in a lurch. Some Nordic species, exceptionally pale, with a spotless blue blazer and well-manicured eyebrows. Gazes at him suspiciously. "Marlene tells me you'd like a cash advance."

Decides to nip this in the bud. "If you call the number on the back, you'll find I've been pre-approved for the full amount."

Blazer nods understanding, eyebrows disagree, but thanks to that conversation between Lorenzo and Charlotte, eyebrows lose this round. Lion's been approved for the max advance.

Eighty grand doesn't fit in a single oversized envelope.

Fits in four.

They fill the main pocket of his sling-pack. He turns down their offer of a complimentary security escort and heads for the door feeling a little like a gangster. The feeling evaporates once he hits the streets. Two steps onto the pavement and he realizes that walking around New York with a satchel of cash is the kind of thing that might attract actual gangsters.

The very first taxi he sees, flagging like a madman.

"Eighty-nine Jane Street, please," sliding into the seat, slamming the door with too much velocity.

Ten minutes later, 89 Jane turns out to be a combination Japanese noodle shop and craft coffee bar. A large rectangle, entirely made of light wood. Floors, walls, ceilings, in monochromatic beach. No name on the door, no decorations inside. Just wood paneling and wood tables.

Entirely robot operated as far as Lion can tell.

He has no idea what to do next, then notices two small squares cut into the back wall. The first holds a comb microphone beside a small screen.

Must be where you place your order.

The other is currently empty. But, as he watches, the back wall descends into a slot in the counter and an old school robotic claw slides out a bowl of noodles. A closer look at the screen reveals there are only two choices on the menu: noodles or coffee.

Extreme minimalism. Touted as an appropriate reaction to choice paralysis, taken, Lion decides, to its logical conclusion.

He orders coffee and waits for the claw. After it arrives, he carries the cup over to a wooden table in the corner, same bleached color as the rest of the room. Putting his back to the wall, Lion notes an emergency exit to his right, and a clear line of sight to the door.

Ten minutes later a familiar ninja saunters into the room. Baltha-zar Jones, one extremely bribable jeweler, two steps behind her. The ninja heads for coffee; Balthazar heads for Lion, taking the seat across from him. Black velvet jacket over a TUPAC FOREVER T-shirt, living screens built into its elbows displaying faux-corduroy patches in vari-ous professorial shades.

"My man," says Balthazar.

"Mr. Jones."

A complicated handshake. A bit of small talk that Lion needs to cut short, as politely as possible.

"Down to business, then," Balthazar says, pulling a purple velvet drawstring bag from an inside pocket. He also removes a black velvet mat no bigger than a credit card and sets it on the table. Out of the bag and onto the mat, a shiny diamond in the two-carat range.

Lion grabs for it, but Balthazar knocks his hand away.

The jeweler reaches into his jacket pocket again, removing a min-iature robo-claw in a bluish metal alloy. Like someone shrank the coffee-serving robot. He uses the claw to flip over the gem, cut side down, revealing a tiny electrode embedded in its back.

"Touch the tips of the grasper to the middle of the stone and it cre-ates a magnetic current, lets you remove it from the circuit board. Put the new one in the same way."

He passes the instrument to Lion.

"How long for the upload. . . . Is that the right word?"

"Tricky. If you want to KO the whole system, almost instantly. But that's not what you asked for. This," pointing at the diamond, "does what you need. As long as there's a wireless device nearby connected to the net, the data will break free. But it could take a while."

"What's a while?"

"If everything works, twelve hours."

"Hey-hey, Lion Zorn," says the ninja, her hair in pigtails, a Hello Kitty backpack over one shoulder and two coffee cups in her hands.

"Hey-hey," says Lion.

"I will kill-kill both of you," snarls Balthazar.

She plops down beside him, not exactly a soft landing. Pigtails bob, coffee comes dangerously close to spilling over.

"Dial me up that 411, Lion Zorn, what's the say-say."

"Woman," growls Balthazar, "I'm tryin' to put my mind inside your mouth. It ain't takin'."

Lion ignores them. "I've got your end," he says, depositing the sling-pack onto the table. "Do you have anything to carry it in?"

The ninja unshoulders the backpack. Lion realizes it's the Goth Kitty model, black cat with pink whiskers, in Cleopatra garb. He glances around the room. Nobody seems to be paying any attention. In four quick motions, he transfers four oversized manila envelopes from bag to bag, then leaves a fifth on the table.

"That's eighty for the diamond," he says. "Can I drop another ten for one more favor?"

"How may I be of service?" asks Balthazar.

"Brother," says Lion, "can I borrow your ninja?"

THEM DAYS ARE GONE

Lion heads east, chewing up the blocks on the way to his meeting with Arctic. Buildings like tall gray soldiers to his left and right, but his eyes are locked dead ahead. A hard left on Sixth Avenue and another stretch of strides brings him to the corner of West Eighteenth.

And no farther.

There's a sizable crowd blocking forward progress. He hears horns blare, metal crunch, and a high-pitched whine, like a gear-stripped motor revving its way to a heart attack.

Can't see over the bodies to source the sound.

"What's going on?" he asks an older Mexican man standing on the edge of the throng.

The man looks him up and down before answering. Lion notices that the silver in this guy's brush mustache matches the piping on his guayabera.

"What we got here," he says eventually, his accent Texas twangy, "a couple Uber Autonomous in a tussle. Started out a fender bender, but then them cars went crazy, tryin' a murder each other."

He points out a woman to his left, a gash below her ear, blood streaking her cheek.

"Lady over there took a hubcap to the head."

Serious proof of life, thinks Lion.

"Use-ta-could talk some sense to an automobile." Shaking his head, "them days are gone."

Lion retreats a few feet but can't find an easy way through the crowd. Backs up a block and heads north.

Another ten minutes and Arctic's brownstone comes into view. No security cameras visible, but Lion figures they're hidden in the bricks, the lamps, the system. A watchful layer of not-quite-consciousness built into everything these days. The human doorman, merely a finishing touch.

"Good afternoon, Mr. Zorn."

So someone's expecting him.

"Good afternoon," he says, taking a step closer. "My assistant's a few minutes behind me. I gave her my Arctic credit card for ID. Can you send her up?"

"Absolutely, sir."

"Just Lion," extending his hand.

"Frank."

"Thanks, Frank," and across the lobby and into an already waiting elevator. Five floors up and Arctic's as remembered. Same red sequined couch in the corner, same Armani-clad enforcer holding down the front desk.

"Mr. Zorn," she says, standing up, "Jenka and Sir Richard are already in the conference room."

"The white-on-white room?"

She starts to step around the desk, blonde ringlets bobbing as she moves.

"No need," he says, walking past her, "I know the way."

The long hall feels longer than remembered. With the adrenaline in his system, it's got a funhouse flavor. Walls warped, windows misshapen. A deep breath, a slow exhale, and the room's door, slightly ajar.

Lion doesn't bother to knock.

Even when he's expecting the assault, the room's whiteness makes him blink. Takes an extra second to lock into focus. Once it does, he spots Jenka in his white suit, sitting with his back to him. And Sir Richard, wearing a denim work shirt rolled at the sleeves and a pair of faded blue jeans to match, sprawled on the beanbag to his left.

"Lion Zorn in the hizzy," he announces.

Richard glances his way, lifts a hand in greeting, then changes his mind and feathers his hair. Like Lion just got dissed by a Ralph Lauren ad circa 1987.

Jenka spins to glare. Lion ignores him, walking around the hotwhite Ping-Pong table, staying far enough away that he can keep the legs in sight. He waits until the diamond glimmer of the Pong sign comes into view, then chooses a chair.

Slides it back, takes his seat, and kicks feet up on table.

This seems to amuse Richard. Not Jenka.

"Where. The fuck. Have you been?"

"No need for profanity," says Richard, rising from the beanbag. "We can behave like gentlemen."

"Pardon me," says Jenka. "Lion, hope you had a pleasant trip, and might I ask, where. The fuck. Have you been?"

Richard sighs.

"I've been parlaying with your man Tajik," says Lion, tossing his sling-pack onto the table. "Same as you."

"Who's Tajik?" asks Richard, pulling out a chair and sitting down.

So Jenka hasn't told Richard the whole story. That might be useful.

"Screw Tajik," says Jenka, "where's Penelope?"

Priming, Fetu once told Lion, is a way of pre-loading the pattern recognition system, tilting implicit memory just enough that the brain makes faster connections between certain ideas over others. People exposed to the word "nurse," for example, will then recognize the word "doctor" more readily than the word "water." Fetu, he thinks, better not be wrong.

"From what I've heard," says Lion, "you screwed everyone. Got little baby Jenkas running around in white suits in like three countries." Clucks his tongue. "Such a slut."

"Slut?" Richard asks Jenka. "What's he talking about?"

"What are you talking about?" demands Jenka.

"Doesn't matter." A dismissive wave of his hand. "Let's talk business." Lion pulls out his cell phone and dials up voice memos. Clicks RECORD and slides it onto the table.

"My contract specified that I try to contact Muad'Dib and see if I could set up a meeting, correct?"

Neither speaks. Lion repeats himself.

"What is this about?" asks Richard.

"Just setting the record straight."

"Go to hell," says Jenka.

"Fine," says Richard. "I'll play. Yes, those were the terms of our agreement."

Lion picks up his phone, glances at the clock. He's got about ninety seconds to kill. "Excellent," he says, setting it back down, looking first at Jenka, next at Richard. "Well, I've spoken to Muad'Dib, and he's not interested in meeting with you."

They simply stare.

"I believe this concludes our affairs."

"You think we're done?" says Jenka.

Thirty-four seconds gone, counting silently in his head.

"Done," he agrees.

"You're out of your fucking mind."

"Language," snaps Richard, doing a fairly convincing imitation of Lion's first-grade teacher. "What do you mean Muad'Dib's not interested?"

Forty-five seconds.

Lion kills another ten by digging through his sling-pack until he finds his Moleskine, then fifteen more flipping through its pages. Sets it down, looks back at Richard. But before he can speak, from the other end of the hallway, the sound of a woman's voice, shouting.

"Jenka, you pompadoured slut! Lose track of time? Lose your wallet? I'm here for my goddamn money."

"Slut?" asks Richard, and right on cue. Chalk one up for Fetu. Priming, works as advertised.

"Sixteen months," shouts the woman, "sixteen motherfucking months of child support, that's what you owe me. Sixteen goddamn motherfucking months—what the hell-hell we s'posed to eat?"

"She's got a sword!" screams the Armani-clad secretary. "She's killing the couch!"

Jenka's on his feet, Richard's in his wake.

"Plus interest!" hollers the woman. "Bitch, you owe me slut tax!"

Both Jenka and Richard dash out the door. Lion wastes no time, diving beneath the table and aiming for the glimmer of the Pong sign. Mini-claw comes out of the left pocket, velvet bag from the right. Starts counting stones, just as Balthazar explained.

A few seconds to find the right one. A crash in the other room and he figures he's got about thirty seconds left.

When he touches the claw to the gem, there's a bright flash and then the shine seems to drain from the whole panel. It happens in an instant. AIs, Lion realizes, die in the same way humans die—with far less fanfare than we think we deserve.

He drops the stone atop the bag, then positions the one Balthazar gave him on the tip of the grasper. The panel flickers back to life once he gets it in place.

"Who the hell are you?" shouts Jenka from the other room.

Lion grabs bag, stone, and claw in one quick swipe, shoving them back into his pocket. He bangs his skull on the table trying to get back to his feet. Rubbing his head with one hand, he snatches his sling-pack with the other, then quick-steps around the table and into the hall.

"Who the hell are you?" she shouts back.

Lion makes it to the waiting room in time to see a familiar ninja standing on the coffee table, kicking magazines and waving her blade.

"Jenka."

"Hell you are," she says, skewering a red sequined pillow, flicking it at him.

"Hell I'm not."

"Shit," says the ninja, lowering her sword, jumping down from the table, "wrong slut."

And then she's out the front door before anyone can react. The couch is in ribbons, the floor red-speckled with sequins.

"Who the hell was that?" demands Richard.

"I have no idea," replies Jenka.

"Who the hell was that?" repeats Richard

"Should I call security?" asks the Armani.

"I think we're done here," says Lion, walking past the mess, stopping by the door to look back at Richard. "It's just my opinion, but you shouldn't do it."

"Why?" demands Jenka.

"Introduce Sietch Tabr as an autism drug. It'll work. It'll help people. Skip the social media barrage. You'll still make a killing."

Richard runs his fingers through his hair, "We don't have time for that."

"We don't," agrees Lion, "but the Rilkeans are not wrong. Empathy is a question you have to live. Jenka thinks you can change culture by force—and he's not wrong either—but there's always a cost."

Then he's out the door, leaving Arctic in the rearview, he hopes, for the very last time.

FANCY A SHAG

All kinds of evil premonitions in the elevator, but when Lion hits the ground floor, he sees only Frank, behind the desk, studying a soccer feed on a tablet-phone. No goons grab him, though he suspects that happens more in the movies. In real life, it's going to be subtler and harder to trace. A hit-and-run, an exotic illness.

He crosses the lobby at a good clip.

Punching through the front door, Lion notices the light has drained from the afternoon. How long was he inside? Maybe twenty minutes? But the soft blues he remembers have gone slate gray, and a cold wind is blowing in from the boroughs.

Then he notices the shiny mobile, parked curbside, Bo leaning against the hood. Dark glasses, dark suit, arms crossed. Did Arctic send him? That's an old KGB trick—use a friend to do the work of an enemy. He flashes on their trip upstate, Bo's surgical precision, and Lion's suspicion that there was something military in his background.

So this is how it's going down.

He looks around. Empty street to his right, left is busier. Safer. Pivots quickly and loads up his legs, preparing to dash.

"Lion," calls Bo, with a wave.

Nothing threatening in the gesture.

"Bo," he replies.

"How's the arm?"

Lion walks over. Doesn't know what this is, doesn't like standing in front of Arctic's building either. Glancing back and forth, he doesn't see a better option. Looks back at Bo.

"It's alright, thanks . . . . What are you doing here?"

"Beside the fact that I work here?"

"Fair point," says Lion, but still edgy.

"I came to give you this," explains Bo, opening the driver's side door and retrieving the dragon box from a pocket in the side panel.

Lion lifts an eyebrow.

"You're one day past a hella-long plane flight. Thought you might want some Ghost Trainwreck."

"That's very cool of you," smiling . . . then not smiling. "How did you know I just got off a long flight?"

Bo walks over to Lion, reaches out a hand and grabs the hood of his sweater. He fishes around inside until he finds what he's looking for. It takes two hands to dislodge the item. A small square of gray metal, same color as his sweater, same size as a match tip.

"Tracker," says Bo.

"You've been tracking me?"

"Not me," walking over to the SUV's side door, opening it up.

Penelope sits inside, red hair braided into a twisted updo, a long navy shawl over an old Joy Division T-shirt, and a pair of reading glasses. The naughty librarian, Lion thinks, retro-meme.

"Fancy a shag, Lion Zorn?"

Bo snorts. Lion blinks. Penelope slips deeper into the car and taps her hand on the now empty seat. He gazes suspiciously at the upholstery, but climbs inside anyway, his desire to get away from Arctic's front door overriding his unease. Bo hops into the front seat, drops the car into gear and slides into the street.

"Kids," says Bo, "where we headed?"

"Where you staying?" Penelope asks him.

"The Truth."

"Yes, Lion, I want the truth."

"The Truth," he says, giving her a look, "for a change." Then, re-directing his gaze toward Bo, "It's a hotel, downtown."

"I know the place," says Bo, flipping on a blinker.

"We're going to the Truth," says Penelope, "to get Lion's baggage— which is considerable. And then we're going to the Ludlow."

"After that I'm out," says Bo, changing lanes. "I still need this gig."

"Copy that," says Penelope.

"And whatever you two need to talk about, I don't need to know about." Bo hits a button on the dash. A partition rises from the back-side of the front seat, sealing them in, hermetically.

"You tracked me again?" says Lion, turning to Penelope, holding the device in his fingers.

She nods.

"Since when?"

"Kuala Lumpur."

He just glares at her.

"In the elevator," she continues, "after leaving Luther on the roof. You had your back to me, I slipped it in."

"Why? Actually, stupid question, I guess I know why."

"I doubt that."

"What's that supposed to mean?"

Smiles. "You're a bampot."

"I'm sure I am."

"I brought you into this," she says, sliding next to him, pressing her knees into his and holding his gaze. "You didn't ask for it."

"True."

She leans over and kisses him softly on the cheek, then whispers into his ear "so I'm going to make damn sure you come out the other side."

And "Down by the Seaside" in cheerful synth tones.

Not taking his eyes off hers, Lion digs his phone out of his jacket pocket and answers, "Hello."

"What did you mean, 'a cost'?"

"Richard?"

"What did you mean, 'there's always a cost'?" Something sharp in his tone that Lion hadn't noticed before.

"Do you know how culture changes?" says Lion, then changes his mind. "Forget that. Do you know the origin story of empathy?"

"No."

"It's a puzzle," he explains, breaking eye contact with Penelope. "Darwin told us we're descended from apes, so scientists studied them to understand us. They wanted to know where our so-called humanity came from. Kindness, patience, loyalty, cooperation, most importantly, empathy."

"And?"

"Couldn't find any of 'em. Not in apes. Not in any primates. They found intelligence, self-awareness, long-term planning, but none of the big-ticket social emotions."

Penelope reaches down and takes his hand in hers, staring out the window the whole time.

"Where'd they come from?" asks Richard.

"Wolves," he says, feeling her flesh press into his. "Forty thousand years ago, humans and wolves teamed up. It began with garbage. Wolves wanted our leftovers, so they started hanging out by our refuse piles. We liked having cleaner camps. Better hygiene, healthier tribe. Over time, it became a partnership. The wolves, especially the ones who weren't afraid of humans, got more food, lived longer lives, had more pups. And the humans, especially the ones who liked wolves, had cleaner camps, less disease, more children."

"Exerting evolutionary pressure."

"Yeah. And adaptation. After starting out garbage cans, wolves became our security guards: barking at danger, keeping us safe. Then we started hunting together. Wolves hear and smell better, so they took over tracking. We had opposable thumbs, so we focused on killing. For both species, these were huge advantages."

"Co-evolution," says Richard, dryly.

"Uh-huh."

"No. Why are you telling me about co-evolution?"

"The partnership changed us. To co-evolve with wolves, we needed to learn to live with wolves. Our pack size grew. A bigger pack might be a stronger pack, but only if the members can cooperate and work toward a common goal. This required more patience, more collaboration, more loyalty, more empathy, than ever existed in our primate past. But once we teamed up with wolves, evolution began selecting for these things. It means our celebrated humanity is actually a collection of traits we learned from wolves."

"Fascinating," says Richard, that classic British snipe.

"You're an idiot," snaps Lion. "Why does Sietch Tabr matter so much? Because the last time we bothered to think like animals we learned how to be goddamn human beings. Loyalty, patience, empathy—fuck you."

Penelope starts laughing.

"Unfortunately," he says, calming down, "I'm actually making a different point. We teamed up with wolves forty thousand years ago, but empathy—the word—didn't show up until the late eighteen hundreds. It took us that long to recognize and name that emotion. We're slow learners. Compress that process, force people through eons of emotional evolution overnight, we're not built for it. Robert Walker, case in point."

There's a long silence on the line.

"Richard?"

"Thank you," and then a click.

Lion stares at the phone, not sure what just happened. The partition begins to slide down, but he doesn't notice.

"The Truth," says Bo.

"What?" asks Lion, finally looking up from his phone.

"We've arrived."

ALL YOU CAN DO IS YOUR INCH

New York at night—a million lights and every one a story.

The lamppost ten stories below Lion, for example. Of the single-arm variety, with steel glow-apron and rounded bulb. Installed by a Russian electrician with a drinking problem and a failing marriage. Worked the graveyard shift—only one he could get—and it was the hours he kept, the exact opposite of his wife's schedule, made worse by his need for a vodka or two before bed, that was the first fault line in their relationship. Or the reflective glimmer of a dog's collar down the block, illuminated suddenly by passing headlights, belonging to a lost schnauzer searching for his human, wanting to go home, and scared, very scared.

Lion doesn't expect he'll tire of this view anytime soon.

He's back at the Ludlow, in the same room he stayed in two weeks ago. Or was it three?

Time slippage. By-product of emo-stim overload. But he can recall salient details just fine.

After snatching his bags from the Truth, Penelope and Lion had said good-bye to Bo and checked in at the Ludlow. They grabbed dinner at the Dirty French. It was dark by the time they made it up to the room.

Penelope unearthed a bottle of Pappy Van Winkle from the hidden reaches of her backpack. She told him the bottle was a gift from Luther, and maybe that was a lie, maybe it was a bribe; either way, the bourbon worked as advertised.

It took two drinks before their clothes came off.

Sometime later, Penelope slid out of bed and headed for the shower. Lion grabbed the freshly restocked dragon box off the nightstand and carried it out to the terrace. Which is where he is now, looking out at the lights of the city, telling stories about each, the electrician who installed the lamppost, the lost dog down the street, just as Fetu had taught him. Another empathy-expansion exercise; keeping the machinery oiled and ready.

In his left pants pocket, he can feel the weight of the Pong diamond. Such a tiny technology, yet big enough to hold the secrets of the Rilkeans. Like a chastity belt for culture, preventing mimetic fertility. No stories, no empathy; no empathy, no culture. Last tango in cyberspace. Which is also why, he suspects, Sir Richard is so concerned about the failure of language.

Either that, or Lion's really stoned.

He can't decide. The only thing clear is that more is probably better than less in this instance. He takes tobacco from his coat pocket, a handful of Ghost Trainwreck from the dragon box, sits down in a chair, rolls 50-50, clicks his lighter and inhales. Bounce light from the hotel room catches his exhale for a Mandelbrot moment, gone as smoke slides off on the breeze.

He thinks of, for no reason he can think of, the woman he gave his copy of *Dune* to. About their dramatic arc, where they started out and where ended up.

"You look pensive."

He glances up and sees Penelope standing on the edge of the terrace, wearing a white hotel robe, her hair unbraided, hanging long and still damp from the shower. "What are you thinking about?"

"Empathy."

"That story you told Richard? About wolves?"

"More like the inverse. I told Richard about wolves, and how empathy evolved. I was thinking about what empathy can do."

"Which is?" she asks.

"All of this," says Lion, pointing at the city, the lights, their stories. "All of this started as an idea in someone's head. But it exists because of wolves."

She takes a few steps closer to the table, reaching slender fingers out for the joint. The motion tugs her robe up her arm, revealing black ravens soaring over pale flesh.

He passes it over.

"Cities from wolves?" she asks, inhaling.

"It's strange to think about," he says, "but wolves forced early humans to expand empathy, to widen their sphere of caring beyond immediate family. A gazillion generations later that's what made us capable of teaming up to turn something as ephemeral as an idea into something as concrete as a city . . ." Then he frowns. "Maybe Richard's right. Maybe faster is better."

"You're changing your mind?" asks Penelope.

"From what to what?"

"From telling the Rilkean side of the story."

Lion flashes on Balthazar explaining that the reprogrammed diamond takes twelve hours to liberate the data. His phone is inside the hotel room. "What time is it?" he asks Penelope.

"A little before midnight, why?"

Lion got to Arctic at noon, counting in his head. Less than an hour to go. "I never said I'd tell the Rilkean side of the story."

"You said you'd think about it."

"I'm still thinking," he says, sliding back from the table, feeling cold stone beneath bare feet as he pads to the edge of the terrace. Down below, the street's asphalt ribbon and a taxicab parked midblock, candy-apple-red blinkers strobing the darkness.

Penelope crosses over to stand beside him. "All you can do is your inch."

He raises an eyebrow.

"It's something Mum used to say. All you can do is your inch. We grab everyone we can carry, put each other onto our backs, and crawl toward the future. Inch by inch—it's all we can do."

"But it's what we do, right?" Turning toward her then. "What we have to do. It's . . . required."

Which is when he hears the music. Far off in the distance and very familiar. *Down by the seaside, the boats go a-sailing, can the people hear, what the little fish are saying?*

What are the little fish saying?

Then he realizes—it's his phone, ringing, from inside the bedroom. Decides to give it a pass. The ringing quiets for a moment, then starts again. Someone is trying very hard to get hold of him.

No time left, to pass the time of day.

And not going to quit trying.

Lion walks inside. His phone, charging on the nightstand, and a number he doesn't recognize.

"Hello?"

"How does culture change?"

"Richard?" Glances at the unfamiliar digits on the screen. "How many numbers do you have?"

"You asked earlier if I knew how culture changed—what did that mean?"

"It doesn't matter," he says, crossing to a small table beside the window, flanked by two gray flannel armchairs. Slides one out, sits down. "I was making the same point."

"Tell me anyway."

Lion glances to his right, sees Penelope standing with her back to him, the joint's ember like a comet caught between her fingers.

"Darwin told us that scarcity drives evolution," he says. "Only two ways to deal with scarcity. Compete, and fight over dwindling resources, or cooperate, and create new resources. Life seems to favor the latter option over the former."

"Favor? How?"

"Ever read *The Major Transitions in Evolution*? John Maynard Smith and Eörs Szathmáry?"

"Missed that one," same dry tone as before.

"They were biologists interested in the fact that life evolves toward greater complexity, from cells to humans to cities to societies. Each step, they found, required greater cooperation. But this also explains why each step is so hard."

"Why?"

"It's a question of stability. Without it, innovation can't spread far enough to be used to make more resources. That's the goal. It's also why innovation can't take place at the center of the system: too much resistance to change. Has to happen on the fringe. In evolution, this is niche creation; in business, a skunk works; in culture, subculture. It's also why I have a job. But my point is that this only happens slowly, over incredibly long stretches of time."

"Exactly-exactly," says Richard, "and I'm man enough to admit it."

"Pardon?"

"You changed my mind, sport. Empathy, it's too radical a shift to force on society."

"I'm sorry, Richard, seems to be some kind of glitch in the matrix. Did I hear you say you're not going through with it?"

"It's not that simple. You changed my mind. Earlier, actually, when we were on the phone. But Jenka's a different story. The woman with the sword—he knew something was up."

Lion feels the temperature drop. "Jenka?"

"The minute you left the office," Richard sighs, "Jenka set the plan in motion. Bloggers, podcasters, stories are already all over the web."

He finds he's tilted his head backward and is now staring straight up at the ceiling. Eggshell-white paint, pale wooden beams evenly spaced.

"Sietch Tabr," continues Richard. "The first batch came off the line a day ago. Packaged, loaded into trucks. The news broke, and within five hours, someone hijacked one of the trucks."

Ceiling beams swim a little. Emo-stim overload threatening the visual cortex. Slow inhale. Slow exhale. Then he remembers the gemstone in his pocket. How much time has passed since he asked Penelope for the time? Five minutes? Ten? Decides he needs to be sure.

"What time is it?" he asks Richard.

"Twelve twelve."

His gaze doesn't move from the ceiling, but he fingers the AI diamond, feeling the soft crush of the velvet bag, feeling the tiny nub of the diode. Almost proof of life in his pocket.

"Might not matter anymore," he tells Richard.

"Why?"

Tilting his head back down, he glances out at Penelope. "It's late, let's talk about this in the morning."

Apparently billionaires don't like being told what to do.

"Richard?"

"Sure."

Before Richard can say another word, Lion hangs up and walks onto the terrace, seeing the city twinkle in the distance, pulling the little velvet bag from his pocket as he goes. Penelope has sat down at the table. He takes a seat beside her, removing the diamond and holding it between his fingers.

"What's that?"

"The Rilkean side of the story," he says, setting the stone in her hand, showing her the nano-diode on its backside. "It's the AI scrubber, the one you've been looking for."

She looks up from the stone and into his eyes and holds the contact. And he feels it then, that rush of we, the god high of serotonin, like blasting off on Molly, like the last time they blasted off on Molly. Sans Molly.

Neat trick.

Takes him a moment to find his way back to his voice. "Remember the Pong sign, made out of diamonds, on the white table, in the white room?"

"Bloody hell. That's the AI?"

"Was the AI. I unplugged it."

Her eyes go wide, but Lion slow-shakes his head against it.

"That was Richard on the phone," he says. "Jenka put the plan into motion. We're already light-years past Go. The story's all over the web, and someone stole about a million hits of Sietch Tabr."

In the distance, rising above the white noise of the city, he hears sirens. Too many sirens.

"But you unplugged the AI?" Penelope says. "People will get to read the Rilkean side of the story?"

He nods.

"Not exactly what Luther had in mind."

"Enough information will get out there," he says. "People can read it, make up their own damn minds."

Penelope stares at the diamond for a long time, then puts it back into his hand, closing his fingers around it, holding his fist in hers. For reasons unknown, the sirens go silent. But that rush of we is back, and who knows, might even stick around for a little while.

"You should keep it," she says eventually. "It's your inch."

LIKE EVERYBODY ON A BUS
WITH NO BRAKES

ion and Penelope spend the next day in the room at the Ludlow. Some kind of problem with gravity. Seems to necessitate they use their body weight to hold down the bed at all times.

In the evening, they walk down the block for Chinese food. One of those improbable New York nights, people cheerful on the streets. One of those impossible New York restaurants, really just a long, narrow counter, two tables wedged against a wall and a flat-screen television in the corner.

Tuned to the news.

Taking a seat at the counter, Lion has that something-not-quite-right feeling. He looks around slowly, then notices a familiar image on the screen. A house in the woods, clapboard modern on a sizable lot.

Double-takes.

Robert Walker's house.

Staring at the television, he sees a blinking red warning banner pop up on the bottom of the screen. The next image will be graphic and may not be suitable for children. Cut to a close-up of Robert Walker's head on the wall.

Even now, it pulls him up short.

"The AI scrubber," he tells Penelope, pointing at the screen, "must have been programmed to erase Walker's story as well."

She stares at the image. Wide shot. The full tartan graveyard, Walker's head dead center.

"So here we go," she says.

He takes a seat at the counter; Penelope sits beside him. Soups, entrees, and some kind of charged ionosphere between them. They eat quickly. The check arrives before they're done, tucked beneath two fortune cookies on a red plastic tray.

"Have mine," he tells Penelope.

"You don't want to know your fortune?"

Shaking his head, "Ironic, I know, for an em-tracker, but I like the mystery."

They spend another day at the Ludlow, exploring the mystery. Sometime in the late afternoon, habit machinery takes over and Lion gets out of bed to make coffee. Carrying the lie that is large cup out on the terrace, he rolls a cigarette and texts his agent to see what's up.

Gets a fast response.

It's a firm offer for that job in Costa Rica, something about em-tracking the first AI that figured out how to teach a 3-D printer how to print another 3-D printer. Proof of not-quite-life getting jiggy is what that is.

And no rest for the wicked. Lion needs to be on a flight out by Sunday latest, that is, if he's interested.

Give me a day to think about it, he texts back.

Stubbing out his cigarette, he calls out to ask Penelope if she's ever been to Costa Rica.

Gets no response.

Pushing mustard velvet curtains out of his way, he steps inside to find her standing in the center of the room, staring at her cell.

"Penelope?" he tries again.

"Shiz," she says, nodding at her phone, "he's everywhere."

Lion crosses over to take a closer look. On her screen, he sees a familiar blue mohawk parading a well-coiffed woman around an airplane, pointing at a spray-painted image on the wall. A Banksy. The bar code cage with bars bent and a leopard stalking toward freedom.

"The scrubber's off," he says, "so, I guess, Shiz is out of hiding."

"Numby fud's been waiting for this moment."

"Waiting to do what with this moment?"

"Just dropped a single," says Penelope, "his first in five years. It's called 'Sietch Tabr, Mon Amour.'"

"Subtle."

"It's already at number one. Global. This," she points at the screen, "is some pimp-my-plane YouTube show, must be part of his press tour."

On the third day, Lion smiles when he sees a familiar number pop up on his phone.

"Lorenzo Boldacci," he says, "are my methods unsound?"

"I don't see any method at all, sir," replies Lorenzo, finishing the quote. And then a strange sound on the line, before Lion realizes, it's Lorenzo, not talking.

"Everything alright?" he asks.

"There's some trouble . . . in Paris."

"You're in Paris?"

"No, but reporters are."

A sinking in his stomach. "What are you talking about?"

"Story broke about a guy named Antoine Bartholomew. He was a . . . a big game hunter."

Lion catches the tense shift. "Was?"

"Check your phone, I just sent you a link."

Lion put Lorenzo on speaker, then clicks his way past his home screen and into messages. Double-clicks the URL. He sees the front page of a news website load, French text, and a photo of a handsome, dark-skinned man looking directly at him, his head mounted to an elegant teak chevron.

"Go wide," says Lorenzo.

Lion places his fingers on his screen and expands the scope of the shot, seeing that the head has been hung in a well-stocked trophy room, different plaid wallpaper this time, same deer, antelope, gazelle, zebra, bear, in a sad row beside it.

"Is this Bartholomew?" he asks, feeling suddenly sick.

"Cops found him this morning," says Lorenzo. "What you can't see in the shot—they also found a couple of lines of silver powder."

"That took less than three days," says Lion.

"He left a note."

"Fucking of course he did. A suicide note?"

"More like an apology, to the animals."

Lion takes a moment to take this in, forcing his gaze away from the head and out the terrace window. A wisp of cloud creeps across blue sky. It doesn't distract, or not enough.

He knows this won't be the last apology. Definitely not the last body. Sietch Tabr is going wide. It's a high-speed empathy-expansion exercise for the masses. Of course there'll be casualties. Like everybody on a bus with no brakes.

Lion glances back at the photo. Which is when he notices something familiar in Bartholomew's eyes. Regret. Remorse. That hard, sad, backward-facing emotion, the evermore cost of progress.

"Either of you doing anything next week?" he asks, his eyes still locked on the image.

"What?" says Lorenzo.

"Who are you talking to?" asks Penelope.

"Both of you," Lion replies, looking away from the photo, pulling his wallet out of his pocket, flipping it open. "I still have Arctic's Amex. Let's hell out of Dodge and go to Costa Rica."

"What's in Costa Rica?" says Lorenzo.

"Toucans."

"Toucans?" asks Penelope.

"We can bring some Sietch Tabr and find out what it's like to have a beak as big as an ice axe."

Lorenzo starts laughing. "Can I invite Charlotte?"

"What kind of question is that, Kemosabe? Absolutely you can invite Charlotte."

"Live the questions," says Lorenzo.

"Live the questions," Penelope agrees.

So Richard was right: The animals are next. Inch by inch, the them become us. One tribe, many umwelten, everyone a story.

"Perhaps you will live along some distant day into the answer," says Lion, but mostly to himself.

And he feels it then, that ratchet-click deep in the reptilian dark of his brain stem, back where they hide the real secrets. Data bit finds data bit and nearly takes his breath away.

FACT FROM FICTION AND OTHER ACKNOWLEDGMENTS

First off, thank you for reading my book. Without you, I might have to get a real job—and we all know how horribly wrong that's gonna go. Of course, if, for reasons unknown, you skipped the book and are just reading the acknowledgments, well, that's odd, but whatever, I hope you find what you're looking for.

Most importantly, this book would not exist without the support of two people. First, my amazing wife, Joy Nicholson, who is my compass, who I'm crazy about, who always, always, always fights for the animals—never could have done this without you.

Also, the mad genius, Michael Wharton. For the past twenty-five years, Michael has been my best friend and frontline editor. A great many of the words I've written have sought his guidance and approval before making their way public—including, of course, his tireless and brilliant work on *Last Tango*. Without you, my brother, doubtful this would have been possible, certain it would have been a lot less fun.

Big thanks are also owed to a few other folks: Joe Alexander consistently ripped me away from my keyboard, got me into the mountains, and kept me laughing throughout. The random, hysterical stuff Joe says on a chairlift inspired the scene at the Virgin Galactic counter. Much appreciated, Joe, it is the prophecy.

Joshua Lauber was the genesis of a lot of the ideas in this book. It was Josh who shared my obsession with the history of Jamaica, the roots of Rastafarianism, and the Rod of Correction. Big up, my friend.

My wonderful mother, Norma Kotler, once again demanded to see this book as soon as it was done, never mind the spelling mistakes, and despite the fact that I warned her repeatedly that there were boatloads of drugs in the story, and some sex and strong language. Still she braved forward. Thanks, Mom!

I also have to thank my agent, Paul Bresnick, for always telling me the truth, and for being such a warrior. Everyone at St. Martin's has been amazing as well, especially my editor, the incredibly talented Peter Wolverton.

Also, the story about the woman whose son got shot in Afghanistan was a variation of an Aaron Sorkin story from *West Wing*. I couldn't figure out how to get the attribution in without ruining the tale and the tale was just so good. . . . So a debt is owed to Mr. Sorkin. You know what they say, "good artists borrow, great artists . . ."

Lastly on the gratitude tip—Vishen Lakhiani and the A-Fest Jamaica posse managed to kick my head sideways enough that I could find the right words to finish this book. Neat trick. And deeply appreciated.

On the science and technology front, pretty much everything I describe—excluding Sietch Tabr—exists in a lab somewhere or is coming into existence in a lab somewhere. And yeah, that includes both the face-reading aquarium and the fact that you can store information in diamonds (though no one has yet built an AI out of the stones). Same goes for the data on empathy. All true. Or as true as we know for now. But either way, Rilke was right. It is our superpower.

As far as Sietch Tabr goes—is it real? Let's just say there are more than a few underground chemists now playing with psychedelics that expand empathy in some darn curious directions. Freaky work for sure, and keep it up.

The William James information is also correct, excluding the letter to his brother, novelist Henry James—though, if you read through their old correspondence, that's pretty much how they spoke to each other.

The Rasta/reggae history and the Rod of Correction story are also both as true and as accurate as possible, though, considering everything there is to consider about the amazing island of Jamaica (and its incredibly outsized impact on culture), "true" and "accurate" may not mean exactly what they normally mean. That said, if you're interested in the question of how religions get assembled, the Rastafarian religion, the eighteenth-largest faith in the world, is pretty much the only one in history created in plain sight. You can literally see the technology as it's being built and the signifiers start to stack up. And, once again, the craziest part: It worked. The Rastas rose out of the most dire, heart-wrenching poverty imaginable to reshape hearts, minds, and culture. Give thanks.

Same goes for the Pokémon subcult in Chile: They really exist; they really do rebel by wet-kissing strangers on the street.

Also, all the information about animals, biodiversity, overpopulation, and the Sixth Great Extinction is sadly, horribly, accurate. We can all do so much better. Enough said.

Finally, whenever I write a book, I seek a few songs that make me feel the way I want the book to make the reader feel. These go on a playlist and get listened to thousands of times along the way. In this case, it was "Goddamn Lonely Love" by the Drive-By Truckers and "Down With the Sickness" by Disturbed. Thank you so much: Art In; Art Out—the way it's supposed to work.

Finally, finally, a closing dedication: This one is for the canids, who taught us about empathy, who still teach us about empathy. Big up, my Bredren.